About the Authors

Sharon Kendrick once won a national writing competition by describing her ideal date: being flown to an exotic island by a gorgeous and powerful man. Little did she realise that she'd just wandered into her dream job! Today she writes for Mills & Boon, featuring often _____ _for_ heroes and the _____ nees. She believes t_____ er want to end. Just l_____

Julia Jam_____ the peaceful verdant co_____ and the wild shores of Cornwall. She also loves the Mediterranean—so rich in myth and history, with its sunbaked landscapes and olive groves, ancient ruins and azure seas. 'The perfect setting for romance!' she says. 'Rivalled only by the lush tropical heat of the Caribbean—palms swaying by a silver sand beach lapped by turquoise waters...what more could lovers want?'

USA TODAY bestseller and RITA® Award winner **Catherine Mann** has penned over fifty novels, released in more than twenty countries. After years as a military spouse bringing up four children, Catherine is now a snowbird—sorta?—splitting time between the Florida beach and somewhat chillier beach in her home state of South Carolina. The nest didn't stay empty long, though, as Catherine is an active board member for the Sunshine State Animal Rescue. www.CatherineMann.com.

Billonaires
COLLECTION

January 2019

February 2019

March 2019

April 2019

May 2019

June 2019

Billionaires:
The Tycoon

SHARON KENDRICK

JULIA JAMES

CATHERINE MANN

MILLS & BOON

First Published in Great Britain 2019
By Mills & Boon, an imprint of HarperCollins *Publishers*
1 London Bridge Street, London, SE1 9GF

BILLIONAIRES: THE TYCOON © 2019 Harlequin Books S.A.

The Billionaire's Defiant Acquisition © 2016 Sharon Kendrick
A Tycoon To Be Reckoned With © 2016 Julia James
The Boss's Baby Arrangement © 2016 Catherine Mann

ISBN: 978-0-263-27557-5

9-0419

Printed and bound in Spain
by CPI, Barcelona

THE BILLIONAIRE'S DEFIANT ACQUISITION

SHARON KENDRICK

With special thanks to fascinating
Fredrik Ferrier, for giving me an
illuminating glimpse into the world of art

And to the fabulous Annie Macdonald Hall,
who taught me so much about horses—and made
me understand why people love them so much.

CHAPTER ONE

IN THE FLESH she looked more dangerous than beautiful. Conall's mouth hardened. She was exquisite, yes…but *faded*. Like a rose which had been plucked fresh for a man's buttonhole before a wild night of partying, but which now lay wilted and drooping across his chest.

Fast asleep, she lay sprawled on top of a white leather sofa. She was wearing a baggy T-shirt, which curved over her breasts and bottom, ending midway along amazingly tanned legs which seemed to go on for ever. Beside her lay an empty champagne glass—the finger-marked crystal upended and glinting in the spring sunshine. A faint breeze drifted in from the open windows leading onto the balcony, but it wasn't enough to disperse the faint fug of cigarette smoke, along with the musky scent of incense. Conall made a barely perceptible click of distaste. Cliché after cliché were all here—embodied in the magnificent body of Amber Carter as she lay with her head pillowed on her arm and her black hair spilling like ink over her golden skin.

If she'd been a man he would have shaken her awake with a contemptuous hand, but she was not a man. She was a woman. A spoilt and distractingly beautiful woman who was now his responsibility and for some reason he didn't want to touch her. He didn't dare.

Damn Ambrose Carter, he thought viciously, remembering the older man's plaintive appeal to him. *You've got to save her from herself, Conall. Someone has to show her she can't carry on like this.* And damn his own stupid conscience, which had made him agree to carry out this crazy deal.

He listened. The apartment was silent—but maybe he should check it was empty. That there were no other bodies sprawled in one of the many bedrooms and able to hear what he was about to say to her.

He prowled from room to room, but, among all the debris of cold pizza lying in greasy boxes and half-empty bottles of vintage champagne, he could find no one. Only once did he pause—when he pushed open a door of a spare bedroom, cluttered with books and clothes and a dusty-looking exercise bike. Half hidden behind a velvet sofa was a stack of paintings and Conall walked over to them, his natural collector's eye making him flick through them with interest. The canvases were raw and angry—with swirls and splodges of paint, some of which had been highlighted with a sharp edging of black ink. He studied them for several moments, until he was forced to remember that he was here for a purpose and he turned away from the pictures and returned to the sitting room, to find Amber Carter lying exactly where he'd left her.

'Wake up,' he growled. And then, when that received no response, he repeated it—more loudly this time. 'I said, wake up.'

She moved. A golden arm reached up to brush aside the thick sweep of ebony hair which obscured most of her face, offering him a sudden unimpeded view of her profile. Her cute little nose and the natural pout of her rosy lips. Thick lashes fluttered open and as she slowly turned her head to look at him he realised that her eyes were the most startling shade of green he'd ever seen. They made the breath dry in his throat, those eyes. They made him momentarily forget what he was doing there.

'What's going on?' she questioned, in a smoky voice. 'And who the hell are you?'

She sat up, blinking as she looked around—but not creating the kind of fuss he might have expected. As if she was used to being woken by strange men who had walked into her apartment at midday. He felt another shimmer of distaste. Maybe she was.

'My name is Conall Devlin,' he said, looking at her face for some kind of recognition, but seeing only a blank and shuttered boredom on her frozen features.

'Oh, yeah?' Those amazing eyes swept over him and then she yawned. 'And how did you get in, Conall Devlin?'

In many ways Conall was the most old-fashioned of men—an accusation levelled at him many times by disappointed women in the past—and in that precise moment he felt his temper begin to flare because it confirmed everything he'd heard about her. That she was careless. That she didn't care about anything or anyone, except herself. And anger was safer than desire. Than allowing himself to focus on the way her breasts jiggled as she moved. Or to acknowledge that as she rose to her feet and walked across the room she moved with a natural grace, which made him want to stare at her and keep staring. Which made his groin begin to harden with an unwilling kind of lust.

'The door was open,' he said, not bothering to hide his disapproval.

'Oh. Right. Someone must have left it open on their way out.' She looked at him and smiled the pretty kind of smile which probably had most men eating out of her hand. 'I had a party last night.'

He didn't smile back. 'Doesn't it worry you that someone could have walked right in and burgled you—or worse?'

She shrugged. 'Not really. Security on the main door is usually very tight. Though come to think of it—you seem to have got past them without too much difficulty. How did you manage that?'

'Because I have a key,' he said, holding it up between his thumb and forefinger so that it glinted in the bright spring sunshine.

She was walking across the room—the baggy T-shirt moving across her bottom to draw his unwilling attention to the pert swell of her buttocks. But his words made her jerk her head back in surprise and a faint frown appeared on her brow as she extracted a pack of cigarettes from a small beaded handbag which was lying on a coffee table.

'What are you talking about, you *have a key*?' she questioned, pulling out a filter tip and jamming it in between her lips.

'I'd rather you didn't light that,' said Conall tightly.

Her eyes narrowed. 'Oh, really?'

'Yes. *Really*,' he gritted back sarcastically. 'Discounting the obvious dangers of passive smoking, I happen to hate the smell.'

'Then leave. Nobody's stopping you.' She flicked the lighter with a manicured thumbnail so that a blue-gold flash of flame flared briefly into life, but she only got as far as inhaling the first drag when Conall crossed the room and removed the cigarette from her mouth, ignoring her look of shock.

'What the hell do you think you're playing at?' she spluttered indignantly. 'You can't do that!'

'No?' he questioned silkily. 'Watch me, baby.' He walked out to the balcony and crushed the glowing red tip between thumb and forefinger, before dropping it into another empty champagne glass, which was standing next to a large pot plant.

When he returned he could see a look of defiance on her face as she took out a second cigarette.

'There are plenty more where that came from,' she taunted.

'And you'll only be wasting your time,' he said flatly. 'Because every cigarette you light I'm going to take from you and extinguish, until eventually you have none left.'

'And if I call the police and have you arrested for trespass and harassment,' she challenged. 'What then?'

Conall shook his head. 'Sorry to disappoint you, but neither of those charges will stand up—since I think the law might find that you are the one who is actually guilty of trespass. Remember what I just told you? That I have a key.' He paused.

He saw her defiance briefly waver. He saw a shadow cross over her beautiful green eyes and he felt a wave of something which felt almost like empathy and he wasn't quite sure why. Until he reminded himself what kind of woman she was. The spoilt, manipulative kind who stood for everything he most despised.

'Yes I know but I'm asking why—and it had better be a good explanation,' she said in a tone of voice which nobody had dared use with him for years. 'Who are you, and why have you come barging in here, trying to take control?'

'I'm happy to tell you anything you want to know,' he said evenly. 'But first I think you need to put on some clothes.'

'Why?' A smile played at the corners of her lips as she put a hand on one angled hip and struck a catwalk pose. 'Does my appearance bother you, Mr Devlin?'

'Actually, no—at least, not in the way I think you're suggesting. I'm not turned on by women who smoke and flaunt their bodies to strangers,' he said, although the latter part of this statement wasn't quite true, as the continued aching in his body testified. He swallowed against the sudden unwanted dryness in his throat. 'And since I don't have all day to waste— why don't you do as I ask and then we can get down to business?'

For a moment Amber hesitated, tempted to tell him to go to hell. To carry through her threat and march over to the phone and call the police, despite the fact that she was enjoying the unexpected *drama* of the situation. Because wasn't it good to feel *something*— even if it was only anger, when for so long now all she had felt had been a terrifying kind of *numbness*? As if she were no longer made of flesh and blood, but was colourless and invisible—like water.

She narrowed her eyes as her mind flicked back through the previous evening. Had Conall Devlin been one of the many gatecrashers at the impromptu party she'd ended up hosting? No. Definitely not. She frowned. She would have remembered him. Definitely. Because he was the kind of man you would never forget, no matter how objectionable you found him.

Unwillingly, her gaze drifted over him. His rugged features would have been perfect were it not for the fact that his nose had obviously once been broken. His hair was dark—though not quite as dark as hers—and his eyes were the colour of midnight. His jaw was dark and shadowed—as if he hadn't bothered shaving that morning, as if he had more than his fair share of testosterone raging around his body. And what a body. Amber swallowed. He looked as if he would be perfectly at ease smashing a pickaxe into a tough piece of concrete—even though she could tell that his immaculate charcoal suit must have cost a fortune.

And meanwhile the inside of her mouth felt as if it had been turned into sandpaper and she was certain her breath must smell awful because she'd fallen asleep without brushing her teeth. Her fingers crept up surreptitiously to her face. Yesterday's make-up was still clogging her eyes and beneath the baggy T-shirt her skin felt warm and sticky. It wasn't how you wanted to look when you were presented with a man as spectacular as him.

'Okay,' she said carelessly. 'I'll go and get dressed.'

She enjoyed his brief look of surprise—as if he

hadn't been expecting her sudden capitulation—and that pleased her because she liked surprising people. She could feel his gaze on her as she padded out of the room towards her bedroom, which had a breathtaking view over some of London's most famous landmarks.

She stared at the perfect circle of the London Eye as she tried to gather her thoughts together. Some women might have been freaked out at having been woken in such a way by a total stranger, but all Amber could think was that it made an interesting start to the day, when lately her days all seemed to bleed into one meaningless blur. She wondered if *Conall Devlin* was used to getting everything he wanted. Probably. He had that unmistakable air of arrogance about him. Did he think she would be intimidated by his macho stance and bossy air? Well, he would soon realise that nothing intimidated *her*.

Nothing.

She didn't rush to get ready—although she took the precaution of locking the bathroom door first. A power shower woke her into life and after she'd dressed, she carefully applied her make-up. A quick blast of the hairdryer and she was done. Twenty minutes later she emerged in a pair of skinny jeans and a clingy white T-shirt to find him still there. Just not where she'd left him—dominating the large reception room with that faintly hostile glint in his midnight-blue eyes. Instead, he was sitting on one of the sofas, busy tapping something into a laptop, as if he had every right to make himself at home. He glanced up as she walked in and she saw a look in his eyes which made her feel faintly uncomfortable, before he closed the laptop and surveyed her coolly.

'Sit down,' he said.

'This is my home, not yours and therefore you don't start telling me what to do. I don't want to sit down.'

'I think it's better you do.'

'I don't care what you think.'

His eyes narrowed. 'You don't care about very much at all, do you, Amber?'

Amber stiffened. He said her name as if he had every right to. As if it were something he'd been re-hearsing. And now she could make out the faint Irish burr in his deep voice. Her heart lurched because sud-denly this had stopped feeling like a whacky alterna-tive to a normal Sunday morning—whatever *normal* was—and had begun to feel rather…disturbing.

But she sat down on the sofa opposite his, because standing in front of him was making her feel like a naughty schoolgirl who had been summoned in front of the headmaster. And something about the way he was looking at her was making her knees wobble in a way which had nothing to do with anger.

She stared at him. 'Just who are you?'

'I told you. Conall Devlin.' He smiled. 'Name still not ringing any bells?'

She shrugged, as something drifted faintly into the distant recesses of her mind and then drifted out again. 'Maybe.'

'I know your brother, Rafe—'

'*Half*-brother,' she corrected with cold emphasis. 'I haven't seen Rafe in years. He lives in Australia.' She gave a brittle smile. 'We're a very fragmented family.'

'So I believe. I also used to work for your father.'

'My father?' She frowned. 'Oh, dear. Poor you.'

The look which greeted this remark showed that she'd irritated him and for some reason this pleased her. Amber reminded herself that he had no right to storm in and sit on one of her sofas, uninvited. Or to sit there barking out questions. The trouble was that he was exuding a disturbing air of confidence and certainty—like a magician who was saving his show-stopping trick right for the end of his act...

'Anyway,' she said, with an entirely unnecessary glance at the diamond watch which was glittering furiously at her wrist. 'I really don't have time for all this. I'll admit it was a novel way to be woken up but I'm getting bored now and I'm meeting friends for lunch. So cut to the chase and tell me why you're here, Mr Conall. Is my dear daddy having one of his occasional bouts of remorse and wondering how his children are getting on? Are you one of his heavies who he's sent to find out how I am? In which case, you can tell him I'm doing just fine.' She raised her eyebrows at him. 'Or has he grown bored with wife number...let me see, which number is he on now? Is it six? Or has he reached double figures? It's *so-o-o* difficult to keep up with his hectic love life.'

Conall listened as she spat out her spiky observations, telling himself that of *course* she was likely to be mixed up and angry and combative. That anyone with her troubled background was never going to end up taking the conventional path in life. Except he knew that adversity didn't necessarily have to make you spoilt and petulant. He thought about what his own mother had been forced to endure—the kind of hardship which would probably be beyond Amber Carter's wilful understanding.

His mouth tightened. He wouldn't be doing her any favours by patting her on her pretty, glossy head and telling her it was all going to be okay. Hadn't people been doing that all her life—with predictable results? Quite frankly, he was itching to lay her across his lap and spank a little sense into her. He felt an unwanted jerk of lust. Though maybe that wasn't such a good idea.

'I have just concluded a business deal with your father,' he said.

'Bully for you,' she said flippantly. 'No doubt he drove a hard bargain.'

'Indeed he did,' he agreed steadily, wondering if she had any idea of the irony of her words—and how much he secretly agreed with them. Because if anyone else had attempted to negotiate the kind of terms Ambrose Carter had demanded, then Conall would have given an emphatic no and walked away from the deal without looking back. But the acquisition of this imposing tower block in this part of London wasn't just something he'd set his heart on—a lifetime dream he'd never thought he'd achieve just shy of his thirty-fifth birthday. It was more than that. He owed the old man. He owed him big time. Because despite Ambrose's own car crash of an emotional life, he had shown Conall kindness at a time when his life had been short of kindness. He had given him the break he'd needed. Had believed in him when nobody else had.

'You owe me, Conall,' he'd said as he had outlined his outrageous demand. 'Do this one thing for me and we're quits.'

And even though Conall had inwardly objected to

the blatant emotional blackmail, how could he possibly have refused? If it weren't for Ambrose he could have ended up serving time in prison. His life could have been very different. Surely it wasn't beyond the realms of possibility that he could teach his mixed-up daughter a few fundamental lessons in manners and survival.

He stared into her emerald eyes and tried to ignore the sensual curve of her mouth, which was sending subliminal messages to his body and making a pulse at his temple begin to hammer. 'Yesterday, I made a significant purchase from your father.'

She wasn't really paying attention. She was too busy casting longing looks in the direction of her cigarettes. 'And your point is?'

'My point is that I now own this apartment block,' he said.

He had her attention now. All of it. Her green eyes were shocked—she looked like a cat which had had a bucket of icy water thrown over it. But it didn't take longer than a couple of seconds for her natural arrogance to assert itself. For her to narrow those amazing eyes and look down her haughty little nose at him.

'You? But...but it's been in his property portfolio for years. It's one of his key investments. Why would he sell it without telling me?' She wrinkled her brow in confusion. 'And to you?'

Conall gave a short laugh. The inference was as clear as the blue spring sky outside the penthouse windows. He wondered if she would have found the news less shocking if the purchase had been made by some rich aristocrat—someone who presumably she would have less trouble twisting around her little finger.

'Presumably because he likes doing business with me,' he said. 'And he wants to free up some of his money and commitments in order to enjoy his retirement.'

Another frown pleated her perfect brow. 'I had no idea he was thinking about retirement.'

Conall was tempted to suggest that if she communicated with her father a little more often, then she might know what was going on in his life, but he wasn't here to judge her. He was here to offer her a solution to her current appalling lifestyle, even if it went against his every instinct.

'Well, he is. He's winding down and as of now I am the new owner of this development.' He drew in a deep breath. 'Which means, of course, that there are going to be a number of changes. The main one being that you can no longer continue to live here rent-free as you have been doing.'

'Excuse me?'

'You are currently occupying a luxury apartment in a prime location,' he continued, 'which I can rent out for an astronomical monthly sum. At the moment you are paying precisely nothing and I'm afraid that the arrangement is about to come to an end.'

Her haughty expression became even haughtier and she shuddered, as if the very mention of money was in some way vulgar, and Conall felt a flicker of pleasure as he realised he was enjoying himself. Because it was a long time since a woman had shown him anything except an eager green light.

'I don't think you understand, Mr...*Devlin*,' she

continued, spitting his name out as if it were poison, 'that you will get your money. I'm quite happy to pay the current market value as rent. I just need to speak to my bank,' she concluded.

He gave a smile. 'Good luck with that.'

She was getting angry now. He could see it in the sudden glitter of her eyes and the way she curled her scarlet fingernails so that they looked like talons against the faded denim of her skinny jeans. And he felt a corresponding flicker of something he didn't recognise. Something he tried to push away as he stared into the furious tremble of her lips.

'You may know my father and my brother,' she said, 'but that certainly doesn't give you the authority to make pronouncements about things which are none of your business. Things about which you know nothing. Like my finances.'

'Oh, I know more about those than you might realise,' he said. 'More than you would probably be comfortable with.'

'I don't believe you.'

'Believe what you like, baby,' he said softly. 'Because you'll soon find out what's true. But it doesn't have to get acrimonious. I'm going to be very magnanimous, Amber, because your father and I go back a long way. And I'm going to make you an offer.'

Her magnificent eyes narrowed suspiciously. 'What kind of offer?'

'I'm going to offer you a job and the chance to redeem yourself. And if you accept, we'll see about giving you an apartment more suited to a woman on a working wage, rather than this—' He gave an expansive wave of his hand. 'Which you have to admit is more suited to someone on a millionaire's salary.'

She was staring at him incredulously, as if she couldn't believe what he'd just said. As if he were suddenly going to smile and tell her that he'd simply been teasing and she could have whatever it was she wanted. Was that how men usually behaved towards her? he wondered. Of course it was. When you looked the way she looked, men would fall over themselves whenever she clicked her beautifully manicured fingers.

'And if I don't accept?'

He shrugged. 'That will make things a little more difficult. I will be forced to give you a month's notice and after that to change the locks, and I'm afraid you'll be on your own.'

She jumped to her feet, her eyes spitting green fire—looking as if she'd like to rush across the room and rake those scarlet talons all over him. And wasn't there a primitive side of him which wished she would go right ahead? Take them right down his chest to his groin. Curve those red nails around his balls and gently scrape them, before replacing them with the lick of her tongue.

But she didn't. She just stood there sucking in a deep breath and trying to compose herself...while his erotic little fantasies meant that he was having to do exactly the same.

'I may not know much about the law, Mr Devlin,' she said, biting out the words like splinters of ice, 'but even I know that you aren't allowed to throw a sitting tenant out onto the streets.'

'But you're not a tenant, Amber, and you never

have been,' he said, trying not to show the sudden triumph which rushed through him. Because although she might be spoilt and thoroughly objectionable, she was going to learn enough of life's harsher lessons in the coming weeks, without him rubbing salt into the wound. He picked his next words carefully. 'Your father has been letting you live here as a favour, nothing more. You didn't sign any agreements—'

'Of course I didn't—because he's my *father*!'

'Which means that your occupancy was simply an act of kindness. And now he has sold it to me, I'm afraid he no longer has any interest or claims on the property. And as a consequence, neither do you.'

Wildly, she shook her head and ebony tendrils of hair flew around it. 'He wouldn't just have sprung it on me like this! He would have told me!' she said, her voice rising.

'He said he'd sent you a letter to inform you what was happening, and so had the bank.'

Amber shot an anguished glance over at the pile of mail which lay unopened on the desk. She had a terrible habit of putting letters to one side and ignoring them. She'd done it for longer than she could remember. Letters only ever contained bad news and all her bills were paid by direct debit and if people wanted her that badly, they could always send an email. Because that was what people did, wasn't it?

But in the meantime, she wasn't going to take any notice of this shadowed-jawed man with the mocking voice and a presence which was strangely unsettling. All she had to do was to speak to her father. There had to be some kind of mistake. There *had to*. Either that, or Daddy's brain wasn't as sharp as it had once been. Why else would he choose to sell one of the jewels in his property crown to this...this *thug*?

'I'd like you to leave now, Mr Devlin.'

He raised dark and mocking brows. 'So you're not interested in my offer? A proper job for the first time in your privileged life? The chance to show the world that you're more than just a vapid socialite who flits from party to party?'

'I'd sooner work for the devil than work for you,' she retorted, watching as he rose from the sofa and moved across the room until he was towering over her, with a grim expression on his dark face.

'Make an appointment to see me when you're ready to see sense,' he said, putting a business card down on the coffee table.

'That just isn't going to happen—be very sure about that,' she said, pulling a cigarette from the pack and glaring at him defiantly, as if daring him to stop her again. 'Now go to hell, will you?'

'Oh, believe me, baby,' he said softly. 'Hell would be a preferable alternative to a minute more spent in *your* company.'

And didn't it only add outrage to Amber's growing sense of panic to realise that he actually *meant* it?

CHAPTER TWO

AMBER'S FINGERS WERE trembling as she left the bank and little rivulets of sweat were trickling down over her hot cheeks. Impatiently brushing them aside, she stood stock-still outside the gleaming building while all around her busy City types made little tutting noises of irritation as they were forced to weave their way around her.

There had to be some kind of mistake. There had to be. She couldn't believe that her father would be so cruel. Or so dictatorial. That he would have instructed that tight-lipped bank manager to inform her that all funds in her account had been frozen, and no more would be forthcoming. But her rather hysterical request that the bank manager stop *freaking her out* had been met with nothing but an ominous silence and now that she was outside, the truth hit her like a sledgehammer coming at her out of nowhere.

She was broke.

Her heart slammed against her ribcage. Part of her still didn't want to believe it. Had the bank manager been secretly laughing at her when he'd handed over the formal-looking letter? She'd ripped it open and stared in horror as the words written by her father's lawyer had wobbled before her eyes and a key phrase had jumped out at her, like a spectre.

Conall Devlin has been instructed to provide any assistance you may need.

Conall Devlin? She had literally *shaken* with rage. Conall Devlin, the brute who had stormed into her apartment yesterday and who was responsible for her current state of homelessness? She would sooner starve than ask *him* for assistance. She would talk her father round and he would listen to her. He always did.

But in the middle of her defiance came an overwhelming wave of panic and fear, which washed over her and made her feel as if she were drowning. It was the same feeling she used to get when her mother would suddenly announce that they were leaving a city, and all Amber's hard-fought-for friends would soon become distant and then forgotten memories.

She mustn't panic. She mustn't.

Her fingers still shaking, Amber sheltered in a shop doorway and took out her cell phone. She rang her father's number, but it went straight through to his personal assistant, Mary-Ellen, a woman who had never been her biggest fan and who didn't bother hiding her disapproval when she heard Amber's voice.

'Amber. This *is* a surprise,' she said archly.

'Hello, Mary-Ellen.' Amber drew in a deep breath. 'I need to speak to my father—urgently. Is he there?'

'I'm afraid he's not.'

'Do you know when he'll be back or where I can get hold of him?'

There was a pause and Amber wondered if she was

being paranoid, or whether it sounded like a very deliberate pause.

'I'm afraid it isn't quite as easy as that. He's gone to an ashram in India.'

Amber gave a snort of disbelief and a passing businessman shot her a funny look. 'My father? Gone to an ashram? To do yoga and eat vegan food? Is this some kind of joke, Mary-Ellen?'

'No, it is not a joke,' said Mary-Ellen crisply. 'He's been trying to get hold of you for weeks. He's left a lawyer's letter with the bank—did you get it?'

Amber thought about the screwed-up piece of paper currently reposing with several sticks of chewing gum and various lipsticks at the bottom of her handbag. 'Yes, I got it.'

'Then I suggest you follow his advice and speak to Conall Devlin. All his contact details are there. Conall is the man who'll be able to help you in your father's absence. He's—'

With a howl of rage, Amber cut the connection and slung her phone back into her bag, before starting to walk—not knowing nor caring which direction she was taking. She didn't want *Conall Devlin* to help her! What was it with him that suddenly his name was on everyone's lips as if he were some kind of god? And what was it with her that she was behaving like some kind of helpless *victim*, just because a few obstacles had been put in her way?

Worse things than this had happened to her, she reminded herself. She'd survived a nightmare childhood, hadn't she? And even when she'd got through that, the problems hadn't stopped coming. She wiped a trickle of sweat away from her forehead. But those

kinds of thoughts wouldn't help her now. She needed
to think clearly. She needed to go back to the apartment to work out some kind of coping strategy until
she could get hold of her father. And she *would* get
hold of him. Somehow she would track him down—
even if she had to hitchhike to the wretched ashram in order to do so. She would appeal to his better
judgement and the sense of guilt which had never
quite left him for kicking her and her mother out onto
the street. Surely he wasn't planning to do that for a
second time? And surely he hadn't *really* frozen her
funds? But in the meantime…

She caught the Tube and got out near her apartment, stopping off at the nearest shop to buy some
provisions since her rumbling stomach was reminding her that she'd had nothing to eat that morning. But
after putting a whole stack of shopping and a pack
of cigarettes through the till, she had the humiliation of seeing the machine decline her card. There
was an audible sigh of irritation from the man in
the queue behind her and she saw one woman nudg-
ing her friend as they moved closer as if anticipating
some sort of scene.

'There must be some kind of mistake,' Amber
mumbled, her face growing scarlet. 'I shop in here
all the time—you must remember me? I can bring
the money along later.'

But as the embarrassed shop assistant shook her
head, she told Amber that it was company policy
never to accept credit. And as she rang the bell underneath her till deep down Amber knew there had been
no mistake. Her father really had done it. He'd *frozen her funds* just as the bank manager had told her.

She thought about her refrigerator at home and its meagre contents. There was plenty of champagne but little else—a tub of Greek yoghurt, which was probably growing a forest of mould by now, a bag of oranges and those soggy chocolate biscuits which were past their sell-by date. Her cheeks growing even hotter, Amber scrabbled around in her purse for some spare change and found nothing but a solitary, crumpled note.

'I'll just take the cigarettes,' she croaked, handing over the note but not quite daring to meet the eyes of the assistant as she scuttled from the shop.

The trouble was that these days everyone *glared* at you if you dared smoke a cigarette and Amber was forced to wait until she reached home before she could light up. Whatever happened to personal freedom? she wondered as she slammed the front door behind her and fumbled around for her lighter with shaking hands. She thought about the way Conall Devlin had snatched the cigarette from her lips yesterday and a feeling of fury washed over her.

On a whim, she tapped out a text to her half-brother, Rafe, as she tried to remember what time it was in Australia.

What do you know about a man called Conall Devlin?

Considering they hadn't been in contact for well over a year, Amber was surprised and pleased when Rafe's reply came winging back almost immediately.

Best mate at school. Why?

So *that* was why the name had rung a distant bell and why Conall's midnight-blue eyes had bored into her when he'd said it. Rafe was eleven years older than her and had left home by the time she'd moved back into their father's house as a mixed-up fourteen-year-old. But—come to think of it—hadn't her father mentioned some Irish whizz-kid on the payroll who'd dragged himself up from the gutter? Was Conall Devlin the one he'd been talking about?

She wanted to ask him more, but Rafe was probably lying on some golden beach somewhere, sipping champagne and surrounded by gorgeous women. Did she inform him she was soon to be homeless and that the Irishman had threatened to have the locks changed? Would he even believe her version of the story if he and Conall Devlin had been *best mates*?

There was a ping as another text arrived.

And why are you texting me at midnight?

Amber bit her lip. Was there really any point in grumbling to a man who was thousands of miles away? What was she expecting him to do—transfer money to her account? Because something told her he wouldn't do it, despite the fortune Rafe had built up for himself on the other side of the world. Her half-brother had been one of the people who were always nagging her to get a proper job. Wasn't that one of the reasons why she'd allowed herself to lose touch with him—because he told her things she preferred not hear?

Her fingers wavered over the touchpad.

Just wanted to say hi.

Hi to you, too! Nice to hear from you. Let's talk soon. X

Amber's eyes inexplicably began to fill with tears as she tapped out her reply: Okay. X.

It was the only good thing which had happened to her all day but the momentary glow of contentment it gave her didn't last long. Amber sat on the floor disconsolately finishing her cigarette and then began to shiver. How *could* her father have gone away to India and left her in this predicament?

She thought about what everyone was saying and the different alternatives which lay open to her, realising there weren't actually that many. She could throw herself on people's mercy and ask to sleep on their sofas, but for how long? And she couldn't even do *that* without enough money to offer towards household expenses. Everyone would start to look at her in a funny way if she didn't contribute to food and stuff. And if she couldn't buy her very expensive round in the nightclubs they tended to frequent, then everyone would start to gossip—because in the kind of circles she mixed in, being broke was social death.

She stared down at the diamond watch glittering at her wrist, an eighteenth-birthday present intended to console her during a particularly low point in her life. It hadn't, of course. It had been one of many lessons she'd learnt along the way. It didn't matter how many jewels you wore, their cold beauty was powerless to fill the empty holes which punctured your soul...

She thought about going to a pawnbroker and wondered if such places still existed, but something told her she would get a desultory price for the watch.

Because people who tried to raise money against jewellery were vulnerable and she knew better than anyone that the vulnerable were there to be taken advantage of.

The sweat of earlier had dried on her skin and her teeth began to chatter loudly. Amber remembered her father's letter and the words of Mary-Ellen, his assistant. *Speak to Conall Devlin.* And even though every instinct she possessed was warning her to steer clear of the trumped-up Irishman, she suspected she had no choice but to turn to him.

She stared down at her creased clothes.

She licked her lips with a feeling of instinctive fear. She didn't like men. She didn't trust them, and with good reason. But she knew their weaknesses. Her mother hadn't taught her much, but she'd drummed in the fact that men were always susceptible to a woman who looked at them helplessly.

Fired up by a sudden sense of purpose, Amber went into her en-suite bathroom and took a long shower. And then she dressed with more care than she'd used in a long time.

She remembered the disdainful look on Conall Devlin's face when he'd told her that he didn't get turned on by women who smoked and flaunted their bodies. And she remembered the contemptuous expression in his navy-blue eyes as he'd said that. So she fished out a navy-blue dress which she'd only ever worn to failed job interviews, put on minimal make-up and twisted her black hair back into a smooth and demure chignon. Stepping back from the mirror, Amber hardly recognised the image which stared back at her. Why, she could almost pose as a body double for Julie Andrews in *The Sound of Music*!

Conall Devlin's offices were tucked away in a surprisingly picturesque and quiet street in Kensington, which was lined with cherry trees. She didn't know what she'd expected to find, but it certainly hadn't been a restored period building whose outward serenity belied the unmistakable buzz of success she encountered the moment she stepped inside.

The entrance hall had a soaringly high ceiling, with quirky chandeliers and a curving staircase which swept up from the chequered marble floor. A transparent desk sat in front of a modern painting of a woman caressing the neck of a goat. Beside it was a huge canvas with a glittery image of Marilyn Monroe, which Amber recognised instantly. She felt a little stab at her heart. Everything in the place seemed achingly cool and trendy, and suddenly she felt like a fish out of water in her frumpy navy dress and stark hairstyle. A fact which wasn't helped by the lofty blonde receptionist in a monochrome minidress who looked up from behind the Perspex desk and smiled at Amber in a friendly way.

'Hi! Can I help you?'

'I want to see Conall Devlin.' The words came out more clumsily than Amber had intended and the blonde looked a little taken aback.

'I'm afraid Conall is tied up for most of the day,' she said, her smile a little less bright than before. 'You don't have an appointment?'

Amber could feel a rush of emotions flooding through her, but the most prominent of them all was a sensation of being *less than*. As if she had no right to be here. *As if she had no right to be anywhere.* She found herself wondering what on earth she was doing in her frumpy dress when this sunny-looking creature looked as if she'd just strayed in from a land of milk and honey, but it was too late to do anything about it now. She put her bag down on one of the modern chairs which looked more like works of art than objects designed for sitting on, and shot the receptionist a defiant look.

'Not a formal appointment, no. But I need to see him—urgently—so I'll just sit here and wait, if you don't mind.'

The smile now nothing but a memory, a faint frown creased the blonde's brow. 'It might be better if you came back later,' she said carefully.

Amber thought of Conall walking into her apartment without knocking. About the smug look on his face as he'd held up the key and warned her that she had four weeks to get out. She was the sister of his best friend from school, for heaven's sake—surely he could find it in his hard heart to show her a modicum of kindness?

She sat down heavily on one of the chairs.

'I'm not going anywhere. I need to see him and it's urgent, so I'll wait. But please don't worry—I've got all day.' And with that she picked up one of the glossy magazines which were adorning the low table and pretended to read it.

She was aware that the blonde had begun tapping away on her computer, probably sending Conall an email, since she could hardly call him and tell him that a strange woman was currently occupying the reception area and refusing to move—not when she was within earshot.

Sure enough, she heard the sound of a door opening on the floor above and then someone walking down the sweeping staircase. Amber heard his steps grow closer and closer but she didn't glance up from the magazine until she was aware that someone was coming towards her. And when she could no longer restrain herself, she looked up.

The breath dried in her throat and there wasn't a thing she could do about it, because yesterday she hadn't been expecting him and today she was. And surely that meant she should have been primed not to react—she was busy telling herself *not* to react—but somehow it didn't work like that. Her heart began to pound and her mouth dried to dust and feelings which were completely alien to her began to fizz through her body. On his own territory he looked even more intimidating than he had done yesterday—and that was saying something.

The urbane business suit had gone and he was dressed entirely in black. A black cashmere sweater and a pair of black jeans, which hugged his narrow hips and emphasised his long, muscular legs. His shadowy presence only seemed to emphasise the sense of power which radiated from him like a dark aura. Against the sombre shade, his skin seemed more golden than she remembered—but his midnight eyes were shuttered and his unsmiling face gave nothing away.

'I thought I told you to make an appointment—although I can't remember if that was before or after you told me to go to hell.' His lips flattened into an odd kind of smile. 'And since you can see for yourself that this place is as far from hell as you can imagine—I'm wondering exactly what it is you're doing here, Amber.'

Amber stared into his eyes and tried to think about something other than the realisation that they gleamed like sapphires. Or that his features were so rugged and strong. He looked so powerful and unyielding, she thought. As if he held all the cards and she held none. She wanted to demand that he listen to her and stop trying to impose his will on her. Until she reminded herself that she was supposed to be appealing to his better nature—in which case it would make sense to adopt a more conciliatory tone, rather than blurting out her demands.

'I've been to the bank,' she said.

He smiled, but it wasn't a particularly friendly smile. 'And the nasty man there informed you that your father has finally pulled the plug on all the freebies you've survived on until now—is that what you were going to say, Amber?'

'That's exactly what I was going to say,' she whispered.

'And?'

He shot the word out like a bullet and Amber began to wonder if she should have worn something different. Something shorter, which might have shown a bit of leg instead of her knees being completely covered by the frumpy dress.

Well, if you're going to dress like a poor orphan from the storm—then at least start behaving like one.

Her voice gave a little wobble, which wasn't entirely fabricated. 'And I don't know what I'm going to do,' she said.

His lips twisted. 'You could try going out to work, like the rest of the human race.'

'But I...' Amber kept the hovering triumph in her voice at bay and replaced it with a gloomy air of resignation. 'I'm almost impossible to employ, that's the trouble. It's a fierce job market out there and I don't have many of the qualities which employers are seeking.'

'Agreed,' he said unexpectedly. 'An overwhelming sense of entitlement never goes down well with the boss.'

She cleared her throat. 'Things are really bad, Conall. I can't get hold of my father, my credit cards have all been frozen and I can't...I can't even *eat*,' she finished dramatically.

'But presumably you can still smoke?'

Her head jerked back and her eyes narrowed...

'And don't bother denying it,' he ground out. 'Because I can smell it on you and it makes me sick to the stomach. It's a disgusting habit—and one you're going to have to kick.'

Amber could feel her blood pressure rising, but she forced herself to stay calm. Be docile, she told herself. Let him believe what he wants to believe.

'Of course I'll give it up if you help me,' she said meekly.

'You mean that?'

Chewing on her bottom lip and making her eyes grow very big, Amber nodded. 'Of course I do.'

He gave a brief nod. 'I'm not sure I believe you, but if you're just playing games, then let me warn you right now that it's a bad idea and you might as well turn around and walk out again. However, if you're really in a receptive place and serious about wanting to change, then I will help you. Do you want my help, Amber?'

It nearly killed her to do so but she gave a sulky nod. 'I suppose so.'

'Good. Then come upstairs to my office and we'll decide what we're going to do with you.' He glanced over at the blonde and Amber was almost certain that he *winked* at her. 'Hold all my calls, will you, Serena?'

CHAPTER THREE

CONALL DEVLIN'S OFFICE was nothing like Amber would have imagined, either. She had expected something brash, or slightly tacky—something which would fit well with his brutish exterior. But she was momentarily lost for words as he took her into a beautifully decorated first-floor room which overlooked the street at the front and a beautiful garden at the back.

The walls were grey—the subtle colour of an oyster shell—and it provided the perfect backdrop for many paintings which hung there. Amber blinked as she looked around. It was like being in an art gallery. He was obviously into modern art and he had a superb eye, she conceded reluctantly. His curved desk looked like a work of art itself and in one corner of the room was a modern sculpture of a naked woman made out of some sort of resin. Amber glanced over at it before quickly looking away, because there was something uncomfortably *sensual* about the woman's stance and the way she was cupping her breast with lazy fingers.

She looked up to find Conall watching her, his midnight eyes shuttered as he indicated the chair in front of his desk, but Amber was much too wired to be able to sit still while facing him. Something told her that being subjected to that mocking stare would be unendurable.

So start clawing some power back, she told herself fiercely. *Be sweet. Make him* want *to help you.*

He was rich enough to give her a temporary stay of execution until her father got back from his ashram and everything could be cleared up. She walked over to one of the windows and stared down onto the street as two teenage girls strolled past, chewing gum and giggling—and she felt a momentary pang of wistfulness for the apparent ease of their lives and a sense of being carefree which had always eluded her.

'I haven't got all day,' he warned. 'So let's cut to the chase. And before you start fluttering those long eyelashes at me, or trying to work the convent-schoolgirl look—which, let me tell you, isn't doing it for me—let me spell out a few things. I'm not giving you money without something in return and I'm not letting you have an apartment which is way too big for you. So if the sole purpose of this unscheduled visit is to throw yourself on my mercy asking for funds—then you're wasting your time.'

For a moment Amber was struck dumb because she couldn't ever remember anyone speaking to her like that. Up until the age of four she'd been a princess living in a palace, and then she'd been catapulted straight into a nightmare when her parents had split up. The next ten years had been several degrees of horrible and she hadn't known which way to turn. And when she'd been brought back to live in her father's house after her mother's accident—seriously cramping his style with wife number whatever it had been—everyone had tiptoed round her.

Nobody had known how to deal with a grieving and angry teenager and neither had she. Her confidence had been completely punctured and so had her self-esteem. Her moods had been wild and unpredictable and she'd quickly realised that she could get people to do what she wanted them to do. Amber had learnt that if her lips wobbled in a certain way, then people fell over themselves to help her. She'd also realised that rubbing your toe rather obsessively over the carpet and staring at it as if it contained the secret of the universe was pretty effective, too, because it made people want to draw you out of yourself.

But there was something about Conall Devlin which made her realise he would see right through any play-acting or attempts at manipulation. His eyes were much too keen and bright and intelligent. They were fixed on her now in question so that, for one bizarre moment, she felt as if he might actually be able to read her thoughts, and that he certainly wouldn't like them if he could.

'Then how am I expected to survive?' she questioned. Defiantly she held up her wrist so that her diamond watch glittered, like bright sunlight on water. 'Do you want me to start pawning the few valuable items I have?'

His eyes gleamed as he plucked an imaginary violin from the empty air and proceeded to play it, but then he put his big hands down on the surface of his desk and stared at her, his face sombre.

'Why don't you spare me the sob story, Amber?' he said. 'And start explaining some of *these*.'

Suddenly he upended a large manila envelope and spread the contents out over his desk and Amber stared at the collection of photos and magazine clippings with a feeling of trepidation.

'Where did you get these?'

He made an expression of distaste, as if they were harbouring some form of contamination. 'Your father gave them to me.'

Amber knew she'd made it into various gossip columns and some of those 'celebrity' magazines which adorned the shelves of supermarket checkouts. Some of the articles she'd seen and some she hadn't—but she'd never seen them all together like this, like a pictorial history of her life. Fanned across his desk like a giant pack of cards, there were countless pictures of her. Pictures of her leaving nightclubs and pictures of her attending gallery and restaurant openings. In every single shot her dress looked too short and her expression seemed wild. But then the flash of the camera was something that she loved and loathed in equal measure. Wasn't she stupidly grateful that someone cared enough to want to take her photo— as if to reassure her that she wasn't invisible? Yet the downside was that it always made her feel like a butterfly who had fluttered into the collector's room by mistake—who'd had her fragile wings pierced by the sharp pins which then fettered her to a piece of card...

She looked up from the photos and straight into his eyes and nobody could have failed to see the condemnation in their midnight depths. *Don't let him see the chink in your armour*, she told herself fiercely. *Don't give him that power.*

'Quite good, aren't they?' she said carelessly as she pulled out the chair and sat down at last.

At that point, Conall could have slammed his fist onto the desk in sheer frustration, because she was shameless. Completely shameless. Worse even than he'd imagined. Did she think he was stupid—or was the effect of her dressing up today like some off-duty nun supposed to have him eating out of her hand?

But the crazy thing was that—no matter how contrived it was—on some subliminal level, the look actually worked. No matter what he'd said and no matter how much he tried to convince himself otherwise, he couldn't seem to take his eyes off her. With her thick black hair scraped back from her face like that, you could see the perfect oval of her face and get the full impact of those long-lashed emerald eyes. Was she aware that she had the kind of looks which would make men want to fight wars for her? Conall's mouth twisted. Of course she was. And she had been manipulating that beauty, probably since she first hit puberty.

He remembered his reaction when Ambrose had asked him for his help and then shown him all the photos. There had been a moment of stunned silence as Conall had looked at them and felt a powerful hit of lust which had been almost visceral. It had been like a punch to the guts. Or the groin. There had been one in particular of her wearing some wispy little white dress, managing to look both intensely pure and intensely provocative at the same time. Guilt had rushed through him as he'd stared at her father and shaken his head.

'Get someone else to do the job,' he'd said gruffly.

'I can't think of anyone else who would be capable of handling her,' had been Ambrose's candid reply. 'Nor anyone I would trust as much as I do you.'

And wasn't that the worst thing of all? That Ambrose *trusted* him to do right by his daughter? So that, not only had Conall agreed, but he was now bound by a deep sense of honour to do the decent thing by the man who had saved him from a life of crime.

It would have been easier if he could just have signed her a cheque and told her to go away and sort herself out, but Ambrose had been adamant that she needed grounding, and he knew the old man's determination of old.

'She needs to discover how to live a decent life and to stop sponging off other people,' he said. 'And you are going to help her, Conall.'

And how the hell was he supposed to do that when all he could think about was what it would be like to unpin her hair and kiss her until she was gasping for breath? About what it would be like to cradle those hips within the palms of his hands as he drove into her until they were both crying out their pleasure?

He stared into the glitter of her eyes, unable to blot out the unmistakable acknowledgement that her defiance was turning him on even more, because women rarely defied him. So what was he going to do about it—give up or carry on? The question was academic really, because giving up had never been an option for him. Maybe he could turn this into an exercise in self-restraint. Unless his standards had really sunk so low that he could imagine being intimate with someone who stood for everything he most despised.

He thought back to the question she'd just asked

and his gaze slid over the pile of photos—alighting on one where she was sitting astride a man's shoulders, a champagne bottle held aloft while a silky green dress clung to her shapely thighs.

'They're good if you want to portray yourself as a vacuous airhead,' he said slowly. 'But then again, that's not something which is going to look good on your CV.'

'Your own CV being whiter than white, I suppose?' she questioned acidly.

For a moment, Conall fixed her with an enquiring look. Had Ambrose told her about the dark blots on his own particular copybook? In which case she would realise that he knew what he was talking about. He'd had his own share of demons; his own wake-up call to deal with. But she said nothing—just continued to regard him with a look of foxy challenge which was making his blood boil.

'This is supposed to be about you,' he said. 'Not me.'

'So go on, then,' she said sarcastically. 'I'm all ears.'

'That's probably the first sensible thing you've said all day.' He leaned back in his chair and studied her. 'This is what I propose you do, Amber. Obviously, you need a job in order to pay the rent but, as you have yourself recognised, your CV makes you unemployable. So you had better come and work for me. Simple.'

Amber went very still because when he put it like that it actually *sounded* simple. She blinked at him as she felt the first faint stirring of hope. Cautiously, she looked around the beautifully proportioned room, with its windows which looked out onto the iconic London street. Outside the trees were frothing with pink blossom, as if someone had daubed them with candyfloss. There was a bunch of flowers on his desk—the tiny, highly scented blooms they called paper-whites, which sent a beguiling drift of perfume through the air. She wondered if the blonde in the minidress had put them there. Just as she wondered who had sent him that postcard of the Taj Mahal, or that little glass dish in the shape of a pair of lips, which was currently home to a gleaming pile of paperclips.

And suddenly she was hit by that feeling which always used to come over her at school, when she was invited to a friend's house for the weekend and the friend's parents were still together. The feeling that she was on the outside looking in at a perfectly ordered world where everything worked the way it was supposed to. She swallowed. Because Conall Devlin was offering her a—temporary—place in that sort of world, wasn't he? Didn't that count for something?

'I'm not exactly sure what your line of business is,' she said, asking the competent kind of question he would no doubt expect.

He regarded her from between those shuttered lashes. 'I deal in property—that's my bread-and-butter stuff. I sell houses and apartments all over London and I have subsidiary offices in Paris and New York. But my enduring love is for art, as you might have gathered.'

'Yes,' she said politely, unable to keep the slight note of amazement from her voice but he picked up on it immediately because his midnight eyes glinted.

'You sound surprised, Amber.'

She shrugged. 'I suppose I am.'

'Because I don't fit the stereotype?' He raised a pair of mocking eyebrows. 'Because my suit isn't pinstriped and I don't have a title?'

'Careful, Mr Devlin—that chip on your shoulder seems like it's getting awfully heavy.'

He laughed at this and Amber was angry with herself for the burst of pleasure which rushed through her. Why the hell feel *thrilled* just because she'd managed to make the overbearing Irishman laugh?

'I deal solely in twentieth-century pieces and buy mainly for my own pleasure,' he said. 'But occasionally I procure pieces for clients or friends or for business acquaintances. I act as a middle man.'

'Why do they need *you* as a middle man?'

He stared briefly at the postcard of the Taj Mahal. 'Because buying art is not just about negotiation—it's about being able to close the deal. And that's something I'm good at. Some of the people I buy for are very wealthy, with vast amounts of money at their disposal. Sometimes they prefer to buy anonymously— in order to avoid being ripped off by unscrupulous sellers who want to charge them an astronomical amount.' He smiled. 'Or sometimes people want to sell anonymously and they come to me to help them get the highest possible price.'

Amber's eyes narrowed as she tried not to react to the undeniable impact of that smile. Somehow he had managed to make himself sound incredibly *fascinating*. As if powerful people were keen to do business with him. Had that been his intention, to show her there was more to him than met the eye?

She folded her hands together on her lap. How hard could it be to work for him? The only disadvantage would be having to deal with *him*, but the property side would be a piece of cake. Presumably you just took a prospective buyer along to a house and told them a famous actress had just moved in along the road and prices had rocketed as a result, and they'd be signing on the dotted line quicker than you could say bingo.

'I can do that,' she said confidently.

His eyes narrowed. 'Do what?'

'Sell houses. Or apartments. Whatever you want.'

He sat up very straight. 'Just like that?' he said silkily.

'Sure. How hard can it be?'

'You think I'm going to let someone like you loose in a business I've spent the last fifteen years building up?' he questioned, raking his fingers back through his thick black hair with an unmistakable gesture of irritation. 'You think that selling the most expensive commodity a person will ever buy should be entrusted to someone who hasn't ever held down a proper job, and has spent most of her adult life falling out of nightclubs?'

Amber bristled at his damning assessment and a flare of fury fizzed through her as she listened to his disparaging words. She wanted to do a number of things in retaliation, starting with taking that jug of water from his desk and upending the contents all over his now ruffled dark hair. And then she would have liked to have marched out of his office and slammed the door very firmly behind her and never set eyes on his handsome face ever again. But that wouldn't exactly help foster the brand-new image she was trying to convey, would it? She wanted him to believe she could be calm and unruffled. She would give him a glimpse of the new and efficient Amber who wasn't going to rise to the insults of a man who meant nothing to her, other than as a means to an end.

'I can always learn,' she said. 'But if you think I'd be better suited to shifting a few paintings, I'll happily give that a go. I…I like art.'

He made a small sound at the back of his throat, which sounded almost like a growl, and seemed to be having difficulty holding on to his temper—she could tell that by the way he had suddenly started drumming his fingertips against the desk, as if he were sending out an urgent message in Morse code.

But when he looked up at her again, she thought she saw the glint of something in his dark blue eyes which made her feel slightly nervous. Was it anticipation she could read there, or simply sheer devilment?

'I think you'll find that selling art involves slightly more of a skill set than one described as *shifting a few paintings*,' he said drily. 'And besides, my plans for you are very different.' He glanced down at the sheet of paper which lay on the desk before him. 'I understand that you speak several languages.'

'Now it's your turn to sound surprised, Mr Devlin.'

He shrugged his broad shoulders and sat back in his seat. 'I guess I am. I didn't have you down as a linguist, with all the hours of study that must have involved.'

Amber's lips flattened. 'There is more than one way to learn a language,' she said. 'My skill comes not from hours sitting at a desk—but from the fact that my mother had a penchant for Mediterranean men. And as a child I often found myself living in whichever new country was the home of her latest love interest.' She gave a bitter laugh. 'And, believe me, there were plenty of those. Consequently, I learnt to speak the local language. It was a question of survival.'

His eyes narrowed as he looked at her thoughtfully. 'That must have been...hard.'

Amber shook her head, more out of habit than anything else. Because sympathy or compassion—or whatever you wanted to call it—made her feel uncomfortable. It started making her remember people like Marco or Stavros or Pierre—all those men who had broken her mother's heart so conclusively and left Amber to deal with the mess they'd left behind. It made her wish for the impossible—that she'd been like other people and lived a normal, quiet life without a mother who seemed to think that the answer to all their problems was *being in love*. And remembering all that stuff ran the risk of making you feel vulnerable. It left you open to pain—and she'd had more than her fair share of pain.

'It was okay,' she said, in a bored tone which came easily after so many years of practice. 'I certainly know how to say "my darling" in Italian, Greek and French. And I can do plenty of variations on the line "You complete and utter bastard".'

Had her flippant tone shocked him? Was that why a faintly disapproving note had entered his voice?

'Well, you certainly won't be needed to relay any of those sentiments, be very clear about that.' He glanced down at the sheet of paper again. 'But be-

fore I lay down the terms of any job I might be prepared to offer—I need some assurances from you.'

'What kind of assurances?'

'Just that I don't have any room in my organisation
for loose cannons, or petulant princesses who say the
first thing which comes into their head. I deal with
people who need careful handling and I need to know
that you can demonstrate judgement and tact before I
put my proposition to you.' His midnight eyes grew
shadowed. 'Because frankly, right now, I'm finding
it hard to imagine you being anything other than...
difficult.'

His words hurt. More than they should have done.
More than she'd expected them to—or perhaps that
had something to do with the way he was looking at
her. As if he couldn't quite believe the person she was.
As if someone like her had no right to exist. And yet
all this was complicated by the fact that he looked so
spectacular, with his black sweater hugging his magnificent body and his sensual lips making all kinds of
complicated thoughts that began to nudge themselves
into her mind. Because her body was reacting to him
in a way she wasn't used to. A way she couldn't seem
to control. She could feel herself growing restless beneath that searing sapphire stare—and yet she didn't
even *like* him.

He was like some kind of modern-day *jailer*. Strut-
ting around in his Kensington mansion with all his
skinny, miniskirted minions scurrying around and
looking at her as if she were something the cat had
dragged in. But she had only herself to blame. He had
backed her into a corner and she had let him. She had
come crawling here today to ask for his help and he

had taken this as permission to give her yet another piece of his mind. Imagine *working* for a man like Conall Devlin.

A familiar sense of rebellion began to well up inside her, accompanied by the liberating realisation that she was under no obligation to accept his dictatorial attitude. Why not show him—and everyone else—that she was a survivor? She might not have a wall covered with degrees, but she wasn't stupid. How hard could it be to find herself a job and a place to live? What about tapping into some of the resilience she'd relied on when she'd been dragged from city to city by her mother?

Rising to her feet, she picked up her handbag, acutely aware of those eyes burning into her as if they were scorching their way through her frumpy navy-blue dress and able to see beneath. And wasn't there something about that scrutiny which excited her as much as terrified her? 'I may be underqualified,' she said, 'but I'm not desperate. I'm resourceful enough to find myself some sort of employment which doesn't involve working for a man with an overinflated sense of his own importance.'

He gave a soft laugh. 'So your answer is no?'

'My answer is more along the lines of *in your dreams*,' she retorted. 'And it's not going to happen. I'm perfectly capable of being independent and that's what I'm going to do.'

'Oh, Amber,' he said slowly. 'You are magnificent. That kind of spirit in a woman is quite something— and if you didn't reek of cigarette smoke and feel that the world owed you some sort of living, you'd be quite worryingly attractive.'

For a moment Amber was confused. Was he insulting her or complimenting her—or was it a mixture of both? She glowered at him before walking over to the door and slamming her way out—to the sound of his soft laughter behind her. But the stupid thing was that she felt like someone who'd jumped out of an aeroplane and forgotten to pull the cord on their parachute. As if she were in free fall. As if the world were rushing up towards her and she didn't know when she was going to hit it.

I'll show them, she told herself fiercely. *I'll show them all.*

CHAPTER FOUR

'I'M SO SORRY!' Quickly, Amber mopped up the spilled champagne and edged away from the table as the customer looked at her with those piggy little eyes which had been trailing her movements all evening. 'I'll get you another drink right away.'

'Why don't you sit down and join me instead?' He leered, patting the seat beside him with a podgy hand. 'And we'll forget about the drink.'

Amber shook her head and tried to hide her ever-present sense of revulsion. 'I'm not supposed to mix with the customers,' she said, grabbing her tray and heading towards the bar on feet which were far from steady. She was used to wearing high heels, but these stilt-like red shoes were so gravity defying that walking in them took every ounce of concentration and it wasn't helped by the rest of the club 'uniform'. Her black satin dress was so tight she could scarcely breathe and meanwhile the heavy throb of the background music was giving her a headache.

And judging by the look on her manager's face, the drink spillage hadn't gone unnoticed. Behind her smile Amber gritted her teeth, wondering if she'd taken leave of her senses when she'd stormed out of Conall's office telling him she didn't want his job. Had she really thought the world would be at her feet, waiting to dole out wonderful opportunities by way of compensation? Because life wasn't like that. She'd quickly discovered that a CV riddled with holes and zero qualifications brought you few opportunities and the only work available was in places like this—an underlit hotel nightclub where nobody looked happy.

'That's the third drink you've spilled this week!' The manager's voice quivered indignantly as Amber grew closer. 'Where did you learn to be so clumsy?'

'I...I moved a bit too quickly. I thought he was going to pinch my bottom,' babbled Amber.

'And? What's the matter with that?' The manager glared. 'Isn't it nice to have a man show his appreciation towards an attractive woman? Why else do you think we dress you up like that? Well, you'll have the cost of the drink taken from your wages, Amber. Now go and fetch him another one and, for goodness' sake, try and be a bit friendlier this time.'

Amber could feel her heart thudding as the bartender put a fresh glass of fizzy wine masquerading as champagne on her tray and she began to walk back towards the man with piggy eyes. *Just put the drink down carefully and then leave*, she told herself. But as she bent down in front of him, he reached out to curve his fat fingers around her fishnet-covered thigh and she froze.

'What...what are you doing?' she croaked.

'Oh, come on.' He leered at her again. 'No need to be like that. With legs like that it's a crime not to touch them—and you look like you could do with a square meal. So how about we go up to my room after you finish? You can order something from room service and we can—'

'How about you get your filthy hand off her right now, before I knock you into kingdom come?' came a low and furious voice from behind her, which Amber recognised instantly.

The podgy hand fell away and Amber turned around to see Conall standing there—his rugged face a study in fury and his powerful body radiating adrenaline as he dominated the space around him. The lurch of trepidation she felt at his unexpected appearance was quickly overridden by the disturbing realisation that she'd never been so glad to see someone in her whole life. He looked so strong. So powerful. He made every other man in the room look weak and insubstantial. Her heart began to pound and she felt her mouth grow dry.

'Conall!' she whispered. 'What are you doing here?'

'Well, I certainly haven't come here for a quiet drink. I tend to be a little more discerning in my choice of venue.' Raising his voice against the loud throb of music, he glanced around at the other cocktail waitresses with a shudder of distaste he didn't bother to hide. 'Get your coat, Amber. We're leaving.'

'I can't leave. I'm working.'

'Not here, you aren't. Not any more. And the subject isn't up for discussion, so save your breath. Either you come willingly, or I pick you up and carry you out of here in a fireman's lift. The choice,' he finished grimly, 'is yours.'

Amber wondered if there was something wrong

with her—there must be—because why else would the thought of the Irishman putting her over his shoulder make her heart race even harder than it was already? She could see her manager saying something to a burly-looking man who was standing beside the bar, and as the music continued its relentless beat she began to dread some awful scene. What if Conall got into a fight with Security—with fists and glasses flying?

'I'll get my coat,' she said.

'Do it,' he bit out impatiently. 'And hurry up. This place is making my skin crawl.'

She headed for the changing room—relieved to strip off the minuscule satin dress and fishnet tights and kick the scarlet shoes from her aching feet. Her skin was clammy and briefly she splashed her face with cold water, dabbing herself dry with a paper towel before slithering into jeans and a sweater. Her heart was racing when she reappeared in the club— thankful to find Conall still standing there, with the bar manager handing over what looked like a wad of cash, with a sour expression on her face.

'Let's go,' he said as she approached.

'Conall—'

'Not now, Amber,' he snapped. 'I really don't want to have a conversation with you here, in earshot of all this low life.'

His expression was resolute and his determination undeniable—so what choice did she have but to follow him through the weaving basement corridors of the hotel until they found the elevator which took them to the main lobby?

They emerged into the dark crispness of a clear

spring night and Amber sucked in a lungful of clean air as a chauffeur-driven car purred to a halt beside the kerb.

'Get in,' said Conall and she wondered if he'd spent his whole life barking out orders like that.

But she did as he asked and a feeling of being cocooned washed over her the moment she climbed onto the back seat, because this level of luxury was reassuringly familiar. A luxury she'd been able to count on before Conall and her father had conspired to take it away from her. She glanced over at his hard profile as he got into the car beside her, and her temporary gratitude began to dissolve into a feeling of resentment.

'How did you find me?' she demanded as the powerful engine began to purr into life.

He turned to look at her and, despite the dim light of the car's interior, the angry glitter in his eyes was unmistakable. 'I had one of my people keep track of you.'

'Why?'

'Why do you think? Because you're so damned irresistible I couldn't keep away from you? I hoped I might be able to tell your father how well you were doing following your dramatic exit from my office.' He gave a short laugh. 'Some hope. I should have guessed that you'd head for the tackiest venue in town in search of some easy money.'

'So why bother coming to look for me if you'd already written me off as useless?' she flared.

Conall didn't answer straight away, because his own motives were still giving him cause for concern. He'd been worried about her ability to adapt to a hard world without the cushion of her wealth—yes. And he'd heard stuff about the club where she was working which made him feel uneasy. Yes. That, too. But there had been something more—something which wasn't quite so easy to quantify—which had nothing to do with his moral debt to her father. Hadn't there been a part of him which had admired the way she'd flounced out of his office? And he didn't just mean the pleasure of watching the magnificent sway of her curvy bottom as she'd done so. The way she'd turned down his offer of a job with a flash of defiance in those emerald eyes had made him think that maybe there was a strong streak of pride hidden beneath her wilful surface. He'd imagined her scrubbing floors, doing anything rather than having to work for him, and he couldn't deny that the idea had appealed to him.

He had been wrong, of course. She had gone for the easy solution. The quick fix. She'd seized the first opportunity to shoehorn her magnificent body into a dress which left very little to the imagination and work in a place which attracted nothing but low life. Clearing his throat, he tried to wipe from his mind the memory of those magnificent breasts spilling over the top of the tight satin gown, but the hard aching in his groin was proving more stubborn to control.

'I felt a certain responsibility towards you.'

'Because of my father?'

'Of course. Why else?'

'Another of Daddy's yes-men,' she said tonelessly.

'Oh, I'm nobody's yes-man, Amber. Be very clear about that.' His voice sounded steely. 'And ask yourself what would have happened if I hadn't turned up when I had. Or have I got it all wrong? Maybe you liked that creep pawing your thigh like that? Maybe you couldn't wait to get back to his room for him to give you a "square meal".'

'Of course I didn't! He was a complete creep. They all were.'

He shook his head in exasperation. 'So why the hell couldn't you have taken a normal job? Worked in a shop? Or a café?'

'Because shops and cafés don't provide accommodation! And the club said if I worked a successful month's trial, then I could have one of the staff rooms in the hotel! Which would have coincided neatly with me being evicted from my apartment.' She glared at him. 'And I don't know why you're suddenly trying to sound like the voice of concern when it's *your* fault I'm going to be homeless.'

He gave an impatient sigh. 'I can't believe you'd be so naïve. You must realise how these places operate.'

'I've been to more nightclubs than you've had hot dinners!' she retorted.

'I don't doubt it—but you went there as a rich and valued customer, not a member of staff! Places like that exploit beautiful women. They expect you to *earn* your bonuses—in a way which is usually some variation of lying flat on your back. Haven't you ever heard the expression that there's no such thing as a free lunch?'

The way she was biting on her lip told him that maybe she wasn't as sophisticated as her foxy appearance suggested, or maybe her wealth had always ensured that she'd frequented a classier kind of club, up until now. Unwillingly, he let his gaze drift over her and once he had started, he couldn't seem to stop. Her black hair was spilling down over the shoulders of her raincoat and her green eyes were heavy with make-up. The fading scarlet streak of her lipstick matched those killer heels she'd been wearing when he'd watched her sashaying across the bar, making him have the sort of unwanted erotic thoughts which involved having her ankles wrapped very tightly around his neck. Hell, it would be easy to have those kinds of thoughts even now—even when she was bundled up in an all-concealing raincoat.

He tapped his fingers against one taut thigh. It would be better to wash his hands of her. To tell Ambrose that she was pretty much a lost cause and maybe he would just have to accept that and let her carry on with an open chequebook and a life of pure indulgence.

But as the car passed a lamp post and the light splashed over her face, he noticed for the first time the dark shadows beneath her long-lashed eyes. She looked as if she hadn't had a lot of sleep lately—and she'd lost weight. Her cheekbones were shockingly prominent in her porcelain skin and the belted raincoat drew definition to the narrowness of her waist. She looked as if a puff of wind might blow her away. As if on cue, her stomach began to rumble and he frowned.

'When did you last eat?'

Her expression was mulish. 'What do you care?'

'Stop being so damned stubborn and just answer the question, Amber,' he growled.

She shrugged. 'At the club they advised you not to

eat for at least four hours before your shift. Actually, it was pretty sound advice because it seemed to be club policy to give you a uniform dress which was at least one size too small.'

'And do you have food back in your apartment?'

'Not much,' she admitted.

'Spent it all on cigarettes, I suppose?' he accused.

She didn't correct him as he leaned forward to tap the glass panel which divided them from the chauffeur and the panel slid open.

'Take us to my club,' he commanded.

'Conall, I'm tired,' she objected. 'And I want to go home.'

'Tough. You can sleep afterwards. You need to eat something.'

He didn't say anything more until the car drew up outside the floodlit classical building a short distance from Piccadilly Circus. A uniformed porter sprang forward to open the car door to let her get out and Conall felt a stab of something he couldn't decipher as he followed her sexy sway as she made her way up the marble steps. As she handed over her raincoat he thought he saw her shiver and he took his own cashmere scarf and wound it around her neck, leaving the ends to dangle concealingly in front of her magnificent breasts.

'Better wear this,' he said drily. But it was more for his benefit than any attempt to conform to the club's rather outdated dress code. This way he wouldn't have to look at the pinpoint tips of her nipples thrusting their way towards him from beneath her sweater and making him imagine what it would be like to lock his lips around each one in turn.

It was very late, but they were shown into the long room known as the North Library which overlooked Pall Mall, where a table was quickly laid up for them. Conall ordered soup and sandwiches for Amber and a brandy for himself. He watched in silence as she devoured the comfort food with the undivided attention of someone who was genuinely hungry and, for the first time that evening, he began to relax.

He sipped his drink. Outside the busy city was slowing down. He could see the yellow lights of vacant cabs and the unsteady weave of people making their way home, while in here all was ordered and calm. It always was. It was one of the main reasons why he'd joined, because it had an air of stability which had always attracted him.

Antique chandeliers hung from the corniced ceiling and at one end of the room was a polished grand piano. Despite its traditional air, it was a club for movers and shakers—the kind of place to which few were granted entry because the membership requirements were so high. But there had been no shortage of proposers keen to get him onto the members' list and Conall had defied the odds brought about by youthful misdemeanour. He'd been proposed by a government minister and seconded by a peer of the realm and that fact in itself still had the ability to make him smile wryly. Whoever would have thought that the boy who had been born with so little would end up here, with the great and the good?

He signalled for a fire to be lit and then watched as Amber dabbed at her lips with a heavy linen napkin. Now that the edge had been taken off her hunger, she relaxed back into the leather armchair and began to look around—like a rescued kitten which had been brought from the cold into the warmth. He wondered what the waiter who came to remove her plate must think, because he didn't usually bring women here, to this essentially male enclave—where deals were done over dinner and alliances formed over summer drinks taken outside on the pretty terrace. On the rare occasions he'd brought a date, they hadn't been dressed in skinny jeans and a sweater, like Amber Carter. They had worn subtle silk, with shoes the same colour as their handbags and make-up which was soft and discreet—not laden on so thickly that from a distance she appeared to have two black eyes.

And yet not one of them had made him feel a fraction of the desire which was currently pulsing through his blood and making him achingly aware of his erection.

'So,' he said heavily, putting his glass down on the table and raising his eyebrows in what he hoped was a stern expression. 'I think you've just proved fairly conclusively that independence is not an option—unless you want to take another job like that. The question is whether or not you're finally ready to knuckle down and see sense.'

Amber didn't answer straight away, even though he was firing that impatient look at her. She felt much better after the food she'd just eaten, no doubt about it—but just as one hunger had been satisfied, so another had been awoken and she wasn't sure how to deal with it.

It wasn't just the unexpectedness of seeing Conall Devlin in this famous London club—which, quite frankly, was the last place she'd ever imagined finding someone like him. And it wasn't just the fact that he currently resembled the human equivalent of a jungle cat—a dark and potentially dangerous predator who had temporarily taken refuge in one of the beautifully worn leather chairs. No, it was more than that. It was the subtly pervasive scent of him invading her nostrils, which was coming from the soft scarf he'd draped around her neck. And hadn't she felt a whisper of pleasure when his fingertips had brushed against her skin, even though it had been the most innocent of touches? Hadn't it made her want more, even though experience had taught her that she always froze into a block of ice whenever a man came close?

She looked into the gleam of his eyes. 'By seeing sense, I presume you mean I should do exactly what *you* say?'

'Well, you could give it a try,' he said drily. 'Since we've seen what happens when you do the opposite.'

'But I don't know exactly what it is you're offering me, Conall.'

Conall stiffened. Was he imagining the provocative flash of her eyes—or was that just wishful thinking on his part? Was she aware that when she looked at him that way, his veins were pulsing with a hot, hard hunger and he could think of only one way of relieving it? She must be. Women like her ate men like him for breakfast.

He needed to pull himself together, before she got an inkling of the erotic thoughts which were clogging up his mind and started using her sexual power to manipulate him. 'I'm offering you a role as an interpreter.'

'Not interested,' she said instantly, with an emphatic shake of her head. 'I'm not sitting in some claustrophobic booth all day with a pair of headphones on, while someone jabbers on and on in my ear about something boring—like grain quotas in the European Union.'

Conall failed to hide his smile. 'I think you'll find my proposal is a little more glamorous than that,' he said.

'Oh?'

She had perked up now and his smile died. Of course she had. Glamour was her lifeblood, wasn't it?

'I'm having a party,' he said.

'What kind of party?'

He picked up his brandy glass and took a sip. 'A party ostensibly to celebrate the completion of my country house. There will be music, and dancing—but I'm also hoping to use the opportunity to sell a painting for someone who badly needs the money.'

'I thought you'd decided that, with my lack of experience, I would be useless when it came to selling paintings.'

'I'm not expecting you to *sell* the paintings,' he said. 'I just want you to be there as a sort of linguistic arm candy.'

'What do you mean?'

He hesitated, wondering if her father would approve of the offer he was about to make to her. It would probably be more sensible to give her a lowly back-room job somewhere in his organisation—preferably as far away from him as possible. But Conall could see now that it would be as ineffective as trying to pass fish paste off as caviar, because Amber Carter wasn't a back-room kind of woman.

No way could someone like her ever fade into the background. So why not capitalise on the gifts she *did* have?

'The painting in question is one of a pair,' he said. 'Two studies of the same woman by a man called Kristjan Wheeler—a contemporary of Picasso and an artist whose worth has increased enormously over the last decade. Both pictures went missing in the middle of the last century and only one has ever been found. That is the one I am trying to sell on behalf of my client, and...'

She looked at him as his words tailed away. 'And?'

'I believe the man who wants to buy the painting is in possession of the missing picture. Which means that the one I'm selling is part of a set, and naturally that makes it much more valuable.'

'Can't you just ask him outright whether he's got it?'

He gave the flicker of a smile. 'That's not how negotiation works, Amber—and especially not with a man like this.' He watched her closely. 'You see, the prospective buyer is a prince.'

'A *prince*?'

Conall watched as she sat bolt upright, her fingers tightening around her glass. Her lips had parted and he could see the moist gleam of her tongue. He thought she looked like a starving dog which had been allowed to roam freely around a kitchen and a quiver of distaste ran through him. He took another sip of his brandy. Had he really thought that the chemistry which sizzled between them was unique? Or was he naïvely pretending that she wasn't like this with every man she came across, and the higher that man's status and the fatter his wallet, the better?

And yet surely that would make her perfect for what he had in mind—didn't they say that Luciano of Mardovia had a roving eye where women were concerned?

'That's right,' he said, his eyes narrowing. 'I want you to come to the party and be nice to him.'

Her eyes narrowed. 'How nice?'

The inference behind her question was clear and Conall felt a wave of disgust wash over him. 'I'm not expecting you to have sex with him,' he snapped. 'Just chat to him. Dance with him. Charm him. I shouldn't imagine you would find any of that difficult, given your track record. He will be accompanied by at least two of his aides and he will converse with them in any language except English. Just like you he speaks Italian, Greek and French and he certainly won't be expecting a woman like you to be fluent in all three.'

A woman like you.

It was odd how hurtful Amber found his throwaway comment, especially when for a minute back then she had been lulled into a false sense of security. Secretly, she had *enjoyed* the way he'd turned up and taken her away so masterfully. He'd brought her here—to this club, which was the epitome of elegance and comfort—and she couldn't deny that she was enjoying watching him sitting bathed in flickering firelight, while he sipped at his brandy. He was very easy on the eye.

But she needed to remember that for him she was just a burden. A problem to be dealt with and then disposed of. No point in starting to have fantasies about Conall Devlin.

'So what you're saying, in effect, is that you want me to spy on this Prince?'

He didn't seem particularly bothered by her accusation, for he responded with nothing more than a faintly impatient sigh.

'Don't be so melodramatic, Amber. If I asked you to have a business meeting with a competitor, I would expect you to find out as much information as possible. So if the Prince should happen to comment to one of his aides in, say, Greek that the wine is atrocious, then it would be helpful to know that.'

A smile flickered over her lips. 'You're in the habit of serving atrocious wine, are you, Conall?'

'What do you think?'

'I'm thinking…no.'

'Look, I'm not asking you to lie about your language skills, but there's no need to advertise them. This is business. All I want is to get the best price possible for my client—and Luciano can certainly afford to pay the best price. So…' His midnight gaze swept over her. 'Do you think you can do it? Play hostess for me for an evening and stick to the Prince's side like glue?'

Amber met his eyes. The food and the fire and the brandy had made her feel sleepy and safe and part of her wished she could hold on to this moment and not have to go and face the chill of the outside world. But Conall was clearly waiting for an answer to his question and the expression on his face suggested he wasn't a man who enjoyed being kept waiting. And deep down she knew she could do something like this in her sleep. Go to some upmarket party and be charming? Child's play.

'Yes,' she said. 'I can do it.'

'Good.' He nodded as his cell phone gave a discreet little buzz and he flicked it a brief glance. 'You'll need to get down to my country house early on Saturday afternoon. Oh, and bring some party dresses with you.' His eyes glittered. 'I don't imagine you'll have too much trouble finding any of those in your wardrobe?'

'No. Party dresses I have in abundance—and plenty of shoes to match.'

'Just wear something halfway decent, will you?'

'What *do* you mean?'

'You know damned well what I mean.' There was a pause. 'I don't want you flaunting your body and looking like a tramp.'

Amber swallowed, knowing that she should be outraged by such a statement, and yet something about the way he said it made her feel all…shivery. She forced her mind back to the practical. 'So what time will I expect the car?'

'The car?' he repeated blankly.

'The car which will be collecting me,' she said, as if she were explaining the rules of a simple card game to a five-year-old.

There was a short silence before he tipped back his dark head and laughed, but when he looked at her again his eyes weren't amused, they were stone cold. 'You still don't get it, do you, Amber?' he said. 'You may be about to deal with a prince, but you're going to have to stop behaving like a princess. Because you're not. You will catch the train like any other mortal.

Speak to Serena and she'll give you details of how to find the house. Oh, and I've got your wages from the nightclub in my pocket. I'll give them to you in the car. I didn't want to hand them over in here.' His eyes glittered. 'It could be a gesture open to misinterpretation.'

CHAPTER FIVE

AMBER HADN'T BEEN on a train for years. Not since that time in Rome when her mother's lover had confessed to having a pregnant wife who had just discovered their affair and was on the warpath. It had been bad enough having to flee the city leaving behind half their possessions, but the journey had been made worse by Sophie Carter's increasingly hysterical sobs as she'd exclaimed loudly that she would be unable to live without Marco. It had been left to her daughter to try to placate her, to the accompaniment of tutting sounds from the other people in the carriage.

Amber sat back against the hard train seat and thought about the bizarre twists and turns of life which had brought her to this bumpy carriage which was hurtling through the English countryside towards Conall's country home. She had been corralled into working for the Irish tycoon—the most infuriating and high-handed man she'd ever met.

And the fact that there didn't seem any credible alternative had made her examine her lifestyle in a way which had left her feeling distinctly uncomfortable.

Yesterday she'd gone to the Devlin headquarters in Kensington for a briefing which hadn't been brief at all. Serena had spent ages telling her boring things like making sure she kept her receipts so that she could submit a travel expenses form. Amber remembered blinking at Conall's assistant with a mixture of amusement and irritation. Receipts! She had wanted to tell the lofty blonde that she didn't *do* receipts, but at that moment the great man himself had walked into the building—a distracting image dressed in all black. Cue an infuriating rocketing of Amber's pulse and the spectacle of various female members of staff cooing around him. And cue the uncomfortable realisation that she *didn't like* seeing him surrounded by all those women.

His gaze had met hers.

'I hope you're behaving yourself, Amber?'

'I'm doing my best,' she'd replied from between gritted teeth.

'I'm just talking Amber through the expenses procedure,' Serena had explained.

'And I'm sure she has been nothing but completely cooperative,' Conall had murmured in response, but there had been a definite flicker of warning in the sapphire depths of his eyes.

She'd wanted to defy him then, because defiance was her default mechanism, yet for the first time in her life she had come up against someone who would not be swayed by her. And wasn't that in some crazy way—*reassuring*?

Amber stared out of the train window, realising there was only an hour to go before her journey's end and that she had better be prepared for her meeting with the Prince. Conall had suggested she find out as much about the royal as possible and so she had downloaded as much as she could find on the Internet and had printed it out. No harm in looking at it again. She pulled out the information sheets and began to doodle little drawings around the edge of one of the pages as she reread it.

She had been unprepared for the impact of Prince 'Luc' and his gorgeous Mediterranean island, when his photograph had first popped up on the screen. With his olive skin, bright blue eyes and thick tumble of black hair, he was as handsome as any Hollywood actor, but his looks left her completely cold. That in itself wasn't unusual, because she'd met enough manipulating hunks through her mother to put her off handsome men for ever. What *was* infuriating was that she kept unfavourably comparing the Prince to Conall—and yet Conall wasn't what you'd call *good-looking*. His jaw was dark and his nose had been broken at one point. And he had a hard, cold stare, which proved distractingly at odds with the way his fingers had brushed her skin as he'd wound his scarf around her neck at his club the other night...

The train juddered to a halt at Crewhurst station and Amber climbed out onto the platform, clutching her case, which contained some of her less-revealing dresses. Blinking, she looked around her and breathed in the fresh air, the bright spring day making her feel like an animal who'd spent the winter in hibernation and was emerging into sunshine for the first time. She sniffed at the air and the scent of something sweet. She couldn't remember the last time she'd been out of the city and in the middle of the countryside like this. Cotton-wool clouds scudded across an eggshell-blue sky and frilly yellow daffodils waved their trumpets in the light breeze.

She had been told to take a taxi, but the rank was empty and when she asked the old man in the ticket office when one might be available, he shook his head with the expression of someone who had just been asked to provide the whereabouts of the Holy Grail.

'Can't say. Driver's gone off to take his wife shopping. It isn't far to walk,' he added helpfully, when she told him where she was headed.

Under normal circumstances Amber would have tapped her foot impatiently and demanded that someone find her a taxi—and quickly. But there was something about the scent of spring which felt keen and raw on her senses. She couldn't remember the last time she'd felt this *alive* and a sudden feeling of adventure washed over her. Her bag wasn't particularly heavy. She was wearing sneakers with her skinny jeans, wasn't she? And a soft silk shirt beneath her denim jacket.

After taking directions, she set off along a sun-dappled country road, walking past acid-green hedges which were bursting with new life. Overhead the sound of birdsong was almost deafening and London seemed an awfully long way away. She found herself thinking that Conall seemed to have his life pretty much sorted, with his successful business and his homes in London and the country. And she found herself wondering whether or not he had a girlfriend. Probably. Men like him always had girlfriends. Or wives. A wife who presumably could only speak English.

This thought produced an inexplicably painful

punch to her heart and she glanced at her watch, calculating she must be about halfway there when she noticed that the sky had grown dark. Looking up, she saw a bank of pewter clouds massing overhead and increased her speed, but she hadn't got much further down the lane when the first large splash of rain hit her and she wondered why she hadn't stopped to consider the April showers which came out of nowhere this time of year.

Because usually you're never far from a shop doorway and completely protected from the elements, that's why.

Well, she certainly wasn't protected now.

She was alone in the middle of a country lane while the rain had started lashing down with increasing intensity, until it was almost like walking through a tropical storm. She thought about ringing someone. Conall? No. She didn't want another lecture on her general incompetence. And it was hardly the end of the world to get caught in an April shower, was it? Sometimes you had to accept what fate threw at you, and just suck it up.

Thoroughly soaked now, she increased her pace, her shirt clinging to her breasts like wet tissue paper and her jeans feeling heavy and uncomfortable as the wet denim rubbed against her legs. She didn't hear the car at first and it wasn't until she heard a loud beep that she turned around to see a low black car coming to a halt on the wet lane with a soft screech of tyres. The muscular silhouette behind the wheel was disturbingly familiar and as the electric window floated down she was confronted by the sight of Conall's face and her heart missed a beat.

'Conall—'

'Get in,' he said.

For a moment she was tempted to tell him that she'd rather walk in the pouring rain than get in a car driven by *him*. But that would be stupid—and wasn't she trying her best to be a bit more sensible? She was cold and she was wet and she was headed for his house and the grown-up thing to do would be to thank him for stopping. Pulling open the passenger door, she threw her bag on the floor, beginning to shiver violently as she slid onto the passenger seat and slammed the car door shut.

'This is getting to be something of a habit,' he said grimly. 'Do you think I have the words "rescue mission" permanently stamped on my forehead?'

His rudeness made her polite response disintegrate. 'I didn't ask you to rescue me.'

'But you accepted my help soon enough, didn't you?'

'Because even I'm not stubborn enough to throw up the chance of getting into a warm car! And now I s-suppose you're going to ch-chastise me for getting wet.' She began to shiver. 'As if I have any control over the weather!'

'I was going to chastise you for walking in the middle of the damned road and not paying any attention!' he retorted. 'If I'd been going any faster I could have run you over.'

Her teeth had started to chatter loudly and the way he was looking at her was making her feel... Beneath her sopping silk shirt, Amber's heart began to hammer. She didn't want to think about the way he was making her feel. How could that cold blue stare make her body spring into life like this? How could it make her feel as if her breasts were being pierced by tiny little needles and make a slow melting heat unfurl deep in her belly?

But he was tugging off his leather jacket and draping it impatiently over her shoulders and as his shadow fell over her Amber was suddenly aware of just how close he was. Coal-black lashes framed the gleaming sapphire eyes and his deeply shadowed jaw seemed to emphasise his own very potent brand of masculinity. An unfamiliar sense of longing began to bubble up inside her and she held her breath as she looked up into his face. For a split second she thought he might be about to kiss her. A second when his mouth was so close that all she needed to do was reach up and hook her hand behind his neck, and bring those lips down to meet hers. And in that same second she saw his eyes narrow. She thought... thought...

Did he read the longing in her eyes? Was that why he suddenly pulled away with a hard smile, as if he'd known exactly what was going through her head? Maybe he was able to make women desire him, even if they didn't want to, just by giving them that intense and rather smouldering look. Instinctively, she hugged the coat closer, the leather feeling unbearably soft against her erect and sensitised nipples.

'Do up your seat belt,' he ordered, turning up the car's heater full blast and glancing in his rear mirror before pulling away. 'And talk me through the reason why you decided to walk from the station. It's miles.'

'Why do you think? Because there was no taxi and the man at the ticket office said it wasn't far.'

'You should have rung me.'

'Make your mind up, Conall. You can't criticise me for not behaving like a normal person and then moan at me when I do. I thought it would be good for me to make my way to the house independently. I thought you might even award me a special gold star for good behaviour.' She glanced at him, a smile playing around her lips. 'And to be honest, I didn't know you were already there.'

Conall said nothing as the car made its way through the downpour, the rhythmical swishing of the wiper blades the only sound he could hear above his suddenly erratic breathing. Of course she hadn't known he'd be at the house—he hadn't known himself. He'd planned to arrive later when everything was in place but something had compelled him to get here earlier, and that something was making him uncomfortable because it was all to do with her.

He'd tried telling himself that he needed to oversee the massive security detail which the Prince of Mardovia's bodyguards had demanded prior to the royal visit. That he needed to check on the painting he was hoping to sell and to ensure it was properly lit. But although both those reasons were valid, they weren't the real reason why he was desperately trying to avert his gaze from the damp denim which outlined the slenderness of her thighs.

Admit it, he thought grimly. *You want her. Despite everything you know about her, you haven't been able to get her out of your head since you saw her lying on a white leather sofa wearing that baggy T-shirt.* Only now the image searing into his brain was the way her wet silk shirt had been clinging to her peak-ing breasts before he'd hastily covered them up with his jacket. Was it shocking to admit that he wanted to rip the delicate fabric aside and lick her on each hard nub until she squirmed with pleasure? To slide the damp denim from her thighs and put his heated hands all over her chilled flesh?

Of course it was shocking. He had been entrusted to look after her, not seduce her. If it was sex he wanted then Eleanor was only a phone call away. Their grown-up and civilised 'friends with benefits' relationship suited them both—even if the physical stimulation it gave him wasn't matched by a mental one.

But for once the thought of Eleanor's blonde beauty paled in the face of the fiery, green-eyed temptress on the seat next to him and he was relieved when the sudden shower began to lessen. The sun broke through the clouds as the car made its way up the long drive, just in time to illuminate his house in a radiant display which emphasised its stately proportions. Golden light washed over the tall chimneys and glinted off the mullioned windows. The emerald lawns surrounding the building looked vivid in the bright sunshine and, on a tranquil pond, several ducks quacked happily. Beside him he felt Amber stiffen.

'But this is…this is *beautiful*,' she breathed as the car drew up outside.

He heard the note of wonder in her voice and his mouth hardened. He wondered if she would have been quite so gushing if she'd known the truth about his background. About the hardship and pain and the sense of being an outsider which had never quite left him.

'Isn't it?' he agreed evenly as he stared at the house. With its acres of parkland and sense of history, places like this didn't come on the market very often and Conall still couldn't quite believe it was his. Coming hot on the heels of his London deal, it had been a heady time in terms of recent property acquisitions. Had he ever imagined being a major landowner, when he was eighteen and mad with rage and injustice? When the walls of the detention centre had threatened to close in on him and he had been looking down the barrel of an extended jail sentence?

He turned off the ignition, his glance straying to Amber's large handbag, and it wasn't the sight of the printout about Prince Luciano which caught his eye— although he was pleased to see she'd been doing her homework—but the intricate doodles on the edge of one of the pages which stirred a faint but enduring memory.

He frowned. 'I remember seeing some drawings like this in your apartment that first day.'

She stiffened. 'What, you mean you were snooping around?'

'They were half hidden behind a sofa. Were they yours?'

'Of course they were mine—why?'

Ignoring the defensive note in her voice, he narrowed his eyes. 'I thought some of them showed real promise and a few were really very good.'

'You don't have to say that. Anyway, I know they're rubbish.'

'I don't say things I don't mean, Amber. And why are they rubbish?'

She shrugged, but the words seemed to take a long

time coming. 'I used to paint a lot when we were in Europe and my mother was otherwise *occupied*. But when I went to live with my father, he made it very clear he thought they were no good—that a kid of six could throw some paint at the canvas and get the same effect, and that I was wasting my time.' She flashed a brittle kind of smile. 'So I stopped trying to be an *artist* and became the society girl that everyone expected. Those paintings you saw were years old. I just...just couldn't bear to throw them away.'

Conall experienced a moment of real, silent rage as he read the brief flash of hurt and helplessness in her eyes. Were adults deliberately cruel to troubled teenagers, or was it simply that they didn't know how to handle them?

But maybe she'd always been difficult to handle—in so many ways. Right now she looked like every teenage boy's fantasy in her wet shirt, with his bulky jacket draped around her slender shoulders, making far too many lustful thoughts crowd his mind. 'I'll show you around the house so you have plenty of time to acclimatise yourself before the party, but the guided tour can wait until later. First you need to get out of those wet clothes.'

As soon as the words had left his lips he wanted to take them back, because they sounded like the words a man would say to a woman just before he began touching her. Silently chastising himself for his own foolishness, he got out of the car and opened the door for her.

Still hugging his jacket to her, Amber followed him inside the house into a huge oak-panelled hallway from which curved a majestic staircase. Enormous bucketfuls of white flowers stood on the floor, obviously waiting to be transplanted into vases, and she could hear the sound of female voices coming from a room somewhere and a radio playing in the distance.

'Last-minute party prep,' he said, in reply to a question she hadn't asked. 'You'll meet the team later. Now come with me and I'll show you to your room.'

Her clothes were still clinging damply to her body and Amber guessed she should have been cold—but cold was the last thing she felt right now. Her blood felt heavy and warm as she followed Conall upstairs and her heart was beating painfully against her ribcage. She barely noticed the beautifully restored woodwork or the walls covered with paintings, so fixated was she on the hard thrust of his buttocks against the black denim of his jeans. She could feel her throat growing dry as she stared at the back of his neck, unable to tear her gaze away. With his black hair curling over the collar of his cashmere sweater and his muscular physique rippling with health and strength, he looked in total command of the situation, which she guessed he was. But the weird thing was that she didn't *do* this. She didn't drool over men who treated her as if she were a naughty schoolgirl. Truth was, she didn't drool over anyone. She bit her lip as she remembered the accusations which had been levelled at her in the past. *Cold. Frigid. Ice queen.* Valid accusations, every one of them. Yet when Conall looked at her, he made her want to melt, not freeze.

Pushing open the door of a second-floor bedroom overlooking the parkland at the back of the house, he put her case down. 'You should be comfortable enough in here,' he said abruptly.

Amber glanced around, suddenly shy to find herself alone in a bedroom with him. Comfortable was an understatement for such a lavish room and she was grateful he'd given her somewhere so lovely to sleep, with its heavy velvet drapes and enormous four-poster bed. She looked up into his face, knowing she ought to be asking intelligent questions about the forthcoming party but it was difficult when all she could think about was the curve of his lips and the shadowed roughness of his jaw.

'What time do you need me?' she said, her words sounding jerky as she moistened the roof of her mouth with her tongue.

'Come downstairs at around seven and I'll show you the painting. The Prince is arriving at eight-fifteen and his timetable is worked out to the nearest second. I'd better warn you that lateness won't be tolerated when you're dealing with royals.'

'I won't be late, Conall.' Amber took off his jacket and handed it to him, feeling chilled as the leather left her skin and missing the subtle scent which was all his. 'And thanks for lending me this.'

But he didn't take the jacket from her. He just stood there as if someone had turned him to stone. His brilliant eyes gleamed from between the dark lashes and his golden skin suddenly seemed taut over his cheekbones. 'You know, you're really going to have to stop doing this, Amber,' he said softly. 'I've given you several chances but my patience is wearing thin and, in the end, I'm only made out of flesh and blood—the same as any other man.'

'What are you talking about?'

'Oh, come on.' His voice was edged with a note

of irritation. 'There are many parts you play exceedingly well, but innocence isn't one of them. Much more of those big green eyes gazing at me like that and licking at your lips like a cat which has just seen a mouse—and I'll be forced to kiss you, whether I want to or not.'

Amber looked at him, genuinely confused. 'Why would you even consider kissing me if you didn't want to?'

He laughed, but his laugh contained something dark and unknown and Amber felt as if she were a non-swimmer paddling on the edge of the shore, not noticing the powerful tug of the undercurrent edging towards her.

'Because you're not my kind of woman and because I am, in effect, your employer.' His voice dipped to a silken whisper. 'But that doesn't mean I don't want to.'

His unmistakable passion mixed with the complexity of her own feelings filled Amber with a sudden sense of power and she tilted her chin to look at him defiantly. 'Well, if you really want to kiss me that badly, why don't you just go ahead and do it?'

'I don't kiss women who smoke.'

There was a pause. 'But I haven't had a cigarette since that day I came to your office.'

'You haven't?' His eyes narrowed. 'Why not?'

Should she tell him the truth? Because he'd told her she smelt disgusting and had made her feel *dirty*. But mainly because she'd wanted to show him she could. Somehow Conall Devlin had succeeded where two very expensive hypnotherapy courses had failed, and she'd quit smoking without a single craving.

'Because I am at heart a very obedient woman.' Shamelessly she batted her eyelashes at him. 'Didn't you know that?'

It was provocation pure and simple and Conall felt something inside him snap, like a piece of elastic which had been stretched beyond endurance. He heard the roar of blood in his ears and felt the jerk of an erection pushing hard against his jeans as he found himself pulling her into his arms and breathing in her warmth.

'The only thing I know is that you are a stubborn and defiant woman who has tested me beyond endurance,' he said, his voice rough. 'And maybe this has been inevitable all along.'

She stared into his eyes. 'You're going to put me across your lap and smack my bottom?'

'Is that what you'd like? Maybe later. But not right now. Right now I'm going to kiss you—but be warned that this is going to spoil you for anyone else. Are you prepared for that, Amber? That every man who kisses you after this is going to make you remember me and ache for me?'

'You are *so* arrogant,' she accused.

But her lips were parting and Conall knew she wanted this just as much as him. Maybe more—for he caught a flash of hunger in her darkening eyes. Sliding one hand around her waist while the other cushioned her still-damp hair, he lowered his mouth onto hers. And didn't part of him *want* her to have lied to him—to discover the stale odour of tobacco on those soft lips so that he could pull away in disgust?

But she hadn't lied. She tasted of peppermint and she smelt of daisies and the way she melted into his body was like throwing a match onto a pile of bone-dry timber. He groaned as he felt the stony stud of her nipples pressing against him and he reached down to cup one between his thumb and forefinger, enjoying the way she squirmed beneath his touch and whispered his name. He was so hard that he was afraid that his jeans might rip open all by themselves and, with something which sounded like a roar, he pushed her against the open door, so that it rocked crazily beneath the sudden urgent force of their bodies.

They kissed as if they'd just discovered how to kiss. Her arms were reaching up to his shoulders, as if she was trying to stop herself from sliding to the ground, and as Conall nudged his thigh between hers he was tempted to do just that. To lay her down on the hard floorboards and rip off their clothes and just *take* her, as he had been wanting to for days. Because if he did that—wouldn't he rid his blood of this fever so that he could just *forget* her? His hand cupped her breast and she gasped, drawing in a shuddering breath as he bent his head and grazed his teeth against the nipple which was hard against her damp silk shirt.

'C-Conall,' she gasped.

'I know,' he ground out as desire shot through him in a potent stream. 'Good, isn't it?' With his middle finger, he rubbed along the seam of her jeans at the crotch and he could feel her heat searing through the thick denim as she wriggled her hips in silent invitation.

The scent of sex and of desire was as potent as any perfume and he groped his hand downwards, reaching for his belt. He tugged it open and was just about to undo the top button of his jeans when some sharp splinter of sanity lanced into his thoughts and reality hit him like a slug to the jaw. He dragged his lips away, his eyes focusing and then refocusing as he stared at her and took a step back. Her shirt was half-open and her magnificent breasts were rising and falling as she struggled to control her breathing. Her black hair was plastered to her head, her eyes streaked with mascara from the rain and her lips were rosy-pink and trembling. He wondered what part of teaching her how to try to be a better person this fell under and a wave of self-disgust shot through him as he thought of what he'd just done. And what he'd been tempted to do...

Since when did he violate another man's trust in him, when he knew all too well how painful the consequences of shattered trust could be?

And since when did he lose control like that?

'Is something...wrong?' she questioned.

But he didn't answer. He was too angry with himself to even try. Did she put out like that for everyone? he wondered furiously. Was he just one in a long line of men she indiscriminately chose to satisfy her sexual needs? He took another step away from her, even though every sinew of his body was screaming out its protest. And yes, at that moment he would have traded his entire fortune to slide her panties down her legs and unzip himself and take her, but some last shred of reason stopped him as he reminded himself of the stark reality. That she was everything he'd spent his life trying to avoid and that wasn't about to change any time soon.

It was difficult to speak when all he could think about was thrusting deep into her and losing himself inside her. Difficult to regain control when his heart was racing so hard that it hurt, but Conall had learnt many lessons in his life and masking his temper had been right at the top of the list. He hid it now, replacing it with a silky reason which was always effective.

'Oh, Amber.' Slowly he shook his head. 'Where did you learn to look at a man like that and make him want to go against everything he believes in?'

Her expression was dazed but for once she wasn't flying back at him with one of her smart comments and that pleased him, for it gave him back the power which had momentarily deserted him.

'Judging by the look on your face and your body language, I imagine you must be greedily anticipating the next time,' he continued, struggling to control his ragged breathing. 'But I'm afraid there isn't going to be one. Because that was something which should never have happened. Do you understand what I'm saying, Amber? From now on we're going to stick to business and only business—so be downstairs at the time I told you so that I can brief you before the Prince arrives.' His mouth hardened into a grim and resolute line. 'And we'll both forget this ever happened.'

CHAPTER SIX

AMBER'S HANDS WERE trembling as she shut the door on Conall and tried to block out the sounds of his retreating footsteps—but it wasn't so easy to blot out the mocking words which still echoed around her head.

Forget it had ever happened?

Was he out of his *mind*?

Her fingers strayed to lips which felt as if they were on fire—as if he'd branded them with that hot and hungry kiss. Leaning back against the door, she closed her eyes. He'd done things to her she shouldn't have allowed him to do. He'd touched her breasts and put his hand in between her legs but instead of feeling outrage or disgust—or even her habitual freezing fear—she had embraced every moment of it. It had been the most erotic thing which had ever happened to her until he had ended it so abruptly. His belt undone, he had pulled away from her with disgust darkening his eyes, his accusatory words making her sound like some sort of predator—as if she were using all her wiles to lure him into her bed. Oh, the irony.

Walking over to the window, she stared out over the beautiful green parkland and thought about the way she'd responded to him. How *infuriating* that a desire which had eluded her all these years had been awoken by a man who made no secret of despising her. Who had looked at her as if she were something he'd discovered in a dark corner of a room and wished he hadn't. And his rejection had hurt. Of course it had—especially coming so fast on the heels of the nice things he'd said about her painting.

What mattered now was how she reacted to it. Why take all the responsibility for something *he* had started? Why not show Conall Devlin just what she was capable of? Show him that she was not going to become some simpering fangirl, but do what she had been brought down here to do.

Quickly she unpacked her case and took a shower—and afterwards studied the couple of dresses she'd brought with her, realising that Conall had only ever seen her in a series of unflattering outfits. She brushed her fingertips over the soft fabrics, unsure which one to pick. The scarlet was more show-stopping and did wonders for her silhouette—but something stopped her from choosing it. Instead she pulled the ivory silk chiffon from one of the hangers and gave a small smile. She might have rejected most of the rules of her upbringing, but she could still remember what they were. That less was more and quality counted—especially if you were dealing with a royal prince.

By six-thirty, and feeling more confident, she was swishing her way down the sweeping staircase into the entrance hall, where the buckets of flowers had been transformed into lavish displays. She could see Conall deep in conversation on his cell phone, but he raised his bent head as Amber reached the bottom of the stairs. His eyes narrowed and she felt a beat of satisfaction as she registered his expression. He looked *amazed*. As if she'd grown a pair of wings in the time it had taken her to get ready and come downstairs. Suddenly she was glad that she'd opted for no jewellery other than a discreet pair of pearl studs at her ears and that her newly washed hair fell simply down over her shoulders.

'Hi, Conall,' she said. 'I do hope I'm appropriately dressed to meet this royal guest of yours.'

Conall didn't often find himself lost for words but right now it was a struggle to know what to say. A raw and visceral reaction began to pound its way through his body as Amber came downstairs. He stared at her with a mixture of anger and desire, feeling his groin begin to inevitably harden beneath the material of his suit trousers. How the hell did she manage to make him *feel* this way—every damned time? As if he would die if he didn't touch her. Unwillingly his gaze drifted over her, lingering in a way he couldn't seem to help. Her dress fell in creamy folds to the ground, beneath which you could just see the peep of a silver shoe. With her black hair a sleek curtain of ebony and her eyes as green as a cat's, she looked...

He swallowed. She looked as if butter wouldn't melt in that hot mouth of hers. Like those girls he used to see when he was growing up and his mother was working at the big house. The kind you were encouraged to look at because they always wanted you to look at them, but were forbidden to touch.

But he was no longer the servant's son who had to accept what he was told, he reminded himself grimly.

He was more than Amber Carter's equal—he was her *boss*—and he was the one calling the shots.

'Very presentable,' he answered coolly. 'And certainly an improvement on anything I've seen you wear before.'

She cocked her head to one side. 'Do you always end a compliment with a criticism?'

He shrugged. 'Depends who I'm talking to. I don't think a little criticism would go amiss in your case. But if the point of you coming down here looking like some kind of goddess is to try to snare the Prince, let me save you the trouble by telling you that he has a bona fide princess in the wings who's waiting for him to marry her.'

She shot him an unfriendly look. 'I'm not interested in "snaring" anyone.'

'Even though acquiring a wealthy husband would be a convenient way out of your current financial predicament?'

'Oh, come on! Which century are you living in, Conall? Women don't have to *sell* themselves through marriage any more. They take jobs like this—working for men whose default mechanism is to be moody and more than a little difficult.'

'Or they get Daddy to support them,' he mocked.

'Not any more, it seems,' she said sweetly. 'So why don't we get the show on the road? You're supposed to be giving me a guided tour of the house and showing me this painting the Prince wants to buy.'

Conall nodded as he gestured her to follow him, but he could feel the growing tension in his body as she walked beside him, aware of the filmy material which drifted enticingly against her body and whispered against every luscious curve. Her arms and her neck were the only skin visible and it was difficult to reconcile this almost ethereal image with the earthy woman who had kissed him so fervently in the bedroom earlier.

Tonight his country house looked perfect, like something you might see in the pages of one of those glossy magazines—but hadn't that always been his intention? Wasn't this the pinnacle of a long-held dream—to acquire a stately home even bigger than the one his mother had worked in during his childhood? A way of redressing some sort of balance which had always felt fundamentally skewed.

He led Amber through the ground floor— furnished and recently decorated in the traditional style—showing her the drawing rooms, the library and the grand conservatory. In the ballroom where the party was being held, a string quartet was tuning up and bottles of pink champagne were being put on ice. Everywhere he looked he could see candlelight and the air was scented with the fragrance of cut flowers and the sweet smell of success.

But Conall felt as if he was just going through the motions of showing Amber his home. As though all this lavish wealth suddenly meant nothing. Was that because the beautiful antiques just looked like bog-standard pieces of furniture when compared to the black-haired beauty by his side? Or because all he wanted to do was to drag her off to some dark corner to finish off what he had begun earlier?

He took her to a galleried room at the far end of the house, outside which a burly guard stood. The velvet drapes were drawn against the night outside and on one bare wall—beautifully lit—hung a painting.

'Here it is,' he said.

Amber was glad to have something to concentrate on other than the man at her side, or the remark he'd made earlier about her looking like a goddess. Had he meant it? A wave of impatience swept over her. *Stop reading into his words. Stop imagining he feels anything for you other than lust.*

Stepping back, she began to study the canvas—a luminous portrait of a young woman executed in oils. The woman was wearing a silver headband in her pale bobbed hair and a silver nineteen-twenties flapper dress. It was painted so finely that the subject seemed to be sending out an unspoken message to the onlooker and there was a trace of sadness in her lustrous dark eyes.

'It's exquisite,' Amber said softly.

'I know it is. Utterly exquisite.' He turned to her. 'And you're clear what you need to do? Stay by the Prince's side all evening and speak only when spoken to. Try to refrain from being controversial and please let me know if he communicates any concerns to one of his aides. Think you can manage that?'

'I can try.'

'Good. Then let's go and wait for the guest of honour.'

They walked towards the ballroom, where Amber could hear the string quartet playing a lively piece which floated out to greet them. 'So who else is coming tonight?' she asked.

'Some old friends are coming down from London. A few colleagues from New York. Local people.'

She hesitated. 'Do you ever see my half-brother, Rafe?'

His footsteps slowed and he shook his head. 'Not for ages. Not since he went out to Australia and cut himself off from his old life and nobody knew why.'

Remembering an offhand remark her father had once made, she glanced up at his rugged profile. 'I think it was something to do with a woman.'

'It's always to do with a woman, Amber. Especially when there's trouble.' He turned his head towards her and gave a hard smile. 'What do the French say? *Cherchez la femme.*'

'Is that cynicism I can hear in your voice? Did some girl break your heart, Conall?'

'Not mine, sweetheart. Mine's made of stone— didn't you know?' His eyes glittered. 'All I heard was that Rafe was heavily disillusioned by some woman and his life was never the same afterwards. It's a lesson for us all.'

He really *was* cynical, thought Amber as he introduced her to the party planner—a freckled redhead who clearly thought Conall was the greatest thing since sliced bread. Along with just about every other female present. Amber wondered if he was oblivious to the way the waitresses looked up and practically melted as they offered their trays of canapés and drinks. Whether he noticed that the female guests were fawning all over him. He *must* do—but, she had to admit, he handled it brilliantly. He was charming but he didn't flirt back—thus risking the wrath of their partners. She watched as he shook hands and made introductions as the room began to fill up, a smile creasing his rugged features.

She moved away, trying to remember that she was here as a member of his staff and not as his guest— wishing that she could retain a little immunity when she was close to him. She found herself a soft drink and stood in an alcove, watching as even more people arrived and the level of chatter increased. There was a discreet buzz of anticipation in the air, as if everyone was waiting for their royal guest, but Amber only became aware of the Prince's arrival when a complete silence suddenly descended on the ballroom.

People instantly parted to create a central path for him and the imposing man who walked in accompanied by two aides was instantly recognisable from the images Amber had downloaded from the Internet. With his immaculately cut dark suit and his golden skin gleaming, he had a charisma which was matched by only one other man in the room, who instantly stepped forward to greet him.

Amber watched as Conall gave a brief bow before shaking Luciano's hand and the string quartet broke into what was obviously the national anthem of Mardovia. And then a pair of midnight eyes were silently seeking her out and she found herself walking towards them, forcing herself to concentrate on the Prince and not on the rugged Irishman who had touched her so intimately.

'Your Royal Highness, this is Amber Carter—one of my assistants. Amber will be on hand tonight to provide anything you should require.'

That horrendous year at finishing school in Switzerland had taught Amber very little other than how to play truant and to ski, but it came up trumps now as she executed a deep and perfect curtsey. She rose slowly to her feet and the Prince smiled.

'Anything?' he drawled, his eyes roving down over her with an appreciative stare.

Amber wondered if she'd imagined Conall's faint frown and imperceptibly she nodded to the hovering waitress. 'Perhaps you would care for something to drink, Your Royal Highness?'

'Certo,' he answered softly in Italian, taking a glass of Kir Royale from the tray and then raising it to her in silent salute.

But Amber found herself enjoying the Prince's unexpected attention. For the first time in a long time she found herself encouraged by the sense that here was something she *could* do. She might not have any real qualifications but she'd watched enough of her father's wives and girlfriends fluttering around to know how *not* to behave if you were trying to play the perfect hostess. Even her mother had been able to pull it out of the bag when the need had arisen.

Unobtrusively she stood by to make sure the Prince wasn't approached by any stray star-struck guests as Conall introduced Luciano to several carefully vetted guests. It seemed he'd recently bought a penthouse apartment through Conall's company and she listened while the two men chatted with a local landowner about the escalating fortunes of the London property market. More waitresses appeared with tiny caviar-topped canapés but she noticed that the Prince refused them all. Eventually he turned to Conall.

'Do you think I have properly fulfilled my role as guest of honour,' he questioned drily, 'and given this occasion the royal stamp of approval?'

'You'd like to see the painting now?'

'I think you have tantalised me with it for long enough, don't you?'

Conall looked at her. 'Amber?'

She nodded, aware of two bodyguards who had suddenly appeared at the entrance to the ballroom and who now walked behind them towards the gallery. She thought what a disparate group they made as they made their way through the empty corridors.

The guard at the door stepped aside and Amber watched Luciano's reaction as he stepped forward to stand directly in front of the canvas. She thought that someone trying to negotiate a better price might have feigned a little indifference towards the painting, but the admiration on his face was impossible to conceal.

'What do you think?' asked Conall.

'It is breathtaking,' the Prince said slowly as he leaned forward to study it more closely. He murmured something in Italian to one of his aides and several minutes passed in silence before eventually he turned to Conall. 'We will discuss prices when you are back in London, not tonight. Business should never be distracted by pleasure.'

Conall inclined his head. 'I shall look forward to it.'

'Perhaps you could check that my car is ready? And in the meantime, I really think I must dance with your assistant who has looked after me so well all evening.' The Prince smiled. 'Unless she has any objections?'

The Prince's bright blue eyes were turned in her direction and Amber felt a stab of satisfaction. The Prince of Mardovia had told everyone that she'd done a good job—even though she'd done nothing more onerous than act as his gatekeeper—and now he wanted to dance with her. It was a long time since she could remember feeling this good about herself.

'I'd love to,' she said simply.

'*Eccellente.*'

She was aware of Conall's fleeting frown before he went to chase up the Prince's transport and aware of the envious glances of the other women in the ballroom as the Prince pulled her into his arms and the string quartet began to play a soft and easy waltz. Amber had been to some flashy parties in her time, but even she knew it wasn't every night of the week that you got to dance with a prince and Luciano ticked all the right boxes. He was supremely handsome and extremely attentive, but the weird thing was that it felt almost like dancing with her *brother*. Innocent and sweet, but almost dutiful. His arms around her waist felt nothing like Conall's had felt when he'd hauled her into his arms earlier. Despite the fact that he'd told her to forget it, she found herself remembering the way he had kissed her. Kissed her so hard that he'd left her feeling dazed.

'Devlin is your lover?' the Prince questioned suddenly, his voice breaking into her thoughts and amplifying them.

Slightly taken aback by his candour, Amber bit her lip. 'No!'

'But he would like to be.'

She shook her head. 'He hates me,' she said without thinking and then remembered that she was supposed to be there in the role of facilitator—not pouring out her heart to a royal stranger. 'I'm sorry—'

But Luciano didn't seem to notice for he lifted his hand to silence her apology. 'He may hate you, but he wants you. He watches you as the snake watches a chicken, just before it devours it whole.'

Amber shivered. 'That's not a very nice image to paint, Your Highness.'

'Maybe not, but it is an accurate one.' He gave her a cool smile. 'And you really should have mentioned that you speak Italian.'

Amber could feel a hot blush rising in her cheeks, so that any thought of denying it went straight out of the window. She looked up into Luciano's bright blue eyes. 'How—?'

'Not difficult.' He smiled. 'When I was speaking to my aide you were trying very hard not to react to what I was saying, but I am adept in observing reactions. I have had enough attempts made on my life to recognise subterfuge, even though I sometimes cannot help but admire it. Tell Conall I had always intended to give him a fair price for the painting.'

Amber tilted her chin. 'She's related to you, isn't she? The woman in the painting?'

He grew still. 'You recognised the family likeness, even though our colouring is quite different?'

Amber nodded. 'I'm…I'm quite good at doing that. I have a lot of half-brothers and sisters.'

'She is the daughter of my great-grandfather's brother who was born at the beginning of the last century. He fell in love with an Englishwoman and eloped with her to America. It caused a great scandal in Mardovia at the time.'

'I can imagine,' commented Amber.

Luciano glanced at his watch. 'At any other time

I would be fascinated to continue this discussion but look over there—the Irishman has returned and his expression tells me that he does not like to see you in my arms like this.'

'And you care what he thinks?'

'No, but I think you do.'

Amber stiffened. 'Maybe I do,' she admitted.

Luciano's eyes narrowed as he swung her round with a flourish, to the final few bars of the music. 'You are not aware of his reputation, I think?'

'With women?'

'With women, yes. And with business,' he commented drily. 'He is known for a detachment and a ruthlessness he has demonstrated tonight by placing a *spy* in my camp.'

Amber felt her cheeks grow pink. Hadn't she accused him of the very same thing? 'I'm sure that wasn't his intention at all,' she said doggedly.

The Prince smiled. 'Ah! Your loyalty to the man is touching—but do not look so alarmed, Amber. Conall and I know one another of old and I have great admiration for someone as ruthless as I am—but I would heed any sensible woman to exercise caution with such a man.'

Amber's cheeks were still burning as the Prince dropped his hands from her waist as Conall returned to escort him to his waiting car.

There was a loud buzz of chatter as the royal party left the room and Amber moved away from the dance floor and went to stand by the cool shelter of a marble pillar. With both men gone she felt like Cinderella— as if she no longer had any right to be here. As if any minute now her beautiful cream dress would turn into rags. She looked around. Maybe she should take the opportunity to slip out of the ballroom and go back to her room before Conall came back. Nobody would miss her. He might even be glad that she was out of his hair and he could party on without compunction.

But suddenly the decision was taken out of her hands because Conall had returned and was standing in the entrance to the ballroom, his dark suit hugging his muscular frame. He had undone a couple of buttons of his white silk shirt and Amber could see the faint smattering of dark hair there.

His eyes searched the room until he'd found her and as he began to walk towards her, her heart began to pound painfully in her chest. Would he be angry with her? She might have rather clumsily allowed the Prince to realise she was a linguist but he hadn't seemed to mind and she had done her best. Surely even Conall could understand that.

He was standing in front of her now, his midnight eyes shuttered. He didn't say a single word, just took her hand and led her onto the dance floor and Amber could feel her pulse rocketing skywards as he pulled her into his arms.

'Wh-what are you doing?' she questioned shakily, because she hadn't felt remotely like this when she'd been dancing with Luciano.

'Taking over where the Prince left off.' His eyes gleamed. 'Unless you have decided that dancing with mere mortals has no appeal compared to the heady delights of having a blue-blooded partner?'

'Don't be ridiculous,' she said. 'I'm quite happy to dance with you as long as you promise not to tread on my foot.'

His hands tightened around her waist. 'And that's your only stipulation, is it, Amber?'

Her eyes were fixed on the sprinkling of chest hair which was now exactly at eye level. 'I could think of plenty more.'

'Such as?'

'I wonder why you want to dance with me when you seem to have been glaring at me all evening.'

'Is that what I've been doing?'

'You know you have. Is it...' She hesitated. 'Is it because the Prince guessed that I spoke Italian?'

He laughed. 'He said you frowned when he used the word assassination. I guess most people would. And no, it's not because of that.'

'What, then?'

His hands tightened around her waist. 'Maybe because I have conflicting feelings about you.'

She lifted her face up and met the hard gleam of his eyes. He had *feelings* for her? She could do absolutely nothing about the sudden race of her heart—only pray he couldn't detect its erratic thumping. 'What do you mean?'

Idly, he began to rub his thumb up and down over her ribcage. 'Just that you arouse me. Deeply and constantly. And I can't seem to get you out of my mind.'

If anyone else had come out and said that Amber would have been shocked or scared, but somehow when Conall said it she was neither. 'And I'm supposed to be flattered by such a statement?'

'I don't know,' he said simply. 'My biggest concern is what I'm going to do about it.'

She could feel danger whispering in the air around them, but far more potent was the sense of excitement which made the danger easy to ignore. 'And the options are?'

'Don't be disingenuous, Amber, because it doesn't suit you.' Almost experimentally, he rolled his thumb over one of her ribs, slowly rubbing along the chiffon-covered bone. 'You know very well what the options are. I can take you upstairs so that we can finish off what we started earlier and maybe rid myself of this damned fever which has been raging in my blood since the moment I first saw you draped all over that white leather sofa.'

Somehow Amber stopped herself from reacting. Since *then*? 'Or?'

'Or I trawl this ballroom looking for someone who would make a more suitable bed partner on so many levels.' His voice dipped to a deep caress so that it sounded like velvet brushing over gravel. 'There's a third choice, of course—but not nearly so inviting. Because I could always go and take a long, cold shower and steer clear of all the complications of sex.'

Amber said nothing. He'd made her sound as disposable as a paper handkerchief. As forgettable as last night's tangled dreams. Yet he wasn't lying to her, was he? He wasn't dressing up his desire with fancy words and meaningless phrases—raising up her hopes before smashing them down again. He wasn't promising her the stars, but his underlying message was that he would deliver on satisfaction. And didn't she want that satisfaction for the first time in her life? Didn't she want to sample what other women just took for granted?

She thought about what the Prince had said to her. That a sensible woman would exercise caution. She guessed he'd been warning her off Conall Devlin, for whatever reason. But she wasn't known for being *sensible*, was she? She was known as a wild child—the party animal who was up for anything. And only she knew the truth—that all her wildness was nothing but a façade behind which she hid, a barrier which nobody had ever been able to break down.

But Conall Devlin had got closer than anyone else.

She closed her eyes as she felt his fingers pressing against her flesh and she was acutely conscious that they were inches away from her breast. Through the delicate fabric of her silk dress it felt as if he were touching her bare skin and she felt a shiver rippling down her spine. How did he *do* that? What power did he have which made her respond to him like this and make her so achingly aware of her own body? The hard jut of his hips and the potent cradle of his masculinity as he pressed himself closer should have intimidated a woman of her laughable experience, but it didn't. It just made her want more. Much more. Was she really prepared to turn her back on this opportunity to become a real woman at last?

Instinct made her lips part as she looked into his eyes and saw the sudden gleam of intensity in his darkened gaze.

'And don't I get a say in what happens?' she questioned, as lightly as if she had this kind of conversation every day of the week.

'Of course. You get to choose—because that is a woman's prerogative. Tell me what *you* want, Amber.'

The mood of the conversation had switched and beneath the teasing banter of his tone she could sense his sudden urgency. But still Amber held back, telling herself to confront the reality of what was happening here. For him this was just a liaison no different from countless others—apart from her name and her hair colour, she was probably as interchangeable as the last woman who had shared his bed.

And for her?

It was going to be no good if she started weakening. If she made the mistake of falling for him. She could only go ahead if she accepted it for what it was. Not stardust and roses, but a powerful sexual hunger. A physical awakening which was long overdue.

Rising up on tiptoe, she put her lips to his ear and only just refrained from sliding her tongue across the lobe.

'I want to have sex with you,' she whispered.

Conall stiffened, thinking he had misheard her. He must have done. She had been feisty and defiant every step of the way—surely she wasn't rolling over and capitulating *that* easily. And didn't he *want* her to go on resisting him for a little while longer, because it was so deliciously rare and because the conquest was never quite as good as the chase...

'You mean that?' he questioned softly, his fingertips continuing to slide over her silk-covered torso.

She nodded, her words uncharacteristically brief. 'Yes. Yes, I do.'

A smile curved the edges of his lips as he felt the heat begin to rise within him. 'Very well. This is what I want you to do. You will go upstairs to your room and wait for me while I say goodbye to my guests. But you will not undress before I arrive.' He paused. 'Because undressing a woman is one of the greatest pleasures known to man. Is that clear?'

She nodded—more obedient than he had ever seen her. 'Very clear.'

'I shall come to you before midnight.' He tilted her chin with his thumb and stared straight into her emerald eyes. 'But if before that you decide—for whatever reason—that you've changed your mind, then you must tell me and we will consider this conversation never to have happened. Do you understand?'

'Yes, Conall.'

He put his lips very close to her ear. 'I'm not quite sure how to cope with this unusually docile Amber.'

She turned her head to meet his gaze. 'Would you prefer defiance, then?'

'I'll let you know in graphic detail exactly what I'd prefer but I think it had better wait until we are alone. Because my words are having an unfortunate but predictable effect on my body, and having you this close to me is making me want to tear that dress off you and see the flesh beneath, and I don't think that would go down very well with my guests, do you?'

She shook her head but, to his surprise, her cheeks flushed a deep shade of pink and he felt a doubling of his desire for her. 'Go upstairs and wait for me,' he said roughly. 'Because the sooner this evening ends, the sooner we can begin.'

CHAPTER SEVEN

AMBER HEARD A CREAK behind her and turned to see the handle turning and the door slowly opening to reveal Conall standing rock still on the threshold of her bedroom. The light from the corridor spilled in from behind him, turning his muscular physique into a powerful silhouette, but not for long—because he closed the door and walked across the room, his eyes shuttered as he grew close and looked down at her. His voice sounded like velvet encasing steel.

'Changed your mind?'

She shook her head. Admittedly, she *had* been having second thoughts about their cold-blooded sexual liaison as she'd been sitting perched on the window seat waiting for him. Not undressing as per his curt instructions and feeling a bit like a sacrificial lamb in her evening dress as she stared out at the bright stars which spattered the night sky and the crescent moon which gleamed against the darkness. But her flutterings of apprehension were nothing compared to the stealthy creep of desire which was making her nerve endings feel so raw and her breasts so heavy and tingling. 'No,' she said unsteadily. 'I haven't changed my mind.'

Conall expelled the breath he hadn't realised he'd been holding because hadn't he almost wished she *had*? He'd been plagued by feelings of guilt the moment she had walked off the dance floor with her pale dress floating around her like a cloud. He had felt tortured by his conscience and even now something told him he should get out while he still could.

'I told your father that I would set you on the right path,' he growled.

She looked up into his face. 'And you have. You know you have. I felt so confident tonight—as if anything was possible and it was because of you and the chance you gave me. A few weeks ago I wouldn't have done that but you've made me see new possibilities. I'm a grown woman, Conall, not a child—so don't treat me like one. And my father is not my keeper.'

Transfixed by the unusually steadfast note in her voice and the rise and fall of her breasts, Conall felt the last of his resistance melting away as he took hold of her hands and lifted her to her feet. In the moonlight her face was almost as pale as her silky dress and, in vivid contrast, her dark hair spilled like ebony over her shoulders. She looked like a witch, he thought longingly. *Was* she a witch? Able to enchant him with things he suspected were the wrong things for a man like him? His mouth hardened. *So make sure she knows your boundaries. Make sure she doesn't read anything into what is going to happen.*

'I guess we'd better have the disclaimer conversation,' he said abruptly.

She blinked up at him. 'Disclaimer conversation?'

'Sure. I'm pretty certain a hard-partying woman like you isn't going to object to a one-night stand on moral grounds but just in case—I'd better make it clear that this is all this is going to be. One night. Great sex. But no more.' He raised his eyebrows. 'Any objections?'

'None from me,' she said, in that flippant way which was so much a part of her, though for a second he wondered if he had imagined the faint shadow which crossed over her face. 'So what are we waiting for?'

Heart pounding, he reached for the zip of her dress and slid it down. One small tug and it had pooled to her ankles and she was standing wearing nothing but her high-heeled silver shoes and her underwear.

Conall frowned because somehow her lingerie didn't match her sassy image. Her plain white bra looked like something a woman might wear to the gym and she had on a pair of those big knickers which had been the butt of a national joke for a while. It was not the lingerie of a woman who had boldly whispered to him on the dance floor that she wanted to have sex with him and that puzzled him.

Had she sensed his disquiet? Was that why she reached behind her and unclipped her bra—as careless as a woman getting changed on the beach? He stilled as her breasts spilled free and he felt a jerk of almost unbearable lust as he stared at them. Did she know that they were the stuff of his fevered fantasies—large yet pert, with their rosy-pink and perfect nipples? Of course she did. With a groan he pulled her into his arms and pushed back the spill of her hair as he kissed her. He kissed her until she was melting and her lips opened eagerly beneath his, until she began to move restlessly in his arms. And when he drew his face away, her eyes looked huge and dark in her face. As if she was completely dazed by that kiss. Conall shook his head a little. Come to think of it—wasn't he a little dazed himself?

'You are the most unfathomable woman I've ever met, Amber Carter,' he groaned, taking each nipple between a finger and a thumb and squeezing them until she squirmed with pleasure.

Her eyelids seemed to be having difficulty staying open. 'And is that a good thing, or a bad thing?'

'I haven't made my mind up yet. It's unusual, that's for sure.' He leaned forward and brushed his lips over hers. 'I keep thinking I've got you all worked out and then you go and confound all my expectations.'

'And what do you have me worked out as?'

He laughed and his voice grew serious as he traced the outline of her lips with his finger. 'One minute you're unbearably spoilt, with a sense of entitlement so strong it almost takes my breath away, while the next...'

But Amber halted his words by leaning forward to kiss him, mimicking the almost careless way he'd just brushed his lips over hers. She guessed what was coming and she didn't want to hear it. She didn't dare. She didn't want to hear about her flaws and she certainly didn't want him to work out why she was feeling out of her depth. He was a sexually experienced man—and a perceptive man—who was doubtless going to make some comment about her seeming gauche and innocent. Some bone-deep instinct told her he would run a mile if he knew the truth—and that was something she wasn't prepared to tolerate. Because she wanted Conall Devlin. She didn't care if it was a one-night stand. She couldn't think beyond the sudden urgent needs of her body and she wanted him more than she could remember wanting anything. More than the security she'd prayed for as a child, or the peace which had always eluded her. More than any of that.

So stop behaving like someone who is a stranger to intimacy. Start being the person he thinks you are.

Looping her arms around his neck, she slanted him a coquettish smile. 'Look, I know the Irish are famous for talking, but do you think we could save this conversation until later?'

And suddenly they seemed to be reading from the same page, because his eyes gleamed. 'Oh, I'm happy to skip the talking, sweetheart,' he promised, his voice laden with silken intent. 'What is it they say—action, not words?'

He picked her up and carried her over to the four-poster bed, laying her down on top of it and bending his head to a nipple. Her eyes closed as his tongue flicked over the puckered skin and his teeth gently grazed the engorged nub, making her wriggle her hips with helpless pleasure before he turned his attention to the other. Sweet sensation speared through her, flooding her body with a sudden rush of honey-eyed warmth as his dark head moved over her sensitive skin. Did he realise that her desire was rapidly building, or could he detect it from the subtle new perfume now scenting the air? Was that why he slipped his hand between her legs, burrowing beneath the plain white fabric of her briefs and brushing over the mound of curls before alighting on the heated flesh beneath?

She felt so wet. Maybe that was why he gave a low laugh which sent shivers down her spine. Amber's mouth dried as he began to move his finger against her so that her little gasp was scarcely more than a sigh. It felt as if he were building a wall of pleasure, brick by delicious brick, and she fell back against the pillows, her thighs parting of their own accord, when suddenly he stopped. Her eyes snapped open, terrified he had changed his mind. Her heart pounded. *He mustn't change his mind!*

But he was smiling as he shook his head. 'No,' he said. 'Not like that. Not the first time.'

He moved away from the bed and began to undress— removing his clothes and producing a small silver packet from his pocket with an efficiency which suggested he'd done this many times before. Of course he had. And although fear that she would somehow disappoint him began to bubble up inside her—it quickly disappeared the moment she saw him in all his naked glory.

Amber shivered. He was like a classical statue you might see in a museum—with broad shoulders tapering down to narrow hips and muscular legs. But statues didn't have tawny skin which glowed with life, nor midnight eyes which gleamed with hunger. Inevitably, her gaze was drawn down towards the cradle of his masculinity where, against a palette of jet-dark curls, his erection was thick and pale and prominent. Amber felt her pulse go shooting skywards. She'd never got this far before—she'd always fallen at much earlier hurdles—and perhaps she should have been daunted by what she saw. But she wasn't. It felt natural. As if it was supposed to happen. As if fate had intended it to happen—before she reminded herself that she wasn't going down that path. Stardust and roses weren't part of this equation, she reminded herself fiercely. This was sex. Nothing but sex. He'd told her that himself.

'I like it,' he murmured as he came over to the bed and pulled her into his arms.

'Wh-what?'

'The look on your face.' He smiled. 'As if this was the first time all over again. Have you spent years perfecting that look of wonder and innocence, Amber—knowing just how much it will turn a man on?'

If she'd written the script herself, there wouldn't have been a better time to tell him but Amber couldn't bring herself to say it. Because now he was kissing her and his hands were starfishing over her breasts and she could feel his hardness pressing against her belly.

'Conall,' she gasped as he pulled back for a moment to slide her panties down and she lifted up her bottom to help him.

'You were the one who didn't want to talk,' he murmured as he fumbled for the silver packet he'd put beside the bed. 'Though maybe you'd better say something to distract me because I've never had so much trouble putting on a damned condom.'

'Be…be careful.'

The smile on his lips died. 'Oh, don't worry, sweetheart. Having a baby with you was never part of my agenda.'

The stark statement was oddly painful and yet somehow it helped. It helped her focus on the way he was making her *feel* and not the conflicting thoughts which were swirling around inside her head.

So she kissed him back with a passion which came

from somewhere deep inside her, and with growing confidence began to explore the warm satin of his skin with her mouth and her fingers. And when he moved over her and parted her thighs, the fear she felt was only fleeting. She was twenty-four years old, for heaven's sake. It was time.

Conall gave a groan as he thrust into her, knowing he was going to have to be very careful because he was so aroused he wanted to come straight away. And she was so *tight*. His heart pounded like some caged animal locked inside his chest. Too tight. He gave a near-silent curse as realisation dawned on him and his body stilled. For a moment he almost achieved the impossible by starting to withdraw from her, but the moment was lost the second she cried out and he couldn't work out if the sound was pain or pleasure. Had he hurt her? He stared down into her face, into eyes which were wide—as if seeking some kind of approval—and instantly he shut his own with grim deliberation, not wanting her to see his anger or his disbelief as he began to move inside her. Part of him wanted to just spill his seed and have done with it, but the pride he took in his reputation as a lover made him take his time…

Duplicitous little *bitch*, he thought as he drove into her—each thrust making her gasp out her pleasure. With almost cold-hearted precision he did all the things to her which women liked best. He tilted up her hips to increase the level of penetration while he played with her clitoris. He rode her hard and he rode her slow, and only when he felt her body begin to tense did he let go—and then it was *his* time for bewilderment. Because it had never happened to him before. Not like this. Not at exactly the same time—as if they'd worked very hard at sexual choreography classes to ensure the ultimate in mutual fulfilment. So that as her back began to arch and her long legs began to splay, he couldn't even watch her—he was too busy focusing on his own orgasm, which was welling up inside him like an almighty wave, before taking him under.

Had he thought that the chase was always more tantalising than the conquest? He had been wrong.

Because all he was aware of was the convulsive jerk of his body and the molten rush of heat. Of the sweetest pleasure he had ever known flooding him... and his shuddered cry drowning out the distant hoot of the night owl.

CHAPTER EIGHT

'You acted…'

Conall's words trailed off and Amber didn't prompt him. She didn't want to talk and she didn't want to hear what he had to say. She didn't want to do anything except lie here and go over what had just happened, second by glorious second. To remember the way he'd kissed her. The way he'd pushed deep inside her—and then the growing awareness of her body's reaction, which had seemed too good to be true. Only it hadn't been. It had been very real and very true. Conall Devlin had made love to her and it had been perfect. She expelled a long, slow breath of satisfaction. Suddenly she could understand all the fuss and hype and everything which went with it. Sex was pretty potent stuff.

But then when it was over, he had withdrawn from her without even looking at her. He had just rolled over onto his back and lain there staring at the ceiling in complete silence. As if he was working out what he was going to say, and something told her she wasn't going to like it…

She was right.

'You acted like you'd been round the block a few times—and then some,' he accused.

She risked a glance at him then and almost wished she hadn't because it triggered off a craving to touch him again and that was the last thing he wanted, judging from the stony look on his face. *You haven't done anything wrong*, she told herself. *And he can only make you feel bad about yourself if you let him.*

'You're objecting to the fact I was a virgin?' she questioned, in a voice which was surprisingly calm. Maybe it was the endorphins rushing through her bloodstream which were responsible—making her feel as if she were floating in the sea, in bright sunshine. 'And you're objecting to the fact that I hadn't *been around the block*, is that what you're saying?'

He turned to look at her, his eyes gleaming in his tawny skin. 'What do you think? You knew what the deal was, Amber.'

'Deal?' she echoed. She raised her eyebrows. 'What deal was that?'

'I told you it was a one-night stand!' he exploded.

'And virgins aren't allowed to have one-night stands?'

'Yes. No! Stop wilfully misunderstanding me!'

'I'm confused, Conall. You still haven't told me why you're so angry.'

He glared at her. 'You know damned well why.'

'No, I don't.'

'There's an unspoken rule about sex—that if you're inexperienced, you tell the man.'

'Why? So that you could be "gentle" with me?'

'So that I could have turned around and walked right out again.'

'Because you didn't want me?'

Conall steeled himself against that uncertain note in her voice, reminding himself that she was a consummate actress. She'd played the vamp to an astonishingly successful degree and had fooled him completely. He'd fantasised about all the sexual tricks she might have learnt over the years. He'd been expecting accomplishment and slickness—not for her to cry out like that when he tore through her hymen. Or to clutch at him like a child with a new toy when he was deep inside her. That wonder on her face had not been feigned, he realised grimly.

'You know I wanted you. My body is programmed to want you. It's a reaction outside my control.'

'Gee. Thanks.'

He shook his head. 'The first time is supposed to be special. It's supposed to *mean* something and if I'd realised, I would have done the decent thing and walked away. But you weren't prepared to let that happen, were you, Amber? You saw something and you just went right ahead and took it because that's the kind of woman you are. Even though you must have known it would never have happened if I'd realised you were a virgin. But Amber always gets what Amber wants, doesn't she?'

'If that's what you want to think, then think it,' she said.

'I just don't understand why.' He frowned. 'How come someone who looks like you and acts like you has never actually had sex before now?'

Amber met the anger in his eyes and wondered how much to tell him. But what was the point in holding back—in trying to pretend that she was a normal woman who'd led a normal life?

'Because I don't really like men,' she said slowly. 'And I certainly don't trust them.'

'Which is why you put out for someone you only met a couple of weeks ago, who hasn't even taken you out on a date?'

Put like that, it made her sound plain stupid. As if she'd been caught scraping the very bottom of the barrel. Amber felt her cheeks growing hot, but she could hardly blame him for speaking the truth—even if it made her feel bad. And was she really going to let him take the moral high ground, just because she hadn't given some embarrassingly graphic explanation before he'd made love to her? Why *would* she ruin the mood and risk spoiling something which had felt so natural?

'I'm sure your colossal ego doesn't need me to tell you why I succumbed to you. You must realise that you're overwhelmingly attractive to women, Conall. I'm sure you've heard it many times before. It must be that blend of Irish charm coupled with a masterful certainty that you always know best.' She snuggled down a little further into the bedclothes, but her skin still felt like ice. 'It must be great to have that kind of unshakeable confidence.'

'We were talking about you, not me,' he growled. 'And you still haven't given me an explanation.'

'Do I have to?'

'Don't you think you owe me one?'

'I don't owe you anything.'

'Okay, then. How about as a favour to me for having given you so much pleasure in the last hour?'

Amber swallowed as she met the arrogant glitter in his eyes. In a way it was easier when he was being hateful because at least that stopped her from fostering any dreamy illusions about him. And she realised that this was the other side of intimacy—not the sex part but the bit where two people were naked in more ways than one. Because for once she couldn't run or hide from the truth. She felt exposed; vulnerable. Conall was demanding an explanation and in her heart she guessed she owed him one.

'Maybe it's because I didn't have the best role models in the world,' she said.

'You're talking about your father?' he questioned curiously.

'Not just my father. There were plenty of others. My mother's lovers, for starters.'

'There were a lot?'

'Oh, yes—you could say that.' She gave a hollow laugh. 'After my parents split, my father gave my mother loads of alimony—I think he was trying to ease his conscience about falling in love with a new woman. With hindsight it was probably a big mistake—because money buys you plenty of things, but not happiness. The biggest cliché in the world, I know, but true.' Amber was aware of the irony of her words. As if it had taken this to make her see things clearly. Because hadn't she experienced the closest thing she'd felt to joy in a long time when she'd been walking in that country lane that afternoon? And then just a few minutes ago, when Conall's naked skin had touched hers and he'd taken her to heaven and back? Only one of those things had cost her...and it couldn't be measured in monetary terms.

'So what happened?' he asked, his deep Irish voice penetrating her thoughts.

'My mother couldn't face staying in England with the humiliation of being replaced by wife number four, who was much younger—as well as being a lingerie model. So she decided to do an extensive tour of Europe—which translated into an extensive tour of European men. The trouble was that she was divorced and predatory, with a child in tow. Not the best combination to help her in her ardent pursuit of a new partner.' She shifted her legs beneath the duvet, taking care to keep them well away from his. 'Oh, there were plenty of men—but the men always seemed to come with baggage, usually in the shape of a wife. We were hounded out of Rome, and Athens, too. We were threatened in Naples and had to slip away in the dead of night. Only in Paris did she achieve any kind of acceptance because there the role of mistress is more or less accepted. Only she didn't like playing second fiddle to other men's wives, and...' Her words tailed off.

'And what?'

A wave of indignation swept over her as she met the hard glitter of his sapphire eyes. Why was he doing this? Interrogating her like some second-rate cop. Was he determined to ruin the amazing memory of what had just happened between them by making her retrace a past it was painful to revisit?

'I'm waiting, Amber,' he said softly.

Stubborn, hateful man. Amber stared straight up at the ceiling. 'I don't want to talk about it,' she said woodenly. 'She died, okay? I was brought back to England, kicking and screaming, and moved in with my father, who by that time was on wife number five. I didn't fit in anywhere—and I knew his latest wife didn't want me there. To him, I was a problem he didn't know how to cope with, so he just threw lots of money at it. I started doing loads of courses but only the ones he thought were suitable and, of course, I never saw them through. I didn't know how to deal with normal life—and I'd known so many creepy men when I was growing up that I simply wasn't interested in getting intimate with any of my own.'

'I see.'

Amber pulled the duvet right up to her neck—noticing he didn't object—before rolling on her side to face him. 'And what *do* you see, Conall?'

He gave a short laugh. 'I can see now why your father was so determined he help you escape from the rut you were in. I detected a sense of remorse in his attitude—a sense that he wanted to try to repair some of the mistakes he'd made in the past. He must have realised that giving you money was having precisely the wrong effect, and that's why he withdrew your funds.'

'Wow. You should be a detective!'

'But you didn't like being broke, did you, Amber?' he continued silkily. 'You didn't like having to knuckle down and do a hard day's work like the rest of the human race.'

'I thought I did a good job for you tonight with the Prince!' she defended, stung.

He nodded reluctantly. 'Oh, you did,' he said. 'He was very impressed with you and who wouldn't be, with your classy dress and your pearls? And, of course, the fact that you were gazing up at him on the dance floor and batting those witchy green eyes certainly didn't do you any harm. But I guess you quickly discovered that he wasn't interested in you and so that quicksilver mind of yours had to come up with an alternative plan.'

'Really? And what *plan* was this, Conall? Do enlighten me—this is absolutely fascinating.'

'I think I can understand why you were a virgin,' he said slowly. 'With a mother who was sexually voracious, you must have realised that virginity is the most prized gift a woman can offer a man. It's unique. A one-off.'

'You've lost me now,' she said faintly.

'Think about it. Because despite your lack of qualifications, you're a super-sharp woman, Amber. You know damned well what I'm talking about. You played the vamp with me. You realised there was real chemistry between us and that all I wanted was casual sex. It was a grown-up agreement between two consenting adults when suddenly you spring this surprise on me. You're a virgin! Though when I stop to think about it, maybe it isn't so surprising after all.' He gave a short laugh. 'Take a previously wealthy woman with nothing to offer but her innocence—and throw her into the arms of an old-fashioned man with a conscience and the result is predictable.'

'What *result*?'

Despite their cold hue, his eyes suddenly looked as if they were capable of scorching her skin.

'It doesn't matter—at least, not right now,' he said, his mouth twisting into a grim line. 'What an impetuous fool I was to have taken you to bed!'

'Then why don't you do us both a favour and get out of it right now?'

She wasn't expecting him to take her at her word, but he did—pushing back the bedclothes with an impatient hand and moving away from the bed as if it were contaminated. But the impact of seeing him unselfconsciously naked as he walked across the room was utterly compelling and Amber couldn't seem to drag her gaze away. He went to stand by the window and all she could see was his magnificent physique, silhouetted against the gleaming moon and scattered stars. And all she could think about was how pale his buttocks looked against the deep tawny colour of his back. How it had felt to have the rough power of his muscular legs entwined with her own, which had felt so light and smooth in comparison.

Only he had made her feel bad about what had happened—and bad about herself. As if she were using her virginity as some kind of bargaining tool. As if she were nothing but a cold-blooded manipulator.

So why did she still want him, despite his wounding words? Why did she want to feel his lips on her lips and his hands on her hips as he positioned himself over her, before thrusting deep inside her? Maybe she was one of those women who were only turned on by men who were cruel to them, just like her mother.

She licked her dry lips. 'Are you going now?' she croaked, because surely it would hurt less if he was gone.

He turned back to face her and at once she could see that he was aroused and, although she tried not to react, something in her face must have given away her thoughts because he gave a cold, hard smile.

'Oh, yes,' he said ruefully. 'I still want you, be in no doubt about that. Only this time I'm not going to be stupid enough to do anything about it.' Grabbing his clothes, he started pulling them on until he was standing in the now-creased suit he'd worn to the party.

'I'm going to bed,' he continued. 'I need to sleep on this and decide what needs to be done. I'll have breakfast sent up here tomorrow morning and then drive you back to London. Make sure you're ready to leave at eight.'

Amber shook her head. 'I don't want to drive back to London with you,' she said. 'I'll get the train, like I did before.'

'It's not a subject which is open for negotiation, Amber. You and I need to talk, but not now. Not like this.'

She lay there wide-eyed after he'd gone, hugging her arms around her chest. And although she went to the bathroom to shower his scent from her skin, it wasn't so easy to erase him from her memory and her night was spent fitfully tossing and turning.

She was up and dressed early next morning, telling herself she wasn't hungry but it seemed her body had other ideas. She devoured grapefruit, eggs and toast with an appetite which was uncharacteristically hearty, before going downstairs to find Conall waiting outside for her with his car engine running.

She tried not to look at him as she climbed beside him and she kept communication brief, but he didn't object to her silence and said very little on the journey back to London. She stared out of the window and thought about yesterday and how green the lush countryside had seemed—and how today it seemed like a once-bright balloon from which all the air had escaped.

He drove her straight to her apartment and as he turned off the engine she couldn't resist a swipe.

'Here we are—home at last,' she said with bright sarcasm. 'Though not for much longer, of course, because soon my big, bad landlord will be kicking me out onto the streets.'

'That's what I want to talk to you about,' he said, pushing open his door.

'You're not planning on coming in?'

'No, not planning,' he said grimly. 'I *am* coming in. And there's no need to look so horrified, Amber—I'm not going to jump on you the moment we get inside.'

Oddly enough, his assurance provided Amber with little comfort. Was it possible that one episode of sex had been enough to kill his desire for her for ever? Because the man who had been so hot and hungry for her last night was deliberately keeping his distance from her this morning.

She waited until they were inside and then she turned to him, noticing the dark shadows around his eyes. As if he had slept as badly as her. 'So. What's the verdict?'

His mouth was unsmiling and his voice was heavy. 'I think we should get married.'

Amber blinked in astonishment and, even though she knew it was *insane*, she couldn't quite suppress the flicker of hope which had started dancing at the edges of her heart. She pictured clouds of confetti and a lacy dress, and a rugged face bending down to kiss her. She swallowed. 'You do?'

'Yes.' Navy eyes narrowed. 'I know it's far from ideal but it seems the only sensible solution.'

'I think I need to sit down,' said Amber faintly, sinking onto one of the white leather sofas beneath the penetrating brilliance of his gaze. And now that her heart had stopped pounding with a hope she realised was stupid, she tried to claw back a little dignity. 'Whatever gave you that idea that I would want to marry you?'

His gaze burned into her. 'Didn't it enter your mind for a moment that giving me your virginity would trouble my conscience? I feel a responsibility towards you—'

'Then don't—'

'You don't understand,' he interrupted savagely. 'I have betrayed the trust of your father by taking advantage of you.' His voice hardened. 'And trust is a very big deal to me.'

'He won't know. Nobody will know.'

'*I* will know,' he said grimly. 'And the only way I can see of legitimising what has just happened is to make you my temporary wife.'

She stared at him defiantly. 'So you want to marry me just to make yourself feel better?'

'Not entirely. It would have certain advantages for you, too.'

She opened her mouth and knew she shouldn't say what she was about to say—but *why not*? He'd seen her naked, hadn't he? He'd been deep inside her body in a way that nobody else had ever been. He'd heard her cry out her pleasure with that broken kind of joy as she'd wrapped her legs around his back. What did she have to lose? 'What, like sex?'

But he shook his head, his hair glinting blue-black in the watery spring sunshine. 'No,' he said. 'Most emphatically not sex. I don't want the complications of that. This will purely be a marriage of convenience— a short-lived affair with a planned ending.'

She screwed up her eyes, trying not to react. One brief sexual encounter and already he'd had enough of her? 'I don't understand,' she said, desperately trying to hide the hurt she felt at his rejection.

He walked over to the window and stared out at the view for a moment before turning back to face her. 'Your father wanted you to stand on your own two feet—and as a wealthy divorcee you'll be able to do exactly that.'

'A wealthy divorcee?' she echoed hoarsely.

'Sure. What else did you think would happen— that twenty-five years down the line we'd be toasting each other with champagne and playing with the grandkids?' He gave a cynical smile. 'We'll get married straight away—because a whirlwind marriage always makes a gullible world think it's high romance.'

'But you don't, I suppose?'

His mouth hardened. 'I'm a realist, Amber—not a romantic.'

'Me, too,' she lied.

'Well, that makes it a whole lot easier, doesn't it? And you know what they say…marry in haste, repent at leisure. Only nowadays there's no need to do that. We'll split after three months and nobody will be a bit surprised. I'll settle this apartment on you and agree to some sort of maintenance. And if you want my advice, you should use the opportunity to go off and do something useful with your life—not go back to your former, worthless existence. Your father will see you blossom and flourish with your new-found independence. He's hardly in a position to berate you for a failed marriage—and my conscience will be clear.'

'You've got it all worked out, haven't you?' she said slowly.

'I deal in solutions.' His gaze drifted to her face. 'What do you say, Amber?'

She looked away, noticing a red wine stain on the white leather of the sofa as he waited for her answer. The trouble was that on some level she wasn't averse to marrying him and she wasn't quite sure why. Was it because she felt safe and protected whenever he was around? Or because she was hoping he'd change his mind about the no-sex part? Surely a virile man like Conall wouldn't be prepared to coexist platonically with a woman—no matter how fake or how short their relationship was intended to be.

And look what he was offering in return. At least as a divorcee she would have a certain respectability. A badge of honour that someone had once wanted her enough to marry her...

Except that he didn't. Not really. He didn't love her and he didn't want her.

That old familiar feeling of panic flooded through her. It felt just like that time when she'd been shipped off to her dad's after her mother had died. He hadn't wanted her, either, not really—and neither did Conall. It was a grim proposition to have to face until she considered the alternative. No money. No qualifications. No control. She swallowed. In an ideal world she would turn around and walk out, but where would she go?

Couldn't this marriage be a stepping stone to some kind of better future?

'Yeah, I'll marry you,' she said casually.

CHAPTER NINE

IT WASN'T A real wedding—so no way was it going to feel like one.

It was a line Amber kept repeating—telling herself if she said it often enough, then sooner or later she'd start believing it. Her marriage was nothing but a farce. A solution to ease Conall's conscience and set her up financially for the future. This way, nobody would have to lose face. Not her and not Conall.

But weddings had a sneaky knack of pressing all the wrong buttons, no matter how much you tried not to let them. Despite the example set by both her parents, Amber found herself having to dampen down instincts which came out of nowhere. Who knew she would secretly yearn for a floaty dress with a garland of flowers in her hair? Because floaty dresses and flowers were romantic, and this had nothing to do with romance—Conall had told her that and she had agreed with him. This was a transaction, pure and simple. As emotionless as any deal her Irish fiancé might cut in the boardroom.

So she opted for a dress she thought would be *suitable* for the civil ceremony—a sleek knee-length outfit by a well-known designer, with her hair worn in a heavy chignon and a minimalist bouquet of stark, arum lilies.

The ceremony was small. Her father, still in his ashram, had not been able to attend—and Conall had insisted on keeping the celebrations short and muted.

'I don't want this to turn into some kind of rent-a-crowd,' he'd growled. 'Inviting a bunch of my friends to meet a woman who isn't going to be part of my life for longer than a few weeks is a waste of everyone's time. As long as we give the press the pictures they want, nobody will care.'

But on some level *Amber* had cared. She tried to convince herself that it was a relief not to have to invite anyone and have to maintain the farce of being a blissfully happy bride. She told herself that she was perfectly cool with the miniskirted Serena and another of Conall's glamorous assistants being their only two witnesses on the day.

But hadn't some stupid part of her *wanted* Conall to take her into his arms when he'd slipped the thin gold band on her finger—and to kiss her with all the passion he'd displayed on that moonlit night in his country house? He hadn't, of course. He had waited until they got outside, where a bank of tipped-off photographers was assembled, and it was only then that he had kissed her. From the outside it must have looked quite something, for he held her close and bent over her in a masterful way which made her heart punch out such a frantic beat that for a minute she felt quite dizzy. But his lips had remained as cold and as unmoving as if they'd been made from marble— and it didn't seem to matter what she said or did, she couldn't remember seeing him smile.

They had taken the honeymoon suite at the Granchester Hotel, even though Conall had an enormous house in Notting Hill, which Amber had visited just twice before. But both occasions had felt dry and rather formal and she'd felt completely overwhelmed by the decidedly masculine elements of his elegant town house.

'I think it's best if we stay on neutral territory for the first few days.' His words had been careful. 'It lets the world know we're man and wife, but it will also allow us to work out some workable form of compromise as to how this...*marriage* is going to work.' He'd paused and his midnight-blue eyes had glinted. 'Plus the hotel is used to dealing with the press.'

The hotel seemed used to dealing with pretty much everything. Their suite was huge, with a dining room laid up to serve them a post-wedding meal, a vast sitting room, and a hot tub on the private and very sheltered rooftop garden. Rather distractingly, the king-sized bed had been liberally scattered with scarlet rose petals—something which had made Conall's mouth harden as he'd walked into the bedroom, while pulling loose his tie.

'Why the hell do they *do* that?' he asked.

Amber paused in the act of removing the pins from her hair, relieved to be able to shake it free after the tensions of the long day, even though a feeling of apprehension about the night ahead was building up inside her. 'Presumably they like to think they're adding to the general air of romance.'

'It's so damned corny.'

Kicking off her cream shoes, Amber sank down

on one of the chairs and looked at him, a trace of defiance creasing her brow. 'So now what?'

It was a question Conall had been dreading and one he still hadn't quite worked out how to answer, despite it looming large in his thoughts during the days since she'd agreed to marry him, while they'd waited for the necessary paperwork to go through. Hadn't he thought she might phone him up and tell him she'd changed her mind? That she'd tell him it was insane in this day and age for two people to go through with a marriage neither wanted, just because they'd had casual sex and she had been a virgin?

There had been a big part of him which had *wanted* her to do that. Because whichever way you looked at it, he was now trapped with her for the next three months. Their relationship had to look real, which meant he'd have to be with her—as a new husband would be expected to be with his wife. And he didn't *do* sustained proximity. He liked his freedom and the ability to come and go. He always demanded an escape route and a get-out clause whenever he was in a relationship. And this *wasn't* a relationship, he reminded himself grimly.

He walked over to the ice bucket, which was sitting next to two crystal flutes and yet more scarlet roses, and pulled out a bottle of vintage champagne.

'I think we deserve a drink, don't you?' he said, glancing over at her as he popped the cork.

'Please.'

Trying hard to avert his gaze from the splayed coltishness of her long legs, he handed her a glass. 'Here.'

Amber took the glass and studied the fizzing

golden bubbles for a moment before looking up into his eyes. 'So what shall we drink to, Conall?'

He sat down opposite, deliberately settling himself as far away from her as possible. What he would *like* to drink to wasn't a request for long life or happiness. No. What he needed right then was to be granted some sort of immunity. A sure-fire way to stop thinking about her sensuality—a sensuality which seemed even more potent now that he'd sampled her delicious body for himself. He wondered how it was possible for a woman to be so damned sexy when she'd only ever had sex once before.

He felt his throat thicken, but he had vowed that he was going to forget that night and put it out of his mind. To push away the ever-creeping temptation to do it to her all over again...and again. He swallowed as he felt the hard throb of desire at his groin and the sudden distracting thunder of his pulse. 'To an argument-free three months?'

She raised her eyebrows. 'You think that's possible?'

'I think anything is possible, if we put our minds to it.'

'Okay. Then—purely on the subject of logistics—I'd like to know how this arrangement is supposed to work when there's only one bed?'

Sipping his champagne, he fixed her with a steady look. 'In case you hadn't noticed, it's a very big bed.'

'And you won't be...'

'Won't be what?'

'I don't know.' She shrugged. 'Tempted?'

'To leap on you?' He gave a short laugh. 'Oh, I'm one hundred per cent certain I'll be tempted because you are an extremely beautiful woman and you blew my mind the other night. But I can resist anything when I put my mind to it, Amber. Even you.'

She put the glass down on the table and tucked her legs up neatly beneath her. It was a demure enough pose—but that didn't stop his body jerking in response, nor prevent the sudden urgent desire to slide his fingers all the way up her silken thighs and to feel if she was wet for him. Was that why a sudden brief look burned between them and why she suddenly started shifting awkwardly on the chair, as if a colony of ants had crawled into her panties?

'Well, we're going to have to do *something* to pass the time.' She glanced around. 'And I haven't noticed any board games.'

'I don't think you'll find board games are the activity of choice in a world-famous honeymoon suite,' he said drily.

'So we might as well find out more about each other. A sort of getting-to-know-you session.' She fixed him with a bright smile. 'It'll come in useful if ever we're forced to compete on one of those terrible *Mr and Mrs* TV shows, before we get our divorce finalised. I've told you plenty of stuff about me but you're still one great big mystery, aren't you, Conall?'

And that was the way he liked it. Conall drank some more champagne. Being enigmatic was a lifestyle choice. Keep people away and they couldn't get close enough to cause you pain. Because pain meant you couldn't think straight. It made you lash out and lose control. He'd lost control once—big time—and it had scared the hell out of him. It had almost ruined his life and he had vowed it would never happen again.

But you lost control with Amber the other night, didn't you? You had sex with her even though you'd told yourself it wasn't going to happen. You plunged deep into her body even though your head was screaming at you to withdraw. And you couldn't. You were like a fly caught in her sticky web.

Briefly, he closed his eyes. The way she'd made him feel had been like nothing else he'd ever experienced—as if he'd been teetering on the brink of some dark abyss, about to dive straight in. If he'd had his way, he would have walked away and never seen her again.

But Amber was his wife now and that changed all the rules. He was with her for the duration and there wasn't a damned thing he could do about it. And they were holed up in this hotel with a self-imposed sex ban. What else were they going to do but talk? Surely he needed something to occupy his thoughts other than how much he'd like to rip that damned white dress from her body. He could always have her sign a confidentiality agreement when the time came to settle the divorce. And in the meantime, wasn't there something *liberating* about for once not having to hide behind the barriers he had erected to stop women from getting too close?

'So what do you want to know about me?' he drawled. 'Let me guess. Why I've never married before? That's usually the number-one question of choice for women.'

'Why are you so cynical, Conall?'

'Maybe life has made me that way,' he said mockingly. 'Is it cynical to state the truth?'

Their gazes clashed. He thought her narrowed eyes looked like bright slithers of green glass in her pale face.

'How come you and my father are so close?'

'I told you. I used to work for him a long time ago.'

'But that doesn't explain the connection between you.' She ran her fingertip around the rim of her champagne glass before shooting him another glance. 'A connection which was intimate enough for him to ask you to take charge of my life. Why does he trust you so much, when there are very few people he does trust?'

Conall's mouth hardened. 'Because once he did me a big favour and I owe him.'

'What kind of favour?'

Putting his glass down, he leaned back in the chair and cushioned his head on his clasped hands. 'It's a long story.'

'I like long stories.'

Conall let his gaze drift over her. Maybe it was better to revisit the uncomfortable landscape of the past, than to sit here uncomfortably thinking about what a beautiful bride she made. 'It started when I won a scholarship to your brother's school,' he said. 'Did you know that?'

She shook her head.

'A full scholarship which enabled the illegitimate son of an Irish housekeeper to attend one of the finest schools in the country. It's where I learnt to ride and to shoot.' He gave a short laugh. 'To behave like a true English gentleman.'

'Except you aren't, are you?' she said slowly. 'Not really.'

He met her faintly mocking gaze. 'No, you're right. I'm not. But you have two choices when you go to a place like that—either you try to blend in and mimic all the other boys around you, or you attempt to stay the person you already are. It was because my mother had been so strict about making me study that I was there in the first place and so I vowed to stay true to my roots. I was determined she would never think I was rejecting her values.' There was silence for a moment. Up here in the totally soundproof hotel suite, he thought that the rest of the world seemed a long way away. 'And I think Ambrose admired that quality. I'd actually met him before I won the scholarship, and became friends with his son. I'd polished the windscreen of his car a couple of times, because my mother worked as housekeeper for some of his friends. The Cadogans.'

She nodded. 'I know the Cadogans.'

'Of course you do. Everyone does. They're one of the most well-connected families in England.' He heard his voice become rough, as if someone had just attacked it with coarse sandpaper. And suddenly it stopped being just a memory. It came back to him and hit him, like an unexpected wave sneaking up behind you and knocking you off your feet. He could feel his heart pounding heavily. His skin felt heated and he wanted suddenly to escape. He wanted to get out of that damned suite and start walking. Or walk right over to the chair where she sat and haul her into his arms.

'You were saying?'

Her cool prompt made the mists clear and he was tempted to tell her that he'd changed his mind and it was none of her business. But he had bottled this up for more years than he cared to remember and mightn't it be therapeutic to let it out and for Amber to see her father in a good light for once? He cleared his throat. 'My mother had worked for the family ever since she'd got off the ferry from Rosslare. They worked her long and hard but she never complained—she was grateful that they'd allowed her to bring her baby into the house.' He raised his eyebrows. 'I guess it's unusual for you to hear it this way round. To hear what life is like *below stairs*?'

'Being rich is no guarantee of happiness,' she said flatly. 'I thought that was one thing you and I agreed on. And please don't stop your story just when it was getting interesting.'

'Interesting? That wouldn't have been my word of choice.' His mouth twisted. He thought that there were some memories which never lost their power to wound...was it any wonder he'd buried it so deeply? 'One day a diamond ring went missing—which just happened to be a priceless family heirloom—and my mother was accused of stealing it by one of the Cadogan daughters.' His heart twisted as he remembered his mother's voice when she'd phoned him and the way she'd tried to disguise her shuddering sobs. Because in all the years of heartbreak—those times when she'd waited vainly for a letter or a card from her family in Ireland—he had never once heard her cry. 'My mother was as honest as the day was long. She couldn't believe she was being labelled a thief by a family whose house she had worked in for all those years. A family she thought trusted her.' There it was again. Trust. That word which didn't mean a damned thing.

A clock chimed in one of the suite's adjoining rooms.

'What happened?' Amber asked as the chimes died away.

He gave a heavy sigh. 'In view of her long service record they decided not to press charges but they sacked her and eventually she found a job as a cleaner in a big girls' school. But she never got over it.' He felt the lump which rose in his throat. The sense of helplessness. Even now. 'She died months later—years before her time.'

'Oh, Conall.'

But he held up his hand in an imperious gesture because he didn't need Amber Carter's pity, or for her to soften her voice like that. He didn't want token *kindness*. 'That might have been the end of it if I hadn't gone back to the house and got one of the daughters to talk to me, to find out what had really happened.'

There was a pause and he noticed she didn't prompt him to continue—maybe if she had he would have stopped—but when he started speaking again he could hear the shakiness in his own voice.

'She told me that the ring had been stolen by her sister's boyfriend—a boy high on drugs and keen to purchase more. It was all hushed up, of course. My mother had simply been the scapegoat.' He gave a bitter laugh. 'So I took it on myself to exact some sort of revenge.'

'Oh, Conall,' she whispered. 'What did you do?'

'Don't look so fearful, Amber. I didn't hurt anyone,

if that's what you're thinking—but I hurt them where I knew it would matter. One night, under the cover of darkness, I took a spray can and let rip—covering their beautiful stately house with graffiti which was designed to let the world know just how corrupt they were. I caused a lot of damage to the place and they called the police. It was my word against theirs. They were one of the oldest and most respectable families in the country while I was just...' he shrugged '...a thug with a motive.'

She was silent for a moment. 'And where did my father come in?' she asked eventually.

Conall stared straight ahead, remembering the stench of unwashed bodies and the sound of voices shouting in the adjoining cells. His own cell had been small and windowless and he'd seen a glimpse of a different path which had lain before him—a path he hadn't wanted to take.

'When I was sitting in the detention centre,' he said slowly, 'with my offer of a place at university having been withdrawn and looking at the possibility of a jail term—Ambrose arrived, and vouched for me. Rafe must have called him. He said I'd been a friend of his son's for many years and that this was a one-off deviation. I don't know if he spoke to the Cadogans but all the charges against me were dropped and he offered me a job in his construction company— at the very bottom rung of the ladder. He told me I needed to prove myself and he never wanted to hear of me wasting my time and my education again. So I worked my way up—determined not to abuse his faith in me. I learnt the building trade from the inside out. I worked every hour that God sent and saved every penny I had, until I could buy my first property. And the rest, as they say, is history.'

Amber understood a lot more about Conall Devlin now—and much of it she admired. But not all. He was hard-working and loyal, but he was also heartless. But at least now she could understand some of his prejudice towards her. *Of course* he would despise someone who represented everything he most deplored. To him she was just another of those spoilt and privileged people who stamped their way through life, not caring who they trod on—just as the Cadogans had done to his mother.

She could see the pain on his face even though he was doing his best to hide it—but hiding pain was something she recognised very well. And despite everything—despite this whole crazy, mixed-up situation—all she wanted was to go up to him and put her arms around him. Sitting there in his wedding suit with his tie pulled loose and his dark hair all ruffled, he looked more approachable than she'd ever seen him and she felt a great wave of emotion welling up inside her. In that moment she hated the Cadogans and what they had done to his mother and she found herself silently applauding the graffiti. The most natural thing in the world would be to go over there and kiss him. To comfort him with her body, which was crying out to be touched by him. But sex was off the menu. He'd told her that.

She glanced at the ornate archway which led through to the bedroom and the vast, petal-strewn bed and wondered how she was going to be able to get through the night—any night—when she was forbidden to touch him. And she wanted to touch him.

She wanted to feel those expert fingers caressing her and to rediscover the pleasures of sex. Should she *accidentally* roll up against him during the night, or pretend she was having a nightmare?

She drank another mouthful of champagne. No. She sensed that she would get nothing from Conall if she was anything other than truthful. He was already furious because she'd kept her virginity a secret—if she started to play games with him now he would have zero respect for her. She could spend the next three months tiptoeing round him while the tension between them grew, or she could do the liberated thing of reaching out for what she most wanted. And what did she have to lose?

'Conall?'

'No more questions, Amber,' he warned impatiently. 'I'm done with talking about it.'

'I wasn't going to ask you any more questions about the past. I was wondering more how we're going to spend this short-lived marriage of ours.' She lifted her shoulders in a shrug, suddenly aware of the softness of her body beneath the heavy material of her wedding dress. And that Conall's dark blue gaze seemed fascinated by the movement. Any movement she made, come to think of it. Should that give her the courage to carry on? 'Because despite what I said earlier, we can't talk all the time, can we? We've already done the past and we both know there isn't going to be any future.'

'You sound like someone asking a question who has already decided what the answer is going to be.'

'Maybe I have.' She hesitated. 'All you have to do is agree with me.'

Their eyes met.

'Agree with *what*, Amber?'

'I'd like…' She licked her lips. 'What I'd really like—is for you to teach me everything you know about sex.'

CHAPTER TEN

FOR A MOMENT Conall thought he must have misheard her because it sounded like one of those fantasies men sometimes had about women. Teach her everything he knew about sex? His mouth hardened. So that she could claw her manicured nails deeper into his flesh and learn more about him than she already did?

'Why, Amber?' he questioned, trying to ignore the sudden flare of heat in his blood.

'Isn't it obvious? Because I know so little and you know so much.' She seemed to be struggling to find the right words, which he guessed wasn't surprising in the circumstances. 'And I...'

'Oh, please, don't stop now,' he said silkily. 'This is just starting to get interesting.'

She wriggled her shoulders again and Conall got a sudden disturbing flashback of how she'd looked when she'd been naked in bed, those green eyes all wide and hungry just before he'd entered her. Another fierce hit of blood made an erection jerk beneath his suit trousers.

'I know this arrangement between us isn't meant to last, but—'

'Let me guess?' he interrupted. 'One day your

knight in shining armour is going to come galloping over the horizon and carry you away, and in the meantime you'd like to learn how best to turn him on?'

A little angrily, she pushed a fallen lock of hair away from her face.

'That wasn't what I was going to say. I told you. I'm not crazy about men but I've realised that I like sex. At least, I don't have very much experience to base it on, but I certainly like the sex I had with you. And it seems a pity not to capitalise on that, don't you think?'

Her cheeks suddenly went pink and, in the silence which followed, Conall could hear the shallow sound of his own breathing.

'You want to treat me like some kind of stud?'

'That's a little defensive, Conall. Couldn't we describe it as making the most of your expertise?'

'And this would be sex without strings?'

'Naturally.'

'With no boundaries?'

'That would depend on the boundaries.'

Conall laughed. This was getting more and more like a fantasy by the minute. Gorgeous, defiant Amber asking him to teach her everything he knew about sex—with no strings?

'So what would you say if I asked you to strip for me right now?'

'I'd say that I have no experience of stripping and would be prepared to give it a try, but…'

He raised his eyebrows as he saw a trace of insecurity cross her features. 'But?'

'I want sex,' she whispered, 'but I don't want you to make me feel like an object.'

And that whispered little appeal somehow pierced

his conscience and made him realise he was behaving like a boor.

'Is that what I was doing?' he said softly.

'Yes.'

He stood up and walked over to her. 'Then I guess I'd better wipe the slate clean and start all over again. Come here and let me see what I can do.'

Amber felt herself melting as he pulled her to her feet and took her face between his hands, before bending to place his lips on hers. She told herself she must be true to her words and not read anything into it, but it wasn't easy. Not when he kept brushing his lips over hers like that, as if he had all the time in the world—teasing her and tormenting her so that she felt like a cat having a cotton reel dangled before its eyes. As he skimmed his palms down over her dress she could feel the instant response of her body.

'Want to take a shower?' he murmured.

'I guess,' she said unsteadily.

He took her by the hand and led her to the giant bathroom which had an enormous wet room attached. Amber was trying to stop herself from trembling because, after having been so upfront about expressing her needs, she could hardly turn round and tell him she was having second thoughts, could she?

Because she was. Suddenly she was scared. She realised that she was going to get exactly what she had asked for—and no more. No matter how good this felt, or how much it mimicked tenderness—she needed to remember that it meant nothing. *So just enjoy it for what it is*, she told herself fiercely. *Don't demand more than he will ever give you.*

The tiled floor felt cool beneath her bare feet and

he was tilting up her chin, so that their eyes were on a collision course, and it gave her a thrill of pleasure to read the raw blaze of hunger in his gaze.

'I don't know the protocol for removing a wedding dress,' he said. 'Are there all kinds of hidden panels?'

'Nope.' She gave the familiar Amber smile as she slid down the zip and stepped out of the gown. The easy, confident smile which had always hidden a multiplicity of insecurities. 'It's all me.'

It was gratifying to see his boggle-eyed look in response to what lay beneath, and maybe on some subliminal level Amber had been hoping for this outcome all along. Last time she'd undressed in front of him she had been wearing her plain bra and those hideous big knickers—which she had now replaced with some of the most provocative lingerie she'd been able to find.

Something blue was what brides traditionally wore and she had chosen a shade of blue for her underwear—the same sapphire hue as his shuttered eyes. Wisps of silk and gossamer-fine lace pushed her breasts together so that they appeared to be spilling out of the bra like ice cream piled high on twin cones. The tiny high-cut panties barely covered her bottom and he gave a small groan of appreciation as he splayed his fingers possessively over the silky triangle at the front.

'Wow. X-rated stuff,' he said softly before peeling them off and unclipping her bra. 'And the kind of lingerie I always imagined you wearing.'

'You did a lot of that, did you?' She tipped her head to one side as he stared at her breasts. 'Thinking about me in my underwear?'

'I refuse to answer that question, on the grounds it might incriminate me. And I think you'd better learn to undress me, Amber. I think my hands are shaking too much to do it with any degree of style.'

Hers were still shaking, too, and she didn't know if he noticed but she didn't care. Because suddenly she was hungry for him. Hungry to feel his hands on her skin again and that slow burst of pleasure as he pushed deep inside her.

She eased the jacket from his shoulders and laid it on a nearby stool. Next came his shirt and she freed each stubborn button until at last she could let it flutter free. She turned her attention to his belt and then slid the zip of his trousers slowly down. She gave an instinctive murmur of delight as he sprang free, hard and proud against the palm of her hand, and, even though this was a totally new experience for her, she told herself not to be shy. *Every woman has to learn some time*, she thought—and suddenly she was grateful to be learning from someone as magnificent as Conall. Experimentally, she trickled a finger down over the stiff shaft but the steely clamp of his fingers around her wrist and the stern look on his face halted her.

'No,' he said. 'To touch a man when he is as aroused as this will make me come all over your fingers and will delay the gratification you are seeking.'

Amber wanted to disagree with him. She wanted to tell him that it would delight her to see him at the mercy of her touch. And she wanted to tell him not to be so anatomical about it all—to protest that surely sex was about more than just physical *gratification*. But she didn't say a word and not just because she didn't have the experience to back up her claim or because his words were so *graphic*. Because he was sliding on a condom and turning on the shower and hot water was gushing freely down into the wet room as he pushed her beneath the jets.

Sweet sensation flooded over her as his arms wrapped around her and he stepped in beside her. She was aware of the hot water gushing over her and the slippery feel of Conall's hair-roughened skin as he drew her closer. His dark head was bent and he closed his lips down over one nipple to suck greedily on the hardened tip. She gasped as his fingers slid between her legs and she couldn't tell whether the warmth which flooded through her came from the shower or from inside her own body. Her head fell back as he thrummed her there insistently, the urgent rhythm building relentlessly inside her.

He had made her come once before when he had been deep inside her—but the sensation of this second orgasm took her by surprise because it happened so quickly. One minute she was revelling in him touching her and the next she was gasping out her pleasure as violent spasms racked through her body. She was still gasping when he wrapped her legs around his hips and eased himself inside her, and she clamped her hands on his shoulders as he levered her back against the tiled wall and drove into her.

He was so big. A slow moan escaped from her lips. So very big. As if he had been made to fit inside her like that. As if her own body had been designed to accommodate him and only him. She could feel the heat building again and she sensed his own sudden restraint, as if he had felt it, too—so that when the spasms exploded deep inside her again, she heard him expel a deep and ragged breath. She felt his own jerking movements and heard him groan and she was completely overcome by the sensation of what was happening to her. She must have been. Why else, when her head flopped helplessly onto his shoulder, should she have the salty taste of tears on her lips?

Her eyes were closed as he turned the shower off and wrapped her in a towel, patting her completely dry before carrying her into the bedroom. He set her down on the floor while, with an impatient hand, he yanked off the bedcover so that all the red rose petals scattered down onto the beautiful Persian rug. Like giant spills of blood, she thought, with a sudden clench of her heart, as he put her into bed and climbed in next to her.

'My hair is going to go crazy if I don't brush it,' she murmured.

'Do you want to brush it?' His lips skated over her neck and his words were muffled as he murmured against her skin. 'Or could you think of something else you'd rather do?'

Her head tipped back to accommodate his lips and her eyes closed. There was really no contest. 'Something else.'

It took longer this time. As if it were happening in slow motion. His fingertips seemed determined to acquaint themselves with every centimetre of skin. His kisses were lazy and his thrusts were deep, and her orgasm seemed to go on and on for ever. Afterwards he held her trembling body very tightly and lay there, just stroking her still-damp hair, while her cheek rested against his chest and she listened to the muffled thunder of his heartbeat.

Her eyes felt heavy and her limbs seemed to be weighed with lead. Just keeping her eyes open felt like the biggest effort in the world but there was something she needed to know, and through fluttering lashes she tipped her head back to look at him.

'Conall?' she said.

'Mmm?'

She hesitated. 'You thought I'd want to know why you'd never married before and seemed surprised when I didn't pursue it.'

'And?'

'I'm pursuing it now.' Her gaze was steady. 'Why not?'

Conall took his hand away from her head, wondering why she had reacted in such a dull and predictable way and so comprehensively ruined the soft mood which had settled over him. Give a woman a little intimacy and she tried to take everything. But maybe this would be the ideal time to drive home his fundamental principles, despite the fact that he'd just enjoyed the most mind-blowing sex. He shook his head in slight disbelief. For someone who was so inexperienced, she was so *hot*. When he touched her he felt a fierce and elemental hunger he had trouble reining in. But Amber needn't know that. He felt the beat of a pulse at his temple. Amber *mustn't* know that.

'I'm surprised that someone with your history should ask that,' he drawled. 'For me, it always seemed like backing a horse with an injured leg.'

'So that's the only reason? Because the odds are stacked against it?'

She was very persistent, he thought. 'You ask too many questions, Amber,' he said softly. 'And a man doesn't like to be interrogated straight after sex.'

She met his gaze and maybe she read something in his eyes which made her realise that his patience was wearing thin.

'Okay. Shall we have some more sex, then?' she questioned guilelessly.

Silently he applauded her lack of inhibition as he thought about some of the things he'd like to do to her. To put his head between her thighs and to taste her, just for starters. He'd like to see what she looked like on all fours, with that magnificent bottom pressed into him as he took her from behind. But he was still feeling *exposed*, from all the things he'd told her, and it was time to regain control. The sex, he decided, could wait.

'Not right now, I'm afraid.'

She sounded disappointed. 'Really?'

He pushed back the sheet and got out of bed, walking over to the wardrobe and rifling through for some of the clothes he'd unpacked before the ceremony. Pulling out a pair of jeans and a sweater, he shot her a regretful glance.

'I have some work I need to do,' he said. 'And you should sleep for a while. It's been a long day. I'll wake you up for dinner later. Would you like to go out somewhere? Or I can have the hotel reserve us a table in one of the restaurants downstairs if you prefer?'

Her body tensing beneath the duvet, Amber stared at him in confusion. Dinner was the last thing on her mind. What she wanted was for him to get in beside her and to cradle her in his arms. She wanted to drift off to sleep with him *beside* her and wake up with his black head on the pillow next to hers, so that she could lean over and kiss him and have him make love to her again. But judging by his body language as he carried his clothes towards the adjoining dressing room—that was the last thing Conall wanted.

'Can't work wait?' she questioned.

'Sorry.' He flicked her a cool look. 'It may have slipped your memory but it's my job which is paying for our stay here.'

It was a statement obviously designed to remind her that she was nothing but one of life's freeloaders, and it didn't miss its mark. Amber flinched as he turned his back on her.

She didn't know how a naked man could walk across a room looking so unbelievably in command, but somehow Conall managed it. The pale jut of his buttocks and the powerful thrust of his thighs were like poetry in motion, she thought, silently willing him to turn around and look at her. Just once.

But he closed the door behind him without a second glance.

CHAPTER ELEVEN

IT WAS LIKE playing a game of cat and mouse. A game which had no rules. But despite Amber's joking remark about boundaries, there were plenty of those.

Don't ask.

Don't expect.

And don't feel. Especially that. Don't feel anything for your enigmatic and gorgeous husband, other than desire, because he certainly won't tolerate any outward show of emotion.

But Amber was fast discovering she wasn't a switch which could be flicked on and off. She couldn't blow hot one minute and cold the next. Unlike Conall.

He had woken her up on that first evening with his hand lazily caressing her breast and, after a blissful hour between the sheets, they had gone downstairs to dine in the Granchester's midnight room. Glowing lights on an indigo ceiling mimicked the night skies and the exotic flowers on every table were all fiery oranges and red. And although the hotel took their guests' privacy seriously, someone in the restaurant managed to capture a photo on their cell phone, which found its way into one of the newspapers. It was funny to look at it. Or not, depending on your viewpoint. Conall was leaning in to listen to something Amber was saying and, for that frozen slice of time, it actually managed to look as if he *cared*. Which was a lie. A falsehood. All he cared about was projecting the right *image*. Of making what they had look real to the outside world. But how could it, when it wasn't real?

After five days of relative confinement and wall-to-wall sex, the newlyweds moved into Conall's Notting Hill house, and Amber found herself living in a brand-new neighbourhood. It was a tall, four-storeyed house, overlooking a central square with a beautiful, gated garden and in any other circumstances, she might have been overjoyed to spend time in such a glorious environment. But she felt displaced, surrounded by Conall's things—with nothing of her own in situ except for her clothes. It was *his* territory and he had neither the need nor the desire to modify it in any way to accommodate her. And what was the point, when she would be moving out again in three months, when their short-lived marriage was over?

'I don't know if you've thought about how you're going to spend your time while I'm at work?' he'd said, eyebrows raised in mild question—after he'd finished showing her how the extremely complicated coffee machine worked.

Amber hadn't really thought about it. The recreational shopping which used to consume her now held no appeal and she seemed to have outgrown the people she'd hung out with before. She guessed the truth was that there was only one person she wanted to spend time with and that was the man she'd married—but that was clearly a one-way street. Because Conall was an expert at compartmentalising his life—a skill which seemed beyond her. Or maybe it was because he simply didn't *have* any feelings for her, beyond those of desire and responsibility.

After wake-up sex, he left the house for work and Amber found herself resenting the fact that Serena got to see him all day, while she had to be content with the few measly hours left by the time he finally made it home. At least the May weather was warm enough for her to sit outside and she bought herself a sketch pad and took a book to read in the garden square beneath one of the lilac bushes which scented the air with its heady fragrance.

She'd been there for a couple of weeks when she received a letter from her father, forwarded by Mary-Ellen, telling her how delighted he was to hear of her marriage to Conall.

He's a man I've always admired. Probably the only man on the planet capable of handling you.

And Amber could have wept, because deep down didn't she agree with her father's words? Didn't she revel in the way her new husband made her feel—like a contented, purring pussycat? Weren't the times she was able to snatch with the powerful Irishman the closest thing to heaven she'd ever known?

But Conall doesn't feel that way, she reminded herself. For him this marriage was nothing but a burden—driven by a longstanding debt to her father and an overdeveloped sense of responsibility.

She found herself thinking about the future, even though she tried not to—about what she would miss when it was all over. The sex, of course—but it was all the other things which were proving so curiously addictive. It was breakfast in bed at the weekends and waking up in the middle of the night to find yourself being kissed. It was walking around London and discovering that it seemed like an entirely different city when you were seeing it through someone else's eyes, even if you were aware that your companion would rather be somewhere else.

She made herself a cup of coffee and walked across the kitchen to stare out of the window at the quiet Notting Hill street. Last night she'd woken up as dawn was breaking and the truth had hit her like an intruder trying to break in through the basement window. The realisation had shocked and scared the life out of her—once she'd finally had the guts to admit it. That she was falling for Conall and wanted to give their relationship a real chance. To work on what they'd got and see if it had the potential to last. She wanted more of him, not less, and wouldn't she spend the rest of her life regretting it if she didn't even *try* to explore its potential?

In a frantic attempt to rewind the tape—and show him she wasn't just some vacuous airhead—she started cooking elaborate meals in the evening. Fragments of a half-finished *cordon bleu* cookery course came back to her, so that she was able to present her bemused husband with a perfect cheese soufflé or the soft meringues floating in custard which the French called *îles flottantes*.

She started reading the international section in the newspaper so she could discuss world affairs with him, over dinner. And if at times she realised she was in danger of becoming a caricature of an old-fashioned housewife, she *didn't care*. She wanted to show him that there was more to flaky Amber than the mixed-up socialite who used to fall out of nightclubs.

But if she was hoping for some dramatic kind of conversion, she hoped in vain. Her cool but sexy husband remained as emotionally distant as he had ever been. And even though she adored the powerful sexual chemistry which fizzed between them, she found herself thinking it would make a nice change to have dinner together without at least one course growing cold, while Conall carried her off to the bedroom.

She wasn't sure if she had communicated some of her restlessness, but one morning Conall paused by the doorway as he was leaving for work.

'You've been cooking a lot lately,' he said. 'I think you're due a break, don't you?'

'Is that a polite way of telling me you're fed up with my food?'

He raised his eyebrows. 'Or a roundabout way of wondering if you'd like to go out for dinner tonight?'

'Even though it's a weeknight?' She tried to clamp down the stupid Cinderella feeling which was bubbling up inside her. 'I'd love to.'

'Good.' He glanced out of the window as his driver pulled up. 'Book somewhere for eight and call the office to let them know where. I'll meet you there.'

Amber booked the table and dressed carefully for dinner, aware that she felt as bubbly and as excited as if this were a bona fide first date. She'd read a lot in the newspapers about the Clos Maggiore restaurant, known as 'London's Most Romantic'. The irony of its reputation wasn't lost on her but she'd also read that the food was superb. And she wasn't asking for *romance*—she knew he didn't do *that*. She was just asking for more of the same.

She picked out a discreetly sexy dress—a silk jersey wrap in scarlet—and she was bubbling over with excitement as she hailed a cab and directed it to Covent Garden.

But her happy and expectant mood quickly began to dissolve because he didn't turn up at eight. Nor at eight-twenty. With tight lips, Amber shook her head as the waiter offered her another glass of champagne. She'd already had one on an empty stomach and now her head was swimming. She felt a bit ridiculous sitting alone when all the other tables were occupied by people talking and laughing with each other. The rustic mirrored room was supposed to resemble a garden and somehow it managed to do just that. Just a few steps away from the world-famous market and you could find yourself sitting beneath a ceiling from which hung sprigs of thick white blossom, which looked so realistic that you almost felt you could reach up and pick one. It looked almost magical, but the feeling of dread which had started to build up inside her made Amber feel anything but magical.

Did she really think that one dinner out meant that everything was suddenly going to be perfect? As if he were suddenly going to stop keeping her locked away in her own tiny little box, which was so separate from the major part of his life. That was, if he could even be bothered to show.

Surreptitiously, she glanced at her watch, not wanting anyone to think she'd been stood up—but what if she *had*?

And then, exactly thirty-five minutes after the appointed time, there was a faint commotion at the door and Conall appeared in the flowered archway. The other diners turned to look at him as he walked over to the table and sat down, ignoring the glass of champagne which the waiter placed before him.

'You're late,' she said.

'I know I am and I'm sorry.'

'What happened?' she demanded. 'Did *Serena* keep you busy?'

He frowned. 'I'm not sure what you're trying to imply, Amber—but I'm not going to rise to it. I was on a call to Prince Luciano and I could hardly cut the negotiations short to tell him I was due at dinner.'

'But it didn't occur to you that *I* might like to be involved, seeing that I was there when you first showed him the painting?'

Conall stared at her. He could see she was angry and he knew it was partly justified, but what the hell did she expect? He hadn't planned to be late, but then—he hadn't planned for the Mardovian royal to ring him to talk about the painting. And no, he hadn't thought to involve Amber in the deal because *this was not her life and it never would be.* Soon she would be gone and their marriage nothing but a memory. Didn't she realise that the boundaries he'd imposed were in place to protect them both? *That* was why he kept an emotional distance from her, why he had never repeated those earlier confidences he had shared with her, when he'd opened up to her more than he'd ever opened up to anyone and had been left feeling raw and vulnerable. What was the point of getting close to someone when the end was already in sight? When he never got close to anyone.

Yet it was harder than he'd imagined to keep his distance from the woman he'd married, or to keep thoughts of her at bay during his working day. Hard not to remember how it felt when she was in his arms at night. The growing sense that he was in danger of losing control. His mouth twisted. Because he would never lose control. Never again.

'No, of course it didn't occur to you,' she continued, her voice shaking. 'Because I'm of no consequence to you, am I? None at all!'

Conall leaned back in his chair, his narrowed eyes wary. This marriage of theirs wasn't real, so why the hell was she making out as if it were? 'You sound a little hysterical, Amber.'

Amber went very still, feeling like a small child who had been reprimanded by a very severe teacher. And suddenly all her words were coming out in a haphazard rush. Words she'd thought often enough but never planned to say, in her determination to be the cool and casual Amber she knew she was supposed to be. 'I'm fed up with being allocated a few hours in the morning before you go to work and then just sandwiched in at night, when you can be bothered to tear yourself away from the office and your beloved Serena. Weekends are better—but you still manage to spend a great deal of time working.'

'Will you please lower your voice?' he demanded.

'No. I will not lower my voice.' She sucked in a breath, aware that two worried-looking waiters were now hovering at the edge of the room and some of the lovey-dovey couples had gone completely quiet and were staring at them with mounting looks of horror on their faces as if registering that a full-blown row was escalating. *This is what it's like for me*, thought Amber miserably, trying not to envy all those couples their closeness and unity, but failing to do so. *This is what it's like for me. This is the reality of my marriage.*

And suddenly she realised how stupid she'd been. What was it they said? That you couldn't make a silk purse out of a sow's ear. Just as you couldn't make a real marriage out of something which had only ever been a coldly executed contract. Why even try?

Had she really thought she could endure three months of this? Of trying to *just* enjoy sex when all the time her heart was becoming more and more involved with this stubborn man and would continue to do so with every second which passed? She was a woman, for heaven's sake—not a machine! She might try but she couldn't keep her emotions locked away, even if her husband had managed to do so with such flair. *Because he doesn't have any emotions!*

She leapt to her feet and some of Conall's champagne slopped over the side of the glass as the cutlery on the table clattered. She saw the dark look of warning in his eyes but she ignored it with a sudden carelessness which felt almost *heady.*

'I'm sick of being married to a man who treats me as if I'm part of the furniture!' she flared. 'Who always puts his damned work first. Who doesn't ever want to talk about stuff. *Real* stuff. The stuff which matters. So maybe I ought to admit what's been staring me in the face right from the start. It's over, Conall. Got that? *Over for good!*'

She tried to tug the gold band from her finger but, stubbornly, it refused to budge. Picking up her handbag, she rushed straight out of the restaurant, aware of Conall saying something to the waiters as he followed, hot on her heels. She'd planned to hail a cab but she didn't have time because Conall had reached her with a few long strides and was propelling her towards his waiting car—holding her by the elbow, the way she'd sometimes seen police do in films when they were arresting someone.

'Get in the car,' he said grimly and as soon as the door was closed behind him he turned on her, his face a mask of dark fury. 'And start explaining if you would—what the *hell* was that all about?'

'What's the point in repeating it? It's the truth. You don't make enough time for me.'

'Of course I don't. Because this isn't real, Amber.' The bewilderment in his tight voice sounded genuine. 'Remember?'

'Well, if it isn't real, then we need to show the watching world that there's discord between us. We can't just break up after our supposedly *romantic* whirlwind marriage without some kind of warning. We need to show that cracks have already begun to appear in our relationship and tonight should have helped.'

There were a few seconds of disbelieving silence.

'You mean,' he said, clearly holding onto his temper only by a shred. 'You mean that the undignified little scene you created back there was all just part of some charade? That you disturbed those people's dinner in order to manufacture a spat between us?'

Wasn't it better to let him think that, rather than reveal the humiliating truth that she'd wanted to search for something deeper? That her stupid aching heart was craving the love he could never give her.

'But it's true, isn't it?' she questioned, biting her lip to stop tears spilling from her eyes. 'There are cracks. It's been cracked right from the get-go. All that stuff you said about me realising some of my talents was completely meaningless. You could have done the courtesy of having me sit in on the conference call with Prince Luciano about the Wheeler painting, but you didn't. You didn't even bother to mention the negotiations. To you I'm nothing but an invisible socialite who happens very inconveniently to turn you on.'

'Well, at least you're right about something, Amber, because you certainly turn me on,' he said grimly. 'And yes, I often find myself wishing that you didn't.'

Something dark and heavy had entered the atmosphere—like the claustrophobic feeling you got just before a thunderstorm. But he didn't say another word until the front door had slammed behind them and Amber thought he might slam his way into his study or take a drink out into the garden, or even shut himself in the spare room, but she was wrong. His gaze raked over her and she saw a flicker of something dark and unknown in the depths of his sapphire eyes.

He moved like a predator, striking without warning—reaching out for her dress and hooking both hands into the bodice. He ripped it open, the delicate material tearing as easily as if it had been made of cotton wool. Amber shivered because cold

air was suddenly washing over her skin and because
the expression in his eyes was making her feel...*excited* and he nodded as he looked into her face, as
if he had seen in it something he recognised, something he didn't like.

'And your desire for me is just as inconvenient,
isn't it, Amber?' he taunted. 'You wish you didn't
want me, but you just can't help it. You want me now.
You're aching for me. Wet for me.'

Her lips were parched as they made a little sound,
though she didn't know what she was trying to say.
She could scarcely breathe, let alone think. Excitement fizzed over her skin even though she told herself
she should have been appalled when her panties suffered the same fate as her dress and fluttered redun-
dantly to the hall floor. Appalled when he started to
unfasten his trousers, struggling to ease the zip down
over his straining hardness.

But she wasn't appalled.

She was relieved—for surely that was a moan of
relief she gave as he eased his moist tip up against her
and then thrust deep inside her. She gasped. Was it
anger which made this feel so raw and so incredible
as she ripped open his shirt to bare his magnificent
torso? Or simply the frustration that this was the only
way she could express her growing feelings for him?
She could bury her teeth into the hair-roughened skin
of his chest and nip at him like a small animal. And
although he was giving a soft laugh of pleasure in
response, she knew he wouldn't be laughing when
it was over.

He didn't even kiss her and she knew better than
to reach her mouth blindly towards his in silent

plea. And anyway, there wasn't really time for kissing. There wasn't time for anything but a few hard and frantic thrusts. It was so wild and explosive that she gave a broken cry as her orgasm took her right under and his own cry sounded like some kind of feral moan—as if something dark had been dragged up from the depths of his soul. It was only when he withdrew from her, seconds later—quickly turning his back so she couldn't see his face—that she realised he had forgotten to use a condom.

He was breathing very heavily and it was several seconds before he had composed himself enough to turn around and stare at her and his eyes looked dark and tortured. He was shaking his head from side to side.

'That should never have happened.' His bitter words sounded as if they had been dipped in acid.

'It doesn't matter.'

'Oh, but it does, Amber. It really does.' His lips twisted. 'I can't believe I just did that. That *we* just did that. It was…it was *out of control*. I don't want to live my life like that, and I won't. This marriage was a mistake and I don't know why I fooled myself into thinking it could be anything else.'

Amber stared into his eyes and saw the contempt written there, along with a whole lot of other things she would rather not have seen. Once before he had looked at her as if she were something which had been dragged in from the dark, and it was the same kind of look he was giving her now. But back then he hadn't known her and now he did. It was rejection in its purest form and it hurt more than anything had ever hurt.

Biting back the sob which was spiralling up inside

her throat, she bent down to grab her tattered panties, before rushing upstairs towards the bedroom and slamming the door behind her.

CHAPTER TWELVE

THE END OF the marriage was played out in the papers, just as the beginning had been, and Amber found herself reading the headlines with a sense of being outside herself. As if she were some random little dot high up on the wall, looking down at the mess she'd made of her life.

And it was a mess, all right. She stared down at the photo taken of them at the Granchester on their wedding night—that false and misrepresentative photo snatched by a fellow diner—while she read the accompanying text.

Whirlwind marriage over. Golden couple split.

But it turned out to be surprisingly easy to dismantle their short-lived union. Or maybe not so surprising. Because a marriage undertaken to settle a long-term debt could never be anything other than doomed, no matter how strong the sexual chemistry between them was.

During their last conversation together, Conall had told Amber he intended being 'generous' in his settlement—but she had shaken her head.

'I don't want your charity,' she'd said, trying desperately to hold on to her equilibrium when all she'd wanted was for him to put his arms around her, and to love her.

'An admirable attitude, if a little misguided,' he'd responded coolly. 'And a waste of everyone's time if you don't accept your side of the deal.'

A waste of everyone's time? She had glared at him then, because glaring helped keep the ever-threatening tears at bay.

'I'm offering you the apartment and a monthly maintenance payment,' he'd said. 'You won't have to move.'

She told herself it was pointless to deliberately make herself homeless and so, even though she rejected his offer of monthly maintenance, she accepted the deeds of the apartment and immediately put it up for sale. She couldn't bear the thought of living in a block owned by Conall and the nightmare prospect of running into him. She would buy somewhere smaller, in a less dazzling and expensive area, and use the profit she made to support herself. She would start living within her means and take no maintenance from him. And she intended to get a job.

She sold her diamond watch—slightly taken aback by how much it was worth—and with the money raised she booked onto a short degree course in translation and interpretation at the University of Bath. It was a beautiful city and far enough away from London to know that there would be no risk of running into Conall. By a fortuitous chance there was a course starting almost immediately and Amber leapt at it eagerly. It gave her something to do. Something to replace the miserable thoughts which were whirling round in her head. She didn't want to do some boring job involving grain quotas, but surely there would be other opportunities open to her? Some which might even involve travel. But first she needed a bona fide qualification and so she moved into a rented room in a house on the outskirts of the city and began to work harder than she'd ever worked in her life.

She'd never shared a flat or lived on a reduced budget before and she soon became used to running out of milk, or eating cornflakes for lunch. She discovered that a cheap meal of pasta could taste fantastic when you shared it with three other people and a bottle of cheap wine. And if at night she found sleep eluding her and tears edging out from between her tightly closed eyes, she would hug her arms around her chest and tell herself that soon Conall Devlin would be nothing but a distant memory.

Would he?

Would she ever forget that rare smile which sometimes dazzled her? That lazy way he had of stroking her hair just after they'd made love?

Had sex, she corrected herself as she tossed and turned in the narrow bed. He'd only married her because of the debt he'd felt he owed her father. Other than that, it had really only ever been about the sex. It must have been—because when she'd told him not to bother contacting her again just before she'd left London, Conall had taken her at her word. To Amber's initial fury and then through the dull pain of acceptance, she realised he was doing exactly as she had asked him to do. He hadn't called. Not once. Not a single text or a solitary email had popped into her inbox to check how she was doing in her new life. All negotiations had been dealt with through his lawyers. And she was just going to have to learn to live with that.

June bled into July and a monumental heatwave brought the country almost to a standstill. Sales of ice cream and electric fans soared. Riverbeds dried and the grass turned a dark sepia colour. There was even talk of water rationing. One evening Amber was sitting in the dusty garden after college, when she heard the doorbell ringing loudly through the silent house. It was so hot she didn't want to move and as a rivulet of sweat trickled down her back she hoped someone else would answer it.

She could hear the distant sound of voices. A deep voice which she didn't really register because she was holding her face up, trying to find the whisper of breeze she thought she had detected on the air. And then she heard footsteps behind her and a deep voice that sent shivers racing down her spine— shivers which should have been welcome in the extreme heat, if they hadn't been underpinned by emotions far too complex to analyse.

She lifted her head slowly, telling herself not to react—but how could she possibly *not* react when she'd spent weeks thinking of him and dreaming of him? Hadn't it been an integral part of some of her wildest fantasies that he should suddenly appear in this house, like this? Greedily, her gaze ran over him. His eyes were as shuttered as they had ever been and his jaw was still shadowed blue-black. His concession to the warmer weather meant he was wearing a T-shirt with his jeans, which immediately made her start wishing it were the dead of winter, because then she wouldn't have to stare at that hard, broad torso. She wouldn't have to remember when those rippling biceps had wrapped themselves so tightly around her before carrying her off to bed.

'Conall!' Her throat felt dry and constricted. Her head felt light. 'What are you doing here?'

'No ideas?'

She shook her head. 'No.'

'Even though there's a question we both know needs answering?'

She licked her lips. 'What question is that?' she said hoarsely.

There was a pause. 'Are you carrying my baby?'

The pause which followed was even longer. 'No.'

Conall was taken aback by the shaft of regret which speared through his body and embedded itself deep in his heart. He was briefly aware of the fact that somewhere inside him a dim light had been snuffed out. He wondered how it was possible to want something more than you'd ever wanted anything, and only discover that once the possibility was gone.

He stared into Amber's pale face. At the tremble of her lips. He thought how different she looked from the woman he'd found fast asleep on that white leather sofa. Calmer. With an air of serenity about her which gave him a brief punch of pleasure. But he could see anger flickering in her grass-green eyes as she drew her shoulders back and brushed a lock of ebony hair away from her face with an impatient hand.

'Okay, you've had the answer you presumably wanted, so now you can go.'

'I'm not going anywhere.'

She narrowed her eyes. 'What I don't understand, Conall, is why you've come all this way in order to ask a question which didn't need to have been asked in person. You could have texted or emailed me. Even phoned. But you didn't.'

'It isn't about the question.'

'No? Then what is it about?'

Conall met her gaze and let her fury wash over him like a fierce tide. He had tried to stay away from her—telling himself that it was for her own good, as well as his. But something just kept drawing him back to her—and now that he was here, he felt curiously exposed. He knew she deserved nothing less than the truth, but that still didn't guarantee him the outcome he longed for. It was fork-in-the-road time, he realised. It was time to stop hiding behind the past. To reject the emotional rules he'd lived by for so long. 'I don't know if you can ever forgive me for the way I behaved on our last evening together,' he said, in a low voice.

She frowned. 'You mean…what happened in the hall?'

'Yes,' he said roughly. 'That's exactly what I mean.'

She shrugged with the expression of someone who planned to say exactly what was on their mind—and to hell with the consequences. 'We had some pretty raw and basic sex, which I thought you'd enjoyed—I certainly did, even if you completely ruined my dress and some perfectly good underwear.'

His mouth gave a flicker of a smile. 'You're missing the point, Amber.'

'Am I?' Her voice went very quiet. So quiet it was almost a whisper. 'Yet you were the one who taught me that no sex was bad sex, unless one person happened to object to it.'

'Yes, I know I did. But I lost control.' He felt a lump in his throat. 'For a moment I saw red. I felt consumed by something which seemed to consume *me*. It was as if I was powerless to stop what was happening and I didn't like that.'

'So what? Everyone loses control some time in their lives—especially after a blistering row. What's the matter, Conall—did you think you were going to run off to find a handy canister of paint and start spraying graffiti all over the walls?' She gave an impatient shake of her head. 'I don't have a degree in psychology, but I've seen enough therapists in my teenage years to realise that what you call *staying in control* means never letting any emotion out—so that when you do, it just explodes. So why not do what everyone else does and just let yourself *feel* stuff?'

Her words made sense and deep down he knew it, but did he have the courage to admit that? The courage to reach inside himself for something he'd buried for as long as he could remember? Because yes, that something was emotion. His mother had been uptight, he recognised that now—she'd allowed herself to be defined by a youthful indiscretion, so keen never to repeat it that she had locked away all her feelings and desires. And hadn't he done the same?

There had been other factors, he recognised that, too. He'd grown up in a house where he'd never fitted in. A house where his intellect and natural athleticism had made him physically and mentally superior to the men who ruled the Cadogan household—but their wealth and power had allowed them to patronise him. Amber had accused him of having a chip on his shoulder right at the beginning of their relationship—and she had been right.

But he'd learnt his lesson. Or tried to. He had come here today with only one thing on his mind, and that thing was her.

He looked at her. 'What if I told you that I agree with every word you say?'

She narrowed her eyes suspiciously. 'And what's the catch?'

'No catch. If you can accept that I've been a fool. That I've been arrogant and stubborn and short-sighted in nearly letting the most wonderful thing which has ever happened to me slip through my fingers. And that is you. You I want. And you I miss.' His voice deepened, but there was a break in it. 'Because I love you, Amber, and I want you back.'

She shook her head, struggling a little as she got out of the deckchair. 'But you don't *do* love,' she said. 'Remember?'

'I didn't do a lot of things. If you want the truth, I didn't really live properly until I met you.' He gave a short laugh. 'Oh, don't get me wrong—to the outside world I had everything. I made more money than I knew what to do with. I ate in fine restaurants and owned amazing houses, with great works of art adorning my walls. I could travel to any place in the world and stay in the best hotels, and date pretty much any woman I wanted.' He stopped speaking and for a few seconds he seemed to be struggling to find the right words.

'But I don't want any other woman but you because everyone pales in comparison to you, Amber,' he said, and his voice was raw. 'I thought you represented everything I didn't want—but it turns out you're everything I do. You're sharp. Irreverent. Adaptable. You make me laugh and, yes, you frustrate the hell out of me, too. But you always challenge me—and I'm the kind of man who needs a challenge. And so...'

'So?' she echoed a little breathlessly as he walked across the scorched brown grass and took her in his arms.

'We did a lot of stuff in public—*for* the public. But this is private. This is just for us. I have something I want to give you, but only if you can tell me something—and I want complete honesty from you.' He swallowed. 'And that is whether you love me back.'

Amber savoured the moment and made him wait for a few seconds—she felt almost as if it was her *duty* to do so. Because Conall had made her feel very insecure in his time and he needed to know that they shouldn't put each other through this kind of thing, ever again. But she couldn't hide the smile which had begun to bloom on her face. It spread and spread, filling her with a delight and a sunny kind of joy.

'Yes, I love you,' she said simply. 'I love you more than I can ever say, my tough and masterful Irishman.'

'Then I guess I'd better do this properly.' He glanced around, but, although the garden was deserted except for a dejected-looking starling pecking at the bare ground, they were still visible to the bedroom windows of the adjoining houses.

'Is there anywhere more private we could go?'

Breathlessly she nodded and laced her fingers in his, leading him up the rickety old stairs until they reached the tiny box room which was her bedroom. She watched his face as he looked around, seeing disbelief become admiration and then avid curiosity. He walked across the bare floorboards to the painting she was halfway through, and stared very hard at the vibrant splashes of yellow and green, edged with black.

Turning round, he looked at her. 'You've been painting,' he said.

'Yes.' Her voice was a little unsteady. 'And I have you to thank for that. I realised that you were right. That you didn't say things you didn't mean—and your praise has somehow managed to resurrect my crushed self-belief.' She smiled. 'I may never be able to sell any of these—I may not even want to. But you made me believe in myself, Conall—and that's worth more to me than anything.'

'I'm hoping this might be worth something to you, too—in purely romantic terms, rather than monetary ones,' he said gruffly as he produced a small box from the back pocket of his jeans.

And to Amber's shock he went down onto one knee as he held up a ring with an emerald at its centre— big as a green ice cube—surrounded by lots of diamonds. 'Will you marry me again, Amber? Only in a church this time. Properly. Surrounded by family and friends?'

Amber felt like a princess as she stared at the glittering ring, even though Conall had once reprimanded her for behaving like one. But this was different and she suddenly realised why. She was *his* princess and she always would be. He'd changed her in many ways, but she'd helped change him, too. He'd tamed her—a bit—and somehow she'd managed to tame him right back.

She drew in a deep breath. 'Yes, Conall, I'll marry you again today, tomorrow, next year or next week. I'll marry you any way you want, because you have given me back something I didn't realise I'd lost— and that something was myself,' she said, and now she didn't bother to hide the tears which were welling up in her eyes, because how could she berate him for not showing emotion and then do exactly the same herself? Even so, it was a couple of minutes until she had stopped crying enough to be able to speak. 'You made me realise that there was something inside the empty shell of a person I'd become,' she whispered. 'And I thank you for that from the bottom of my heart. It's one of the many reasons why I love you with every cell of my body, my darling. And why I always will.'

EPILOGUE

OUTSIDE, THE NIGHT was dark and the snow tumbled down like swirling pieces of cotton wool. Conall looked at the layer of white on the ground which was steadily growing thicker. In a few short hours it had transformed the Notting Hill garden into a winter wonderland.

'I really think...' he turned away from the window and walked over to where his wife was just finishing brushing her hair '...that we ought to think about leaving.'

Amber put the brush down and looked at him, a lazy smile on her face. 'In a minute. There's plenty of time—even with the snow. The table isn't booked until eight. Kiss me first.'

'You, Mrs Devlin, are a terror for wanting kisses.'

Her eyes danced in response. 'And you're not, I suppose?'

'I confess to being rather partial to them,' he admitted, pushing her hair away from her face and bending his head towards her, kissing her in a way which never failed to satisfy and frustrate him in equal measure. He never kissed her without wanting her and he couldn't ever imagine not wanting her.

They couldn't get enough of each other in every way that mattered, and he thanked God for the day he'd walked into her life and seen her lying fast asleep amid the debris of a long-forgotten party.

His vow to marry her *properly* had remained true and deeply important to him and their wedding had taken place in a beautiful church not far from their country house. He remembered slowly turning his head to look at Amber as she walked down the aisle, his heart clenching with love and pride. She'd looked like a dream in her simple white dress, fresh flowers holding in place a long veil which floated to the ground behind her. As Conall had remarked to her quietly at the reception afterwards, if there was any woman on the planet who was qualified to wear virginal white, it was her. And when challenged on the subject by his feisty wife, he agreed that it gave him a feeling of utter contentment to know he was the only man she had ever been intimate with. And although she might have teased him about his old-fashioned attitude, deep down he knew she felt the same.

Ambrose had returned from his ashram in time for the ceremony, bronzed a deep colour, with clear eyes and looking noticeably thinner. He'd announced that he'd fallen in love with his yoga teacher and she was planning on joining him in England, just as soon as she got her visa sorted. Amber had briefly raised her eyebrows, but told Conall afterwards that she had learnt you had to live and let live, and that nobody was ever really in a position to judge anyone else. And Conall had opened up her mind to the realisation that her father wasn't all bad—he just had flaws and weaknesses like everyone else. They all did.

And families could be complicated. She knew that, but she also knew it felt better when they were together, rather than apart. She'd encouraged Conall to trace some of his mother's relatives, discovering that the world had moved on and nobody was remotely bothered by the fact that a grown man had been born not knowing who his father was. Several of his aunts were still alive and he had lots of cousins who were eager to meet him, which was one of the reasons why they'd chosen Ireland as their honeymoon destination.

Her half-brother Rafe even made it back from Australia in time for the wedding—causing something of a stir among the women present. Almost as much as the guest of honour—Prince Luc—who could be overheard telling Serena that he had played matchmaker to the happy couple.

The Prince had bought the Wheeler portrait and it now hung next to its sister painting in his Mediterranean palace and next month Conall and Amber were visiting the island of Mardovia, to see them together—at the Prince's invitation. Amber was very excited about the prospect of speaking Italian in front of her husband, very aware that it turned him on to listen to her saying stuff he simply didn't understand! Just as she was excited by the part-time art course she'd started to attend in London, where her tutor encouraged her distinctive style of painting just as much as her husband did.

But tonight they were going to Clos Maggiore—their favourite restaurant—where they'd had the furious row which had been such a flashpoint in their relationship, but where tonight they would sit happily beneath the boughs of white blossom, as contented as any of the other couples who ate there. And Amber would refuse her customary glass of pink champagne and tell Conall what she suspected he would be delighted to hear, even though it had come as something of a shock to her when she'd found out. She thought they'd been so careful...

She looked up into his shuttered eyes. Would he be a good father? A lump rose up in her throat. The very best. Just as he was the very best husband, lover and friend a woman could ever want.

'I love you, Conall Devlin,' she whispered.

His eyes crinkled into a smile—a faint question in their midnight depths. 'I love you, too, Amber Devlin.'

And suddenly she didn't want to wait until they were in the restaurant, gorgeous though it was. This was private, just for them, just like the time when he'd knelt on the bare floorboards of her tiny room in Bath and produced an emerald ring as big as a green ice cube. Feeling stupidly emotional, she tightened her arms around his neck and brushed her lips over his as the excitement grew and grew inside her. 'And this might be a good time to tell you my news...'

* * * * *

A TYCOON TO
BE RECKONED
WITH

JULIA JAMES

For IHV,
who gave me my love of opera.

CHAPTER ONE

'You know, it's you I blame.'

Bastiaan's aunt tried to laugh as she spoke, but it was shaky, Bastiaan could tell.

'It was you who suggested Philip go and stay in your villa at Cap Pierre!'

Bastiaan took the criticism on board. 'I thought it might help—moving him out of target range to finish his university vacation assignments in peace and quiet.'

His aunt sighed. 'Alas, it seems he has jumped out of the frying pan into the fire. He may have escaped Elena Constantis, but this female in France sounds infinitely worse.'

Bastiaan's dark eyes took on a mordant expression. 'Unfortunately, wherever in the world Philip is he will be a target.'

'If only he were less sweet-natured. If he had your... *toughness*,' Bastiaan's aunt replied, her gaze falling on her nephew.

'I'll take that as a compliment,' Bastiaan replied dryly. 'But Philip will toughen up, don't worry.' *He'll need to*, he thought caustically. Just as he himself had had to.

'He's so impressionable!' his aunt cried. 'And so handsome. No wonder these wretched girls make a beeline for him.'

And, of course, so rich, Bastiaan added cynically—but silently. No point worrying his already anxious aunt further. It was Philip's wealth—the wealth he would be inheriting from his late father's estate once he turned twenty-one in a couple of months—that would attract females far more dangerous than the merely irksome spoilt teenage princess Elena Constantis. The real danger would come from a very different type of female.

Call them what one liked—and Bastiaan had several names not suitable for his aunt's ears—the most universal name was a familiar one: gold-diggers. Females who took one look at his young, good-looking, impressionable and soon to be very rich cousin and licked their lips in anticipation.

That was the problem right now. A woman who appeared to be licking her lips over Philip. And the danger was, Bastiaan knew, very real. For Philip, so Paulette, his housekeeper at Cap Pierre, had informed him, far from diligently writing his essays, had taken to haunting the nearby town of Pierre-les-Pins and a venue there that was most undesirable for a twenty-year-old. Apparently attracted by an even more undesirable female working there.

'A singer in a nightclub!' his aunt wailed now. 'I cannot believe Philip would fall for a woman like that!'

'It *is* something of a cliché...' Bastiaan allowed.

His aunt bridled. 'A cliché? Bastiaan, is that all you have to say about it?'

He shook his head. 'No. I could say a great deal more—but to what purpose?' Bastiaan got to his feet. He was of an imposing height, standing well over six feet, and powerfully built. 'Don't worry...' he made his voice reassuring now '... I'll deal with it. Philip will *not* be sacrificed to a greedy woman's ambitions.'

His aunt stood up, clutching at his sleeve. *'Thank you,'* she said. 'I knew I could count on you.' Her eyes misted a little. 'Take care of my darling boy, Bastiaan. He has no father now to look out for him.'

Bastiaan pressed his aunt's hand sympathetically. His maternal uncle had succumbed to heart disease when Philip had just started at university, and he knew how hard her husband's death had hit his aunt. Knew, too, with a shadowing of his eyes, how losing a father too young—as he himself had when not much older than Philip—left a void.

'I'll keep Philip safe, I promise you,' he assured his aunt now, as she took her leave.

He saw her to her car, watched it head down the driveway of his property in the affluent outskirts of Athens. Then he went back indoors, his mouth tightening.

His aunt's fears were not groundless. Until Philip turned twenty-one Bastiaan was his trustee—overseeing all his finances, managing his investments—while Philip enjoyed a more than generous allowance to cover his personal spending. Usually Bastiaan did nothing more than cast a casual eye over the bank and credit card statements, but an unusually large amount—twenty thousand euros—had gone out in a single payment a week ago. The cheque had been paid into an unknown personal account at the Nice branch of a French bank. There was no reason—no *good* reason—that Bastiaan could come up with for such a transfer. There was, however, one very bad reason for it—and that he *could* come up with.

The gold-digger had already started taking gold from the mine....

Bastiaan's features darkened. The sooner he disposed of this nightclub singer who was making eyes at his cousin—and his cousin's fortune—the better. He headed purposefully to his study. If he was to leave for France in the morning, he had work to do tonight. Enterprises with portfolios the size of Karavalas did not run themselves. His cousin's fortune might be predominantly in the form of blue chip stocks, but Bastiaan preferred to diversify across a broad range of investment opportunities, from industry and property to entrepreneurial startups. But, for all their variety, they all shared one aspect in common—they all made him money. A *lot* of money.

The cynical curve was back at Bastiaan's mouth as he sat himself down behind his desk and flicked on his PC. He'd told his aunt that her son would toughen up in time—and he knew from his own experience that that was true. Memory glinted in his dark eyes.

When his own father had died, he'd assuaged his grief by partying hard and extravagantly, with no paternal guardian to moderate his excesses. The spree had ended abruptly. He'd been in a casino, putting away the champagne and generally flashing his cash lavishly, and it had promptly lured across a female—Leana—who had been all over him. At just twenty-three he'd been happy to enjoy all she'd offered him—the company of her luscious body in bed included. So much so that when she'd fed him some story of how she'd stupidly got herself into debt with the casino and was worried sick about it, he'd grandly handed her a more than handsome cheque, feeling munificent and generous towards the beautiful, sexy woman who'd seemed so keen on him...

She'd disappeared the day the cheque had cleared—heading off, so he'd heard, on a yacht belonging to a seventy-year-old Mexican millionaire, never to be seen again by Bastiaan. He'd been royally fleeced and proved to be a complete mug. It had stung, no doubt about it, but he'd learnt his lesson, all right—an expensive one. It wasn't one he wanted Philip to learn the same way. Apart from taking a large wedge of his money, Leana had damaged his self-esteem—an uncomfortably sobering experience for his younger self. Although it had made him wise up decisively.

But, unlike Bastiaan, Philip was of a romantic disposition, and a gold-digging seductress might wound him more deeply than just in his wallet and his self-esteem. That was not something Bastiaan would permit. After his experience with Leana he'd become wise to the wiles women threw out to him, and sceptical of their apparent devotion. Now, into his thirties, he knew they considered him a tough nut—ruthless, even…

His eyes hardened beneath dark brows. That was something this ambitious nightclub singer would soon discover for herself.

Sarah stood motionless on the low stage, the spotlight on her, while her audience beyond, sitting at their tables, mostly continued their conversations as they ate and drank.

I'm just a divertimento, she thought to herself, acidly. *Background music.* She nodded at Max on the piano, throat muscles ready, and he played the opening to her number. It was easy and low-pitched, making no demands on her upper register. It was just as well—the last thing she wanted to do was risk her voice singing in this smoky atmosphere.

As she sang the first bars her breasts lifted, making her all too aware of just how low-cut the bodice of her champagne satin gown was. Her long hair was swept over one bare shoulder. It was, she knew, a stereotypical 'vamp' image—the sultry nightclub singer with her slinky dress, low-pitched voice, over-made-up eyes and long blonde locks.

She tensed instinctively. Well, that was the idea, wasn't it? To stand in for the club's missing resident *chanteuse*, Sabine Sablon, who had abruptly vacated the role when she'd run off with a rich customer without warning.

It hadn't been Sarah's idea to take over as Sabine, but Max had been blunt about it. If she didn't agree to sing here in the evenings, then Raymond, the nightclub owner, lacking a *chanteuse*, would refuse to let Max have the run of the place during the day. And without that they couldn't rehearse…and without rehearsals they couldn't appear at the Provence en Voix music festival.

And if they didn't appear there her last chance would be gone.

My last chance—my last chance to achieve my dream!

Her dream of breaking through from being just one more of the scores upon scores of hopeful, aspiring sopranos who crowded the operatic world, all desperate to make their mark. If she could not succeed now, she would have to abandon the dream that had possessed her since her teenage years, and all the way through music college and the tough, ultra-competitive world beyond as she'd struggled to make herself heard by those who could lift her from the crowd and launch her career.

She'd tried so hard, for so long, and now she was on the wrong side of twenty-five, racing towards thirty, with time against her and younger singers coming up behind her. Everything rested on this final attempt—and if it failed… Well, then, she would accept defeat. Resign herself to teaching instead. It was the way she was currently earning her living, part-time at a school in her native Yorkshire, though she found it unfulfilling, craving the excitement and elation of performing live.

So not yet—*oh, not yet*—would she give up on her dreams. Not until she'd put everything into this music festival, singing the soprano lead in what she knew could only be a high-risk gamble: a newly written opera by an unknown composer, performed by unknown singers, all on a shoestring. A shoestring that Max, their fanatically driven director and conductor, was already stretching to the utmost. Everything, but *everything*, was being done on a tiny budget, with savings being made wherever they could. Including rehearsal space.

So every night bar Sundays, she had to become Sabine Sablon, husking away into the microphone, drawing male eyes all around. It was not a comfortable feeling—and it was a million miles away from her true self. Max could tell her all he liked that it would give her valuable insight into roles such as *La Traviata*'s courtesan Violetta, or the coquettish Manon, but on an operatic stage everyone would know she was simply playing a part. Here, everyone looking at her really thought she *was* Sabine Sablon.

A silent shudder went through her. Dear God, if anyone in the opera world found out she was singing here, like this, her credibility would be shot to pieces. No one would take her seriously for a moment.

And neither Violetta nor Manon was anything like her role in Anton's opera *War Bride.* Her character was a romantic young girl, falling in love with a dashing soldier. A whirlwind courtship, a return to the front—and then the dreaded news of her husband's fate. The heartbreak of loss and bereavement. And then a child born to take his father's place in yet another war...

The simple, brutal tale was told as a timeless fable of the sacrifice and futility of war, repeated down the ages, its score haunting and poignant. It had captivated Sarah the first moment she'd heard Max play it.

What must it be like to love so swiftly, to hurt so badly? she'd wondered as she'd started to explore her role. For herself, she had no knowledge—had never experienced the heady whirlwind of love nor the desolation of heartbreak. Her only serious relationship had ended last year when Andrew, a cellist she had known since college, had been offered a place in a prestigious orchestra in Germany. It had been his breakthrough moment, and she had been so glad for him—had waved him off without a thought of holding him back.

Both of them had always known that their careers must come first in their lives, which meant that neither could afford to invest in a deeply emotional relationship which might jeopardise their diverging career paths. So neither had grieved when they'd parted, only wished each other well. Theirs had been a relationship based primarily on a shared passion for music, rather than for each other—friendship and affection had bound them, nothing more than that.

But this meant she knew that in order to portray her character now—the War Bride—as convincingly as she could, she would need to call on all her imagination. Just as she would need all her operatic abilities to do credit to the challenging vocal demands of the hauntingly beautiful but technically difficult music.

She reached the end of her song to a smattering of applause. Dipping her head in acknowledgement, she shifted her weight from one high-heeled foot to the other. As she straightened again, sending her gaze back out over the dining area, she felt a sudden flickering awareness go through her. She could hear Max start the introduction to her next number but ignored it, her senses suddenly on alert. She heard him repeat the phrase, caught him glancing at her with a frown, but her attention was not on him—not on the song she was supposed to have started four bars earlier. Her attention was on the audience beyond.

Someone was looking at her. Someone standing at the back of the room.

He had not been there a moment ago and must have just come in. She shook her head, trying to dismiss that involuntary sense of heightened awareness, of sudden exposure. Male eyes gazed at her all the time—and there was always movement beyond the stage…diners and waiters. They did not make her pause the way this had—as if there were something different about him. She wanted to see him more clearly, but the light was wrong and he was too far away for her to discern anything more than a tall, tuxedo-clad figure at the back of the room.

For the third time she heard Max repeat the intro—insistently this time. And she knew she had to start to sing. Not just because of Max's impatient prompt but because she suddenly, urgently, needed to do something other than simply stand there, pooled in the light that emphasised every slender curve of her tightly sheathed body. Exposed her to that invisible yet almost tangible scrutiny that was palpable in its impact on her.

As she started the number her voice was more husky than ever. Her long, artificial lashes swept down over her deeply kohled eyes, and the sweep of her hair dipped halfway across her jawline and cheekbone. She forced herself to keep singing, to try and suppress the frisson of disturbed awareness that was tensing through her—the sense of being the object of attention that was like a beam targeted at her.

Somehow she got through to the end of the number, pulling herself together to start the next one on time and not fluff it. It seemed easier now, and she realised that at some point that sense of being under scrutiny had faded and dissipated. As if a kind of pressure had been lifted off her. She reached the end of the last number, the end of her set, with a sense of relief. She made her way off-stage, hearing canned music starting up and Max closing down the piano.

One of the waiters intercepted her. 'There's a guy who wants to buy you a drink,' he said.

Sarah made a face. It wasn't unusual that this happened, but she never accepted.

The waiter held up a hundred-euro note. 'Looks like he's keen,' he informed her with a lift of his brow.

'Well, he's the only one who is,' she said. 'Better take it back to him,' she added. 'I don't want him thinking I pocketed it and then didn't show.'

Her refusal got Max's approval. 'No time for picking up men,' he said, flippantly but pointedly.

'As if I would...' She rolled her eyes.

For a moment, it crossed her mind that the invitation to buy her a drink might be connected to that shadowy figure at the back of the room and his disturbing perusal of her, but then she dismissed the thought. All she wanted to do now was get out of her costume and head for bed. Max started opera rehearsals promptly every morning, and she needed to sleep.

She'd just reached her dressing room, kicking off her high heels and flexing her feet in relief, when there was a brief knock at the door. She only had time to say, 'Who is it?' before the door opened.

She glanced up, assuming it would be Max, wanting to tell her something that couldn't wait. But instead it was a man she'd never seen before in her life.

And he stilled the breath in her lungs.

CHAPTER TWO

BASTIAAN'S EYES ZEROED in on the figure seated at the brightly lit vanity unit with its trademark light-bulb-surrounded mirror. Backlit as she was by the high-wattage bulbs, her face was in shadow.

But the shadows did nothing to dim her impact. If anything it emphasised it, casting her features into relief. On stage, she'd been illuminated in a pool of light, her features softened by the distance at which he'd sat. He'd deliberately taken a table at the rear of the room, wanting at that point only to observe without being noticed in return.

It hadn't taken him more than two moments to realise that the female poised on the stage possessed a quality that signalled danger to his young, impressionable cousin.

Allure—it was an old-fashioned word, but that was the one that had come to his mind as his eyes had rested on the slender figure sensuously draped in low-cut clinging satin, standing in a pool of soft, smoky light, her fingers lightly curved around her microphone, the lustrous fall of her long blonde hair curled over her bare shoulder like a vamp from the forties.

Her mouth was painted a rich, luscious red, her eye make-up was pronounced, with long, artificial lashes framing luminous eyes. Seeing her now, close up, she was even more alluring.

No wonder Philip is smitten!

His eyes completed his swift scrutiny and he was interested to see a line of colour running along her cheekbones. *Curious...* he thought. Then the tightening of her mouth told him what had accounted for that reaction. It was not a blush—a woman like her probably hadn't blushed since puberty—it was annoyance.

Why? he found himself wondering. Women were not usually annoyed when he paid them attention. Quite the reverse. But this *chanteuse* was. It was doubly unusual because surely a woman in her profession was well used to male admirers courting her in her dressing room.

An unwelcome thought crossed his mind—was it his cousin's wont to hang out here? Did she invite him to her changing room?

Just how far has she got with him?

Well, however far it was, it was going to stop from now on. Whatever story she'd trotted out to Philip in order to get him to give her money, the gold mine was closing down...

She was looking at him still, that scarlet mouth of hers pressed tightly, and something sparking now in her eyes.

'*Oui?*' she said pointedly.

His eyelids dipped over his eyes briefly. 'Did the waiter not pass on my invitation?' he asked, speaking in French, which he spoke as well as English and a couple of other languages as well.

Her arched eyebrows rose. 'It was you?' she said. Then, without bothering to wait for a reply, she simply went on, 'I'm afraid I don't accept invitations to share a drink with any of the club's guests.'

Her tone was dismissive, and Bastiaan felt a flicker

of annoyance at it. Dismissive was not the kind of voice
he was used to hearing in women he was speaking to. Or
indeed from anyone he was speaking to. And in someone
whose career relied on the attention and appreciation of
others, it was out of place.

*Perhaps she thinks she does not need to court her au-
dience any longer? Perhaps she thinks she already has
a very comfortable exit from her profession lined up?*

The flicker of annoyance sparked to something
sharper. But he did not let it show. Not now—not yet. At
the moment, his aim was to disarm her. Defeating her
would come afterwards.

'Then allow me to invite you to dinner instead,' he responded. Deliberately, he infused a subtly caressing note
into his voice that he'd found successful at any other time
he'd chosen to adopt it.

That line of colour ran out over her cheekbones again.
But this time there was no accompanying tightening of
her red mouth. Instead she gave a brief smile. It was civil
only—nothing more than that, Bastiaan could see.

'Thank you, but no. And now...' the smile came again,
and he could see that her intention was to terminate the
exchange '...if you will excuse me, I must get changed.'
She paused expectantly, waiting for him to withdraw.

He ignored the prompt. Instead one eyebrow tilted
interrogatively. 'You have another dinner engagement?'
he asked.

Something snapped in her eyes, changing their colour,
he noticed. He'd assumed they were a shade of grey, but
suddenly there was a flash of green in them.

'No,' she said precisely. 'And if I did, *m'sieu*—' the
pointedness was back in her voice now '—I don't believe
it would be any of your concern.' She smiled tightly, with
less civility now.

If it were with my cousin, mademoiselle, it would indeed be my concern... That flicker of more than annoyance came again, but again Bastiaan concealed it.

'In which case, what can be your objection to dining with me?' Again, there was the same note in his voice that worked so well with women in general. Invitations to dine with him had never, in his living memory, been met with rejection.

She was staring at him with those eyes that had gone back to grey now, the flash of green quite absent. Eyes that were outlined in black kohl, their sockets dramatised outrageously with make-up, their lashes doubled in length by artificial means and copious mascara.

Staring at him in a way he'd never been stared at before.

As though she didn't quite believe what she was seeing. Or hearing.

For just a second their eyes met, and then, as if in recoil, her fake lashes dropped down over her eyes, veiling them.

She took a breath. '*M'sieu*, I am desolated to inform you that I also do not accept invitations to dine with the club's guests,' she said. She didn't make her tone dismissive now, but absolute.

He ignored it. 'I wasn't thinking of dining here,' he said. 'I would prefer to take you to Le Tombleur,' he murmured.

Her eyes widened just a fraction. Le Tombleur was currently the most fashionable restaurant on the Côte D'Azur, and Bastiaan was sure that the chance to dine at such a fabulous locale would surely stop her prevaricating in this fashion. It would also, he knew, set her mind instantly at rest as to whether he was someone possessed of sufficient financial means to be of interest to her. She would not wish to waste her time on someone who was not in the same league as his young cousin. Had she but known, Bastiaan thought cynically, his own fortune was considerably greater than Philip's.

But of course Philip's fortune was far more accessible to her. Or might be. If she were truly setting Philip in her sightline, she would be cautious about switching her attentions elsewhere—it would lose her Philip if he discovered it.

A thought flickered across Bastiaan's mind. She was alluring enough—even for himself... Should *that* be his method of detaching her? Then he dismissed it. Of course he would not be involving himself in any kind of liaison with a woman such as this one. However worthy the intention.

Dommage... He heard the French word in his head. *What a pity*...

'*M'sieu*...' She was speaking again, with razored precision. 'As I say, I must decline your very...*generous*... invitation'.

Had there been a twist in her phrasing of the word 'generous'? An ironic inflection indicating that she had formed an opinion of him that was not the one he'd intended her to form?

He felt a new emotion flicker within him like a low-voltage electric current.

Could there possibly be more to this woman sitting there, looking up at him through those absurdly fake eyelashes, with a strange expression in her grey-green eyes—more green now than grey, he realised. His awareness of that colour-change was of itself distracting, and it made his own eyes narrow assessingly.

For just a fraction of a second their eyes seemed to

meet, and Bastiaan felt the voltage of the electric current surging within him.

'Are you ready to go yet?'

A different voice interjected, coming from the door, which had been pushed wider by a man—a youngish one—clad in a dinner jacket, half leaning his slightly built body against the doorjamb. The man had clearly addressed Sabine, but now, registering that there was someone else in her dressing room, his eyes went to Bastiaan.

He frowned, about to say something, but Sabine Sablon interjected. 'The gentleman is just leaving,' she announced.

Her voice was cool, but Bastiaan was too experienced with women not to know that she was not, in fact, as composed as she wanted to appear. And he knew what was causing it…

Satisfaction soared through him. Oh, this sultry, sophisticated *chanteuse*, with her vampish allure, her skin-tight dress and over-made-up face, might be appearing as cool as the proverbial cucumber—but that flash in her eyes had told him that however resistant she appeared to be to his overtures, an appearance was all it was…

I can reach her. She is vulnerable to me.

That was the truth she'd so unguardedly—so unwisely—just revealed to him.

He changed his stance. Glanced at the man hovering in the doorway. A slight sense of familiarity assailed him, and a moment later he knew why. He was the accompanist for the *chanteuse*.

For a fleeting moment he found himself speculating on whether the casual familiarity he could sense between the two of them betokened a more intimate relationship. Then he rejected it. Every male instinct told him that whatever lover the accompanist took would not be female.

Bastiaan's sense of satisfaction increased, and his annoyance with the intruder decreased proportionately. He turned his attention back to his quarry.

'I shall take my leave, then, *mademoiselle*,' he said, and he did not trouble to hide his ironic inflection or his amusement. Dark, dangerous amusement. As though her rejection of him was clearly nothing more than a feminine ploy—one he was seeing through…but currently choosing to indulge. He gave the slightest nod of his head, the slightest sardonic smile.

'*A bientôt.*'

Then, paying not the slightest attention to the accompanist, who had to straighten to let him pass, he walked out.

As he left he heard the *chanteuse* exclaim, 'Thank goodness you rescued me!'

Bastiaan could hear the relief in her tone. His satisfaction went up yet another level. A tremor—a discernible tremor—had been audible in her voice. That was good.

Yes, she is vulnerable to me.

He walked on down the corridor, casually letting himself out through the rear entrance into the narrow roadway beyond, before walking around to the front of the club, where his car was parked on the forecourt. Lowering himself into its low-slung frame, he started the engine, its low, throaty growl echoing the silent growl inside his head.

'*Thank goodness you rescued me!*' she had said, this harpy who was trying to extract his cousin's fortune from him.

Bastiaan's mouth thinned to a tight, narrow line, his eyes hardening as he headed out on to the road, setting his route back towards Monaco, where he was staying tonight in the duplex apartment he kept there.

Well, in that she was mistaken—most decidedly.

No one will rescue you from me.

Of that he was certain.

He drove on into the night.

'Give me two minutes and I'll be ready to go,' Sarah said.

She strove for composure, but felt as if she'd just been released from a seizure of her senses that had crushed the breath from her lungs. How she'd managed to keep her cool she had no idea—she had only know that keeping her cool was absolutely essential.

What the hell had just happened to her? Out of nowhere...the way it had?

That had been the man whose assessing gaze she'd picked up during her final number. She'd been able to feel it from right across the club—and when he'd walked into her dressing room it had been like...

Like nothing I've ever known. Nothing I've ever felt—

Never before had a man had such a raw, physical impact on her. Hitting her senses like a sledgehammer. She tried to analyse it now—needing to do so. His height, towering over her in the tiny dressing room, had dominated the encounter. The broad shoulders had been sleekly clad in a bespoke dinner jacket, and there had been an impression of power that she had derived not just from the clearly muscular physique he possessed but by an aura about him that had told her this man was used to getting his own way.

Especially with women.

Because it hadn't just been the clear impression that here was a wealthy man who could buy female favours—his mention of Le Tombleur had been adequate demonstration of *that*—it had been far, far more...

She felt herself swallow. *He doesn't need money to impress women.*

No, she acknowledged shakily, all it took was those piercing dark eyes, winged with darker brows, the strong blade of his nose, the wide, sensual curve of his mouth and the tough line of his jaw.

He was a man who knew perfectly well that his appeal to women was powerful—who knew perfectly well that women responded to him on that account.

She felt her hackles rise automatically.

He thought I'd jump at the chance!

A rush of weakness swept through her. Thank God she'd had the presence of mind—pulled urgently out of her reeling senses—to react the way she'd managed to do.

What was it about him that he should have had such an effect on me?

Just what had it been about that particular combination of physique, looks and sheer, raw personal impact that had made her react as if she were a sliver of steel in the sudden presence of a magnetic field so strong it had made the breath still in her body?

She had seen better-looking men in her time, but not a single one had ever had the raw, visceral, overpowering impact on her senses that this man had. Even in the space of a few charged minutes...

She shook her head again, trying to clear the image from her mind. Whoever he was, he'd gone.

As she got on with the task of turning herself back into Sarah, shedding the false eyelashes, heavy make-up and tight satin gown, she strove to dismiss him from her thoughts. *Put him out of your head,* she told herself brusquely. *It was Sabine Sablon he wanted to invite to dinner, not Sarah Fareham.*

That was the truth of it, she knew. Sabine was the

kind of woman a man like that would be interested in—sophisticated, seductive, a woman of the world, a *femme fatale*. And she wasn't Sabine—she most definitely was not. So it was completely irrelevant that she'd reacted to the man the way she had.

I haven't got time to be bowled over by some arrogantly smouldering alpha male who thinks he's picking up a sultry woman like Sabine. However much he knocked me sideways.

She had one focus in her life right now—only one. And it was *not* a man with night-dark eyes and devastating looks who sucked the breath from her body.

She headed out to where Max was waiting to walk her back to her *pension*, some blocks away in this harbourside *ville* of Pierre-les-Pins, before carrying on to the apartment he shared with Anton, the opera's composer.

As they set off he launched into speech without preamble. 'I've been thinking,' he said, 'in your first duet with Alain—'

And he was off, instructing her in some troublesome vocal technicalities he wanted to address at the next day's rehearsal. Sarah was glad, for it helped to distance her mind from that brief but disturbing encounter in her dressing room with that devastating, dangerous man.

Dangerous? The word echoed in her head, taking her aback. *Had* he been dangerous? Truly?

She gave herself a mental shake. She was being absurd. How could a complete stranger be dangerous to her? Of course he couldn't.

It was absurd to think so.

CHAPTER THREE

'BASTIAAN! FANTASTIC! I'd no idea you were here in France!' Philip's voice was warm and enthusiastic as he answered his mobile.

'Monaco, to be precise,' Bastiaan answered, strolling with his phone to the huge plate-glass window of his high-rise apartment in Monte Carlo, which afforded a panoramic view over the harbour, chock-full of luxury yachts glittering in the morning sunshine.

'But you'll come over to the villa, won't you?' his cousin asked eagerly.

'Seeking distraction from your essays…?' Bastiaan trailed off deliberately, knowing the boy had distraction already—a dangerous one.

As it had done ever since he'd left the nightclub last night, the seductive image of Sabine Sablon slid into his inner vision. Enough to distract anyone. Even himself…

He pulled his mind away. Time to discover just how deep Philip was with the alluring *chanteuse*. 'Well,' he continued, 'I can be with you within the hour if you like?'

He did not get an immediate reply. Then Philip was saying, 'Could you make it a bit later than that?'

'Studying so hard?' Bastiaan asked lightly.

'Well, not precisely. I mean, I *am*—I've got one essay

nearly finished—but actually, I'm a bit tied up till lunch-time…'

Philip's voice trailed off, and Bastiaan could hear the constraint in his cousin's voice. He was hiding something.

Deliberately, Bastiaan backed off. 'No problem,' he said. 'See you for lunch, then—around one… Is that OK?' He paused. 'Do you want me to tell Paulette to expect me, or will you?'

'Would *you*?' said Philip, from which Bastiaan drew his own conclusion. Philip wasn't at the villa right now.

'No problem,' he said again, making his voice easy still. Easier than his mind…

So, if Philip wasn't struggling with his history essays at the villa, where was he?

Is he with her now?

He could feel his hackles rising down his spine. Was that why she had turned down dining with him at Le Tombleur? Because she'd been about to rendezvous with his cousin? Had Philip spent the night with her?

A growl started in his throat. Philip might be legally free to have a relationship with anyone he wanted, but even if the *chanteuse* had been as pure as the driven snow, with the financial probity of a nun, she was utterly unsuitable for a first romance for a boy his age. She was nearer thirty than twenty…

'Great!' Philip was saying now. 'See you then, Bast—gotta go.'

The call was disconnected and Bastiaan dropped his phone back in his pocket slowly, staring out of the window. Multi-million-pound yachts crowded the marina, and the fairy tale royal palace looked increasingly besieged by the high-rise buildings that maximised the tiny footprint of the principality.

He turned away. His apartment here had been an excellent investment, and the rental income was exceptional during the Monaco Grand Prix, but Monte Carlo was not his favourite place. He far preferred his villa on Cap Pierre, where Philip was staying. Better still, his own private island off the Greek west coast. That was where he went when he truly wanted to be himself. One day he'd take the woman who would be his wife there—the woman he would spend the rest of his life with.

Although just who she would be he had no idea. His experience with women was wide, indeed, but so far not one of his many female acquaintances had come anywhere close to tempting him to make a relationship with her permanent. One thing he was sure of—when he met her, he'd know she was the one.

There'd be no mistaking that.

Meantime he'd settle himself down at the dining table, open his laptop and get some work done before heading off to meet Philip—and finding out just how bad his infatuation was…

'I could murder a coffee.' Sarah, dismissed by Max for now, while he focussed his attentions on the small chorus, plonked herself down at the table near the front of the stage where Philip was sitting.

He'd become a fixture at their rehearsals, and Sarah hadn't the heart to discourage him. He was a sweet guy, Philip Markiotis, and he had somehow attached himself to the little opera company in the role of unofficial runner—fetching coffee, refilling water jugs, copying scores, helping tidy up after rehearsals.

And all the time, Sarah thought with a softening of her expression, he was carrying a youthful torch for her that glowed in every yearning glance that came her way. He was only a few years older than her own sixth-formers, and his admiration for her must remain hopeless, but she would never dream of hurting his feelings. She knew how very real they seemed to him.

Memory sifted through Sarah's head. She knew what Philip was experiencing. OK, she could laugh at herself now, but as a music student she'd had *the* most lovestruck crush on the tenor who'd taken a summer master class she'd attended. She'd been totally smitten, unable to conceal it—but, looking back now, what struck her most was how tolerant the famous tenor had been of her openly besotted devotion. Oh, she probably hadn't been the only smitten female student, but she'd always remembered that he'd been kind, and tactful, and had never made her feel juvenile or idiotic.

She would do likewise now, with Philip. His crush, she knew perfectly well, would not outlast the summer. It was only the result of his isolation here, with nothing to do but write his vacation essays…and yearn after her hopelessly, gazing at her ardently with his dark eyes.

Out of nowhere a different image sprang into her head. The man who had walked into her dressing room, invaded her space, had rested his eyes on her—but not with youthful ardour in them. With something far more powerful, more primitive. Long-lashed, heavy-lidded, they had held her in their beam as if she were being targeted by a searchlight. She felt a sudden shimmer go through her—a shiver of sensual awareness—as if she could not escape that focussed regard. Did not want to…

She hauled her mind away.

I don't want to think about it. I don't want to think about him. He asked me out, I said no—that's it. Over and done with.

And it hadn't even been *her* he'd asked out, she reminded herself. The man had taken her for Sabine, sultry and seductive, sophisticated and sexy. She would have to be terminally stupid not to know how a man like that, who thought nothing of approaching a woman he didn't know and asking her to dinner, would have wanted the evening to end had 'Sabine' accepted his invitation. It had been in his eyes, in his gaze—in the way it had washed over her. Blatant in its message.

Would I have wanted it to end that way? If I were Sabine...?

The question was there before she could stop it. Forcibly she pushed it aside, refusing to answer. She was *not* Sabine—she was Sarah Fareham. And whatever the disturbing impact that man had had on her she had no time to dwell on it. She was only weeks away from the most critical performance of her life, and all her energies, all her focus and strength, had to go into that. Nothing else mattered—*nothing*.

'So,' she said, making her voice cheerful, accepting the coffee Philip had poured for her, 'you're our one-man audience, Philip—how's it going, do you think?'

His face lit. 'You were *wonderful*!' he said, his eyes warm upon her.

Damn, thought Sarah wryly, she'd walked into that one. 'Thank you, kind sir,' she said playfully, 'but what about everyone else?'

'I'm sure they're excellent,' said Philip, his lack of interest in the other performers a distinct contrast with his enthusiasm for the object of his devotion. Then he frowned. 'Max treats you very badly,' he said, 'criticising you the way he does.'

Sarah smiled, amused. 'Oh, Philip—that's his job. And it's not just me—he's got to make sure we all get it right and then pull it together. He hears *all* the voices— each of us is focussing only on our own.'

'But yours is *wonderful*,' Philip said, as though that clinched the argument.

She gave a laugh, not answering, and drank her coffee, chasing it down with a large glass of water to freshen her vocal cords.

She was determined to banish the last remnants from the previous night's unwanted encounter with a male who was the very antithesis of the one sitting gazing at her now. Philip's company eased some of the inevitable tension that came from the intensity of rehearsals, the pressure on them all and Max's exacting musical direction. Apart from making sure she did not inadvertently encourage Philip in his crush on her, sitting with him was very undemanding.

With his good-natured, sunny personality, as well as his eagerness and enthusiasm for what was, to him, the novelty of a bohemian, artistic enterprise, it wasn't surprising that she and the other cast members liked him. What had been more surprising to her was that Max had not objected to his presence. His explanation had not found favour with her.

'*Cherie*, anyone staying at their family villa on the *Cap* is loaded. The boy might not throw money around but, believe me, I've checked out the name—he's one rich kid!' Max's eyes had gone to Sarah. 'Cultivate him, *cherie*—we could do with a wealthy sponsor.'

Sarah's reply had been instant—and sharp. 'Don't even *think* of trying to get a donation from him, Max!' she'd warned.

It would be absolutely out of the question for her to take advantage of her young admirer's boyish infatuation, however much family money there might be in the background. She'd pondered whether to warn Philip that Max might be angling for some financial help for the cash-strapped ensemble, but then decided not to. Knowing Philip, it would probably only inspire him to offer it.

She gave a silent sigh. What with treading around Philip's sensibilities, putting her heart and soul into perfecting her performance under the scathing scrutiny of Max, and enduring her nightly ordeal as Sabine, there was a lot on her plate right now. The last thing she needed to be added to it was having her mind straining back with unwelcome insistence to that unnerving visitation to her dressing room the night before.

At her side, Philip was glancing at his watch. He made a face.

'Need to go back to your essays?' she asked sympathetically.

'No,' he answered, 'it's my cousin—the one who owns the villa on the *Cap*—he's turned up on the Riviera and is coming over for lunch.'

'Checking you aren't throwing wild all-night parties, is he?' Sarah teased gently, although Philip was the last type to do any such thing. 'Or holding one himself?'

Philip shook his head. 'Bastiaan's loads too old for that stuff—he's gone thirty,' he said ingenuously. 'He spends most of his time working. Oh, and having hordes of females trailing around after him.'

Well, thought Sarah privately, if Cousin Bastiaan was from the same uber-affluent background as Philip, that wouldn't be too surprising. Rich men, she supposed, never ran short of female attention.

Before she could stop it, her mind homed back to that incident in her dressing room the night before. Her eyes darkened. Now, *there* was a man who was not shy of flaunting his wealth. Dropping invitations to flash restaurants and assuming they'd be snapped up.

But immediately she refuted her own accusation.

He didn't need money to have the impact he had on me. All he had to do was stand there and look at me...

She dragged her mind away. She had to stop this—she *had* to. How many times did she have to tell herself that?

'Sarah!' Max's imperious call rescued her from her troubling thoughts.

She got to her feet, and Philip did too. 'Back to the grindstone,' she said. 'And you scoot, Philip. Have fun with your cousin.' She smiled, lifting a brief hand in farewell as she made her way back to the stage.

Within minutes she was utterly absorbed, her whole being focussed only on her work, and the rest of the world disappeared from sight.

'So,' said Bastiaan, keeping his voice studiedly casual, 'you want to start drawing on your fund, is that it?'

The two of them were sitting outside on the shaded terrace outside the villa's dining room. They'd eaten lunch out there and now Bastiaan was drinking coffee, relaxed back in his chair.

Or rather he appeared to be relaxed. Internally, however, he was on high alert. His young cousin had just raised the subject of his approaching birthday, and asked whether Bastiaan would start to relax the reins now. Warning bells were sounding.

Across the table from him, Philip shifted position. 'It's not going to be a problem, is it?' he said.

He spoke with insouciance, but Bastiaan wasn't fooled. His level of alertness increased. Philip was being evasive.

'It depends.' He kept his voice casual. 'What is it you want to spend the money on?'

Philip glanced away, out over the gardens towards the swimming pool. He fiddled with his coffee spoon some more, then looked back at Bastiaan. 'Is it such a big deal, knowing what I want the money for? I mean, it's *my* money…'

'Yes,' allowed Bastiaan. 'But until your birthday I… I *guard* it for you.'

Philip frowned. 'For me or *from* me?' he said.

There was a tightness in his voice that was new to Bastiaan. Almost a challenge. His level of alertness went up yet another notch.

'It might be the same thing,' he said. His voice was even drier now. Deliberately he took a mouthful of black coffee, replaced the cup with a click on its saucer and looked straight at Philip. 'A fool and his money…' He trailed off deliberately.

He saw his cousin's colour heighten. 'I'm not a fool!' he riposted.

'No,' agreed Bastiaan, 'you're not. But—' he held up his hand '—you could, all the same, be made a fool *of*.'

His dark eyes rested on his cousin. Into his head sprang the image of that *chanteuse* in the nightclub again—pooled in light, her dress clinging, outlining her body like a second skin, her tones low and husky…*alluring*…

He snapped his mind away, using more effort than he was happy about. Got his focus back on Philip—not on the siren who was endangering him. As for his tentative attempt to start accessing his trust fund—well, he'd made his point, and now it was time to lighten up.

'So just remember…' he let humour into his voice now '…when you turn twenty-one you're going to find yourself very, *very* popular—cash registers will start ringing all around you.'

He saw Philip swallow.

'I do know that…' he said.

He didn't say it defiantly, and Bastiaan was glad.

'I really won't be a total idiot, Bast—and…and I'm not ungrateful for your warning. I know—' Bastiaan could hear there was a crack in his voice. 'I know you're keeping an eye on me because…well, because…'

'Because it's what your father would have expected—and what your mother wants,' Bastiaan put in. The humour was gone now. He spoke with only sober sympathy for his grieving cousin and his aunt. He paused. 'She worries about you—you're her only son.'

Philip gave a sad smile. 'Yes, I know,' he said. 'But Bast, please—do reassure her that she truly doesn't need to worry so much.'

'I'll do that if I can,' Bastiaan said. Then, wanting to change the subject completely, he said, 'So, where do you fancy for dinner tonight?'

As he spoke he thought of Le Tombleur. Thought of the rejection he'd had the night before. Unconsciously, his face tightened. Then, as Philip answered, it tightened even more.

'Oh, Bast—I'm sorry—I can't. Not tonight.'

Bastiaan allowed himself a glance. Then, 'Hot date?' he enquired casually.

Colour ran along his cousin's cheekbones. 'Sort of…' he said.

'Sort of hot? Or sort of a date?' Bastiaan kept his probing light. But his mood was not light at all. He'd wondered last night at the club, when he'd checked out the *chanteuse* himself, whether he might see Philip there as well. But there'd been no sign of him and he'd been relieved. Maybe things weren't as bad as he feared. But now—

'A sort of date,' Philip confessed.

Bastiaan backed off. He was walking through landmines for the time being, and he did not want to set one off. He would have to tread carefully, he knew, or risk putting the boy's back up and alienating him.

In a burst, Philip spoke again. 'Bast—could I...? Could you...? Well, there's someone I want you to meet.'

Bastiaan stilled. 'The hot date?' he ventured.

Again the colour flared across his cousin's cheeks. 'Will you?' he asked.

'Of course,' Bastiaan replied easily. 'How would you like us to meet up? Would you like to invite her to dinner at the villa?'

It was a deliberate trail, and it got the answer he knew Philip had to give. 'Er...no. Um, there's a place in Les Pins—the food's not bad—though it's not up to your standards of course, but—'

'No problem,' said Bastiaan, wanting only to be accommodating. Philip, little did he realise it, was playing right into his hands. Seeing his cousin with his *inamorata* would give him a pretty good indication of just how deep he was sunk into the quicksand that she represented.

'Great!'

Philip beamed, and the happiness and relief in his voice showed Bastiaan that his impressionable, vulnerable cousin was already in way, way too deep...

CHAPTER FOUR

BEYOND THE SPOTLIGHT trained on her, Sarah could see Philip, sitting at the table closest to the stage, gazing up at her while she warbled through her uninspiring medley. At the end of her first set Max went backstage to phone Anton, as he always did, and Sarah stepped carefully down to the dining area, taking the seat Philip was holding out for her.

She smiled across at him. 'I thought you'd be out with your cousin tonight, painting the Côte d'Azur red!' she exclaimed lightly.

'Oh, no,' said Philip dismissively. 'But speaking of my cousin...' He paused, then went on in a rush, 'Sarah, I hope you don't mind... I've asked him here to meet you! You *don't* mind, do you?' he asked entreatingly.

Dismay filled her. She didn't want to crush him, but at the same time the fewer people who knew she appeared here nightly as Sabine the better. Unless, of course, they didn't know her as Sarah the opera singer in the first place.

Philip was a nice lad—a student—but Cousin Bastiaan, for all Sarah knew, moved in the elite, elevated social circles of the very wealthy, and might well be acquainted with any number of people influential in all sorts of areas...including opera. She just could not afford to jeopardise what nascent reputation the festival might build for her—not with her entire future resting on it.

She thought rapidly. 'Look, Philip, I know this might sound confusing, but can we stick to me being Sabine, rather than mentioning my opera singing?' she ventured. 'Otherwise it gets…complicated.'

Complicated was one word for it—*risky* was another.

Philip was looking disconcerted. 'Must I?' he protested. 'I'd love Bastiaan to know how wonderful and talented you really are.' Admiration and ardent devotion shone in his eyes.

Sarah gave a wry laugh. 'Oh, Philip, that's very sweet of you, but—'

She got no further. Philip's gaze had suddenly flicked past her. 'That's him,' he announced. 'Just coming over now—'

Sarah craned her neck slightly—and froze.

The tall figure threading its way towards their table was familiar. Unmistakably so.

She just had time to ask a mental, *What on earth?* when he was upon them.

Philip had jumped to his feet.

'Bast! You made it! Great!' he cried happily, sticking to the French he spoke with Sarah. He hugged his cousin exuberantly, and went on in Greek, 'You've timed it perfectly—'

'Have I?' answered Bastiaan. He kept his voice studiedly neutral, but his eyes had gone to the woman seated at his cousin's table. Multiple thoughts crowded in his head, struggling for predominance. But the one that won out was the last one he wanted.

A jolt of insistent, unmistakable male response to the image she presented.

The twenty-four hours since he'd accosted her in her

dressing room had done nothing at all to lessen the impact she made on him. The same lush blond hair, deep eyes, rich mouth, and another gown that skimmed her shoulders and breasts, moulding the latter to perfection...

He felt his body growl with raw, masculine satisfaction. The next moment he'd crushed it down. So here she was, the sultry *chanteuse*, making herself at home with Philip, and Philip's eyes on her were like an adoring puppy's.

'Bastiaan, I want to introduce you to someone very special,' Philip was saying. A slight flush mounted in the young man's cheeks and his glance went from his cousin to Sarah and back again. 'This...' there was the slightest hesitation in his voice '...this is Sabine.' He paused more discernibly this time. 'Sabine,' he said self-consciously, 'this is my cousin Bastiaan—Bastiaan Karavalas.'

Through the mesh of consternation in Sarah's head one realisation was clear. It was time to call it, she knew. Make it clear to Philip—and to his cousin Bastiaan— that, actually, they were already 'acquainted.' She gave the word a deliberately biting sardonic inflection in her head.

Her long fake lashes dipped down over her eyes and she found herself surreptitiously glancing at the dark-eyed, powerfully built man who had just sat down, dominating the space.

Dominating her senses...

Just as he had the night before, when he'd appeared in her dressing room.

But it wasn't this that concerned her. It was the way he seemed to be suddenly the only person in the entire universe, drawing her eyes to him as irretrievably as if he were the iron to her magnetic compass. She couldn't look away—could only let her veiled glance fasten on him, feel again, as powerfully as she first had, the raw impact he had on her, that sense of power and attraction that she could not explain—did not want to explain.

Call it. She heard the imperative in her head. *Call it—say that you know him—that he has already sought you out...*

But she couldn't do anything other than sit there and try to conjure up some explanation for why she couldn't open her mouth.

Into her head tumbled the overriding question—*What the hell is going on here?*

Because something was—that was for sure. A man she'd never seen before in her life had turned up at the club, bribed a waiter to invite her to his table, then confronted her in her dressing room to ask her out... And then he reappeared as Philip's cousin, unexpectedly arrived in France...

But there was no time to think—no time for anything other than to realise that she had to cope with the situation as it was now and come up with answers later.

'*Mademoiselle...*'

The deep voice was as dark as she remembered it—accented in Greek, similar to Philip's. But that was the only similarity. Philip's voice was light, youthful, his tone usually admiring, often hesitant. But his cousin, in a single word, conveyed to Sarah a whole lot more.

Assessing—guarded—sardonic. Not quite mocking but...

She felt a shiver go down her spine. A shiver she should not be feeling. Should have no need of feeling. Was he *daring* her to admit they'd already encountered one another?

'*M'sieu...*' She kept her voice cool. Totally neutral.

A waiter glided up, seeing a new guest had arrived.

The business of Bastiaan Karavalas ordering a drink—
a dry martini, Sarah noted absently—gave her precious
time to try and grab some composure back.

She was in urgent need of it—whatever Bastiaan Karavalas was playing at, it was his physical presence that
was dominating her senses, overwhelming her with his
raw, physical impact just the way it had last night in her
dressing room. Dragging her gaze to him set her heart
quickening, her pulse surging. What *was* it about him?
That sense of presence, of power—of dark, magnetic attraction? The veiled eyes, the sensual mouth…?

Never had she been so aware of a man. Never had her
body reacted like this.

'For you, *mademoiselle*?' the deep, accented voice
was addressing her, clearly enquiring what she would
like to drink.

She gave a quick shake of her head. 'Thank you—no.
I stick to water between sets.'

He dismissed the waiter with an absent lift of his hand
and the man scurried off to do his bidding.

'Sets?' Bastiaan enquired.

His thoughts were busy. He'd wanted to see whether
she would disclose his approach to her the previous evening, and now he was assessing the implications of her
not doing so.

He was, he knew, assessing a great deal about her…
Predominantly her physical impact on him. Even though
that was the thing least relevant to the situation.

Or was it?

The thought was in his head before he could stop it.
So, too, was the one that followed hard upon its heels.

Her reaction to him blazed from her like a beacon.
Satisfaction—stabbing through him—seared in his veins.
That, oh, *that*, indeed, was something he could use…

He quelled the thought—this was not the time. She had taken the first trick at that first encounter, turning down the invitation he'd so expected her to take. *But the game, Mademoiselle Sabine, is only just begun...*

And he would be holding the winning hand!

'Sa...Sabine's a singer,' Philip was saying, his eyes alight and sweeping admiringly over the *chanteuse* who had him in her coils.

Bastiaan sat back, his eyes flickering over the slinkily dressed and highly made-up figure next to his cousin. 'Indeed?'

It was his turn to use the French language to his advantage—allowing the ironic inflection to work to her discomfiture...as though he doubted the veracity of his cousin's claim.

'Indeed, *m'sieu*,' echoed Sarah. The ironic inflection had not been lost on her and she repaid it herself, in a light, indifferent tone.

He didn't like that, she could see. There was something about the way his dark brows drew a fraction closer to each other, the way the sensual mouth tightened minutely.

'And what do you...sing?' he retaliated, and one dark brow lifted with slight interrogation.

'Chansons d'amour,' Sarah murmured. 'What else?' She gave a smile—just a little one. Light and mocking.

Philip spoke again. 'You've just missed Sabine's first set,' he told Bastiaan.

His glance went to her, as if for reassurance—or perhaps, thought Bastiaan, it was simply because the boy couldn't take his eyes from the woman.

And nor can I—

'But you'll catch her second set!' Philip exclaimed enthusiastically.

'I wouldn't miss it for the world,' he said dryly. Again, his gaze slid to the *chanteuse.*

A new reaction was visible, and it caught his attention. Was he mistaken, or was there, somewhere beneath the make-up, colour suffusing her cheekbones?

Had she taken what he'd said as sarcasm?

If she had, she repaid him in the same coin.

'You are too kind, *m'sieu,*' she said.

And Bastiaan could see, even in the dim light, how her deep-set eyes, so ludicrously enhanced by false eye-lashes and heavy kohled lids, flashed fleetingly to green.

A little jolt of sexual electricity fired in him. He wanted to see more of that green flash...

It would come if I kissed her—

'Sa...Sabine's voice is wonderful.'

Philip cut across his heated thoughts. Absently, Bastiaan found himself wondering why his cousin seemed to stammer over the singer's name.

'Even when she's only singing *chan—*'

Sarah's voice cut across Philip's. 'So, M'sieu Karavalas, you have come to visit Philip? I believe the villa is yours, is it not?'

She couldn't care less what he was doing here, or whether he owned a villa on Cap Pierre or anywhere else. She'd only spoken to stop Philip saying something she could see he was dying to say, despite her earlier plea to him—

Even when she's only singing chansons *in a place like this.*

I don't want him to mention anything about what I really sing—that I'm not really Sabine!

Urgency filled her. And now it had nothing to do with not wanting Bastiaan Karavalas to know that Sarah Fareham moonlighted as Sabine Sablon. No, it was for a quite different reason—one that right now seemed far more crucial.

I can't handle him as Sarah. I need to be Sabine. Sabine can cope with this—Sabine can cope with a man like him. Sabine is the kind of sophisticated, worldly-wise female who can deal with such a man.

With the kind of man who coolly hit on a woman who'd taken his eye and aroused his sexual interest, arrogantly assuming she would comply without demur. The kind of man who rested assessing, heavy-lidded eyes on her, drawing no veil over what he saw in her, knowing exactly what impact his assessment of her was having.

That kind of man...

Philip's enthusiastic voice was a relief to her.

'You ought to spend some time at the villa, Bast! It really is a beautiful place. Paulette says you're hardly ever there.'

Bastiaan flicked his eyes to his cousin. 'Well, maybe I should move across from Monaco and stay awhile with you. Keep you on the straight and narrow.'

He smiled at Philip, and as he did so Sarah suddenly saw a revelation. Utterly unexpected. Gone—totally vanished—was the Bastiaan Karavalas she'd been exposed to, with his coolly assessing regard and his blatant appraisal, and the sense of leashed power that emanated from him. Now, as he looked across at Philip, his smile carved deep lines around his mouth and lightened his expression, made him suddenly seem... different.

She felt something change inside her—uncoil as if a knot had been loosened...

If he ever smiled at me like that I would be putty in his hands.

But she sheered her mind away. Bastiaan Karavalas

was unsettling enough, without throwing such a smile her way.

'Make me write all my wretched essays, you mean—don't you, Bast?' Philip answered, making a face.

But Sarah could see the communication running between them, the easy affection. It seemed to make Bastiaan far less formidable. But that, she knew with a clenching of her muscles, had a power of its own. A power she must not acknowledge. Not even as Sabine.

'It's what you came here for,' Bastiaan reminded him. 'And to escape, of course.'

His dark eyes flickered back to Sarah and the warmth she'd seen so fleetingly as he'd smiled at his young cousin drained out of them. It was replaced by something new. Something that made her eyes narrow minutely as she tried to work out what it was.

'I offered the villa to Philip as a refuge,' he informed Sarah in a casual voice. 'He was being plagued by a particularly persistent female. She made a real nuisance of herself, didn't she?' His glance went back to his cousin.

Philip made another face. 'Elena Constantis *was* a pain,' he said feelingly. 'Honestly, she's got boys buzzing all over her, but she still wanted to add *me* to her stupid collection. She's so immature,' he finished loftily.

A tiny smile hovered at Sarah's lips, dispelling her momentary unease. Immaturity was a relative term, after all. For a second—the briefest second—she caught a similar smile just tugging at Bastiaan Karavalas's well-shaped mouth, lifting it the way his smile at Philip had done a moment ago.

Almost, *almost* she felt herself starting to meet his eyes, ready to exchange glances with him—two people so much more mature than sweet, young Philip...

Then the intention was wiped from her consciousness.

Its tempting potency gone. Philip's gaze had gone to her. 'She couldn't be more different from *you*,' he said. The warmth in his voice could have lit a fire.

Sarah's long, fake eyelashes dipped again. Bastiaan Karavalas's dark gaze had switched to her, and she was conscious of it—burningly conscious of it. Conscious, too, of what must have accounted for the studiedly casual remark he'd made that had got them on to this subject.

Surely he can't think I don't realise that Philip is smitten with me?

Bastiaan was speaking again. 'Sabine is certainly much *older*,' he observed.

The dark eyes had flicked back to her face—watching, she could tell, for her reaction to his blunt remark. Had he intended to warn her? To show her how real his cousin's infatuation with her was?

How best to respond…? 'Oh, I'm ancient, indeed!' she riposted lightly. 'Positively creaking.'

'You're not old!' Philip objected immediately, aghast at the very idea. Adoration shone in his eyes. Then his gaze shifted to the dance floor in front of the stage, where couples had started to congregate. His face lit. 'Oh! Sabine—will you dance with me? Please say yes!'

Indecision filled her. She never danced with Philip or did anything to encourage him. But right now it would get her away from the disturbing, overpowering impact of Bastiaan Karavalas.

'If you like,' she replied, and got to her feet as he leapt eagerly to his and walked her happily out on to the dance floor.

Thankfully, the music was neither very fast—fast dancing would have been impossible in her tight gown— nor so slow that it would require any kind of smoochy embrace. But since most of the couples were in a traditional ballroom-style hold with each other, that was the hold she glided into.

Philip, bless him, clearly wasn't too *au fait* with so formal a dancing style, but he manfully did his best. 'I've got two left feet!' he exclaimed ruefully.

'You're doing fine,' she answered encouragingly, making sure she was holding him literally at arm's length.

It seemed an age until the number finally ended.

'Well done,' she said lightly.

'I won't be so clumsy next time,' he promised her.

She let her hand fall from his shoulder and indicated that he should let go of her too—which he did, with clear reluctance. But Philip's crush on her was not uppermost in her mind right now.

She was just about to murmur something about her next set, and this time make sure she headed off, when a deep voice sounded close by.

'Mademoiselle Sabine? I trust you will give me equal pleasure?'

She started, her head twisting. Bastiaan Karavalas was bearing down on them as the music moved on to another number. A distinctly slower number.

He gave her no chance to refuse. An amused nod of dismissal at his cousin and then, before she could take the slightest evasive action, Sarah's hand had been taken, her body was drawn towards his by the placing of his large, strong hand at her waist, and she was forced to lift her other hand and let it rest as lightly as she could on his shoulder. Then he was moving her into the dance—his thigh pressing blatantly against hers to impel her to move.

Instinctively Sarah tried to preserve her composure, though her heart was pounding in her ribcage. Her body was as stiff as a board, her muscles straining away from him as if she could increase the narrow gap between their bodies. His answer was to curve his fingers into her waist, and with effortless strength secure his hold on her again.

He smiled down at her.

It was a smile of pure possession.

Sarah could feel her blood surging in her body, quickening in every vein, heating her from within as she moved against his possessive clasp.

'So, *mademoiselle*, on what shall we converse?'

His smile had given way to a question in which both irony and amusement were mingled. And something else too—something she could not give a name to, but which seemed to send yet another quiver of excruciating physical awareness of his closeness to her.

Yet again she found herself clinging to the persona of Sabine. Sabine could cope with this—Sabine could let the potently powerful Bastiaan Karavalas sweep her off and yet keep her cool about it. Keep her composure. So what would Sabine do...say...?

'The choice is yours, *m'sieu*,' she answered, managing to keep her tone somewhere between insouciant and indifferent. Social...civil...just this side of courteous. She made herself meet his gaze, the way Sabine undoubtedly would—for what would Sabine be overset by in those dark, sensual eyes? And Sabine's ridiculously long fake lashes helped, Sarah thought with gratitude, because their length made it easier for her to look at him with a veiled expression—helped her feel protected from the impact those deep, dark eyes were having on her...

Abruptly, he spoke, yanking her back to full focus. 'Why did you not mention that you had already made my acquaintance?' he said.

Sarah felt her eyes widening. There was only one answer to give. 'Why didn't *you*?' she said. She sought to copy the dismissive inflection that Sabine would surely give.

Her answer was a sudden opacity in his gaze. 'You must know why—' he said.

From his dark, deep-set eyes a message blazed that was as clear as day...as old as time.

Sarah could feel her breath catch in her throat, her pulse leap—and suddenly Sabine, with all her worldly defences, felt a long, long way away.

'Why did you refuse to come to dinner with me?' Again, the question was blunt—challenging. Taking her by surprise.

'You were a complete stranger.' She sought for the only explanation that was relevant—whether or not it was one that Sabine would have made.

Thoughts flickered across her mind like random electric currents. Would Sabine have found that objectionable? Or would she have made her decision about whether to let a man take her to dinner—and what might follow—on quite different grounds?

Such as if the man were the most devastating male she'd ever set eyes on—who'd had the most powerful impact on her she'd ever experienced—who'd stilled the breath in her lungs and sent her pulse into overdrive...

But she was given no opportunity to think coherently about that, or about anything at all, because now his eyes had a glint in them that was setting her pulse racing even faster.

'Well, I am not a stranger now.'

Not when I hold you in the intimacy of this embrace... your soft, satiny body in my arms, the warmth of your palm against mine, the brush of your thighs as we move to the music together...

He felt the flush of heat beating in his veins. Telling him how susceptible he was to what she possessed.

The power to make him desire her…

His senses were overpowering him. There was a lingering perfume about her—not cloying, as he might have expected, but faintly floral. Her hair, curved around her shoulder as it was, was not sticky with spray but fine and silky. He wanted to feel it running through his fingers. Wanted to drink in the fine-boned beauty of her face, see again that flash of emeralds in her eyes…

A sudden impulse possessed him. To wipe her complexion free of the mask of make-up covering it and see her true beauty revealed.

'Why do you wear so much make-up?' His question came from nowhere—he hadn't meant to ask it.

She looked momentarily startled. 'It's stage make-up,' she answered. She spoke as if she found it hard to believe he'd asked.

He frowned. 'It does not flatter you,' he stated.

Now, *why* had he said that? he grilled himself. Why tell this woman such a thing?

Because it is the truth—she masks her true beauty, her true self, behind such excess.

Her expression changed. 'It's not designed to flatter— only to withstand the stage lighting. You don't imagine that I wear these spiders on my eyes for any other reason, do you?' Her voice was dry.

'Good,' he said, giving a brief nod.

Even as he did so he realised he was way off agenda. What on earth was he *doing*, talking about her stage make-up? Let alone expressing approval—relief?—that it *was* only make-up. He sought to resume the line of enquiry he'd started. That was the reason he was dancing with her—so that he could continue his assessment of her. Purely for the purposes for which he'd arrived in France, of course...

To free his cousin from her.

Free her from Philip—

The thought was there—indelible, inadmissible. He wiped it instantly. There was no question of freeing *her* from his cousin. It was Philip—only Philip—he was concerned about. That was what he had to remember.

Not the way her body was moving with his to the soft, seductive cadences of the music, drawing them closer and closer to each other...

Not the way her fragrance was coiling into his senses. Not the way his eyes were lingering on her face...her parted lips... The way he was feeling the soft breath coming from her...intoxicating him...

The melody ended. He stopped abruptly. Even more abruptly she disengaged herself from his grasp. But she did not move—simply stood there for a moment, continuing to gaze at him. As if she could not stop...

Her breasts, Bastiaan could see, were rising and falling as if her breathing were rapid—her pulse was more rapid still. Colour was in her cheeks, beneath the thick layer of foundation. He could just see it...sense it...

Her gaze was dragged from him, back across to where Philip was sitting, his expression a mixture of impatience at her absence, discontent that she had been dancing with his cousin, and his usual fixed regard of uncritical admiration.

She walked across to him—her dress felt tighter suddenly, and she was all too conscious of the swaying movement of her hips. She could almost *feel* Bastiaan Karavalas watching her...

She reached the table. Philip stood up immediately, his chair scraping.

'Phew!' she said, pointedly not resuming her seat. 'I'm worn out by dancing. Two dances and two partners—quite an evening for me!' She spoke with deliberate lightness, obvious humour. Reaching for her glass of water, she took a quick gulp, finding she needed it, then set it down. 'I must go backstage,' she said. 'Prep for my next set.'

Conscious that Philip's cousin was standing behind her, she could say very little else to Philip. She took a step away, encompassing Bastiaan Karavalas in her movement.

'I'll bid you goodnight,' she said, making her voice sound nothing more than effortlessly casual.

She had to get control back—the way Sabine would. Sabine would have been utterly unfazed by that slow, seductive dance with Bastiaan Karavalas. Sabine wouldn't have felt as if her whole body were trembling, her senses overwhelmed. No, Sabine would stay composed, unruffled—would be well used to men like Bastiaan Karavalas desiring her.

Philip was speaking and she made herself pay attention, drag her thoughts away from his cousin.

'I'll see you tomorrow at the…here…?' he asked.

Sarah was relieved that he'd just avoided saying *at the rehearsal*.

She smiled. A warm smile. Because she didn't want to hurt him, and his feelings were so transparent. 'Why not?' she said lightly. 'Unless…' And now her eyes found Bastiaan again. 'Unless you and your cousin have plans…? You must make the most of him while he's here.'

Dark lashes flickered over even darker eyes. She saw it—caught it. 'I may well be here some time,' Bastiaan Karavalas said. 'It all depends…'

She made no answer—could only give a vague, brief

smile and bestow a little wave on Philip, because she wanted to be nice to him, and he was so young, and felt so much…

And then she was gone, whisking away through a little door inset into the wall beside the low stage.

Slowly, Bastiaan sat down. Philip did too, but Bastiaan said nothing—his head was full. Far too full. Only one thought was predominant—he wanted to hear her sing… he wanted to feast his eyes on her again.

Feast so much more than his eyes…

CHAPTER FIVE

As Sarah took her place on the stage she was burningly aware of those dark, heavy eyes upon her. It was the same sensation she'd had the previous night, when she hadn't known who was watching her—had only been able to feel it. As she felt it now, again, that same sense of exposure. But now there was so much more—now there was a frisson running through her body, her veins, that came from his heavy-lidded perusal.

Why? The question kept circling in her head. Why was she reacting like this? Why was this man—this dark, disturbing cousin of Philip—able to arouse such a response in her? Never, *never* before had she been so affected by a man.

By a man's desire for her.

Because it is a desire that echoes in me too...

That was the truth of it. Out of nowhere, like a bolt of lightning crashing into tinder-dry trees, he'd set her alight....

A sense almost of panic swept over her.

I can't handle it. I'm not used to it. No man has ever made me feel this way—like I'm on fire, burning from the inside. I don't know what to do—how to react...

Nothing with Andrew had prepared her for this. Nothing!

I didn't know it was possible to feel this way. To feel this overwhelmed—this helpless.

This aroused...

Standing there in the spotlight, knowing that the dark, heavy eyes of Bastiaan Karavalas were resting on her, that she was exposed to his view, her body had reacted as if her flesh were aflame.

She wanted to run, bolt from the stage, but that was impossible. Impossible to do anything but continue to stand there, the microphone between her fingers, her voice intimate.

While Bastiaan Karavalas looked his fill of her.

No! The cry came from within. *It isn't me he's gazing at—it's Sabine. Sabine is standing here, feeling like this.*

And Sabine—Sabine could handle it. Of course she could. Sabine was not helpless or overwhelmed by the blatant desire in those dark, heavy eyes.

Or by her own desire...

Sabine was who she must be to cope with what was happening to her, with the fire that was running in her veins, burning her senses. That was what she clung to as she worked her way through her numbers.

Never had her set seemed longer, and how she got through it she wasn't sure, but in the end she was heading off stage, filled with relief.

As she gained her dressing room she saw Philip waiting. He launched in as soon as he could.

'Sarah—this Sunday—will you...will you come over to the villa for lunch?' He got the words out in a rush, his eyes filled with eager hope. 'I've been wanting to ask you, but it was Bast who suggested it.'

She felt a quiver inside her, even though she strove to stanch it. *Why? Why had Bastiaan Karavalas suggested inviting her to his villa?*

And the only answer she could think of sent that quiver vibrating through her again, quickening her pulse.

I don't have time for this. I don't have time to have Bastiaan Karavalas looking at me the way he does, have the impact on me he does. I just don't have time—not now. And I can't cope with it anyway—can't cope with him. I don't know how to respond or react. And, anyway, it isn't me he's inviting—it's Sabine! Sabine's the one he's drawn to—not me. He wants what Sabine would offer him...

The hectic thoughts tumbled through her mind, incoherent and confused. She had to answer somehow—but what? And how?

'So, will you come? Please say yes,' Philip's eager voice pressed.

She pulled herself together forcibly. 'I'm...I'm not sure...' she got out.

'What's this you're plotting?'

Max's voice sounded behind her. It sounded amused, but with a pointedness in it that Sarah was not deaf to.

Philip turned. 'I was asking Sarah if she would come over to the villa for lunch on Sunday with my cousin and me,' he relayed.

'Cousin?' Max raised his eyebrows.

'My cousin—Bastiaan Karavalas,' supplied Philip. 'It's his villa I'm staying at. He's visiting me from Greece.'

'Karavalas...' murmured Max.

Sarah knew he was storing the information away and would check it out later—just as he'd checked out Philip's name. Any cousin of Philip's would be rich as well, and for that reason she knew she might be disheartened by what Max said next, but she could not be surprised.

Max smiled at Philip. 'Why wait till Sunday?' he said

blandly. 'Make it tomorrow—I'll rejig the schedule so Sarah can get away at noon. How would that be?'

Philip's face lit. 'Fantastic! I'll go and tell Bast now. Brilliant!'

He beamed at Sarah and Max, and then rushed off to front of house.

Sarah turned to Max. 'Max—' she began, about to remonstrate.

Max held up a hand. 'Say nothing. I know your opinion about asking Philip for money. But...' his voice changed 'But this Bastiaan Karavalas, the cousin—well, that's a different matter, isn't it? A grown man who owns a villa on Cap Pierre—and presumably a whole lot else—doesn't require kid-glove-handling, does he? So, *cherie*, off you go to lunch with these lovely rich people and make yourself agreeable to them.'

Sarah's expression hardened. 'Max, if you think—'

'*Cherie*, it's just lunch—nothing more than that. What did you *think* I was suggesting?'

He sounded amused, and it irritated Sarah. 'I don't know and I don't care,' she shot back, shutting her dressing room door in his face.

Consternation was flooding through her. She did not *want* to go over to Bastiaan Karvalas's villa and spend the afternoon there. She didn't want to spend a single moment more in his company. Didn't want another opportunity for him to work his dark, potent magic on her senses...

I don't need this distraction. I have to focus on the festival—it's all that's important to me. Nothing else. I want Bastiaan Karavalas gone—out of my life!

She stilled suddenly as she started to change out of her costume. Her mind raced.

Maybe going to the villa wasn't so bad an idea after

all. Maybe she could turn the invitation to her advantage. Find an opportunity to get Bastiaan Karavalas on his own and suggest that it would be a really good idea for him to whisk Philip away. Distance would soon cause his youthful crush to atrophy.

And it would take Bastiaan Karavalas away as well... Stop him disturbing her the way he did so that she could get back to the only important thing in her life now: preparing for the festival. Not being swept away by what was in his dark, desiring eyes.

Yes. She took a steadying breath. That, surely, would make it worth enduring an afternoon of his company. Because there was no other reason for wanting to spend an afternoon with Bastiaan Karavalas.

Liar, said a voice inside her head. A voice that whispered to her in Sabine's soft, seductive tones...

'She'll come over tomorrow!' Philip exclaimed happily as he re-joined Bastiaan.

'How surprising...' murmured Bastiaan.

Of course Mademoiselle Sabine had jumped at the invitation to get a foot...literally...in the door.

His cousin completely missed the sardonic note in his voice. 'Isn't it?' he answered. 'Considering how—' he stopped short.

Bastiaan cocked an eyebrow. 'Considering...?' he prompted.

'Oh, nothing,' Philip answered hastily, but looked as if he were hiding something.

Yet again the question fired in Bastiaan's head. *How far has this infatuation gone? What is Philip hiding?*

But surely his instincts were correct? Philip was not radiating the aura of a young man who had achieved possession of the object of his desire and devotion. He was still worshipping at the altar.

A silent growl of raw, male satisfaction rasped through him. Its occurrence did not please him. Just the opposite. Damnation—the very thought that he could be *glad* that Philip was still merely mooning over the delectable blonde singer for any other reason than that it meant that it would be easier separating him from Sabine, extricating him from her toils, was unacceptable.

He changed the subject deliberately. 'So—tonight... Do you want to come over to Monte? We can eat out and you can stay at my apartment.'

Again, it was a deliberate trail, to discover whether Philip would otherwise have been heading towards La Belle Sabine for a midnight tryst...

To his satisfaction Philip was perfectly amenable to this suggestion, helping Bastiaan to confirm his judgement that, however besotted Philip was with the woman, it had not yet progressed to anything more...tangible.

Then another, more unwelcome thought struck him. *Is she holding out on bestowing herself upon him until he has control over his own funds?*

Was that her game plan? His expression hardened as they left the club. He was looking forward to lunch tomorrow—it would give him more time to study her. Assess her.

All for the sake of rescuing his cousin, of course. Not for any other reason...

None that he would permit.

'Stop!' Max threw his hand up impatiently. 'I said *sostunuto*, not *diminuendo*! If you can't tell the difference, Sarah, believe me—I can! Take it again.'

Sarah drew her breath in sharply but said nothing,

though her jaw was set. Max was being particularly tyrannical this morning, and Alain, her tenor, playing The Soldier, was fractious. So was she, she admitted to herself. She was hitting vocal difficulties all over the place, and it was frustrating the hell out of her. The rehearsal session was not going smoothly and Max was finding fault with all of them. Nerves were getting jittery all round.

She shut her eyes to center herself.

'In your own time, Sarah,' came Max's sarcastic prompt.

Somehow her next attempt managed to assuage him, and he turned his exacting attention to Alain and his apparently many flaws, before resuming his attack on Sarah for the next passage that displeased him.

By the time he dismissed her Sarah felt ragged. She definitely needed fresh air and a change of environment. For the first time she actually felt grateful that she was to have the afternoon off, courtesy of Philip's invitation. As she scooped up her bag she heard Max start in on the alto and the baritone, and hurried to make her escape from the fraught atmosphere.

Philip had texted to say he'd pick her up from her *pension*, where she headed now to change into something suitable for having lunch at a millionaire's villa on the exclusive Cap Pierre.

Just what constituted 'suitable'? she pondered.

In the end there was only one outfit that was possible. It was one she'd bought when she'd first arrived in France to join the opera company, after the school term had ended. It wasn't her usual floaty, floral style, but a chic sixties-style shift in a shade of green that suited her fair colouring.

She pushed her hair back with a white band, and completed the retro look with pastel lipstick, frosted eye-shadow and a lot of eyeliner.

She studied her reflection—yes, definitely more Sabine than Sarah. Just what she needed.

'Oh, my goodness!' she exclaimed as she stepped outdoors and immediately saw the low, lean, bright red Ferrari parked there.

'Isn't it a beauty?' Philip said lovingly. 'It's Bast's. He keeps it in Monte Carlo—he has an apartment there as well—and he's letting me drive it today.'

He sounded awestruck at the prospect.

'Bast's already at the villa,' Philip explained, helping her into the low, luxurious passenger seat. 'So...' He looked at her expectantly, his eyes alight, as he started the engine with a throaty growl. 'What do you think?'

She gave a laugh. 'Terrifying!' she said feelingly.

He laughed, as though he could not possibly believe her, and moved off. He was obviously thrilled by driving such a powerful, fabulous car, and Sarah wisely let him concentrate. The road leading out on to the *Cap* was a residential one, with a modest speed limit.

It was only five minutes to the villa, and she could see Philip's reluctance to abandon the vehicle when he arrived. It seemed, she thought dryly, and not with regret, that she finally had a rival.

Well, any rival was to be welcomed, even one with wheels. What she really wanted to conjure up, though, was a flesh and blood rival to take his mind off *her*—someone suitable for his age and circumstances. She frowned slightly. What had Bastiaan Karavalas been saying the previous evening? About dispatching Philip to his villa in the first place because he'd been pursued by some spoilt teen in Greece? That was a *good* sign, because it could only mean that Philip's cousin would be amenable to her suggesting that another rescue was needed.

Except that I'm going to have to speak to him alone.

That was *not* something she wanted to have to do. Not even behind the protection of being Sabine. But right now she would grab any protection she could.

Walking into the white-plastered, low-rise villa, set in spacious grounds out on the promontory of the *Cap*, she felt the need of Philip's familiar innocuous presence as they crossed the cool, stone-floored hall into a wide reception room and she saw the tall, sable-haired figure of Bastiaan Karavalas strolling in from the vine-shaded terrace beyond to greet them.

As she had the night before, and the first time she'd laid eyes on him, Sarah felt an instinctive, automatic reaction to him. It was like a switch being thrown inside her—a buzz of electric current in her veins, a kick in her heartbeat. She saw his dark eyes narrow as they lit on her, and the electric current ran again—and then Philip was greeting him and ushering her forward.

'Here we are, Bast,' he said cheerfully. 'Is lunch ready? I'm starving. Are we eating out on the terrace?'

'We've time for a drink first,' Bastiaan replied, and Sarah saw that he was carrying a champagne bottle in one hand and three glasses loosely by their stems in the other. 'But let's head out anyway. *Mademoiselle...?*'

He stepped aside from the door to let her go through first. It meant passing close to him, and she felt his eyes on her as she walked out on to the terrace. Then all thoughts of the disturbing Bastiaan Karavalas left her.

'Oh, this is *beautiful*!' she heard herself exclaim.

The wide, shady terrace, roofed by vines and vivid bougainvillaea, opened to verdant lawns beyond, which were edged with richly foliated bushes and sloped down to a glittering azure pool, behind which stretched the even more glitteringly azure reaches of the Mediterranean Sea.

'Welcome to my villa, Sabine,' said Bastiaan.

She turned at the accented voice. His eyes were sweeping over her and she could feel their impact. Feel the electricity course through her again.

Not in a tuxedo, as she had previously seen him, but in a pair of long, pale grey chinos and a short-sleeved, dark burgundy open-necked polo shirt, which moulded his powerful torso. He looked lean, lithe and devastatingly attractive. She felt her stomach give a little clench of appreciation.

'Sab—come and sit down,' Philip was saying, indicating the ironwork table set for lunch.

He'd taken to calling her 'Sab' on the way there, and Sarah was glad. It might make him less likely to call her Sarah. She was also glad about her choice of outfit. OK, so she was probably slightly too smartly dressed for what was clearly going to be an al fresco meal, with Bastiaan in casual clothes and Philip in his customary designer-labelled T-shirt and jeans, but her retro-chic dress felt almost like a costume—and that *had* to help her be Sabine and not Sarah, who was perilously out of her depth in such deep waters as swirled about this powerfully, devastatingly sensual male...

As she carefully seated herself where Philip was holding a chair out for her, in a position that afforded her a view right out over the gardens, she could feel those heavy-lidded eyes on her while Bastiaan settled himself at the head of the table.

'May I tempt you to champagne, Sabine?' The deep-voiced question required an answer.

'Thank you,' she said politely. Inside, the inner voice

that whispered to her so seductively in Sabine's husky tones was teasing her... *You tempt me to so much more...*

She silenced it sharply, making herself look not at the man who drew her eyes, but instead out over the beautiful gardens to the sea beyond. Her expression softened. It really was absolutely beautiful, she thought with genuine pleasure. Private, verdant, full of flowers, with the azure sea sparkling beyond—a true Mediterranean idyll.

'What a beautiful spot this is!' she could not help exclaiming warmly. 'If it were mine I'd never leave!'

'Oh, Bast has an entire island to himself at home,' Philip answered. 'This place is tiny in comparison.'

Sarah's eyes widened. Bastiaan saw it as he busied himself opening the champagne. *Thank you, Philip*, he thought, *that was helpful*. His appreciation was sincere— he wanted to see how Sabine reacted to his wealth. Whether it would cause her to turn her attentions to him instead of his cousin.

And would that be helpful too? Again he found himself contemplating using that method to detach her from Philip. It might be so much...*swifter*.

Enjoyable...

His eyes rested on her as he filled their glasses. He was still trying to get past his first reaction to her when he'd walked out on to the terrace. It had been—*surprise*.

Oh, he'd known, obviously, that she wouldn't turn up for lunch in a skin-tight evening gown and a face full of stage make-up. But he'd expected her to wear some kind of flashy strapless brief sundress, exposing a lot of thigh and with a slashed décolletage, and to be adorned with jangly gold jewellery, her hair in a tousled mane. But her stylishly retro look had a chicness to it that drew his eye without condemnation.

Interesting, he found himself thinking. She had

changed her image decisively. At the nightclub she had been all sultry vamp. Today she had moved on a couple of decades to the swinging sixties—almost as though she'd made a costume change between acts...

But then, he thought caustically, putting on an act was what a woman like Sabine was all about, wasn't it? From standing on a stage singing throaty, amorous numbers for strangers, to manipulating the emotions of a smitten, impressionable youth.

His eyes hardened minutely as they rested on her. *You will find it harder to manipulate me, mademoiselle...*

If there was any manipulating to be done, then it would be coming from *him*—not her. He would be the one to steer her in the precise direction he wished her to go— away from Philip. *And to me instead?* Again the thought played in his mind provocatively. Temptingly.

'I imagine a private island is just about *de rigueur* for a Greek tycoon, isn't it?' she was saying now, lightly, with a clear infusion of amusement in her voice.

Bastiaan sat back in his chair, lifting his glass. 'Do you take me for a tycoon, *mademoiselle*?' he riposted.

But there was a deep timbre in his voice all the same. She felt it like a low vibration in her body.

'Oh, surely you could be nothing less, *m'sieu*?' she answered in kind. 'With your private island in the Aegean!'

She had matched the slight tinge of ironic inflection that had been in his voice and suddenly there seemed to be a flicker in his dark eyes, a slight curve of his mouth, as if for her alone... Something she didn't want to be there. Something she did...

No, no I don't. And, anyway, isn't it bad enough that I've got to deal with Philip's bad attack of calf love? The last thing I need is to develop a crush of my own on his cousin.

She paused. Crush? Was *that* what she was calling this strange, disturbing electricity between them? This ridiculous, absurd awareness of his overpowering physical impact on her? A *crush*?

Negation leapt in her. No, this was no crush. There was only one cause for what she was feeling about this man who had walked into her dressing room that night, who had taken her in his powerful, controlling clasp on the dance floor, who was now watching her, his heavy eyes half lidded, waiting for her to reply in similar vein...

Desire. Raw, insistent desire. Desire bred of her burning awareness of his presence, of his physical existence— the way the tough line of his jaw squared his face, the way the strong column of his throat rose from the open neck of his polo, the way the sable darkness of his hair feathered the broad brow, the way his shirt moulded across the strength of his shoulders, his torso...

Desire—that was the only word for it. The only name to give what she was feeling now as her body flushed with heat, with awareness...

Desperation spiked in her. It was like a sideways sweeping wave, knocking her askew, derailing her. And she could not allow it to happen. Not with her whole life's ambition consuming her right now. That was all she must think of—that was all she must focus on.

Not on this man who can make my pulse catch just by letting his dark, dark eyes rest on me, setting my senses afire...

It was a fire she had to quench—and fast.

She reached for her champagne, needing its potency to regain control of herself.

'Bast's island's in the Ionian Sea, not the Aegean,' Philip was saying. 'Off the west coast of Greece. Not far from Zakynthos.'

Sarah turned her head towards him, half reluctant, half grateful to drag her gaze away from his darkly disturbing cousin. 'I don't know Greece at all,' she said. 'I've never been.'

'I'd love to show you. You'd love Athens!' Philip replied immediately, his voice full of enthusiasm.

A low laugh came from the other end of the table. 'A city full of ancient ruins? I doubt it. I'm sure Sabine would prefer sophisticated cities, like Milan or Paris.'

She didn't correct him. The real Sabine, wherever she was right now, probably *would* prefer such cities, and at the moment that persona was hers. She'd better let the issue lie.

She gave a very Gallic shrug, as she had so often seen her French mother give.

'I like warm climates,' she answered, which seemed an unrevealing comment to make, and was true as well. The Yorkshire winters she'd grown up with had never been her favourite, nor her mother's either. She had preferred the soft winters of her native Normandy. She looked at Philip again. 'I couldn't stand the frozen East Coast USA winters you have at uni.'

Philip shivered extravagantly. 'Neither can I!' He laughed. 'But we get snow in Greece sometimes—don't we, Bast?'

'There is even skiing in the mountains,' his cousin agreed.

'Bast skis like a champion!' Philip exclaimed, with open admiration for his older cousin.

'I was at school in Switzerland,' Bastiaan said laconically, by way of explanation.

Sarah's glance went back to Bastiaan. 'Is that why your French is so good?' she asked.

'Oh, Bast's fluent in German as well—aren't you,

Bast? And English, of course. *My* English is probably better than my French, actually, so really we should be speaking—'

'Tell me more about your private island.' Sarah's voice cut across Philip, preventing him from finishing his sentence. She was starting to think that this was ridiculous—all this stuff about her being Sabine. She should just come right out with it—trust Philip's cousin with her real identity and be done with it.

But she was conscious of a deep reluctance to do so. Partly, she knew, for the reason she'd given Philip—but that was not the overwhelming reason. Being Sabine gave her...*protection*. Protection from the onslaught on her senses that Bastiaan Karavalas was making on her.

'My private island?' Bastiaan echoed her. 'What can I tell you? Acreage? Location? Value?'

There was a quizzical expression in his voice, and he spoke lightly, yet Sarah could see a twist at the corner of his mouth. She found herself wondering at it, but her focus had to be on continuing the conversation. She didn't really care that much about Bastiaan Karavalas's island, but it had been the first thing she'd been able to think of asking about in order to interrupt Philip.

'What do you do on it?'

The quizzical expression came again, but this time she had the feeling it was genuine—as if her question had been unexpected. She watched him lift his champagne flute to his mouth.

'Do?' he said. 'Very little.' He gave a sudden smile, taking a mouthful of champagne. 'I take a dinghy out sometimes...swim, chill...not much else. Oh, I read sometimes too—or just watch the sun set with a glass of beer at my side. Nothing exciting. You, *mademoiselle*, would find it very dull.'

Even as he spoke Bastiaan found himself wondering. Why hadn't she followed up on his deliberate mentions of its size and value? Gone on to draw him out about the other properties he owned? Like his villa in the Caribbean, his condo in Manhattan, his apartment in London, his mansion in Athens... It was inconsistent of her. She'd been keen to get him to talk about owning the island in the first place, getting him to reveal to her just how wealthy he actually was.

'Au contraire,' she riposted, and Bastiaan became aware of the greenness of her eyes. 'It sounds very relaxing.'

She held his gaze a moment, and into his head sprang the image of just how he might 'relax' with such a woman on his private island... He felt a kick go through him— one that told him her impact on him was as powerful as ever.

Should I respond to it? Respond to the allure she has for me? Use it for my own purpose?

The questions came—but not the answers... And the very fact that the questions were forming in his mind indicated the temptation they presented. Showed him the answers he wanted to give...

His thoughts were interrupted by Paulette, emerging with the lunch tray. Philip got to his feet to take it from her and was rewarded by a beaming smile—clearly his young cousin had become a favourite of the housekeeper. As he and Philip started to unload it, he noticed Sabine was helping as well, passing plates of *charcuterie* and *fromage*, salads and crusty baguette slices.

'Would you like wine, or are you happy to stick to champagne?' Bastiaan enquired of his guest courteously.

Sarah smiled. 'What girl wouldn't be happy to stick to champagne?' she replied humorously.

She was working hard to keep her tone light, inconsequential. After lunch she must find an opportunity to get Bastiaan on his own, to broach to him her recommendation that it might be best to remove his young cousin to another place that offered less distraction. But even as she determined to do it she found herself dreading it. Dreading being on her own with Bastiaan Karavalas for any time at all.

Roughly, she shook such thoughts from herself. Sought to find something innocuous to say... 'Though if I drink too much at lunchtime I may well fall fast asleep in the afternoon.'

Bastiaan laughed, and yet again Sarah felt her pulse quicken. 'You would be quite welcome,' he said, and indicated the sun loungers that were set out on the lawn beneath the shade of a parasol.

'Don't tempt me,' she riposted, reaching for a piece of bread.

But you do *tempt me, Mademoiselle Sabine—you tempt me greatly...*

Again, the words took shape in his head before he could unsay them. Unthink them...

As he started to help himself to lunch Bastiaan could feel thoughts swirling. Would it *really* be so bad to let his interest in Sabine take the direction in which he could feel it drawing him? Had since his first moment of setting eyes on her.

She tempts me—and without a doubt she feels desire for me, answering my desire for her...

He could hear the arguments in his head already—as tempting as this beautiful woman was.

It would achieve the end I seek...the purpose of my journey—it would take her away from Philip, set him free from his infatuation. And give me what I want...

There was so much in its favour. Why should he reject such a solution to the problem?

Through half-veiled eyes he watched as Philip fussed over her, offering her dishes from the table.

'Chicken, brie and grapes would be lovely,' she said.

Her smile on his cousin was warm, and Bastiaan could see Philip drinking it in. Out of nowhere, a needle pricked Bastiaan beneath the skin.

I want her to smile like that at me.

Jerkily, he reached for the champagne bottle, refilled their glasses.

'So...' said Sarah, glancing between the two of them, casting about for something else to say that would be innocuous. 'Philip seems very smitten with that scarlet monster of yours that he picked me up in.'

'Monster?' said Philip immediately. 'She's a beauty!'

'Her growl is terrifying!' Sarah countered, with a little laugh.

'Wait till I drive you fast in it!' Philip exclaimed. 'Then you'll hear her *roar*!'

She shuddered extravagantly, but Bastiaan addressed Philip directly. 'No,' he said firmly. 'I know you love the idea of racing around in a car that powerful, but I'm not having you smash yourself up. Or, worse, my *car*,' he added, to lighten the rejection.

A mutinous look flashed briefly across Philip's face. Sarah could see it.

'Sab would be perfectly safe with me.'

Bastiaan shook his head. Inside, his thoughts were not just on the safety of Philip driving the powerful performance car. No way was Sabine going to use *his* car to further her aims with his cousin. It was not Sabine who needed to be kept safe—it was Philip.

'Come out with me instead,' he said. 'I'll show you

its paces. We'll do the Grande Corniche. How about to-morrow?' he suggested.

Philip's face lit. 'Great!' he enthused. His expression changed. 'But…er…in the afternoon, OK?'

Bastiaan nodded. 'Yes. Do your studies in the morning, then I'll reward you with a spin after lunch.' He turned to Sabine. 'As you know,' he said deliberately, 'my cousin is here first and foremost to complete his university vacation assignments. Not to jaunt around on holiday, entertaining *you*.'

Sarah's face tightened. 'Yes, I am aware of that,' she said coolly. Did he think *she* was inciting Philip to neglect his studies? Well, all the more reason to confront him this afternoon—warn him that he needed to remove Philip yet again.

And I need Bastiaan gone too. I haven't got time for distractions—least of all by a man like this.

His gaze held hers, and for a moment, timeless and impossible, she felt as if her heart had stopped beating.

What power does he have? The question coiled in her mind like smoke. And the answer twisted in the same sinuous shape… *Too much.*

'Good,' replied Bastiaan. Her eyes had darkened in colour again. He wondered at it. Then a more potent thought overrode that. *Emeralds*, he found himself thinking—that was the jewel for her. *Emeralds with the slightest hint of aqua—at her throat, her ears…*

The vision of her draped in such jewels was instant, vivid. They would enhance her blonde beauty, catching the fire of her emerald eyes, displaying that beauty for him and him alone. He felt desire, raw and insistent, growl within him whenever he succumbed to the temptation of thinking about this beautiful, alluring woman—so unsuitable for his naive, infatuated cousin…

But for me it would be different.

Of course it would—to him she presented no danger. Sophisticated, worldly-wise, closer to his age than to Philip's... Whatever his opinion of women who sought to part impressionable young men from their money, *he* was not susceptible to such wiles. *He* was not vulnerable to a woman like her.

But she... Ah, *she* would be vulnerable to *him*. Vulnerable to the desire for him that he could read in her like a book—a desire he shared and made no attempt to conceal. Why should he? For him there was no risk in succumbing to the flame that ran between them.

He took another fortifying mouthful of champagne, making his decision. Resolution streamed within him. *Yes, he would do it!*

Long lashes dipped over his dark eyes. He reached forward across the table, moving a bowl of ripe, succulent peaches towards Sabine. 'May I entice you?' he asked. And in his eyes was an expression that in no way indicated that it was to the fruit he was referring...

Her eyes flickered. He could see it. See the hint of green fire that signalled just as much as her dilating pupils that her sexual awareness of him was radiating out on all frequencies. He smiled, drawing an answering smile from her—an instinctive response. She took a peach and he was minutely aware of the delicate length of her fingers, the pale gloss of her nails.

'Thank you,' she murmured, and dragged her gaze away from him, as though she found it difficult to do so.

He saw the heightened colour on her cheeks as she placed the peach on her plate and started to slice it diligently, head bowed a little, as if she needed to focus on her task. Her chest was rising and falling a little faster than it had been before. Bastiaan sat back, lifting his champagne glass, satisfaction in his eyes.

Philip was helping himself from the fruit bowl as well, but unlike Sarah he bit enthusiastically into the peach from his hand, spurting juice. 'These are *really* good,' he said enthusiastically.

Sarah flicked her eyes to him. 'Aren't they?' she agreed. 'Just ripe and perfect.'

She was glad to talk about the ripeness of the fruit. Glad to turn her head to Philip and talk about something else. Glad to do *anything* to drag her consciousness away from the man at the opposite end of the table. Glad, too, a few minutes later, when Paulette arrived with a tray of coffee.

Sarah started to gather up the used plates, but the housekeeper snatched them from her, muttering darkly and casting meaningful glances between her and Philip.

Surely she doesn't think I'm encouraging Philip? Sarah thought.

Another thought struck her, even more unwelcome. Did *Bastiaan* think that as well?

No, he couldn't. Of course not! She was doing her utmost to be nothing more than casually friendly— easy-going and relaxed, spending most of her time deflecting his compliments to her. A man as worldly-wise as Bastiaan Karavalas would surely be able to read her reaction to Philip's youthful ardency as easily as if she had written it large.

As easily as he must be able to read my reaction to him...

She felt her stomach clench. The knowledge that Bastiaan Karavalas could see into her feelings towards him was both dismaying and arousing. Fiercely she tried to suppress the arousal, but even as she tried she felt her eyes going to him, almost meeting his as they did so, before she continued handing plates to the unappreciative Paulette. And she felt, in that fleeting mingling before she dipped her lashes to veil her eyes, the tremor of attraction flare and catch.

He knows how he affects me—knows how he makes me feel. It's impossible to hide it from him.

A thought speared into her troubled consciousness. Coming without volition. What if *Philip* knew how attracted she was to his cousin? What if she responded openly to Bastiaan Karavalas's desire for her—hers for him? Would that destroy Philip's crush for her in an instant? Surely it would. It might be harsh, but it would be effective.

And it would give me a reason to succumb to what is happening to me.

As if standing on the edge of a precipice, she hauled herself back from the brink. Was she *insane* to think such a thing? She must be. Whether she was being Sabine or herself, whether Philip did or did not have a hopeless infatuation with her, Bastiaan Karavalas had no place in her life—*none*. Whatever the power of his sensual impact on her, she must ignore it. Suppress it. Walk away from it.

Speak to Bastiaan this afternoon—explain how he should take Philip away—and then get back to what is important. The only thing that is important to you at this time.

Making her final attempt to launch her professional career. Nothing else. *No one* else.

'Sab, did you bring your swimming costume?'

Philip's question cut across her thoughts. She looked startled. 'No—no, I didn't.'

His face fell, then brightened as Bastiaan spoke.

'No problem. There's a wide collection of assorted

swimwear in the guest suites. I'm sure there'll be something to fit you.' Bastiaan's eyes glanced over her, as if assessing her figure's size, and her eyes automatically went to his as he spoke.

'Great!' exclaimed Philip. 'When we've had coffee I'll show you where to change.'

She gave him a flickering uncertain smile. She ought to make her excuses and leave—try and have that word she needed with Bastiaan before she did so. But as she sat sipping her coffee, replete with lunch, champagne coursing gently in her veins, she had no energy to make such a move.

Her gaze slipped out over the beautiful gardens beyond the terrace. Out of nowhere she felt a different mood take hold as she committed herself to staying longer. It really was *so* beautiful here, with the gardens and the dazzlingly blue sea beyond. All she ever saw of the Côte d'Azur was the walk back to her *pension* and the local shops around the harbour. By day she was focussed only on rehearsals, by night she posed as Sabine. A relentless schedule of work. Why not relax a little now?

Why don't I make the most of being here? Who could ask for anything more lovely and enjoyable? And surely the longer I spend in Bastiaan's company the more used I'll get to him—the more immune I'll feel. The less I'll react to him.

Yes, that was the way to look at it. Extended exposure to him would surely help to dissipate this ridiculous flaring of her senses every time he glanced at her...

It was a confidence that was comprehensively annihilated as she emerged from the villa in the swimsuit Philip had found for her. Even though it was a one-piece, and she had a matching turquoise sarong wrapped around her, she burned with self-consciousness as she felt Bastiaan's eyes go straight to her from where he and Philip waited by the pool loungers.

But it was not just her own body that she was so conscious of. Nor was it the sight of Philip, his slenderly youthful physique clad in colourful board shorts with a fashionable logo, sporting snazzy wrap-around sunglasses that was causing her breath to catch. No, it was the way her eyes had gone immediately to the powerful torso of Bastiaan…to the sculpted pecs and abs, the strong biceps and wide shoulders. His hip-hugging dark blue trunks were sober compared with Philip's. His eyes were not shaded by dark glasses, and she could feel the impact of his gaze full on, even through her own sunglasses.

She made a play of making herself comfortable on a sun lounger, and then—again self-consciously—she unknotted the sarong and let it fall to either side of her, exposing her swimsuit-clad body and bare thighs.

'The bikinis didn't tempt you?'

Bastiaan's deep voice threw the question at her and Sarah gave an inner shudder at the thought of exposing even more flesh to Bastiaan Karavalas.

'They're hopeless for swimming in,' she said lightly. She relaxed her shoulders into the cushioned lounger and lifted her face to the sun. 'Oh, this is *gorgeous*,' she said feelingly, as the heat of the sun started to penetrate her skin after the cool of the interior of the house.

'Are you a sun-worshipper?' Bastiaan asked, amusement in his voice.

'When I can be,' she answered, still lightly.

'I'm surprised you're not more tanned, given that you only work nights,' he said.

She glanced towards him uncertainly. The reason she was pale was because she'd spent the first part of the summer in the north of England, teaching, and her days here were spent in rehearsal. But all she could say—again in that same deliberately light voice—was, 'I'm working on it!' Then, in order to avoid any more awkward questions, she gave a little yawn. 'Do you know, I really *do* think I might have a little siesta? Champagne at lunchtime has made me sleepy.' She slid her dark glasses off her face—no point getting white circles around her eyes—and gave a swift smile to her hosts. 'Wake me up if I start snoring,' she warned them humorously.

'You could *never* snore!' Philip said immediately, clearly aghast at the idea of his goddess doing anything so un-goddess-like.

His cousin gave a low laugh. He found that her throwaway comment, so insouciantly self-mocking, appealed to him. But then, of course, almost everything about Mademoiselle Sabine was appealing. Everything physical, at least.

Bastiaan's eyes clouded meditatively as he let his gaze rest on her slim, lissom body. Her eyes were closed, and that allowed him to study her face at leisure, while his cousin busied himself fiddling with his iPod's playlist and fishing out earphones now that the object of his admiration was so annoyingly determined to doze off.

She really is incredibly lovely to look at.

That was the thought uppermost in Bastiaan's consciousness. She had taken off her make-up, he realised, presumably to replace it with sun cream, but it had not dimmed her beauty in the least. He found himself studying her face as she lay there with her eyes studiedly closed. Curious thoughts flitted across his mind. Now she was neither *film noir* vamp nor sixties siren.

So who is she?

The question was in his mind…but he was finding no answer.

He frowned. What did it matter what image Sabine Sablon chose to present to him? What did it matter that she appeared to have an engaging sense of humour about herself? What did it matter that as she lay there, her face bare of make-up, being blessed by the sun's rays, all he could see in her was beauty…?

All he could feel was desire…?

He settled himself on his lounger and started to make his plans. The first step, he knew, must be to remove Philip from the vicinity—and for that he had an idea forming already.

Then it would be time to turn his attentions to the woman—the beautiful, alluring woman who was lying so close to him—and bring her right up close and very, *very* personal…

CHAPTER SIX

SARAH SAT, MERMAID-LIKE, on the sun-warmed rock at the sea's edge, watching Bastiaan approach her through the water with swift, powerful strokes. He and Philip were racing each other from the shore to the pontoon moored a little way off. Philip was on the pontoon now, timing Bastiaan.

She watched Bastiaan getting closer to her and tensed. She really must grab this moment to try and speak to him. She'd been looking for an opportunity since she'd woken from her siesta and they'd all headed down to the sea. So far Philip had stuck to her like glue, delighted to introduce her to the delights of the villa's private stretch of rocky shoreline and encouraging her to swim out with him to the pontoon.

As Bastiaan's long arm touched the rock and he twisted in the water, his muscles bunched to start on his return, she leant forward.

'Bastiaan…?'

It was the first time she'd addressed him by his name directly, and it sounded odd to her. Almost…*intimate.*

Dark eyes lifted to her immediately, a question in them. 'Yes?' There was impatience in his voice, and more, too.

'Can I… can I speak with you privately…before I go?'

Dark brows tugged together, then relaxed. 'Of course,'

Bastiaan said smoothly. 'I am at your service, Sabine. But not right now.'

Was he being sarcastic, ironic, or was he just in a hurry to complete his race? Maybe the latter, for he twisted his powerful torso and plunged back into his strokes, face-down in the water, threshing with fast, vigorous movement towards the pontoon.

Sarah breathed out, feeling her tension ease a tad. Well, she'd done it, but she didn't look forward to it—didn't want *any* private conversation with Bastiaan Kara-valas on any subject whatsoever.

In her head, silent but piercing, came a single word. *Liar.*

An hour or so later, after a refreshing dip in the villa's pool, she announced that she needed to be going. She glanced at Bastiaan, hoping he would remember her request to speak to him.

Smoothly, he took her cue. 'Let me show you back to where you got changed,' he said.

He gestured with his arm towards the villa's interior and Sarah walked ahead of him, glad that the sarong around her was veiling her somewhat.

As they gained the marble-floored hall she heard him speak.

'So, what is it you want to say to me?'

His tone was neutral, yet Sarah felt that she could hear in its timbre a kind of subtext. She paused at the foot of the stairs and turned. Now that the moment had come she felt excruciatingly awkward. Should she *really* tell this forbidding man who had such dangerous power over her senses that his young cousin was hopelessly enamoured of her? Did he need telling in the first place? Wasn't it obvious that Philip was smitten? Maybe she didn't have to broach the subject at all—

But her cowardly hopes were dashed by the pointedly enquiring look in his dark eyes and the mordant expression in them.

She lifted her chin. 'It's about Philip—' she blurted out.

One eyebrow rose quizzically. She became crushingly conscious of his bared torso, tanned and muscular, and his still damp hip-hugging swim shorts. Of the way his wet hair was slicked back, accentuating the sculpted line of his cheekbones and jaw.

'I... I think it might be a good idea if he went...went somewhere else to complete his essays.' The words came out in a rush.

Something changed in Bastiaan's eyes. 'Why?' he asked bluntly.

She felt colour run into her cheeks, which were already hot from exposure to the sun. 'Isn't it obvious?' she returned. Her voice was husky, her words reluctant to come, resonating with the awkwardness she felt.

Long lashes dipped over deep-set eyes, and suddenly his expression was veiled.

'Ah, yes,' he said slowly. He inclined his head minutely towards her. 'Well, I shall see what I can do to accomplish what I can in that respect.' His eyes met hers. 'It may take a day or two, but I think I can see a way.'

His eyes were still holding hers, and his expression was still veiled. For a moment—just a fraction of a moment—she wondered whether she'd made her predicament plain to him.

Then he was speaking again. His tone of voice had changed. 'The bedroom you changed in is the third along the landing,' he informed her. 'Please make use of the en suite bathroom to shower and wash your hair if you wish.' Then he'd turned away and was heading back outside.

Sarah mounted the staircase with a sense of relief. It was done—she'd given Bastiaan Karavalas the warning about Philip that she'd needed to, and now she could leave him to it. Whatever plan he came up with to remove Philip from his villa and her vicinity, he would, she was pretty sure, do it effectively. Everything about him told her that he was a man who achieved everything he set himself to do. Of that she had no doubt whatsoever.

Bastiaan stood in the night-dark garden of his villa, contemplating the dim vista of the sea beyond. It was way gone midnight, but he was not tired. After Philip had driven Sabine back to the *ville*, openly thrilled to be let loose with his cousin's Ferrari again, even on the tame roads of the *Cap,* they'd both headed out to dine in Villefranche. It had been a relaxed meal, and their conversation mostly about cars, with Philip grilling him on competing makes and models and which was the absolute best amongst them all.

Bastiaan had been glad to indulge him, even though he knew that his aunt lived in terror of her son's eager enthusiasm for such powerful and potentially deadly machines—but anything that took Philip's mind off the siren charms of Sabine Sablon was to be welcomed.

Well, Philip would not be available for very much longer. Bastiaan was setting his plans in place.

He was refining them now as he stood in the cool night, with stars pricking out in the heavens and catching the swell of the sea with their trickles of light. Across the bay he could hear faint music, coming from one of the restaurants along the harbour. On his island in the Ionian there was no sound from any source other than nature.

A slight frown drew his brows together. Sabine had said how relaxing his remote island sounded—had she meant it? It was unlikely—nothing about Sabine Sablon indicated that her natural habitat was anything that resembled a small, unpopulated island where the nearest night-life was a fast speedboat away.

And yet today at the villa she had seemed happy to while away the afternoon swimming and sunbathing, openly enjoying the easy-going, lazy relaxation of it all. She had been admiring of the gardens and the sea views, appreciative of the peace and quiet, content to do nothing but let the time pass.

Confounding his expectations of her.

His expression changed. Until, of course, the very end of the afternoon. When she'd made her move on him... changing her allegiance from Philip to himself.

Bastiaan's mouth twisted. That request of hers to speak to him privately had been transparent in its objective. As transparent as her suggestion, made in an intimate husky voice, that their path would be smoother without young Philip to get in their way. Well, in that he would oblige her—and be glad to do so. For she was, of course, playing right into his hands with her suggestion.

The twist at his mouth turned into a smile. A smile of satisfaction.

Of anticipation.

Soon—very soon now—his cousin would be safe from her charms, and *he* would be enjoying them to the hilt.

Sarah's voice was low, throaty, as she finished the last number of her final set of the evening. It had been days since she'd spent the afternoon at Bastiaan Karavalas's villa, and Philip had been noticeable by his absence. He hadn't shown up at the next morning's rehearsal, and she'd picked up an apologetic text from him mid-morning, saying that he was working on his essays, then heading off with Bastiaan in the Ferrari. Nor had he turned up at the club in the evening—another apologetic text had said he was staying at Bastiaan's Monte Carlo apartment. Since then there'd been silence.

Sarah knew why—Bastiaan was doing his best to keep Philip preoccupied and away from her. She could only be grateful: it was, after all, what she'd asked him to do, and what she knew was best for Philip. For herself too.

And not just because it was keeping the disturbing impact of Bastiaan himself away from her—essential though that was for her fractured peace of mind. More than ever she needed to focus on her work. She could afford no distraction at all—not now. Least of all now.

Anxiety bit at her. She was hitting a wall—a wall that was holding her back, holding them all back, and making Max tear into her mercilessly.

They had reached the scene where the War Bride received news of her husband's death. Her aria in it was central to the drama—the fulcrum on which it turned. Although technically it was hard to sing, it was not that that was confounding her.

Max had been brutal in his criticism.

'Sarah—your husband is *dead*! A brief while ago you were rapturously in love—now all that has been ripped from you—*destroyed*! We *have* to hear that! We have to hear your despair, your disbelief. But I don't hear it! I don't hear it at *all*!'

However hard she'd tried, she hadn't been able to please him. Had not been able to get through that wall.

He'd made her sing an earlier aria, declaring her love, dazzled by the discovery of her headlong tumbling into its lightning-swift ecstasy, so that she could use it to contrast with her plunge into the depths of grief at its loss. But she still hadn't been able to please him.

'You've gone from love to grief in *days*—from bride to widow. We need to hear that unbearable journey in your voice. We need to hear it and believe it!'

She'd thrown up her hands in frustration. 'But *that's* what I can't do! I can't *believe* in it! People don't fall in love just like that only for it to end a few days later. It doesn't happen.'

In her head she remembered how she had wondered, on first hearing the tragic tale, what it must be like to love so swiftly, to hurt so badly. Unreal...quite unreal...

Her mind skittered onto pathways she should not go down.

Desire—yes. *Desire* at first sight—that was real. *That* she could not deny. Across her vision strolled Bastiaan Karavalas, with his night-dark eyes and his hooded, sensual regard that quickened her blood, heated her body. Desire had flamed in her the moment she had seen him, acknowledged his power over her...

But desire isn't love! It's not the same thing at all. Of course it isn't.

She recalled Max's exasperated rasp. 'Sarah, it's a *fable*! These characters are archetypes—timeless. They're not people you see in the street. Anton—talk to her—*make* her understand!' He'd called across to where the composer had been sitting at the piano.

But it didn't matter how much Anton went through the text with her, elucidated the way his music informed and reinforced the words she sang, she was still stuck. Still could not break through.

Max's tension cast a shadow over them all as he stepped up the intensity of their rehearsals, becoming ever more exacting. Time, as he constantly reminded them all, was running increasingly short, and their performance was not yet up to the standard it had to be.

Time and again he halted them in mid-song, demanding they repeat, improve, perfect their performance. Nerves were jittery, tempers fraying, and emotions were running high amongst them all.

Now, standing on the stage, finally lowering the microphone as she took a smattering of applause for Sabine's tedious repertoire, Sarah felt resentment fill her. Max was working them all hard, but he was working her harder than everyone else. She knew it was for her own good, for the good of her performance, the good of them all, but she was giving everything she had and it was still not enough. From somewhere, somehow, she had to find more.

Tiredness lapped at her now, and the lazy, sunlit afternoon she'd spent at the villa seemed a long time ago—far longer than a handful of days.

Memory played back the verdant flower-filled gardens, the graceful loggia and the vine-shaded terrace, the sparkling water of the pristine pool and the deep azure of the glorious Mediterranean beyond. The complete change of scene—to such a beautiful scene—had been a tonic in itself, a respite both from the rigours of rehearsal and the banal tiresomeness of performing her nightly cabaret. It had been relaxingly enjoyable despite the disturbing presence of Bastiaan Karavalas.

Because of it...

The realisation was disquieting—and yet it sent a little thrill through her at the same time. She tried to quell it. She felt it, she told herself sternly, only because she was standing here with the hot spotlight on her, in her skin-tight gown, just as she had been that first night when she'd felt his unknown eyes upon her.

More memories stirred. Her eyes moved briefly to the dance floor between the tables and the stage, and warmth flushed through her, as if she could still feel the firm, warm clasp of Bastiaan Karavalas's hands on her as they'd danced. Still feel the shimmering awareness of his physical closeness, the burning consciousness of her overpowering attraction to him.

An attraction she could not explain, could not cope with and certainly could not indulge .

She must not think about him—there was no point. He and Philip were both gone, and her only focus must be the festival performance ahead of her. So what was the point of the strange little pang that seemed to dart into her, twisting as it found its mark somewhere deep within? None. Bastiaan Karavalas was gone from her life and she must be glad of it.

I must!

She straightened from her slight bow, glancing out over the dining tables beyond before making ready to leave the stage.

And looked straight at Bastiaan Karavalas.

As her eyes lighted on the dark, familiar form, she felt a kick inside her that came from the same place as had that pang, only moments earlier. She hurried off the stage, aware that her heart was beating faster. *Why was he here?* Just to tell her how he'd removed Philip? Or was there another reason—a reason she would not give name to?

But Max did. 'You've lost your young, rich admirer, I see, *cherie*, and replaced him with a new one. Cultivate him—I've looked him up and he's worth a fortune!'

Sarah's jaw tightened, and she would have said something harsh, but there were tight lines of ingrained stress around Max's mouth and she could see tiredness in his face. He was working as hard as any of them—*harder*. And if she was working late nights, then so was he.

'I don't know what he's doing here,' she replied with a shrug.

Max gave his familiar waspish smile. 'Oh, come now—do you need it spelled out?'

She gave another shrug, not bothering to respond. Bastiaan thought she was Sabine—not Sarah. For a moment a thought struck her. Should she introduce Max to Bastiaan—see if he couldn't persuade him to sponsor their production? But that would mean explaining that she was Sarah, not Sabine—and all her objections to that disclosure still held. She just could not afford to let her role as Sabine contaminate her identity as an opera singer, compromise her future reputation.

'Well?' Max prompted. 'Off you go to him—it's you he's here to see, that's obvious. Like I say, be nice to him.' His eyes were veiled for a moment. 'Just don't be late for rehearsal tomorrow, OK?'

'Oh, for God's sake!' she snapped at his implication.

Whether he was joking or not, she didn't care. She was too tired to care. But if Bastiaan had taken the trouble to turn up here, she had better return the courtesy.

Max was now on his phone to Anton and she left him to it, making her way through to the front of house. Her emotions were mixed. She felt strange—both a sense of reluctance and a stirring of her blood. They warred within her.

As she approached Bastiaan's table he got to his feet. He seemed taller than ever—and suddenly more forbidding, it seemed to her, his lean body sheathed in a custom-made tuxedo. Was it because of the momentary tightening of his features? The veiling of his dark eyes? Whatever it was, she felt a shimmer go through her. Not just of an awareness that was quickening her pulse, but of its opposite as well—a kind of instinctual reserve.

She would keep this as brief as possible—it was the only sensible thing to do.

'M'sieu Karavalas,' she greeted him, with only the slightest smile at her mouth, a nod of her head.

An eyebrow lifted as he held a chair for her. 'Bastiaan, surely?' he murmured. 'Have we not advanced that far, *mademoiselle*?'

There was light mockery in his invitation to use his given name while reserving more formality for his own addressing of her. A mockery that played upon what he knew—*must* know—about her receptiveness to his masculine potency, his own appreciation of her charms...

She made no reply, merely gave a flickering social smile as she sat down while he resumed his seat.

'So, what have you done with Philip?' she asked. She kept her tone light, but this was, after all, the only reason that his cousin was here.

She saw a dark flickering cross his eyes. 'I've just returned from driving him to Paris,' he answered.

Sarah's eyes widened in surprise. *'Paris?'*

Bastiaan lifted his cognac glass. 'Yes,' he said smoothly. 'He's meeting his mother there, and visiting family friends.'

'So, how long will he be away?' she asked. She sought to keep her tone light, still, but it was hard—every nerve-ending was quivering with the overpowering impact this man had on her.

'Long enough.'

There was a hint of a drawl in his voice and it made her stare at him. She tried to quash the sudden flare in her veins as his veiled, unreadable gaze rested on her. A gaze that suddenly seared its message into her.

'And now, having disposed of the problem of my young cousin,' Bastiaan was saying, his voice dragging across her nerve-endings and making them flare with a kind of internal shiver that she felt in every cell of her body, 'we can move on to a far more interesting subject.'

Something in his face changed and he shifted slightly, relaxing back, it seemed to her, and lifting his cognac glass, his long, strong fingers curved around the bowl. His eyes rested on her with an open expression in them that was pinioning her where she sat.

She could not answer him. Could only sit, lips slightly parted, feeling her heart start to race. The rest of the room had disappeared. The rest of the *world* had disappeared. There was only her, sitting there, her body shimmering with a sensual awareness of what this man could do to her…

And then a smile flashed suddenly across his features. 'Which is, Mademoiselle Sabine, the subject of where we should dine tonight.' He paused, a light in his eyes. 'Last time you disdained my suggestion of Le Tombleur. But, tell me, does it meet with your approval tonight?'

'Tonight?' Her echo of his question was hollow, hiding the shock beneath. Hiding the sudden, overwhelming spike of adrenaline that had shot into her veins as she'd realised what he intended.

Amusement played about his well-shaped mouth. 'Do we need to wait any longer, Sabine?'

All pretence at formality was gone now. All pretence at denial of what had flared between them from the very first. There was only one reality now—coursing through her veins, pounding in her heart, sheering across her skin, quickening in her core.

This man—this man alone—who had walked into her life when she'd least expected it, least wanted it, could least afford to acknowledge it. This man who could set her pulse racing…in whose dark, disturbing presence her body seemed to come alive.

Temptation overwhelmed her. The temptation to say *Yes! Yes!* to everything he was offering. Simply to let his hand reach across the table to hers, to let him raise her to her feet, lead her from here and take her where he wanted…

To a physical intimacy, a sensual intensity, an embarkation into realms of sensuous possibility that she had never encountered before.

And why not? *Why not?* She was free, an adult and independent woman. Her emotional ties to Andrew, such as they'd been, were long gone. She was no ingénue—she knew what was being offered to her…knew it was something that would never come again in her life. For there could never be another man who would affect her the way this man could.

She could go with him as Sabine—the woman he took her to be—as assured as he in the world that this dark, powerful man moved in. A world of physical affairs that sated the body but left the heart untouched. As Sabine she could indulge in such an affair, could drink it to the full, like a glass of heady champagne that would intoxicate the blood but leave her clear-headed the following day.

The temptation was like an overpowering lure, dominating her senses, her consciousness. Then, like cold water douching down upon her, she surfaced from it.

She was not Sabine.

She was Sarah. Sarah Fareham. Who had striven all her life towards the moment that was so close now—the moment when she would walk out on stage and give the performance upon which her future life would depend.

I can't go with him—I can't.

She felt her head give a slow, heavy shake.

'*C'est impossible.*'

The words fell from her lips and her eyes were veiled beneath the ludicrously over-long false eyelashes.

His face stilled. 'Why?'

A single word. But she did not answer. Could not. Dared not. She was on a knife's edge—if she did not go now, right now, she would sever her resolve. Give in to the temptation that was lapping at her like water on a rising tide.

She shook her head again, drained her coffee cup with a hand that was almost shaking. She got to her feet. Cast one more look at him. One last look.

The man is right—the time is wrong.

'Goodnight, *m'sieu*,' she said, and dipped her head and walked away. Heading to the door beside the low stage, moving back towards her dressing room.

Behind her, Bastiaan watched her go. Then, slowly, he reached for his cognac. Emotion swelled within him but he did not know what it was. Anger? Was that it? Anger that she had defied his will for her?

Or anger that she had denied what burned between them like a hot, fierce flame?

I want her—and she denies me my desire...

Or was it incomprehension?

He did not know, could not tell—knew only that as his fingers clenched around the bowl of his cognac glass he needed the shot of brandy more than he needed air to breathe. In one mouthful he had drained it, and then, his expression changing, he pushed to his feet and left the club. Purpose was in every stride.

CHAPTER SEVEN

SARAH'S FINGERS FUMBLED with the false eyelashes as she peeled them off her eyelids, then with shaky hands wiped the caking foundation off her face, not bothering to tackle her dark eye make-up. She felt as if she was shaking on the inside, her mind shot to pieces. She'd made herself walk away from him, but it hadn't seemed to help.

All she could see in her vision was Bastiaan Karavalas, saying in his low, deep voice, 'Do we need to wait any longer?'

Emotion speared in her—a mix of panic and longing, confusion and torment. An overwhelming urge to get away as swiftly as possible, to reach the safe haven of her room in the *pension*, surged through her. She wouldn't wait to change. She simply grabbed her day clothes, stuffing them into a plastic bag and seizing up her purse, then headed for the rear exit of the club. Max was long gone and she was glad.

She stepped out into the cool night air of the little road that ran behind the club—and stopped dead.

Bastiaan's Ferrari blocked the roadway and he was propped against it, arms folded. Wordlessly he opened the passenger door.

'Give me one reason,' he said to her, 'why you will not dine with me.'

His voice was low, intense. His eyes held hers in the dim light and would not release them. She felt her mouth open to speak—but no words came out. In her head was a tumult, a jumble of thoughts and emotions and confusion.

He spoke for her. 'You can't, can you? Because this has been waiting to happen since I first set eyes on you.'

The intensity was still in his voice, in his gaze that would not let her go.

She was still trying to find the words she had to find, marshal the thoughts she had to think, but it was impossible. Impossible to do anything but succumb. Succumb to the emotions that were coursing through her. Impelling her forward. She felt one last frail, hopeless thought fleeting through her tumbling mind.

I tried—I tried to stop this happening. Tried to deny it, tried to prevent it. But I can't—I can't deny this any longer. I can't.

It was all she could manage. Then, as she sank into the low, plush seat of the powerful, sleek car, she felt herself give in entirely, completely, to what was happening. Succumbing to the temptation that was the darkly devastating man closing the door on her, lowering himself in beside her, reaching to the ignition to fire the powerful engine and moving off into the night with her at his side.

Taking her where he wanted to take her.

Where she wanted to go.

She stole a sideways look at him. Their gazes clashed. She looked away again, out over the pavements and the buildings along the roadway. She knew what she was doing—and why. Knew with every pulse of blood in her veins and in the jittering of her nerves, which were humming as if electricity were pouring through her— a charge that was coming out of the very atmosphere itself.

Enclosed as she was, only a few inches away from the long, lean body of the man next to her, she felt the low, throaty vibration of the ultra-powerful engine of the car—was aware of the sleek, luxurious interior, of the whole seductive ambience of sitting beside him.

She knew that her body was outlined by her stage dress, that her image was that of a woman in the full glamour of her beauty. And that the man beside her, clad in his hand-made tuxedo, with the glint of gold of his watch, the cufflinks in his pristine cuffs, the heady, spiced scent of his aromatic aftershave, had contrived to make the situation headily seductive.

She gave herself to it. It was too late now for anything else. Far too late.

'Where are we going?' she asked. Her voice was low-pitched and she could not quite look at him. Could not quite believe that she was doing what she was doing.

He glanced at her, with half a smile curving his sensual lips. 'I attempted once before to take you to Le Tombleur—perhaps this time you will acquiesce?'

Had there been a huskiness discernible in his voice as he'd said the word 'acquiesce'? She couldn't be sure—could only be sure that there was some kind of voltage charging her body right now, one she had never experienced before. Somewhere inside her, disappearing fast, there was a voice of protest—but it was getting feebler with every moment she was here with Bastiaan, burningly conscious of his powerful masculine presence, of the effect he had on her that she could not subdue.

Beyond the confines of the car the world was passing by. But it was far, far away from her now. Everything was far, far away.

It did not take long to get to the restaurant, set in the foothills of the Alpes-Maritimes above the crowded coastline of the Riviera. She was helped from the car, ushered inside by the tall, commanding man at her side. The *maître d'* was hurrying forward, all attention, to show them to a table out on the terrace, looking down on where the lights of the Riviera glittered like a necklace of jewels.

She eased into her seat, ultra-aware of the tightness of her gown, the voluptuousness of her figure. Her eyes went yet again to the man sitting opposite her, studying his menu. What was it about him that he could affect her the way he did? Why was she so overwhelmed by him? Why had she been so fatally tempted to succumb to what she knew she should not be doing? To dine here with him *à deux*…

And what would happen afterwards…?

Her mind skittered away. She did not think—did not dare think. Dared only to go on sitting there, occupying herself by opening the menu, glancing blindly down at the complex listings. Was she hungry? She could not tell. Could tell only that her heart rate was raised, that her skin was flushed with heat…that her eyes wanted only to go on resting on the man opposite her.

'So, what would you like to eat?'

Bastiaan's voice interrupted her hopeless thoughts and she was glad. She made herself give a slight smile. 'Something light,' she said. 'In this dress anything else is impossible!'

It had been a mistake to make such a remark, however lightly it had been said. It drew a wash of scrutiny from the dark, long-lashed eyes. She felt her colour heighten and had to fight it down by studying the menu again. She found a dish that seemed to fit the bill—scallops in a saffron sauce—and relayed it to Bastiaan. He too chose fish, but a more robust grilled monkfish, and then there followed the business of selecting wine to go with it.

Choices made, he sat back, his eyes resting on her at his leisure. Satisfaction soared through him. Her yielding had not surprised him in the least, but it had gratified him. Now, at last, he had her to himself.

His sensation of satisfaction, of the rightness of it all, increased. Yes, seducing her would, as he had always planned, achieve his goal of quashing any ambitions she might have had concerning his cousin, but as they sat there on the secluded terrace, with the night all around them, somehow his young cousin seemed very…irrelevant.

'So,' he began, 'tell me about yourself, Sabine?' It was an innocuous question—and a predictable one—but he could see a veil flicker over her eyes.

'Myself?' she echoed. 'What is there to tell that is not evident? I am a singer—what else?' She sounded flippant, unconcerned. Studiedly so.

'What part of France do you come from?' Another innocuous polite enquiry—nothing more than that. Yet once again he saw that flicker.

'Normandy,' she answered. 'A little place not far from Rouen.' Her mother's birthplace, it was the part of France she knew best, and therefore it seemed the safest answer to give.

'And have you always wanted to be a singer?'

The lift of a shoulder came again. 'One uses the talents one is given,' she replied. It was as unrevealing an answer as she could think to give.

Bastiaan's eyes narrowed minutely.

Sarah saw the narrowing. Could he tell she was being as evasive as she could? She was glad that the sommelier arrived at that moment, diverting Bastiaan. But as the man departed, and Bastiaan lifted his wine glass, she felt his dark eyes upon her again.

'To our time together,' he said, and smiled.

She made herself lift her own glass and meet his eyes. It was like drowning in dark velvet. She felt her blood quicken, her breath catch. A sense of unreality over-whelmed her—and yet this was real...vividly, pulsingly real. She was sitting here, so close to the man who could set her senses on fire with a single glance.

Oh, this was ridiculous. To be so...so overcome by this man. She *had* to claw back her composure. If she were going to take refuge in being Sabine then she must be as poised and cool as that protection provided. With an inner breath she set down her glass and then let her glance sweep out across the glittering vista far below.

'If the food is as exceptional as the location, I can un-derstand why this place has such a reputation,' she mur-mured. It seemed a safe thing to say—and safe things were what she was clutching at.

'I hope both please you,' he replied.

His lashes dipped over his eyes. It was clear to him that she did not wish to talk about herself, but her very evasiveness told him what he wanted to know—that she was, indeed, a woman who presented to the world what she chose to present. For himself, he did not care. Sabine Sablon would not, after all, be staying long in his life.

'Does this have a Michelin star yet?' Sarah asked, bringing her gaze back to him. Another safe thing to ask.

'One. But a second is being targeted,' he answered.

'What makes the difference, I wonder?' Sarah asked. Safe again...

He lifted his wine glass. Talking about Michelin stars was perfectly acceptable as a topic. It lasted them until their food arrived, and then they moved on to the subject of the Côte d'Azur itself—how it had changed and developed, what its charms and attractions were.

It was Bastiaan who talked most, and he soon became aware that Sabine was adept at asking questions of him, keeping the conversation flowing.

And all the time, like a deep, powerful current in a river on whose surface aimless ripples were circling, another conversation was taking place. One that was wordless, silent, yet gaining strength with every politely interested smile, every nod, every lift of a fork, of a glass, every glance, every low laugh, every gesture of the hand, every shift in body position…every breath taken.

It was a conversation that could lead to only one end… take them to only one destination.

The place he had determined she should go. The place she could no longer resist him taking her to.

Sarah climbed back into the car and Bastiaan lowered his tall frame into the driving seat beside her. Immediately the space confining them shrank. Her mind was in a daze. Wine hummed in her veins—softening her body so that it seemed to mould to the contours of the leather seat. She heard the throaty growl of the engine and the powerful car moved forward, pressing her further into her seat. She could feel the low throb of her beating heart, the flush of heat in her skin.

But it was in *Sabine's* breast that her heart was beating. It was Sabine whose senses were dominated by the presence of this magnetic, compelling man beside her. Sabine who was free to do what she was doing now—ignoring everything in the world except this man, this night…

Sabine, alluring, sensual and sophisticated, could yield to the overpowering temptation that was Bastiaan Karavalas and all that he promised. Sabine had led her to this place, this time, this moment—a moment that Sabine would wish to come…would choose to be in…

This is going to happen. It is going to happen and I am not going to stop it. I want it to happen.

She did. It might be rash, it might be foolish, it might be the thing she had least expected would happen during this summer, but she *was* going to go with Bastiaan Karavalas.

This night.

And as for tomorrow…

She would deal with that then. Not now.

Now there was only her, and him, and being taken to where he was taking her. Wordless. Voiceless. Irreversible.

He took her to his apartment in Monte Carlo.

It was as unlike the villa on Cap Pierre as she could imagine. In a modern high-rise block, its decor sleek and contemporary. She stood by the huge-paned glass windows, gazing out over the marina far below, seeing the glittering lights of the city scintillating like diamonds, feeling the rich sensuality of her body, the tremor in her limbs.

Waiting…

Waiting for the man standing behind her, his presence, his scent overpowering her. Waiting for him to make his move…to take her into his arms…his embrace…his bed.

She heard him murmur something, felt the warmth of his breath on the nape of her neck, the drift of his hands around her shoulders, so light, feather-light, and yet with a silken power that made her breath catch, her lips part as the tremor in her limbs intensified. She felt the powerful touch of his palms glide down her bare arms, fasten on her wrists, and with a movement as subtle as it was irresistible, she felt him turn her towards him.

She lifted her face to him, lips parted, eyes deep and lustrous. She was so close she could feel the strength and heat of his body, feel the dark intensity of his gaze, of those eyes holding hers, conveying to her all that she knew was in her own eyes as well.

He smiled. A slow pull of his mouth. As if he knew what she was feeling, as if he were colluding with the strange, strong, heavy pulse of the blood in her veins. His eyes worked over her face leisurely, taking in every contour, every curve of her features.

'You are so beautiful…' It was a husky statement. 'So very beautiful…'

For one long, timeless moment his eyes poured into hers as they stood there, face to face, and then his hands closed around her slender, pliant waist and drew her to him slowly, very slowly, as if each increase in the pressure of his hands drawing her to him was almost against his will and yet as impossible for him to resist as it was for her to resist.

Nor did she want to—she wanted only to feel his mouth making its slow descent to hers, wanted him to fuse his lips to hers, to take her mouth, possess it, mould it to his, open it to his…

And when he did her eyes could only close, her throat could only sigh with a low sound of absolute pleasure, as with skill and sensual slowness his mouth found hers to take it and taste it. Somewhere inside her, very dimly, she could feel heat pooling. Her heart seemed to cease its beating as she felt the rich, sensual glide of his lips on hers, his mouth opening hers to him, his kiss deepening.

His hold on her waist tightened, strengthened, as the shift of his stance changed so that she was being cradled against him, and with a little shimmer of shocked response she felt how aroused he was.

His arousal fired hers so that her blood surged, her breath caught, the melding of her mouth to his quickened and deepened. Her hands lifted, closing around the strong breadth of his back, splaying against the smooth fabric of his dinner jacket. She felt her breasts crush against the wall of his chest. She heard his low growl, felt his palms pull her tighter against him.

Excitement flared through her. Every cell in her body was alive, sensitive, eager for more of what she was already experiencing. And then, as if on a jerking impulse, he swept her body into his arms, as if she were nothing more than a feather. He was striding away with her, his mouth still fastened upon hers, and the world beyond whirled as he deposited her heavily upon the cold satin surface of a wide, soft bed and came down beside her.

His mouth continued devouring hers, and one thigh was thrown over her as a kind of glory filled her. Desire, open and searing, flooded her. She felt her breasts tighten and tingle and threw back her head to lift them more. Another low growl broke from him, and then her arms were being lifted over her head and pinioned with one hand while his palm closed possessively over the sweet, straining mound of her breast. She gasped with pleasure, groaning, her head moving restlessly from side to side, her mouth, freed from his, abandoned and questing.

Was this her? Could it be her? Lying like this, flaming with a desire that was consuming her, possessing her, shameless and wanton?

His heavy thigh lay between hers and she felt her hips writhe against it, wanting more and yet more of the sensations that were being loosened within her. Did she speak? And if she did, what did she say? She did not know—knew only that she must implore him to bestow upon her what she was craving, yearning for, more and more and more...

Never had she felt like this, so deeply, wildly aroused. As if she were burning with a flame that she had never known.

He smiled down at her. 'I think it is time, *cherie*, that we discarded these unnecessary clothes...'

He jack-knifed to his feet, making good on his words. She could not move—could only gaze at him in the dim light as he swiftly, carelessly, disposed of what he was wearing. And then his hard, lean body was lowering down beside her, his weight indenting the mattress. She felt his nakedness like a brand, and suddenly, out of nowhere, her cheeks were flaring, her eyelids veiling him from her sight.

He gave a low, amused laugh. 'Shy?' he murmured. 'At *this* point?'

She couldn't answer him—could only let her eyes flutter open. And for an instant—just an instant—she thought she saw in the dim light a question suddenly forming in his...

But then it was gone. In its place a look of deep, sensual appreciation.

'You are beautiful indeed, *cherie*, as you are...but I want to see your beauty *au naturel.*'

A hand lifted to her shoulders, easing the straps away first on one side, then the other. With a kind of sensual delicacy he peeled her gown down her body to her waist, letting his gaze wander over her in that lazy, leisurely fashion that made the heat pool in her body. Then he tugged it further still, over her hips, taking with it her panties, easing the material down her thighs to free her legs. Now only her stockings remained, and with a sense of shock she realised what it was he was seeing of her...

'Shall I make love to you like this?' he asked, and there was still that lazy, sensual amusement in his voice.

She answered him. No, she would *not* be arrayed like that for him.

With swift decision she sat up, peeling her stockings from her body, tossing them aside with the belt that fastened them. Her hair was tumbling now, free and lush over her breasts, as she sat looking at him where he lay back on the coverlet, blatant in his own nakedness. She gazed down at him, pushing back her hair with one hand. He was waiting—assured, aroused, confident—conspiring with her to make the next move, and she was glad to do so.

Draping her long hair around one shoulder, she leant forward. Her breasts almost grazed his bared chest as she planted her hands either side of him.

'Where shall I start?' she heard herself murmur, with the same warm, aroused amusement in her voice as his had held.

An answering amusement glittered in his dark eyes. 'Take me,' he said, and the amusement was there in his deep voice too. 'I am yours.'

She gave a low, brief laugh, and then her mouth was gliding, skimming over the steel-hard contours of his chest. Lightly...arousingly.

For interminable moments he endured it, his arousal mounting unbearably, as she deliberately teased and tempted him. And then, with an explosive edge, he knew he could take it no longer. He hauled her down on him—fully on him—and the satisfaction he knew as he heard her gasp was all he needed to hear. He rolled her over beneath him, and with a thrust of his thigh parted her.

His mouth found hers—claiming and clinging, feasting and tasting. Urgency filled him. He wanted her *now*.

Almost he succumbed to the overwhelming urge to possess her as she was. But that would be madness—insanity. With a groan of self-control he freed himself, flung out an arm sideways and reached into the bedside drawer.

She was seeking to draw him back, folding her hands around him, murmuring, and he could hear the breathless moans in her throat as she sought him.

'Wait—a moment only...'

It was almost impossible for him to speak. His arousal was absolute...his body was in meltdown. He *had* to have her—he *had* to possess her. Had to complete what he had wanted to do from the very first moment of laying eyes upon her lush, alluring body, since he had first felt the response in those emerald eyes...

Oh, she might be as mercenary as he feared, as manipulative as he suspected, but none of that mattered. Only this moment mattered—this urgency, this absolute overriding desire for her that was possessing him.

A moment later he was ready, and triumph surged through him. At last he could take what he wanted—possess *her*, this woman who would belong to no one else but him...

She was drawing him down on her, her thighs enclosing his as her body opened to him, and with a relief that flooded through him he fused his body deep, deep within her own...

Immediately, like a firestorm, sensation exploded within him and he was swept away on burning flames that consumed him in a furnace of pleasure. For an instant so brief he was scarcely conscious of it, he felt dismay that he had not waited for her. But then, with a reeling sense of amazed wonder, he realised that she had come with him into the burning flames...that she was clinging to him and crying out even as he was, and that their bodies were wreathed in a mutual consummation that was going on and on and on...

Never before had he experienced such a consummation. Never in all his wide and varied experience had the intensity been like this. It was as if his whole mind and body and being had ignited into one incredible, endless sensation—as if their bodies were melding together, fusing like molten metal into each other.

When did it change? When it did it start to ebb, to take him back down to the plane of reality, of consciousness? He didn't know—couldn't say. Could only feel his body shaking as it returned slowly, throbbingly, to earth. His lungs were seizing and he could feel his heart still pounding, hear his voice shaking as he lifted himself slightly from her, aware that his full weight was crushing her.

He said something, but he did not know what.

She was looking at him—gazing up with an expression in her eyes that mirrored what he knew was in his own. A kind of shock. She was stunned by what had happened.

For one long moment they seemed just to stare at each other disbelievingly. Then, with a ragged intake of breath, Bastiaan managed to smile. Nothing more than that. And he saw her eyes flutter closed, as if he had released her. A huge lassitude swept over him, and with a kind of sigh he lowered himself again, settling her sideways against him, pulling her into his warm, exhausted body.

Holding her so close against him was wonderful, reassuring, and all that he wanted. His hands spread across her silken flanks, securing her against him, and he heard her give a little sigh of relaxation, felt one of her hands close over his, winding her fingers into his, and then, with a final settling of her body, she was still, her breathing quietening as she slipped into sleep.

In his final moment of remaining consciousness Bastiaan reached back to haul the coverlet over them both and then, when they were cocooned beneath, he wrapped his arm around her once more and gave himself to sleep, exhausted, replete, and in that moment possessing all that he wanted to possess on earth.

Something woke her—she wasn't sure what. Whatever it was, it had roused her from the deep slumber into which she'd fallen...a slumber deeper and sweeter than she had ever known.

'Good morning.'

Bastiaan, clad in a towelling robe, was looking down at her. His dark eyes were drinking her in. She did not answer. Could not. Could only hear in her head the words that had forced their way in.

What have I done? Oh, God, what have I done?

But she didn't need to ask—the evidence was in her naked body, in her lying in the bed of Bastiaan Karavalas.

Memory burned like a meteor, scorching through the sky. Awareness made her jack-knife. 'Oh, God—what time is it?' She stared at him, horror-struck.

His face pulled into a frown. 'Of what significance is that?' he demanded.

But she did not answer him—did not do anything except leap from the bed, not caring that she was naked. Not caring about anything except snatching, from wherever she could see them, her clothes from the previous night.

Dismay and horror convulsed her. She pushed into the bathroom, caught sight of herself in the huge mirror, and gave a gasping groan. Three minutes later she stumbled out—looking ludicrous, she knew, with her tangled hair tumbling over her shoulders, her evening dress from the night before crumpled and idiotic on her. But she didn't care—couldn't care. Couldn't afford to care.

She might be wearing Sabine's clothes, left over from the night before, but Sabine herself was gone. Sarah was back—and she was panicking as she had never panicked before.

'What the *hell*…?' Bastiaan was staring at her.

'I have to go.'

'*What?* Don't be absurd.'

She ignored him. Pushed right past him out into the reception room and stared desperately around, looking for her bag. Dimly she remembered that her day clothes were in a plastic bag that must, she thought urgently, still be in the footwell of Bastiaan's car. But there was no time for that now. No time for anything except to get out of here and find a bus stop…

Oh, God, it will take for ever to get back. I'll be late—so late. Max will be furious!

She felt her arm caught, her body swung round. 'Sabine—what is going on? Why are you running away?'

She stared, eyes blank with incomprehension. 'I have to go,' she said again.

For a second there was rejection in his eyes, and then, as if making a decision, he let her go.

'I'll call a cab—' he said.

'No!'

He ignored her, crossed to a phone set by the front door, spoke swiftly to someone she assumed was the concierge. Then he hung up, turned to look at her.

'I don't know what is going on, or why. But if you insist on leaving I cannot stop you. So—go.' His voice was harsh, uncomprehending. His expression blank.

For one timeless moment she was paralysed. Could

only stare at him. Could only feel as if an explosion was taking place inside her, detonating down every nerve, along every vein.

'Bastiaan, I—'

But she could not speak. There was nothing to say. She was not Sabine. She was Sarah. And she had no place here…no place at all…

He opened the front door for her and she stumbled through.

As she ran for the elevator she heard the door slam behind her. Reverberating through every stricken cell in her body.

CHAPTER EIGHT

BASTIAAN WAS DRIVING. Driving as though he were being chased by the hounds of hell. The road snaked up, high into the Alpes-Maritimes, way beyond the last outpost of the Riviera and out into the hills, where bare rock warred with the azure skies. Further on and further up he drove, with the engine of the car roaring into the silence all around him.

At the top of the pass he skidded to the side, sending a scree of stones tumbling down into the crevasse below. He cut the engine but the silence brought no peace. His hands clenched over the steering wheel.

Why had she run from him? *Why?* What had put that look of absolute panic on her face?

Memory seared across his synapses. What had flamed between them had been as overwhelming for her as it had been for him—he knew that. Knew it with every male instinct he possessed. That conflagration of passion had set them both alight—*both* of them.

It has never been like that for me before. Never.

And she had gazed at him with shock in her eyes, with disbelief.

Had she fled because of what had happened between them? Had it shocked her as it had shocked him? So that she could not handle it, could not cope with it?

*Something is happening, Sabine, between us—
something that is not in your game plan. Nor in mine.*

He stared out over the wide ravine, an empty space
into which a single turn of the wheel would send his car—
himself—hurtling. He tried to make himself think about
Philip, about why he had come here to rescue him from
Sabine Sablon, but he could not. It seemed...irrelevant.
Unimportant.

There was only one imperative now.

He reached for the ignition, fired the engine. Nosed
the car around and headed back down to the coast with
only one thought in his head, driving him on.

Max lifted his hand to halt her. 'Take it again,' he said.
His voice was controlled, but barely masking his exasperation.

Sarah felt her fingers clench. Her throat was tight,
and her shoulders and her lungs. In fact every muscle in
her body felt rigid. It was hopeless—totally, absolutely
hopeless. All around her there was a tension that was
palpable. Everyone present was generating it, feeling it.
She most of all.

When she'd arrived at rehearsal, horrendously late,
Max had turned his head to her and levelled her with a
look that might have killed her, like a basilisk's. And then
it had gone from bad to worse...to impossible.

Her voice had gone. It was as simple and as brutal as
that. It didn't matter that Max wasn't even attempting to
get her to sing the aria—she could sing nothing. Nothing at all.

But it was not the mortification of arriving so late to
rehearsal, her breathless arrival and hectic heartbeat that
were making it impossible for her to sing. It was because

inside her head an explosion had taken place, wiping out everything that had once been in it.

Replacing it only with searing white-hot memory.

Her night with Bastiaan.

It filled her head, overwhelming her, consuming her consciousness, searing in her bloodstream—every touch, every caress, every kiss. Impossible to banish. Impossible for anything else to exist for her.

'Sarah!' Max's voice was sharp, edged with anger now.

She felt another explosion within her. 'I *can't.*' The cry broke from her. 'I just can't! It isn't there—I'm sorry… I'm *sorry!*'

'What the hell use is sorry?' he yelled, his control clearly snapping.

And suddenly it was all too much. Just too much. Her late arrival and the collapse of her voice were simply the final straw.

Alain, her tenor, stepped forward, put a protective arm around her shoulder. 'Lay off her, Max!' he snapped.

'And lay off the rest of us too!' called someone else.

'Max, we're exhausted. We *have* to have a break.'

The protests were mounting, the grumbling turning into revolt. For a dangerous moment Max looked as if he wanted to yell at them all, then abruptly he dropped his head.

'OK,' he said. 'Break, everyone. Half an hour. Get outside. Fresh air.'

The easing of the fractured tension was palpable and the company started to disperse, talking in low, relieved voices.

Alain's hand dropped from Sarah's shoulder. 'Deep breaths,' he said kindly, and wandered off to join the general exodus outdoors.

But Sarah couldn't move. She felt nailed to the floor. She shut her eyes in dumb, agonised misery.

Dear God, hadn't she said she must have no distractions. *None*. And then last night—!

What have I done? Oh, what have I done!

It was the same helpless, useless cry she'd given as she'd stood in Bastiaan's apartment naked, fresh from his bed.

Anguish filled her—and misery.

Then, suddenly, she felt her hands being taken.

'Sarah, look at me,' said Max.

His voice had changed—his whole demeanour had changed. Slowly, warily, she opened her eyes. His expression was sympathetic. Tired lines were etched around his eyes.

'I'm sorry,' he said. 'We're all burning out and I'm taking it out on you—and you don't deserve it.'

'I'm so sorry for arriving late,' she replied. 'And for being so useless today.'

But Max squeezed her hands. 'You need a break,' he said. 'And more than just half an hour.'

He seemed to pause, searching her strained expression, then he nodded and went on.

'Should I blame myself?' he asked. There was faint wry humour in his dry voice. 'Wasn't I the one who told you not to be late this morning? Knowing who'd turned up to see you? No, no, *cherie*—say nothing. Whatever has happened, it's still going on in your head. So...'

He took a breath, looking at her intently.

'What I want you to do is...go. Go. Whatever it takes—do it. I don't want to see you again this week. Take a complete break—whether that's to sob into your pillow or... Well, whatever! If this rich cousin of Philip is good for you, or bad, the point is that *he's* in your head and your work is not.' His voice changed. 'Even without last night you've hit the wall, and I can't force you through it. So you must rest, and then—well, we shall see what we shall see.'

He pressed her hands again, his gaze intent.

'Have faith, Sarah—have faith in yourself, in what you can accomplish. You are so nearly there! I would not waste my genius on you otherwise,' he finished, with his familiar waspish humour.

He stepped back, patting her hands before relinquishing them.

'So—go. Take off. Do anything but sing. Not even Sabine's dire ditties. I'll sort it with Raymond—somehow.'

He dropped a light kiss on her forehead.

'*Go!*' he said.

And Sarah went.

Bastiaan nosed the car carefully down the narrowing street towards the harbour. She was here somewhere—she had to be. He didn't know where her *pension* was, but there were a limited number, and if necessary he would check them all out. Then there was the nightclub as well—someone there at this time of day would know where she might be.

I have to find her.

That was the imperative driving him. Conscious thought was not operating strongly in him right now, but he didn't care. Didn't care that a voice inside his head was telling him that there was no reason to seek her out like this. One night with her had been enough to achieve his ends—so why was he searching for her?

He did not answer—refused to answer. Only continued driving, turning into the area that fronted the harbour, face set, eyes scanning around as if he might suddenly spot her.

And she was there.

He felt his blood leap, his breath catch.

She was by the water's edge, seated on a mooring bollard, staring out to sea. He felt emotions surge through him—triumph shot through with relief. He stopped the car, not caring whether it was in a parking zone or not. Got out. Strode up to her. Placed a hand on her shoulder.

'Sabine…' His voice was rich with satisfaction. With possession.

Beneath his hand he felt her whole body jump. Her head snaked around, eyes widening in shock.

'Oh, God…' she said faintly.

He smiled. 'You did not truly believe I would let you go, did you?' he said. He looked down at her. Frowned suddenly. 'You have been crying,' he said.

There was disbelief in his voice. Sabine? Weeping? He felt the thoughts in his head rearrange themselves. Felt a new one intrude.

'What has made you cry?' he demanded. It was not *him*—impossible that it should be him.

She shook her head. 'It's just…complicated,' she said.

Bastiaan found himself hunkering down beside her, hands resting loosely between his bunched thighs, face on a level with hers. His expression was strange. His emotions stranger. The Sabine who sat here, her face tear-stained, was someone new—someone he had never seen before.

The surge of possessiveness that had triumphed inside him a moment ago on finding her was changing into something he did not recognise. But it was moving within him. Slowly but powerfully. Making him face this new emotion evolving within him.

'No,' he contradicted, and there was something in his voice that had not been there before. 'It is very simple.' He looked at her, his eyes holding hers. 'After last night, how could it be anything else?'

His gaze became a caress and his hand reached out softly to brush away a tendril of tangled hair that had escaped from its rough confines in a bunched pleat at the back of her head. He wanted to undo the clasp, see her glorious blond mane tumble around her shoulders. Although what she was wearing displeased him, for it seemed to be a shapeless tee shirt and a pair of equally shapeless cotton trousers. And her face was blotchy, her eyes strained.

Yet as he spoke, as his hand gently brushed the tendril from her face, he saw her expression change. Saw the strain ebb from her eyes, her blotched skin re-colour.

'I don't know why you ran from me,' he heard himself say, 'and I will not ask. But…' His hand now cupped her chin, feeling the warmth of her skin beneath his fingertips. 'This I *will* ask.'

His eyes rested on hers—his eyes that had burned their way into hers in the throes of exquisite passion. But now they were simply filled with a single question. The only one that filled his head, his consciousness.

'Will you come with me now? And whatever complications there are will you leave them aside?'

Something shifted in her eyes, in the very depths of them. They were green—as green as emeralds. Memory came to him. He remembered how he'd wanted to drape her in emeralds. It seemed odd to him just then. Irrelevant. Unimportant. Only one thing was important now.

The answer she was giving him with her beautiful, emerald-green eyes, which were softening even as he held them. Softening and lightening and filling with an expression that told him all he needed to know.

He smiled again. Not in triumph this time, nor in possession. Just smiled warmly upon her.

'Good,' he said. Then he drew her to her feet. His smile deepened. 'Let's go.'

He led her to his car and helped her in.

The rest of this week, thought Sarah.

The wealth of time seemed like largesse of immense proportions. The panic that had been in her breast and the tension that had bound her lungs with iron, her throat with barbed wire, were gone. Just...*gone*. They had fallen from her as she had risen to her feet, had her hand taken by Bastiaan. Her feet felt like cushions of air.

I've been set free!

That was what it felt like. As if she had been set free from all the complications that had been tearing into her like claws and teeth ever since she'd surfaced that morning, realizing what she'd done. What *she*—Sarah, not Sabine—had done. And now... Oh, now, it didn't matter—didn't matter who she was.

Max understood—understood the entire impossibility of what had been tying her in knots for days now, ever since Bastiaan Karavalas had walked into her life.

Right man—wrong time.

But no more—not for a precious handful of glorious, wonderful, liberating days.

I can do what I've been longing to do—what I succumbed to doing last night. This man alone is different from any I've ever known. What happened last night was a revelation, a transformation.

She quivered with the memory of their passion as he

started the car, gunning the engine. She turned to look at him, her eyes as bright as stars.

'Where are we going?' she asked.

She had asked that last night and he had taken her to a new, glittering realm of enchantment and desire, passion and fulfilment.

'My villa,' he answered, his eyes warm upon her before he glanced back to steer the car out of the little town, along the road that curved towards the *Cap*.

Gladness filled her. The apartment in Monte Carlo was glitzy and glamorous, but it did nothing for her. It was his villa that charmed her.

'Wonderful…' she breathed. She felt as light as air, floating way, way up into the sky—the carefree, bright blue sky, where there were no complications to tether her down.

I'm free from everything except seizing with both hands this time now! Right man—right time. Right now!

Her spirits soared, and it seemed they were at the villa in minutes. For a brief interlude Sarah felt self-conscious about encountering Paulette again. If the woman had considered her a threat to Philip, what might she think of her cavorting with her employer? But Paulette, she discovered, had a day off.

'So we'll have to make our own lunch,' Bastiaan told her.

He didn't want to make lunch—he wanted to make love. But his stomach was growling. He was hungry. Hungry for food, hungry for her. He would sate both appetites and life would be good. *Very* good.

He had Sabine back with him, and right now that was all he wanted.

As he headed towards the kitchen he glanced out of the French windows to the terrace beyond. Only a few days ago they had lunched there, all three of them—he and Sabine and Philip.

It seemed a long time ago.

'So...' Bastiaan set down his empty coffee cup on the ironwork table on the villa's shady terrace and leant back in his chair, his eyes resting on Sabine. 'What shall we do now?'

The expression in his eyes made it totally clear what he would like to do—he'd sated his hunger for food, and now he wanted to sate a quite different hunger.

Across from him, Sarah felt her pulse give a kick—when Bastiaan looked at her like that it was hard to respond in any other way. Lunch had been idyllic. Simple *charcuterie* and *fromage*, with huge scarlet tomatoes and more of the luscious peaches they'd had the other day. It had felt a little odd to be here again, receiving such intimacy from Bastiaan.

Has it really happened? Am I really here with Bastiaan, and are we lovers?

But it was true—it really was—and for the rest of this glorious week it could go on being true.

A rich, sensuous languor swept through her as his gaze twined with hers. A wicked sparkle glinted in her own.

'The pool looks irresistible...' she murmured provocatively.

She almost heard him growl with frustration, but gallantly he nodded. 'It does indeed—especially with you in it.' His eyes glinted too. 'Do you want me to guide you back to the room you changed in last time? Or—' and now there was even more of a wickedly intimate glint in his eyes '—shall we dispense with swimsuits altogether?'

She laughed in answer, and disappeared off to change.

Maybe they could go skinny-dipping at night, under the stars…?

The water was wonderfully refreshing, and so was Bastiaan's company. There was a lot of playful frolicking, and from her more covert—and not so covert—appreciation of his strong, muscled physique. A thrill went through her. For now—for this brief, precious time—he was hers. How wonderful was that?

Very wonderful—and more than wonderful: incredible.

It was incredible when, on retiring to the bedroom in the villa to shower in the en-suite bathroom, she discovered Bastiaan could wait no longer.

He stepped inside the shower, hands slicking down her wet, tingling body. She gasped in shock and then in arousal as skilfully, urgently and devastatingly he took possession of her. As her legs wrapped around him and he lifted her up her head fell back in ecstasy, and it seemed to her that she had been transformed into a different person. A person who was neither the sultry Sabine nor the soprano Sarah, but someone whose only existence was to meld herself with this incredible, sensual male, to fuse her body with his, to burn with him in an explosion of physical pleasure and delight.

Afterwards, as they stood exhausted, with the cooling water streaming over them, her breath coming in hectic pants, he cut the shower, reached for huge fleecy towels and wrapped her up as if she were a precious parcel.

He let his hands rest over her damp shoulders, his eyes pouring down into hers. 'What do you do to me?' he asked. There was a strange quality in his voice, a strange expression in his dark eyes.

She let her forehead rest on his chest, the huge lassitude of the aftermath of passion consuming her now.

She could not answer him for it was a question that was in her own being too.

He swung her up into his arms, carried her through into the bedroom, lowering her down upon the cool cotton coverlet, coming down beside her. He drew her into his sheltering embrace, kissed her nape with soft, velvet kisses. And then exhausted, sated, complete, they slept.

When they awoke they made love again, slowly and softly, taking their time—all the time in the world—in the shuttered late-afternoon light of the cool room. And this time Bastiaan brought her to a different kind of ecstasy—a slow, blissful release that flowed through her body like sweet water after drought.

Afterwards they lay a little while in each other's loose embrace, and then Bastiaan lifted his head from the pillow.

'I know,' he told her, 'a great way to watch the sunset.'

It was indeed, Sarah discovered, a wonderful way to watch the sunset.

He took her out to sea in a fast, sleek motor launch that they boarded from the little quay at the rocky shore below the villa. Exhilaration filled her as Bastiaan carved a foaming wake in the darkening cobalt water, the sun low on the surface, turning the Mediterranean to gold as it kissed the swell.

He cut the engine, letting the silence settle around them, and she sat next to him, his arm casually around her shoulder, his body warm against hers. She could feel the gentle bob of the waves beneath the hull, feel the warmth of the sun on her face as she lifted it to its lingering rays. It was as if they were the only people in the world. Here out on the water, with Bastiaan's arm around her, she felt as if all that lay beyond had ceased to be.

Here there were no complications.

Here there was only Bastiaan.

What is happening to me?

The question wound in her mind between the circuits of her thoughts, seeking an answer she was not ready to find. It was far easier simply to go on sitting there, with the warm air like an embrace, the hugeness of the sea all around them, the rich gold of the setting sun illuminating them. This—now—was good. This was all she wanted. This was her contentment.

They headed back to shore in the gathering dusk.

'Would you like to eat out or at the villa?' Bastiaan asked.

'Oh, don't go out,' she said immediately. Then frowned. 'But I'm not very good at cooking, and I don't want you to have to...' she said uncertainly. Could a man like Bastiaan Karavalas really cook a meal?

He gave a laugh. 'We'll have something delivered,' he told her. 'What would you like?'

'Pizza?' she suggested.

He laughed again. 'Oh, I think we can do better than that,' he said.

And indeed they could.

On the Côte d'Azur, when money was no object, it seemed that gourmet meals could be conjured out of thin air.

As she took her place at the table on the terrace, in the warm evening air, it was to discover that a team of servers had arrived from a nearby Michelin-starred restaurant and were setting out their exquisite wares.

She and Bastiaan had already shared a glass of champagne before the meal arrived, and she felt its effervescence in her veins. Now, as the team from the restaurant departed, Bastiaan lifted a glass of rich, ruby Burgundy.

'To our time together,' he said. It was the same toast he'd given the night before, at Le Tombleur.

Sarah raised her own glass.

Our time together...these few precious days...

She felt emotion pluck at her.

From his seat, Bastiaan rested his eyes on her. She looked nothing like she had the night before when they had dined. And he was glad of it. She was wearing a pale blue kimono that he had found in a closet. In sheerest silk, it was knotted at the waist and had wide sleeves, a plunging neckline that gave the merest hint of the sweet swell of her breasts. Her glorious hair was loose, cascading down her back. She wore no make-up. Needed not a scrap of it.

How beautiful she is. How much I desire her!

He tried to remember why it was he had seduced her. Tried to remember his fears for Philip. Tried to remember how he had determined to foil her machinations. But his memory seemed dim. Flawed.

As he gazed on her they seemed unreal, those fears. Absurd...

Did I misjudge her?

That was the question that uncoiled itself in his mind. The question that pressed itself against his consciousness. The question which, with every passing moment he spent with her, seemed more and more...*unnecessary.*

Thoughts flitted through his mind. What evidence, after all, *was* there against her? Oh, Philip was lovestruck—that was undeniable. His every yearning gaze told Bastiaan that. But what of her? What of her behaviour towards Philip?

I thought her nothing more than a blatant gold-digger—trying to exploit Philip's youth and vulnerability. But is she—was she?

I thought that she had blatantly switched her attentions to me—had manoeuvred me to get rid of Philip from the scene.

But why, then, had she been so reluctant to go with him when he'd sought her out on his return from Paris? And why had she fled from him in his apartment that first morning? If she'd been no better than he'd thought her, wanting him for his wealth, she should have clung to him like glue. Not wept by the quayside while he'd searched so urgently for her.

Was that the behaviour of the woman he'd thought her to be? It couldn't be—it just *couldn't*.

There is no evidence against her. From the very start she has confounded my suspicions of her—time after time. All I have to go on, other than my fears for Philip, is that payment that he made.

That was the truth of it. Had he been conjecturing everything else about her? Feeding his suspicions simply because he'd wanted to protect his young cousin? He took a breath, fixed his eyes on her as she lifted her wine glass to answer his toast, looked across at him and smiled—her eyes like incandescent jewels, rich and glowing.

Emotion leapt in him, and in his head he heard his own voice, searing across his thoughts.

There could be an explanation for why Philip paid out that money. All I have to do is ask him. There is no reason—none—to fear that it was to Sabine. She could be completely innocent of the suspicions I've had of her.

As innocent as he wanted her to be. Wanted so much for her to be...

'To us,' he said, and let his eyes mingle and meld with hers—the eyes of this woman who could be everything he wanted her to be. And nothing he did not.

From this moment on he would not let his fears, his

suspicions, poison him. Would not let anything spoil his enjoyment of this moment, this time with her.

And nothing did—that was the bliss of it. Cocooned with her at the villa, he made love to her by day and by night—and *every* time it took him by storm. A storm not only of the senses but of something more.

What is it you do to me?

That was the question that came every time she lay cradled in his arms, her head on his chest, her arm like a silken bond around his waist, her body warm and flushed with passion spent.

The question had no answer—and soon he did not seek an answer. Soon he was content simply to let the hours pass with her. Time came and went, the sun rose and set, the stars wheeled in the clear sky each night as they lay out on the pool loungers, gazing upwards, hand in hand, the cool midnight breeze whispering over their bodies, the moon rising to cast its silver light upon them.

Who *was* this woman? Bastiaan asked of himself, thinking of all that he knew of her. It no longer seemed to matter. Not any more.

Sometimes he caught fragments of her life—a passing mention of the garden at a house in Normandy where, so he surmised, she must have grown up. The climate and the terrain so different from this sun-baked southern shore. Once he tried to draw her out about her singing, but she only shook her head and changed the subject with a smile, a kiss.

Nor did she talk to him about *his* life—only asked him about Greece. How it was to live there, with so much history, the history of millennia, pressing all around him. Of how he made his money, his wealth, she never spoke. She seemed quite oblivious to it. She did not ask to leave the villa—was content to spend each day within its confining beauty.

Meals were delivered, or concocted by them both—simple, hearty food, from salads and *charcuterie* to pasta and barbecues, prepared with much laughter and consumed with appetite. An appetite that afterwards turned to passion for each other.

I didn't know it would be like this—having Sabine with me. I didn't think it would be this...this good.

He tried to think back to a time when it had not been like this—when Sabine had not been with him, when all he'd had were his fears for Philip, his suspicions of her. But it seemed very far away—blurring in his head. Fading more and more with each hour. All that mattered to him now was being as they were now, lying side by side beneath the stars, hand in hand.

He felt her thumb move sensuously, lightly over his as their clasped hands hung loosely between them. He turned his head towards her, away from the moon above. She was gazing across at him, her face dim in the moonlight, her eyes resting on him. There was a softness in her face, in her eyes...

'Bastiaan...' Her voice was low, a sweet caress.

His eyes found hers. Desire reached into his veins. He drew her to her feet and wound his fingers into hers. Speared his hand into her hair, let his mouth find hers.

Passion, strong and sweet and true, flared at his touch. Drove them indoors to find each other, again, and yet again, in this perfect, blissful time they had together.

CHAPTER NINE

'MY *PENSION* IS just there,' Sarah said, pointing to the corner of the street. 'I won't be five minutes.'

Bastiaan pulled the car over to the kerb and she dashed inside. She wanted to change into something pretty for the day. They were finally emerging from the villa, and Bastiaan was set on taking her to a place he was amazed she hadn't seen yet.

The picturesque little town of St Paul de Vence, up in the hills behind the coastline, was famous as a place frequented by artists. She was happy enough to go there—happy enough to be anywhere in the world right now, providing Bastiaan was with her and she with him.

Bastiaan. Oh, the name soared in her head, echoed deep inside her. She was seizing all that he was holding out to her so that there was nothing else except being with him, day after precious day, night after searing night.

It's as if I were asleep and he has woken me. Woken my senses, set them alight.

In her head, in her heart, emotion hovered like a fragile bubble, iridescent and glistening with light and colour. A bubble she longed to seize but dared not—not now, not yet. But it filled her being, made her breathless with delight, with joy. Joy that brought a smile to her face now, as she ran into the *pension*, eager to be as quick as possible so she could re-join Bastiaan without delay.

Five minutes later she was running down the stairs again, pausing only to snatch at the mail in her room's pigeonhole, dropping the envelopes into her handbag before emerging out onto the roadway. She jumped into the car and off they set.

Bastiaan's gaze was warm upon her before he focussed on the way ahead.

She's changed her image yet again, he found himself thinking. This one he liked particularly, he decided. Her hair was in a long plait, her make-up no more than a touch of mascara and lip gloss, and her skin had been warmed by the sun of the past few days to a golden honey. Her outfit was a pretty floral calf-length sundress in pale blue and yellow. She looked fresh and summery and beautiful.

And *his*. Oh, most definitely, definitely his!

Emotion surged within him. What it was, he didn't know—and didn't care. Knew only that it felt good—*so* good...

The route out of the *ville* took them past the nightclub where she sang. As they drove by he saw her throw it a sideways glance, almost looking at it askance, before turning swiftly away. He was glad to have passed it too—did not want to think about it. It jarred with everything that was filling him now.

He shook his head, as if to clear it of unwelcome thoughts. At the villa, safe in its cocoon, the outside world had seemed far, far away. All that belonged in it far, far away.

Well, he would not think of it. He would think only of the day ahead of them. A day to be spent in togetherness, on an excursion, with lunch in a beautiful place, a scenic drive through the hinterland behind the coast.

The traffic lights ahead turned red and he slowed down to a halt, using the opportunity to glance at Sabine beside him. She was busying herself looking at the contents of an envelope she'd taken out of the bag on her lap. It was, he could see, a bill from the *pension*. She gave it a cursory check, replaced it in her bag, then took out another envelope. Bastiaan could see it had a French stamp on it, but she was turning it over to open it, so he could not see the writing on the front.

As she ripped it open and glanced inside she gave a little crow of pleasure. 'Oh, how sweet of him!'

Then, with a sudden biting of her lip, she hurriedly stuffed the envelope back inside her handbag, shutting it with a snap.

Abruptly the traffic lights changed, the car behind him sounded its horn impatiently, and Bastiaan had to move off. But in the few seconds that it took a chill had gone down inside him.

Had he really seen what he'd thought he'd seen?

Had that been a cheque inside that envelope?

He threw a covert sideways glance at her, but she was placing her bag in the footwell, then getting out her phone and texting someone, a happy smile playing around her mouth.

Bastiaan found he was revving the engine, his hands clenching momentarily around the steering wheel. Then, forcibly, he put the sudden burst of cold anger out of his head. Why should Sabine *not* receive mail? And if that mail were from a man what business was it of his? She might know any number of men. Very likely did...

Another emotion stabbed at him. One he had not experienced before. One he never had cause to experience. Rigorously, he pushed it aside. Refused to allow his mind to dwell on the question that was trying to make itself heard. He would *not* speculate on just who might be sending her correspondence that she regarded as 'sweet.' He would not.

He risked another sideways glance at her as he steered through the traffic. She was still on her phone, scrolling through messages. As his gaze went back to the road he heard her give a soft chuckle, start to tap a reply immediately.

Bastiaan flicked his eyes towards her phone screen, hard though it was to see it from this angle and in the brightness of the sun. In the seconds his glance took a face on the screen impinged—or did it? It was gone as she touched the screen to send her message, but he could feel his hands clenching on the wheel again.

Had that been Philip?

The thought was in his head before he could stop it. He forced it out. It had been impossible to recognise the fleeting photo. It could have been anyone. *Anyone*. He would not let his imagination run riot. His fears run riot…

Instead he would focus only on the day ahead. A leisurely drive to St Paul de Vence…strolling hand in hand through its narrow pretty streets, thronged with tourists but charming all the same. Focus only on the easy companionable rightness of having Sabine at his side, looking so lovely as she was today, turning men's heads all around and making a glow of happy possession fill him.

It would be a simple, uncomplicated day together, just like the days they'd spent together at his villa. Nothing would intrude on his happiness.

Into his head flickered the image of her glancing at the contents of that envelope in her lap. He heard again her little crow of pleasure. Saw in his mind the telltale printing on the small piece of paper she'd been looking at…

No!

He would not think about that—*he would not.*

Leave it be. It has nothing to do with you. Let your suspicions of her go—let go completely.

Resolutely he pushed it from his mind, lifting his free hand to point towards the entrance to the famous hotel where they were going to have lunch. She was delighted by it—delighted by everything. Her face alight with pleasure and happiness.

Across the table from him Sarah gazed glowingly at him. She knew every contour of his face, every expression in his eyes, every touch of his mouth upon her...

Her gaze flickered. Shadowed. There was a catch in her throat. Emerging from the villa had been like waking from a dream. Seeing the outside world all around her. Being reminded of its existence. Even just driving past the nightclub had plucked at her.

The days—the nights—she'd spent with Bastiaan had blotted out everything completely. But now—even here, sitting with people all around them—the world was pressing in upon her again. Calling time on them.

Tomorrow she must leave him. Go back to Max. Go back to being Sarah again. Emotion twisted inside her. This time with Bastiaan had been beyond amazing—it had been like nothing she had ever known. *He* was like no man she had ever known.

But what am I to him?

That was the question that shaped itself as they set off after lunch, his powerful, expensive car snaking its way back towards Cap Pierre. The question that pierced her like an arrow. She thought of how she'd assumed that a man like him would be interested only in a sophisticated seductive affair—a passionately sensual encounter with a woman like Sabine.

Was that still what she thought?

The answer blazed in her head.

I don't want it to be just that. I don't want to be just Sabine to him. I want to be the person I really am— I want to be Sarah.

But did she dare? That was what it came down to. As Sabine she had the protection of her persona—that of a woman who could deal with transient affairs…the kind a man like Bastiaan would want.

Would he still want me if I were Sarah?

Or was this burning passion, this intensity of desire, the only thing he wanted? He had said nothing of anything other than enjoying each hour with her—had not spoken of how long he wanted this to last or what it meant to him, nor anything at all of that nature.

Is this time all he wants of me?

There seemed to be a heaviness inside her, weighing her down. She stole a sideways look at Bastiaan. He was focussed on the road, which was building up with traffic now as they neared Nice. She felt her insides give a little skip as her gaze eagerly drank in his strong, incisive profile—and then there was a tearing feeling in its place.

I don't want to leave him. I don't want this to end. It's been way, way too short!

But what could she do? Nothing—that was all. Her future was mapped out for her and it did not include any more time with Bastiaan.

Who might not want to spend it with her anyway. Who might only want what they were having now. And if that were so—if all he'd wanted all along was a kind of fleeting affair with Sabine—then she must accept it.

Sabine would be able to handle a brief affair like this—so I must be Sabine still.

As Sarah she was far too vulnerable...

She took a breath, steeling herself. Her time with Bastiaan was not yet up—not quite. There was still tonight—still one more precious night together.....

And perhaps she was fearing the worst—perhaps he wanted more than this brief time.

Her thoughts raced ahead, borne on a tide of emotion that swelled out of her on wings of hope. Perhaps he would rejoice to find out she was Sarah. Would stand by her all through her final preparations for the festival—share her rejoicing if they were successful or comfort her if she failed and had to accept that she would never become the professional singer she had set her sights on being.

Like an underground fire running through the root systems of a forest, she felt emotions flare within her. What they were she dared not say. Must not give name to.

Right man—wrong time...for now...

But after the festival Bastiaan might just become someone to her who would be so much more than this incandescent brief encounter.

'Shall we stop here in Nice for a while?'

Bastiaan's voice interrupted her troubled thoughts, bringing her back to the moment.

'They have some good shops,' he said invitingly.

The dress she was wearing was pretty, but it was not a designer number by any means. Nor were any of the clothes she wore—including that over-revealing evening gown she wore to sing in. He found himself wanting to know just how a dress suitable for her beauty would enhance her. Splashing out on a wardrobe for her would be a pleasure he would enjoy. And shopping with her would keep at bay any unnecessary temptation to worry about the cheque she had exclaimed over. He would not think about it—would not harbour any suspicions.

I'm done with such suspicions. I will banish them— not let them poison me again.

But she shook her head at his suggestion. 'No, there's nothing I need,' she answered. She did not want to waste time shopping—she wanted to get back to the villa. To be with Bastiaan alone in the last few dwindling hours before she had to go.

He smiled at her indulgently. 'But much, surely, that you *want*?'

She gave a laugh. She would not spoil this last day with him by being unhappy, by letting in the world she didn't want to think about. 'What woman doesn't?' was her rejoinder.

Then, suddenly, her tone changed. Something in that world she didn't want to let in yet demanded her attention. Attention she must give it—right now.

'Oh, actually…could we stop for five minutes? Just along here? There's something I've remembered.'

Bastiaan glanced at her. She was indicating a side street off the main thoroughfare. Maybe she needed toiletries. But as he turned the car towards where she indicated, a slight frown creased his forehead. There was something familiar about the street name. He wondered why—where he had seen it recently.

Then she was pointing again. 'Just there!' she cried.

He pulled across to the pavement, looked where she was pointing, and with an icy rush cold snaked down his spine.

'I won't be a moment,' she said as she got out of the car. Her expression was smiling, untroubled. Then, with a brief wave to him, she hurried into the building.

It was a bank. And Bastiaan knew, with ice congealing in his veins, exactly which bank it was—a branch of the bank that Philip's cheque for twenty thousand euros had been paid into...

And in his head, imprinted like a laser image, he saw again the telltale shape of the contents of that envelope she'd opened in the car that morning, which had caused her to give a crow of pleasure. Another cheque that he knew with deadly certainty she was now paying into the very same account...

A single word seared across his consciousness with all the force of a dagger striking into his very guts.

Fool!

He shut his eyes, feeling cold in every cell of his body.

'All done!' Sarah's voice was bright as she got back into the low-slung car. She was glad to have completed her task—glad she'd remembered in time. But what did *not* gladden her was having had to remember to do it at all. Letting reality impose itself upon her. The reality she would be facing tomorrow...

Conflict filled her. How could she want to stay here as Sabine—with Bastiaan—when Sarah awaited her in the morning? Yet how could she bear to leave Bastiaan—walk away from him and from the bliss she had found with him? Even though all the hopes and dreams of her life were waiting for her to fulfil them...

I want them both!

The cry came from within. Making her eyes anguished. Her heart clench.

She felt the car move off and turned to gaze at Bastiaan as he drove. He'd put on dark glasses while she'd been in the bank, and for a moment—just a moment— she felt that he was someone else. He seemed preoccupied, but the traffic in the middle of Nice was bad, so she did not speak until they were well clear and heading east towards Cap Pierre.

'I can't wait to take a dip in the pool,' she said lightly. She stole a glance at him. 'Fancy a skinny-dip this time?' She spoke teasingly. She wanted to see him smile, wanted the set expression on his face to ease. Wanted her own mood, which had become drawn and aching, to lighten.

He didn't answer—only gave a brief acknowledging smile, as fleeting as it was absent, and turned off the main coastal route to take the road heading towards Pierre-les-Pins.

She let him focus on the road, her own mood strained still, and getting more so with every passing moment. Going through Pierre-les-Pins was harder still, knowing that she must be there tomorrow—her time with Bastiaan over.

Her gaze went to him as he drove. She wanted, needed, to drink him in while she could. Desire filled her, quickening in her veins as she gazed at his face in profile, wanting to reach out and touch, even though he was driving and she must not. His expression was still set and there was no casual conversation, only this strained atmosphere. As if he were feeling what she was feeling...

But how could he be? He knew nothing of what she must do tomorrow—nothing of why she must leave him, the reality she must return to.

Urgency filled her suddenly. *I have to tell him—tell him I am Sarah, not Sabine. Have to explain why...*

And she must do it tonight—of course she must. When else? Tomorrow morning she would be heading back to the *ville*, ready to resume rehearsals. How could she hide that from him? Even if he still wanted her as Sarah she could spend no more time with him now—

not with the festival so close. Not with so much work for her yet to do.

A darker thought assailed her. Did he even *want* more time with her—whether as Sarah or Sabine? Was this, for him, the last day he wanted with her? Had he done with her? Was he even now planning on telling her that their time together was over—that he was leaving France, returning to his own life in Greece?

Her eyes flickered. His features were drawn, with deep lines around his mouth, his jaw tense.

Is he getting ready to end this now?

The ache inside her intensified.

As they walked back inside the villa he caught her hand, stayed her progress. She halted, turning to him. He tossed his sunglasses aside, dropping them on a console table in the hallway. His eyes blazed at her.

Her breath caught—the intensity in his gaze stopped the air in her lungs—and then, hauling her to him, he lowered his mouth to hers with hungry, devouring passion.

She went up like dry tinder. It was a conflagration to answer his, like petrol thrown on a bonfire. Desperation was in her desire. Exultation at his desire for her.

In moments they were in the bedroom, shedding clothes, entwining limbs, passions roused, stroked and heightened in an urgency of desire to be fulfilled, slaked.

In a storm of sensation she reached the pinnacle of her arousal, hips straining to maximise his possession of her. His body was slicked with the sheen of physical ardour as her nails dug into his muscled shoulders and time after time he brought her to yet more exquisite pleasure. She cried out, as if the sensation was veering on the unbearable, so intense was her body's climax. His own was as dramatic—a great shuddering of his straining body, the cords of his neck exposed as he lifted his head, eyes blind with passion. One last eruption of their bodies and then it was over, as though a thunderstorm had passed over a mountain peak.

She lay beneath him, panting, exhausted, her conscious mind dazed and incoherent. She gazed up at him, her eyes wide with a kind of wonder that she could not comprehend. The wildness of their union, the urgency of his possession, of the response he'd summoned from her, had been almost shocking to her. Physical bliss that she had never yet experienced.

And yet she needed now, in the aftermath, to have him hold her close, to cradle her in his arms, to transform their wildness to comfort and tenderness. But as she gazed upwards she saw that there was still that blindness in his eyes.

Was he still caught there, on that mountain peak they'd reached together, stranded in the physical storm of their union? She searched his features, trying to understand, trying to still the tumult in her own breast, where her heart was only slowly climbing down from its hectic beating.

Confusion filled her—more than confusion. That same darkening, disquieting unease that had started as they'd driven back from Nice. She wanted him to say something—anything. Wanted him to wrap his arms about her, hold her as he always did after the throes of passion.

But he did no such thing. Abruptly he was pulling away from her, rising up off the bed and heading into the en-suite bathroom.

As the door closed behind him an aching, anxious feeling of bereavement filled her. Unease mixed with her confusion, with her mounting disquiet. She got out of bed, swaying a moment, her body still feeling the aftermath of what it had experienced. Her hair was still in its plait, but it was dishevelled from their passion. Absently she smoothed it with her hands. She found that they were trembling. With the same shaky motion she groped for her clothes, scattered on the floor, tangled up with his.

From the bathroom came the sound of the shower, but nothing else.

Dressed, she made her way into the kitchen. Took a drink of water from the fridge. Tried to recover her calm.

But she could not. Whatever had happened between them it was not good. How could it be?

He's ending it.

Those were the words that tolled in her brain. The only words that could make sense of how he was being. He was ending it and looking to find a way of doing so. He would not wish to wound her, hurt her. He would find an…*acceptable* way to tell her. He would probably say something about having to go back to Athens. Maybe he had other commitments she knew nothing about. Maybe…

Her thoughts were jumping all over the place, as if on a hot plate. She tried to gather them together, to come to terms with them. Then a sound impinged—her phone, ringing from inside her bag, abandoned in the hallway when Bastiaan had swept her to him.

Absently she fished it out. Saw that it was Max. Saw it go to voicemail.

She stared blindly at the phone as she listened to his message. He sounded fraught, under pressure.

'Sarah—I'm really sorry. I need you to be Sabine tonight. I can't placate Raymond any longer. Can you make it? I'm really sorry—' He rang off.

She didn't phone back. Couldn't. All she could do was start to press the keys with nerveless fingers, texting her reply. Brief, but sufficient.

OK.

But it wasn't OK. It wasn't at all.

She glanced around the kitchen, spotted a pad of paper by the phone on the wall. She crossed to it, tore off a piece and numbly wrote on it, then tucked it by the coffee machine that was spluttering coffee into the jug. She picked up her bag and went out into the hallway, looked into the bedroom. The tangled bedclothes, Bastiaan's garments on the floor, were blatant testimony to what had happened there so short a while ago.

An eternity ago.

There was no sign of Bastiaan. The shower was still running.

She had to go. Right now. Because she could not bear to stay there and have Bastiaan tell her it was over.

Slowly, with a kind of pain netting around her, her mind numb, she turned and left the villa.

Bastiaan cut the shower, seizing a towel to wrap himself in. He had to go back into the bedroom. He could delay it no longer. He didn't want to. He didn't want to see her again.

Wanted to wipe her from existence.

How could I have believed her to be innocent? How could I?

He knew the answer—knew it with shuddering emotion.

Because I wanted her to be innocent—I didn't want her to have taken Philip's money, didn't want it to be true!

That was what was tearing through him, ripping at him with sharpest talons. Ripping his illusions from him.

Fool! Fool that he had been!

He closed his eyes in blind rage. In front of his very eyes she'd waltzed into that bank in Nice, paid in whatever it was she'd taken from Philip—or another man. It didn't matter which. The same branch of that bank—the very same. A coincidence? How could it be?

A snarl sounded in his throat.

Had that cheque she'd paid in this afternoon been from Philip too? Had that postmark been from Paris? Had it been his writing on the envelope? His expression changed. The envelope would still be in her bag, even if the cheque were not. That would be all the proof he needed.

Is she hoping to take me for even more?

The thought was in his head like a dagger before he could stop it. Was that what was behind her ardency, her passion?

The passion that burns between us even now, even right to the bitter end...

Self-hatred lashed at him. How could he have done what he'd just done? Swept her to bed as he had, knowing what she truly was? But he'd been driven by an urge so strong he hadn't been able to stop himself—an urge to possess her one final time...

One final time to recapture all that they'd had—all he'd thought they'd had.

It had never been there at all.

The dagger thrust again, into the core of his being.

He wrenched open the door.

She was not there. The rumpled bed was empty. Her clothes gone.

Emotion rushed into the sudden void in his head like

air into a vacuum. But quite what the emotion was he didn't know. All he knew was that he was striding out of the room, with nothing more than a towel snaked around his hips, wondering where the hell she'd got to.

For a numb, timeless moment he just stood in the hallway, registering that her handbag was gone too, so he would not be able to check the writing on the envelope. Then, from the kitchen, he heard the sound of the coffee machine spluttering.

He walked towards it, seeing that the room was empty. Seeing the note by the coffee jug. Reading it with preternatural calm.

Bastiaan—we've had the most unforgettable time. Thank you for every moment.

It was simply signed 'S.'

That was all.

He dropped it numbly. Turned around, headed back to the bedroom. So she was walking out on him. Had the sum of money she'd extracted this time been sufficient for her to afford to be able to do so? That was what Leana had done. Cashed his cheque and headed off with her next mark, her geriatric protector, laughing at the idiot she'd fooled and left behind.

His mouth tightened. Well, things were different now. *Very* different. Sabine did not know that he was Philip's trustee, that he knew what she had taken and could learn if she'd taken yet more today. She had no reason not to think herself safe.

Is she still hoping to take more from Philip?

Memory played in his head—how Philip had asked him to loosen the purse strings of his main fund before his birthday—how evasive he'd been about what he wanted the money for. All the suspicions he'd so blindly set aside leapt again.

Grim-faced, he went to fetch his laptop.

And there it was—right in his email inbox. A communication today, direct from one of Philip's investment managers, requesting Bastiaan's approval—or not—for Philip's instruction to liquidate a particular fund. The liquidation would release over two hundred thousand euros...

Two hundred thousand euros. Enough to free Sabine for ever from warbling in a second-rate nightclub.

He slammed the laptop lid down. Fury was leaping in his throat.

Was that what Philip had texted her about? Bastiaan hadn't been mistaken in recognizing him as the sender— he could not have been. Was that why she'd given that soft, revealing chuckle? Was that why she'd bolted now, switching her allegiance back to Philip?

Rage boiled in Bastiaan's breast. Well, that would never happen—*never*! She would *never* go back to Philip.

She can burn in hell before she gets that money from him!

His lips stretched into a travesty of a smile. She thought herself safe—but Sabine Sablon was *not* safe. She was not safe at all...

And she would discover that very, very shortly.

CHAPTER TEN

SARAH REACHED FOR the second false eyelash. Glued it, like the first, with shaky hands. She was going through the motions—nothing more. Hammers seemed to be in her brain, hammering her flat. Mashing everything inside her. Misery assailed her. She shouldn't be feeling it—but she was. Oh, she was.

It was over. Her time with Bastiaan was over. A few precious days—and now this.

Reality had awaited her. Max had greeted her with relief—and apology. And with some news that had pierced the misery in her.

'This is your last night here. Raymond insisted you show up just for tonight—because it's Friday and he can't be without a singer—but from tomorrow you're officially replaced. Not with the real Sabine—someone else he's finally found. And then, thank God, we can all decamp. We've been given an earlier rehearsal spot at the festival so we can head there straight away.'

He'd said nothing else, had asked no questions. Had only cast an assessing look at her, seeing the withdrawal in her face. She was glad of it, and of the news he'd given her. Relief, as much as she could feel anything through the fog of misery encompassing her, resonated in her. Now there was only tonight to get through. How she would do it, she didn't know—but it would have to happen.

As she finished putting on her lipstick with shaky hands she could feel hope lighting inside her. Refusing to be quenched. *Was* it over? Perhaps it wasn't. Oh, perhaps Bastiaan *hadn't* been intending to end it all. Perhaps she'd feared it quite unnecessarily. Perhaps, even now, he was missing her, coming after her...

No! She couldn't afford to agonise over whether Bastiaan had finished with her. Couldn't afford to hope and dream that he hadn't. Couldn't afford even to let her mind go where it so wanted to go—to relive, hour by hour, each moment she'd spent with him.

I can't afford to want him—or miss him.

She stared at her reflection. Sabine was more alien than ever now. And as she did so, the door of her dressing room was thrust open. Her head flew round, and as her gaze fell upon the tall, dark figure standing there, her face lit, joy and relief flaring in her eyes. Bastiaan! He had come after her—he was not ending it with her! He still wanted her! Her heart soared.

But as she looked up at him she froze. There was something wrong—something wrong with his face. His eyes. The way he was standing there, dominating the small space. His face was dark, his eyes like granite. He was like nothing she had seen before. This was not the Bastiaan she knew...not Bastiaan at all...

'I have something to say to you.'

Bastiaan's voice was harsh. Hostile. His eyes were dark and veiled, as if a screen had dropped down over them.

Her heart started to hammer. That dark, veiled gaze pressed down on her. Hostility radiated from him like a force field. It felt like a physical blow. What was happening? Why was he looking at her like this? She didn't know—didn't understand.

A moment later the answer came—an answer that was incomprehensible.

'From now on stay away from Philip. It's over. Do you understand me? *Over!*' His voice was harsh, accusing. Condemning.

She didn't understand. Could only go on sitting there, staring at him, emotion surging through her chaotically. Then, as his words sank in, a frown convulsed her face.

'Philip?' she said blankly.

A rasp of a laugh—without humour, soon cut short— broke from him. 'Forgotten him already, have you? Well, then…' and now his voice took on a different note—one that seemed to chill her deep inside '…it seems my efforts were not in vain. I have succeeded, it seems, in… *distracting* you, *mademoiselle*.' He paused heavily and his eyes were stabbing at her now. 'As I intended.'

His chest rose and fell, and then he was speaking again.

'But do not flatter yourself that my….*attentions* were for any purpose other than to convince you that my cousin is no longer yours to manipulate.'

She was staring at him as if he were insane. But he would not be halted. Not now, when fury was coursing through his veins—as it had done since the veils had been ripped from his eyes—since he'd understood just how much a fool she'd made of him. Not Philip—*him!*

I so nearly fell for it—was so nearly convinced by her.

Anger burned in him. Anger at her—for taking him for a fool, for exploiting his trusting, sensitive cousin and for not being the woman he'd come to believe, to hope, that she was.

The woman I wanted her to be.

The irony of it was exquisite. He'd seduced her because he'd believed her guilty—then had no longer been able to believe that she was. Then all that had been ripped and up-ended again—back to guilt.

A guilt he no longer wanted her to have, but from which there could be no escape now. *None.*

He cut across his own perilous thoughts with a snarl. 'Don't play the innocent. If you think you can still exploit his emotional vulnerability to you…well, think again.'

His voice became harsh and ugly, his mouth curling, eyes filled with venom.

'You see, I have only to tell him how you have warmed *my* bed these last days for his infatuation to be over in an instant. Your power over him extinguished.'

The air in her lungs was like lead. His words were like blows. Her features contorted.

'Are you saying…?' She could hardly force the words from her through the pain, through the shock that had exploded inside her, 'Are you saying that you seduced me in order to…to separate me from Philip?' There was disbelief in her voice. Disbelief on so many levels.

'You have it precisely,' he said heavily, with sardonic emphasis. 'Oh, surely you did not believe I would not take action to protect my cousin from women of your kind?'

She swallowed. It was like a razor in her throat. 'My kind…?'

'Look at yourself, Sabine. A woman of the world—isn't that the phrase? Using her *talents*—' deliberately he mocked the word she'd used herself when she'd first learnt who he was '—to make her way in the world. And if those *talents*—' the mockery intensified '—include catching men with your charms, then good luck to you.' His voice hardened like the blade of a knife. 'Unless you set your sights on a vulnerable stripling like my cousin—

then I will wish you only to perdition! And ensure you go there.'

His voice changed again.

'So, do you understand the situation now? From now on content yourself with the life you have—singing cheap, tawdry songs in a cheap, tawdry club.'

His eyes blazed like coals from the pit as he gave his final vicious condemnation of her.

'A two-cent *chanteuse* with more body than voice. That is all that you are good for. Nothing else!'

One last skewering of his contemptuous gaze, one last twist of his deriding mouth, and he was turning on his heel, walking out. She could hear his footsteps—heavy, damning—falling away.

Her mouth fell open, the rush of air into her lungs choking her. Emotion convulsed her. And then, as if fuse had been lit, she jerked to her feet. She charged out of the dressing room, but he was already stepping through the door that separated the front of house from backstage. She whirled about, driven forward on the emotion boiling up inside her. A moment later she was in the wings at the side of the stage, seizing Max by the arm, propelling him forward.

Anger such as she had never felt before in her life, erupted in her. She thrust Max towards the piano beside the centre spot where her microphone was. She hurled it into the wings, then turned back to Max.

'Play "Der Hölle Rache".'

Max stared at her as if she were mad. *'What?'*

'Play it! Or I am on the next plane to London!'

She could see Bastiaan, threading his way across the dining room, moving towards the exit. The room was busy, but there was only one person she was going to sing for. Only one—and he could burn in hell!

Max's gaze followed hers and his expression changed. She saw his hands shape themselves over the opening chord, and with a last snatch of sanity took the breath she needed for herself. And then, as Max's hands crashed down on the keyboard, she stepped forward into the pool of light. Centre stage.

And launched into furious, excoriating, maximum *tessitura*, her full-powered *coloratura* soprano voice exploding into the space in front of her to find its target.

Bastiaan could see the exit—a dozen tables or so away. He had to get out of here, get into his car and drive... drive far and fast. *Very* fast.

He'd done it. He'd done what he'd had to do—what he'd set out to do from that afternoon in Athens when his aunt had come to see him, to beg him to save her precious young son from the toils of a dangerous *femme fatale*. And save him he had.

Saved more than just his cousin.

I have saved myself.

No!

He would not think that—would not accept it. Would only make for the exit.

He reached the door. Made to push it open angrily with the flat of his hand.

And then, from behind him, came a crash of chords that stopped him.

He froze.

'Der Hölle Rache.' The most fiendishly difficult soprano aria by Mozart. Fiendish for its cripplingly punishing high notes, for the merciless fury of its delivery. An aria whose music and lyrics boiled with coruscating rage as *Die Zauberflöte*'s 'Queen of the Night' poured out seething venom against her bitter enemy.

'Hell's vengeance boils in my heart!'

Like a remotely operated robot, turning against his will, Bastiaan felt his body twist.

It was impossible. Impossible that this stabbing, biting, fury of a voice should be emanating from the figure on the stage. Absolutely, totally impossible.

Because the figure on the stage was *Sabine*. Sabine— with her tight sheath of a gown, her *femme fatale* blonde allure, her low-pitched voice singing huskily through sultry cabaret numbers.

It could not be Sabine singing this most punishing, demanding pinnacle of the operatic repertoire.

But it was.

Still like a robot he walked towards the stage, dimly aware that the diners present were staring open-mouthed at this extraordinary departure from their normal cabaret fare. Dimly aware that he was sinking down at an unoccupied table in front of the stage, his eyes pinned, incredulous, on the woman singing a few metres away from him.

The full force of her raging voice stormed over him. There was no microphone to amplify her voice, but she was drowning out everything except the crashing chords of the piano accompanying her. This close, he would see the incandescent fury in her face, her flashing eyes emerald and hard. He stared—transfixed. Incredulous. Disbelieving.

Then, as the aria *furioso* reached its climax, he saw her stride to the edge of the stage, step down off it and sweep towards him. Saw her snatch up a steak knife from a place setting and, with a final, killing flourish, as her scathing, scything denunciation of her enemy was hurled from her lips, she lifted the knife up and brought it down in a deadly, vicious stab into the tabletop in front of him.

The final chords sounded and she was whirling around, striding away, slamming through the door that led backstage. And in the tabletop in front of him the knife she'd stabbed into it stood quivering.

All around him was stunned silence.

Slowly, very slowly, he reached a hand forward and withdrew the knife from the table. It took a degree of effort to do so—it had been stabbed in with driving force.

The entire audience came out of their stupor and erupted into a tremendous round of applause.

He realised he was getting to his feet, intent on following her wherever she had disappeared to, and then was aware that the pianist was lightly sprinting off the stage towards him, blocking his route.

'I wouldn't, you know,' said the pianist, whom he dimly recognised as Sabine's accompanist.

Bastiaan stared at him. 'What the *hell* just happened?' he demanded. His ears were still ringing with the power of her voice, her incredible, unbelievable voice.

Sabine's accompanist made a face. 'Whatever you said to her, she didn't like it—' he answered.

'She's a *nightclub* singer!' Bastiaan exclaimed, not hearing what the other man had said.

The accompanist shook his head. 'Ah, no...actually, she's not. She's only standing in for one right now. Sarah's real musical forte is, as you have just heard, opera.'

Bastiaan stared blankly. 'Sarah?'

'Sarah Fareham. That's her name. She's British. Her mother is French. The real Sabine did a runner, so I cut a deal with the club owner to get free rehearsal space in exchange for Sarah filling in. But he's hired a new singer now—which is very convenient as we're off tomorrow to the festival venue.'

Bastiaan's blank stare turned blanker. 'Festival...?' He

seemed to be able to do nothing but echo the other man's words, and Bastiaan had the suspicion, deep down, that the man was finding all this highly amusing.

'Yes, the Provence en Voix Festival. We—as in our company—are appearing there with a newly composed opera that I am directing. Sarah,' he informed Bastiaan, 'is our lead soprano. It's a very demanding role.' Now the amusement was not in his voice any more. 'I only hope she hasn't gone and wrecked her voice with that ridiculous "Queen of the Night" tirade she insisted on.' His mouth twisted and the humour was back in his voice, waspish though it was. 'I can't think why—can you?'

Bastiaan's eyes narrowed. It was a jibe, and he didn't like it. But that was the absolute, utter least of his emotions right now.

'I have to speak to her—'

'Uh-uh.' The pianist shook his head again. 'I really wouldn't, you know.' He made a face again. 'I have *never* seen her that angry.'

Bastiaan hardly heard him. His mind was in meltdown. And then another question reared, hitting him in the face.

'Philip—my cousin—does *he* know?'

'About Sarah? Yes, of course he does. Your cousin's been haunting this place during rehearsals. Nice kid,' said Max kindly.

Bastiaan's brows snapped together uncomprehendingly. Philip *knew* that 'Sabine' was this girl Sarah? That she was in some kind of opera company? Why the hell hadn't he told him, then? He spoke that last question aloud.

'Not surprisingly, Sarah's being a bit cagey about having to appear as Sabine,' came the answer. 'It wouldn't do her operatic reputation any good at all if it got out.

This festival is make-or-break for her. For *all* of us,' he finished tightly.

Bastiaan didn't answer. Couldn't.

She trusted Philip with the truth about herself—but she never trusted me with it!

The realisation was like a stab wound.

'I have to see her.'

He thrust his way bodily past the pianist, storming down the narrow corridor, his head reeling, trying to make sense of it all. Memory slashed through him of how he'd sought her out that first evening he'd set eyes on her. His face tightened. Lies—all damn lies.

Her dressing room door was shut, but he pushed it open. At his entrance she turned, whipping round from where she was wrenching tissues from a box on her dressing table.

'Get out!' she yelled at him.

Bastiaan stopped short. Everything he had thought he'd known about her was gone. Totally gone.

She yelled at him again. 'You heard me! Get out! Take your foul accusations and *get out*!'

Her voice was strident, her eyes blazing with the same vitriolic fury that had turned them emerald as she'd hurled her rage at him in her performance.

'Why didn't you *tell* me you weren't Sabine?' Bastiaan cut across her.

'Why didn't *you* tell *me* that you thought me some sleazy slut who was trying it on with your precious cousin?' she countered, still yelling at him.

His expression darkened. 'Of course I wasn't going to tell you that, was I? Since I was trying to separate you from him.' A ragged breath scissored his lungs. 'Look, Sabine...'

'I am *not* Sabine!'

Sarah snatched up a hairbrush from her dressing table and hurled it at him. It bounced harmlessly off his broad chest. The chest she'd clung to in ecstasy—the chest she now wanted to hammer with her fists in pure, boiling rage for what he'd said to her, what he'd thought of her...

What he'd done to her...

He took me to bed and made love to me, took me to paradise, and all along it was just a ghastly, horrible plot to blacken me in Philip's eyes.

Misery and rage boiled together in the maelstrom of her mind.

'I didn't know you weren't Sabine. Do *not* blame me for that,' Bastiaan retaliated, slashing a hand through empty air. He tried again, attempting to use her real name now. 'Look... Sarah...'

'Don't you *dare* speak my name. You know *nothing* about me!'

His expression changed. Oh, but there *was* something he knew about her. From the shredded remnants of his mind, the brainstorm consuming him, he dragged it forth. Forced it across his synapses.

She might be Sabine, she might be Sarah—it didn't matter—

'Except, of course,' he said freezingly, each word ice as he spoke it, 'about the money. Philip's money.'

She stilled. 'Money?' She echoed the word as if it were in an alien tongue.

He gave a rough laugh. Opera singer or nightclub singer—why should it be different? His mouth twisted. Why should 'Sarah' be any more scrupulous than 'Sabine'?

'You took,' he said, letting each word cut like a knife, 'twenty thousand euros from my cousin's personal account. I know you did because this afternoon you paid another cheque into the very same bank account that the twenty thousand euros disappeared into.'

Her expression was changing even as he spoke, but he wouldn't let her say anything—anything at all.

'And this very evening, after you'd oh-so-conveniently cut and run from my villa, I got a request to release *two hundred thousand* euros from my cousin's investment funds.' His eyes glittered with accusation. 'Did you not realise that as Philip's trustee I see *everything* of his finances—that he needs my approval to cash that kind of money? Running back to him with whatever sob story you're concocting will be in vain. Is *that* why you left my bed this afternoon?'

'I left,' she said, and it was as if wire were garrotting her throat, 'because I had to appear as Sabine tonight.'

She was staring at him as if from very far away. *Because I thought you'd had all you wanted from Sabine.*

And he had, hadn't he? That was the killing blow that struck her now. He'd had exactly what he'd wanted from Sabine because all he'd wanted was to separate her from Philip and to keep his money safe.

Behind the stone mask that was her face she was fracturing into a thousand pieces…

Her impassivity made him angry—the anger like ice water in his veins. 'I'll tell you how it will be,' he said. 'Philip will go back to Athens, safely out of your reach. And you—Sabine, Sarah, whoever the hell you are— will repay the twenty thousand euros that he paid into your bank account.'

Her eyes were still on him. They were as green and as hard as emeralds.

'It wasn't my bank account,' she said.

Her voice was expressionless, but something had changed in her face.

A voice came from the doorway. 'No,' it said, 'it was mine.'

CHAPTER ELEVEN

SARAH'S EYES WENT to Max, standing in the doorway.

'What the *hell* have you done?' she breathed.

He got no chance to answer. Bastiaan's eyes lasered him. 'Are you claiming the account is yours? *She* went into that bank this afternoon.'

'To pay in a cheque for three thousand euros my father had just sent me to help with the expenses of mounting the opera. I paid it directly into Max's account.'

She was looking at Bastiaan, but there was no expression in her face, none in her voice. Her gaze went back to Max.

'You took Philip for *twenty thousand euros*?' There was emotion in her voice now—disbelief and outrage.

Max lifted his hands. 'I did not ask for it, *cherie*. He offered.'

Bastiaan's eyes narrowed. Emotion was coursing through him, but right now he had only one focus. 'My cousin *offered* you twenty thousand euros?'

Max looked straight at him. 'He could see for himself how we're stretched for funding—he wanted to help.' There was no apology in his voice.

Bastiaan's eyes slashed back to Sarah. 'Did you know?'

The question bit at her like the jaws of a wolf. But it was Max who answered.

'Of course she didn't know. She'd already warned me not to approach him.'

'And yet,' said Bastiaan, with a dangerous silkiness in his voice, 'you still did.'

Max's eyes hardened. 'I told you—he offered it without prompting. Why should I have refused?' Something in his voice altered, became both defiant and accusing. 'Are we supposed to starve in the gutter to bring the world our art?'

He got no answer. The world, with or without opera in it, had just changed for Bastiaan.

His eyes went back to Sarah. Her face was like stone. Something moved within him—something that was like a lance piercing him inside—but he ignored it. He flicked his eyes back to Max, then to Sarah again.

'And the two hundred thousand euros my cousin now wishes to lavish on a fortunate recipient?' Silk over steel was in his voice.

'If he offered I would take it,' said Max bluntly. 'It would be well spent. Better than on the pointless toys that rich men squander their wealth on,' he said, and there was a dry bitterness in his words as he spoke.

'Except—' Sarah's voice cut in '—that is exactly what Philip is planning to do.'

She opened a drawer in the vanity unit, drew out her phone, called up a text, pointed the screen towards Bastiaan.

'This is the text he sent me today, while we were driving to St Paul de Vence.' Her voice was hollow.

His eyes went to it. Went to a photo of the latest supercar to have been launched—one of those he and Philip had discussed over dinner in Villeneuve.

The accompanying text was simple.

Wouldn't this make a great twenty-first birthday present to myself? I can't wait!

Underneath, he could read what she had replied.

Very impressive! What does Bastiaan think? Check with him first!

Sarah was speaking. 'I was as tactful as I could be— I always have been. I don't want him hurt, whatever he thinks he feels about me, but I never wanted to encourage him. And not about this, either,' she replied, in the same distant, hollow voice. 'I know you're not keen on him having such a powerful car so young.'

Harsh realisation washed through Bastiaan like a chilling douche. Philip had been so evasive about why he wanted money released from his funds...

But it wasn't for her—none of the money was for her...

And she was not, and never had been, the person he'd thought her...not in any respect whatsoever. Neither nightclub singer, nor gold-digger, nor any threat at all, in any way, to Philip.

My every accusation has been false. And because of that...

His mind stopped. It was as if he were standing at the edge of a high cliff. One more step forward and he would be over the edge. Falling to his doom.

Sarah was getting to her feet. It was hard, because she seemed to be made of marble. Nothing seemed to be working inside her at all. Not in her body, not in her head. She looked at Bastiaan, at the man she'd thought he was. But he wasn't. He was someone quite different.

'You'd better go,' she said. 'My set starts soon.' She

paused. Then, 'Stay away from me,' she said. 'Stay away—and go to hell.'

From the doorway, Max tried to speak. 'Sarah...'

There was uncertainty in his voice, but she just looked at him. He gave a slight shrug, then walked away. Her eyes went back to Bastiaan, but now there was hatred in them. Raw hatred.

'Go to hell,' she said again.

But there was no need to tell him that. He was there already.

He turned and went.

Sarah stood for one long motionless, agonising, end-less moment, her whole body pulled by wires of agony and rage. Then tears started to choke her. Tears of fury. Tears of misery.

Aching, ravening misery.

His aunt was staring at him from across her drawing room in Athens. Bastiaan had just had lunch with her and Philip, and now, with Philip back at his studies, his aunt was cornering him about his mission to the Riviera.

'Bastiaan, are you telling me that this girl in France is actually some sort of opera singer and *isn't* trying to entrap Philip?'

He nodded tautly.

His aunt's expression cleared. 'But that's wonderful.' Then she looked worried. 'Do you think he's still... *enamoured*, though? Even if she isn't encouraging him?'

He shook his head. 'I don't think so. He's full of this invitation to go to the Caribbean with Jean-Paul and his family.' He cast his aunt a significant look. 'Plus, he seems to be very taken with Jean-Paul's sister, whose birthday party it is.'

Philip's mother's face lit. 'Oh, Christine is a sweet

girl. They'd be so well-suited.' She cast a grateful look at her nephew. 'Bastiaan—*thank you*. I cannot tell you how grateful I am for setting my mind at rest about that singer and my boy!'

His eyes were veiled for a moment, and there was a fleeting look that he hid swiftly. His expression changed. 'I made one mistake, though,' he said.

More than one...

His throat closed, but he forced himself to continue. 'I let Philip drive my car while we were there—now he's determined to get one of his own.'

His aunt's face was spiked with anxiety. 'Oh, Bastiaan—please, stop him. He'll kill himself!'

He heard the fear in her voice, but this time he shook his head. 'I can't stop him—and nor can you. He's growing up. He has to learn responsibility. But—' he held up a hand '—I *can* teach him to drive a car like that safely. That's the deal I've struck with him.'

'Well…' her acquiescence was uneasy, but resigned '…if you do your best to keep him safe…'

'I will,' he said.

He got to his feet. He needed to be out of there. Needed it badly. He was heading off to his island, craving solitude. Craving anything that might stop him thinking. Stop him feeling…

No—don't go there. Just...don't.

As he walked towards the front door Philip hailed him from his room. 'Bast! You will come, won't you? To Sarah's premiere? It would be so great if you do. You only ever saw her as Sabine—she'd love you to see what she can really do. I know she would.'

His eyes veiled. What Sarah would love was to see his head on a plate.

'I'll see,' he temporised.

'It's at the end of next week,' Philip reminded him.

It could be tomorrow or at the end of eternity for all the difference it would make, Bastiaan knew. Knew from her brutal, persistent refusal to acknowledge any of his texts, his emails, his letters. All of them asking... *begging* one thing and one thing only...

His mind sheered away—the way he was training it to. Day by gruelling day. But it kept coming back—like a falcon circling for prey. He could sail, he could swim, he could walk, he could get very, very drunk—but it would not stay out of his head.

Three simple words. Three words that were like knife-thrusts to his guts.

I've lost her.

'Sarah?'

Max's voice was cautious. It wasn't just because of the thorny issue of Philip's generosity and Max's ready acceptance. He was treating her with kid gloves. She wished he wouldn't. She wished he would go back to being the waspish, slave-driving Max she knew. Wished that everyone would stop tiptoeing around her.

It was as if she had a visible knife wound in her. But nothing was visible. Her bleeding was internal...

It was their first rehearsal day at the festival site, a small but beautiful theatre built in the grounds of a château in northern Provence. She was grateful—abjectly grateful—to be away from the Riviera...away from the nightclub. Away from anything, everything, that might remind her of what had happened there...

But it was with her day and night, asleep and awake, alone and with others, singing or not.

Pain. A simple word. Agonizing to endure.

Impossible to stop.

'Are you sure you want to start with that aria?' Max's enquiry was still cautious. 'Wouldn't you rather build up to it?'

'No,' she said.

Her tone was flat, inexpressive. She wanted to do this. Needed to do it. The aria that she had found impossible to sing was now the only one she wanted to sing.

She took her position, readied herself—her stance, her throat, her muscles, her breathing. Anton started to play. As she stood motionless, until her entry came, thoughts flowed through her head...ribbons of pain...

How could I not understand this aria? How could I think it impossible to believe in it—believe in what she feels, what she endures?

Her bar came. Max lifted his hand to guide her in as the music swelled on its pitiless tide. She gazed blindly outward, not seeing Max, not seeing the auditorium or the world. Seeing only her pain.

And out of her pain came the pain of the War Bride, her anguished voice reaching out over the world with the pain of hopes destroyed, happiness extinguished, the future gone. The futility, the loss, the courage, the sacrifice, the pity of war...all in a single voice. *Her* voice.

As her voice died away into silence...utter silence... Anton lifted his hands from the keyboard. Then he got to his feet, crossed to her. Took her hands. Kissed each of them.

'You have sung what I have written,' he told her, his voice full. It was all he said—all he needed to say.

She shut her eyes. Inside her head, words came. Fierce. Searing.

This is all I have. And it will be enough. It will be enough!

But in the deepest recesses of her consciousness she could hear a single word mocking her.

Liar.

Bastiaan took his seat. He was up in the gods. He'd never in his life sat so high above the stage, in so cheap a seat. But he needed to be somewhere where Philip, down in the stalls, could not see him.

Bastiaan had told him that, regrettably, he could not make it to the opening night of *War Bride*.

He had lied.

What he did not want—could not afford—was for Philip to let Sarah know he would be there.

But he could no more have stayed away than remained in a burning building.

Emotion roiled within him as he gazed down. Somewhere behind those heavy curtains she was there. Urgency burned in him. She had blocked him at every turn, denied him all access.

Even Max, when he'd asked for his intervention, had simply replied, 'Sarah needs to work now. Don't make any more difficulties for her.'

So he'd stayed away. Till now.

Tonight—tonight I have to speak to her. I have to.

As the house lights went down and the audience started to settle, conversation dimming, he felt his vision blur. Saw images shape themselves—tantalizing, tormenting.

Sabine, her eyes glowing with passion, gazing up at him as they made love.

Sabine, smiling, laughing, holding his hand.

Sabine—just being with her, hour by hour, day by day, as they ate, as they swam, as they sunbathed and star-gazed.

Sabine—so beautiful, so wonderful.

Until I threw her away.

He had let fear and suspicion poison what they'd had. Ruin it.

I did not know what I had—until I lost it.

Could he win it back? Could he win *her* back?

He had to try—at least he had to try.

'OK, Sarah, this is it.' Max was pressing his hands on her shoulders, his eyes holding hers. 'You can do it—you know you can.'

She couldn't respond, could only wait while he spoke to the others, reassuring them, encouraging them. He looked impeccable in white tie and tails, but she could see the tension in him in every line of his slight body. She could hear the audience starting to applaud and the tuning up of the players in the orchestra die away as Max, their conductor for the evening, took the podium.

She tried to breathe, but couldn't. She wanted to die. Anything—anything at all to avoid having to do what she was going to have to do. What she had been preparing for all her life. What she had worked for in every waking second, allowing nothing else to lay claim to an instant of her time, a moment of her concentration.

Least of all the man who had done what he had to her. Least of all him. The man who was despicable beyond all men, thinking what he had of her, judging and condemning her as he had, while all the while…all the while…

He made love to me and thought me nothing better than a cheap little gold-digger. Right from the start— from the very moment he laid eyes on me. Everything was a lie—everything! Every moment I spent with him was a lie. And he knew it the whole time!

No, she had not allowed such vicious, agonizing thoughts into her head. Not one. She'd kept them all at bay—along with all those unbearable texts and voice-mails that she'd deleted without reading or listening to. Deleted and destroyed, telling him to go to hell and stay there. Never, ever to get in touch again.

Because all there was in her life now was her voice—her voice and her work. She had worked like a demon, like one possessed, and blocked out everything else in the universe. And now this moment, right now, had come. And she wanted to die.

Dear God, please let me do OK. Please let me get it right—for me, for all of us. Please.

Then the small chorus was filing out on to the stage, and a moment later she heard Max start the brief overture. She felt faint with nerves. As they took their places the familiar music, every note of which she knew in every cell of her body, started to wind its way through the synapses of her stricken brain. The curtain rose, revealing the cavern of the auditorium beyond, and now the chorus was starting their low, haunting chant—their invocation to vanishing peace as the storm clouds of war gathered.

She felt her legs tremble, turning to jelly. Her voice had gone. Completely gone. Vanished into the ether. There was nothing—nothing in her but silence…

She saw the glare of the stage lights, the dimness of the auditorium beyond, and on his podium Max, lifting his baton for her entrance cue. She fixed her eyes on him, took a breath.

And her voice came.

High and pure and true. And nothing else in the universe existed any more except her voice.

Unseen, high above in the gods, Bastiaan sat motionless and heard her sing.

The knife in his guts twisted with every note she sang.

For the whole duration of the opera, as it wound to its sombre conclusion, Bastiaan could not move a muscle, his whole being riveted on the slender figure on the stage. Only once did he stir, his expression changing. During the heartrending aria of grief for her young husband's death, with the agony of loss in every note. His eyes shadowed. The poignancy of the music, of her high, keening voice, struck deep within him.

Then the drama moved on to its final scene, to her song to the unborn child she carried, destined to be another soldier, in yet another war. And she, the War Bride, would become in her turn the Soldier's Mother, destined to bury her son, comfort his widow—the next War Bride, carrying the next unborn soldier...

As her voice faded the light on the stage faded too, until there was only a single narrow spot upon her. And then that, too, faded, leaving only the unseen chorus to close the timeless tragedy with a chorale of mourning for lives yet to be lost in future conflicts. Until silence and darkness fell completely.

For a palpable moment there was complete stillness in the house—and then the applause started. And it did not stop. Did not stop as the stage lights came up and the cast were there, Sarah, and the other soloists stepping forward. The applause intensified and the audience were rising to their feet as Max walked out on to the stage with Anton at his side, and then both of them were taking Sarah by the hand, leading her forward to a crescendo of applause.

Bastiaan's palms were stinging, but still the applause continued, and still his eyes were only for her— for Sarah—now dropping hands with Max, calling her tenor forward, and the other soloists too, to take their share of the ovation, breaking the line to let the chorus take theirs, and then all the cast joined in with applause for the orchestra taking their bows.

He could see her expression—beatific, transfigured.

He could stay still no longer. He rose from his seat, jolted down the staircase to the ground floor, out into the fresh night air. His heart was pounding, but not from exertion. Walking swiftly, purposefully, he pushed open the stage door, walked up to the concierge's booth.

'This is for Max Defarge. See that he gets it this evening.' He placed the long white envelope he'd taken from his inside jacket pocket into his hand, along with a hundred-euro note to ensure his instruction was fulfilled. Then he walked away.

He couldn't do this. What the hell had he been thinking? That he could just swan into her dressing room the way he had that first night he'd seen her sing?

Seen Sabine sing—not Sarah!

But the woman he'd heard tonight had not been Sabine—had been as distant from Sabine as he was from the stars in the sky. That knife twisted in his guts again, the irony like acid in his veins. That he should now crave only the woman he had thrown away....distrusted and destroyed.

His mobile phone vibrated. Absently he took it out—it was a text from Philip.

Bast, you missed a sensation! Sarah was brilliant and the audience is going wild! Gutted you aren't here. Am staying for the after-party soon as the audience clears. Can't wait to hug her!

He didn't answer, just slid the phone away. His heart as heavy as lead.

CHAPTER TWELVE

SARAH WAS FLOATING at least six inches off the ground. The champagne that Max had splashed out on was contributing, she knew, but mostly it was just on wings of elation—the buoyancy of abject relief and gratitude that she had given the performance of her life.

Elation filled them all—hugs and kisses, tears and laughter and joy lifting them all above the exhaustion that their efforts had exacted from them. But no one cared about exhaustion now—only about triumph.

She could scarcely believe it, and yet it was true. All true. Finally all true.

'Am I dreaming this?' she cried to her parents as they swept her into their arms. Her mother's face was openly wet with tears, her father's glowing with pride.

Her mother's hand pressed hers. 'Whoever he is, my darling—the man you sang about—he's not worthy of you.' Her voice was rich with sympathy and concern.

Sarah would not meet her mother's eyes.

Her mother smiled sadly. 'I heard it in your voice. You were not singing of the loss of your soldier. It was real for you, my darling—*real*.'

Sarah tried to shake her head, but failed. Tried to stop the knife sliding into her heart, but failed. She could only be grateful that Max was now embracing her—for the millionth time—and drawing her off to one side. He found a quiet spot in the foyer area where the after-party was taking place and spoke.

'This has just been given to me,' he said.

His voice was neutral. Very neutral. Out of his pocket he took a folded piece of paper and opened it, handing it to Sarah. She took it with a slight frown of puzzlement. Then her expression changed.

'I'm glad for you,' she said tightly. It was all she could manage. She thrust the paper back at Max.

'And for yourself?' The question came with a lift of the brow, speculation in his eyes, concern in his voice.

She gave her head a sharp, negative shake. Turned away bleakly. Heading back into the throng, she seized up another glass of champagne, more hugs, more kisses. And suddenly, a huge bear hug enveloping her.

'Oh, Sarah… Sarah—you were brilliant. Just *brilliant*! You were *all* brilliant!'

It was Philip—sweet, lovely Philip—his face alight with pleasure for her. She hugged him back, glad to see him. But automatically, fearfully, she found her gaze going past him. And there was another emotion in her eyes—one she did not want to be there but which leapt all the same.

It died away as he spoke again. 'I just *wish* Bast could've been here. I told him I really, *really* wanted him to hear you do your real stuff—not all that inane Sabine garbage.' He released her from his hug.

She smiled fondly. 'Thank you for all your loyalty and support. It means a great deal to me,' she said sincerely, because his youthful faith in her had, she knew, been a balm to her. 'And Philip?' She pressed his hands, her voice serious now. 'Listen—don't *ever* let types like Max take money off you again. He was out of order.'

He coloured again. 'I wanted to help,' he said.

For a second, just a second, her eyes shadowed with pain. Philip's 'help' had exacted a price from her and she had paid heavily. Was still paying.

Would pay all her life...

'You did,' she said firmly. 'And we're all grateful—you helped make all this possible!' She gestured widely at the happy scene around them.

'Great!' He grinned, relieved and reassured.

She, too, was relieved and reassured. Philip's crush on her was clearly over, there was no light of longing in his eyes any more. Just open friendliness. 'We all liked you hanging around—with or without that hefty donation to us. Oh, and Philip?' Her face was expressive. 'That monster car you want to get for yourself—please, just do *not* smash yourself up in it!'

He grinned again. 'I won't. Bast's teaching me to drive it safely.' He blew her a kiss as he headed off. 'One day I'll deliver you to the artists' entrance at the Royal Opera House Covent Garden in it—see if I don't.'

'I'll hold you to that,' she said fondly.

She turned away. Covent Garden... Would she make it there? Was what had happened tonight the first step on her journey there?

Fierce emotion fired through her.

I have to make it. I have to!

Work and work alone must consume her now. No more distractions.

The words echoed in her head, mocking her. How often had she said them?

Even right from the start, when her eyes had set on the man who had invaded her dressing room that night, invaded her life...

Invaded my heart...

She felt a choke rising in her throat, constricting her breathing. She forced it back. She would not give in to it. Would not give in to the bleakness that was like a vacuum inside her, trying to suck all the joy out of this moment for her.

My work will be enough—it will be!

That was all she had to remember. All she had to believe.

Lie though it was…

An hour later she had had enough of celebration. The exhaustion she'd blanked out was seeping through her again.

Her parents had gone, yawning, back to their hotel in the nearby spa town. Philip was getting stuck into the champagne with the chorus, with a lot of laughter and bonhomie.

Helping herself to a large glass of water, Sarah found her feet going towards the French windows. Cool fresh air beckoned her, and she stepped out onto a paved area. There was an ornate stone-rimmed pond at the end of a pathway leading across the lawn, with soft underwater lights and a little fountain playing. She felt herself wandering towards it.

Her elation had gone. Subsumed not just by exhaustion but by another mood. Seeing Philip had not helped her. Nor had what Max had disclosed to her. Both had been painful reminders of the man she wanted now only to forget.

But could not.

She reached the pond, trailed her fingers in the cool water, her gaze inward. Back into memory.

Sun sparkling off the swimming pool as Bastiaan dived into it, his torso glistening with diamond drops of water.

His arm tight around her as he steered the motorboat towards the gold of the setting sun. His eyes burning down at her with passion and desire. His mouth, lowering to hers...

She gave a little cry of pain. It had meant nothing—nothing to him at all. False—all false!

Bitter irony twisted inside her.

I thought he wanted me to be Sabine—a woman of the world, alluring and sensual, willing and eager for an instant romance. But all along Sabine was the woman he wanted to destroy.

And destroy her he had.

Too late she had discovered, after a few brief, fleeting days of passion and desire, how much more she wanted. Wanted as Sarah—not Sabine.

Pain shot through her again. And too late she had discovered what she was to Bastiaan…what she had been all along, through every kiss, every caress, every moment she'd spent with him.

Discovered that she had lost what she had never had at all.

The choke rose in her throat again, but she forced it back. She would not weep, would not shed tears. She snatched her hand from the water, twisted around, away from the stone pond.

And looked straight at Bastiaan.

He walked towards her. There was a numbness in him, but he kept on walking. She stood poised, motionless, looking so achingly beautiful, with her gold hair coiled at her nape, her slender body wreathed in an evening gown of pale green chiffon.

As he drew closer, memory flashed. The two of them sitting behind the wheel of his boat, moving gently on the low swell of the sea, her leaning into him, his arm around her waist, as he turned its nose into the path of the setting sun, whose golden rays had burnished them as if in blessing.

Another memory, like a strobe light, of them lying together, all passion spent, during the hours of the night, her slender body cradled in his. Another flash, and a memory of the fragrance of fresh coffee, warm croissants, the morning sun reaching its fingers into the vine-shaded terrace as they took their breakfast.

Each memory became more precious with every passing hour.

Each one was lost because of him. Because of what he'd done to her.

He could not take his eyes from her. Within him emotion swelled, wanting to overtake him, to impel him to do what he longed to do—sweep her into his arms. He could not—dared not. Everything rested on this moment—he had one chance...one only.

A chance he must take. Must not run from as he had thought to do, unable to confront her in the throng inside, at the moment of her triumph in her art. But now as she stood there, alone, he must brave the moment. Reclaim what he had thrown from him—what he had not known he had possessed.

But I did know. I knew it with every kiss, every embrace, every smile. I knew it in my blood, my body—my heart.

As he came up to her, her chin lifted. Her face was a mask. 'What are you doing here? Philip said you weren't here. Why did you come?'

Her words were staccato. Cold. Her eyes hard in the dim light.

'You must know why I am here,' he said. His voice was low. Intense.

'No. I don't.' Still staccato, still that mask on her face. 'Is it to see if I'm impressed by what you've done for Max? All that lavish sponsorship! Is it by way of apology for your foul accusations at me?'

He gave a brief, negating shake of his head and would have spoken, but she forged on, not letting him speak.

'Good. Because if you want to sponsor him—well, you've got enough money and to spare, haven't you? I want none of it—just like I never wanted Philip's.' She took a heaving breath, 'And just like I want nothing more to do with you either.'

He shut his eyes, receiving her words like a blow. Then his eyes flared open again. 'I ask only five minutes of your time, Sab—Sarah.'

He cursed himself. He had so nearly called her by the name she did not bear. Memory stabbed at him—how he had wondered why Philip stammered over her name.

If I had known then the truth about her—if I had known it was not she who had taken money from Philip...

But he hadn't known.

He dragged his focus back. What use were regrets about the past? None. Only the future counted now—the future he was staking this moment on.

She wasn't moving—not a muscle—and he must take that for consent.

'Please...please understand the reasons for my behaviour.'

He took a ragged breath, as if to get his thoughts in order. It was vital, crucial that he get this right. He had one chance...one chance only...

'When Philip's father died I promised his mother I would always look out for him. I knew only too well that he could be taken advantage of. How much he would become a target for unscrupulous people.'

He saw her face tighten, knew she was thinking of what Max had done, however noble a cause he'd considered it.

He ploughed on. 'Especially,' he said, looking at her without flinching, 'women.'

'Gold-diggers,' she said. There was no expression in her voice.

'Yes. A cliché, but true all the same.'

A frown creased between Bastiaan's eyes. He had to make her understand what the danger had been—how real it could have been.

If she had truly been the woman I feared she was.

'I know,' he said, and his mouth gave a caustic curl of self-derision, 'because when I was little older than Philip, and like him had no father to teach me better, a woman took me to the cleaners and made a complete fool of me.'

Did he see something change in her eyes? He didn't know—could only keep going.

'So when I saw that twenty thousand euros had gone from Philip's account to an unknown account in Nice... when I heard from Paulette that Philip had taken to hanging around a nightclub endlessly and was clearly besotted with someone, alarm bells rang. I *knew* the danger to him.'

'And so you did what you did. I know—I was on the receiving end.'

There was bitterness in her voice, and accusation. She'd had enough of this—*enough*. What was the point of him going on at her like this? There wasn't one. And it was hell—just hell on earth—to stand here with him so close, so incredibly close.

So unutterably distant… Because how could he be anything else?

She made herself say the words that proved it. 'I get the picture, Bastiaan. You seduced me to safeguard Philip. That was the only reason.' There was a vice around her throat, but she forced the words through.

She started to turn away. That vice around her throat was squeezing the air from her. She had to get out of here. Hadn't Bastiaan Karavalas done enough to her without jeopardizing everything she had worked to achieve?

'*No.*'

The single word, cutting through the air, silenced her.

'No,' he said again. He took a step towards her. 'It was not the only reason.'

There was a vehemence in the way he spoke that stilled her. His eyes were no longer veiled…they were burning—burning with an intensity she had never seen before.

'From the moment I first saw you I desired you. Could not resist you even though I thought you were Sabine, out to exploit my cousin. *Because* I thought that it gave me…' he took a breath '…a justification for doing what I wanted to do all along. Indulge my desire for you. A desire that you returned—I could see that in every glance you gave me. I knew you wanted me.'

'And you used that for your own ends.' The bitterness was back in her voice.

He seemed to flinch, but then he was reaching for her wrist to stay her, desperate for her to hear what he must say—*must* say.

'I regret everything I did, Sarah.' He said her name with difficulty, for it was hard—so hard—not to call her by the name he'd called her when she was in his arms. 'Everything. But not—not the time we had together.'

She strained away from him. 'It was fake, Bastiaan. Totally fake.' There was harshness in her voice.

'Fake?' Something changed in his voice. His eyes. His fingers around her wrist softened. 'Fake…?' he said again.

And now there was a timbre to his voice that she had heard before—heard a hundred times before…a thousand. She felt a susurration go through her as subtle as a breath of wind in her hair. As caressing as a summer breeze.

'Was *this* fake?' he said,

And now he was drawing her towards him and she could not hold back. The pulse in her veins was whispering, quickening. She felt her breath catch, dissolve.

'Was *this* fake?' he said again.

And now she was so close to him, so close that her head was dropping back. She could catch the scent of his body, the warmth of it. She felt her eyes flutter shut and then he was kissing her, the softness of his lips a homage, an invocation.

He held her close, and closer still, cupping her nape to deepen his kiss.

Bliss eased through her, melting and dissolving. Dissolving the hard, bitter knot of pain and anger deep inside her. He let her lips go, but his eyes were pouring into hers.

'Forgive me—I beg you to forgive me.' His voice was husky, imploring. 'I wronged you—treated you hideously. But when I made those accusations at you—oh, they were tearing me to pieces. To have spent those days with you, transforming everything in my life, and then that final day…' He shut his eyes, as if to shut out the memory, before forcing himself to open them again, to speak to her of what had haunted him. 'To think myself duped—

because how could you be that woman I'd feared you were when what we had was so…so wonderful.'

His voice dropped.

'I believed all my fears—and I believed the worst fear of all. That you were not the woman I had so wanted you to be…'

He gazed down at her now, his hand around her nape, cradling her head, his eyes eloquent with meaning. And from his lips came the words he had come here to say.

'The woman I love—Sabine or Sarah—*you* are the woman I love. Only you.'

She heard the words, heard them close, as close as her heart—the heart that was swelling in her breast as if it must surely become her very being, encompassing all that she was, all that she could be.

She pressed her hand against the strong wall of his chest, glorying in feeling her fingers splay out over the hard muscle beneath his shirt. Feeling the heat of his body, the beat of his heart beneath her palm.

Wonder filled her, and a whitening of the soul that bleached from her all that she had felt till now—all the anger and the hurt, the fury and the pain. Leaving nothing but whitest, purest bliss.

She gazed up at him, her face transformed. He felt his heart turn over in his breast, exultation in it.

'I thought it impossible…' she breathed. 'Impossible that in a few brief days I could fall in love. How could it be so swift? But it was true—and oh, Bastiaan, it hurt so *much* that you thought so ill of me after what we'd had together.'

To love so swiftly—to hurt so badly…

She saw him flinch, as if her words had made a wound, but he answered her.

'The moment I knew—that hellish moment when I knew everything I'd feared about you, all I'd accused you of was false...nothing but false... I knew that I had destroyed everything between us. You threw me out and I could do nothing but go. Accept that you wanted nothing to do with me. Let you get on with your preparations for tonight without my plaguing you.'

His voice changed. 'But tonight I could keep silent no longer. I determined to find you—face you.' A rueful look entered his dark eyes. 'I bottled it. I was too... too scared to face you.' His gaze changed again, becoming searching. 'What you've achieved tonight—what it will bring you now—will there be room for me? *Can* there be?'

She gave a little cry. 'Oh, Bastiaan, don't you see? It's *because* of what I feel—because now I know what love is—that I can achieve what I have tonight...what will be in me from now for ever.'

She drew back a little.

'That aria I sang, where the War Bride mourns her husband's death...' She swallowed, gazing up at him with all her heart in her eyes. 'She sings of love that is lost, love that burns so briefly and then was gone. I couldn't sing it. I didn't understand it until—'

He pulled her into his arms, wrapping them tight around her. 'Oh, my beloved, you will *never* feel that way again. Whatever lessons in love you learn from me will be happy ones from now. Only happy ones.'

She felt tears come then, prickling in her eyes, dusting her lashes with diamonds in the starlight. Bastiaan—*hers*. Her Bastiaan! After such torment, such bliss! After such fears, such trust. After such anger, such love...

She lifted her head to his, sought his mouth and found

it, and into her kiss she poured all that was in her heart, all that she was, all that she would be.

An eternal duet of love that they would sing together all their lives.

EPILOGUE

SARAH LAY ON the little sandy beach, gazing up at the stars which shone like a glittering celestial tiara overhead. There was no sound but the lapping of water, the night song of the cicadas from the vegetation in the gardens behind. But her heart was singing—singing with a joy, a happiness so true, so profound, that she could still scarcely credit it.

'Do you remember,' the low, deep voice beside her asked, 'how we gazed up at the stars by the pool in my villa at Cap Pierre?'

She squeezed the hand that was holding hers as she and Bastiaan lay side by side, their eyes fixed on eternity, ablaze overnight in the Greek sky.

'Was it then?' she breathed. 'Then that I started to fall in love with you?'

'And I with you?'

Her fingers tightened on his. Love had come so swiftly she had not imagined it possible. And hurt had followed.

But the pain I felt was proof of love—it showed me my own heart.

Now all that pain was gone—vanished and banished, never to return! Now, here with Bastiaan, as they lay side by side on the first night of their married life together, they were sealing their love for ever. He had asked her where she wanted to spend her honeymoon but she had seen in his eyes that he already knew where he wanted them to be.

'I always said,' he told her, 'that I would bring my bride to my island—that she alone would be the one woman I would ever want here with me.'

She lifted his hand to her mouth, grazing his knuckles with a kiss.

'I also always said—' and his voice was different now, rueful and wry '—that I would know who that woman would be the moment I set eyes on her.'

She laughed. She could do that now—now that all the pain from the way he had mistrusted and misused her was gone.

'How blind I was! Blind to everything that you truly were! Except...' And now he hefted himself on to one elbow, rolled on to his hip to gaze down at her—his beloved Sarah, his beloved bride, his beloved wife for all the years to come. 'Except to my desire for you.'

His eyes blazed with ardour and she felt her blood quicken in its veins as it always did when he looked at her like that, felt her bones melting into the sand beneath her.

'That alone was true and real! I desired you then and I desire you now—it will never end, my beautiful, beloved Sarah!'

For an instant longer his gaze poured into hers, and then his mouth was tasting hers and she was drawing him down to her. Passion flared and burned.

Then, abruptly, Sarah held him off. 'Bastiaan Karavalas—if you think I am going to spend my wedding night and consummate my marriage on a beach, with pebbles digging into me and sand getting into places I don't even want to think about, then you are—'

'Entirely right?' he finished hopefully, humour curving his mouth.

'Don't tempt me,' she said huskily, feeling her resolve weaken even as she started to melt again.

But you do tempt me...

The words were in Bastiaan's head, echoing hers, taking him back—back to the time when he had been so, so wrong about her. And so, so right about how much he wanted her. He felt his breath catch with the wonder of it all. The happiness and joy that blazed in him now.

He got to his feet, crouched beside her, and with an effortless sweep scooped her up into his arms. She gave a little gasp and her arms went around his neck, clinging to him.

'No,' he said firmly, 'you're right. We need a bed. A large, comfortable bed. And, as it happens, I happen to have one nearby.'

He carried her across the garden into the house behind. It was much simpler than the villa in Cap Pierre, but its privacy was absolute.

The grand wedding in Athens a few hours ago, thronged with family and friends, with Sarah's parents, his aunt and his young cousin—Philip having been delighted at the news of their union—and even his own mother, flown in from LA, seemed a world away.

Max had delivered Sarah fresh from rehearsals for a production of *Cavalleria Rusticana*—with himself directing and Sarah singing 'Santuzza' at a prestigious provincial opera house in Germany—making it very clear to her that the only reason he was tolerating her absence was because she happened to be marrying an extremely wealthy and extremely generous patron of the opera, whose continued financial sponsorship he fully intended to retain.

'Keep the honeymoon short and sweet!' Max had ordered her. 'With your career taking off, it has to come first!'

She'd nodded, but had secretly disagreed. Her art and her love would always be co-equal. Her life now would be hectic, no doubt about that, and future engagements were already being booked up beyond her dreams, but they would never—*could* never—displace the one person who for all her life would stand centre stage to her existence.

She gazed up at him now, love blazing in her eyes, as he carried her into the bedroom and lowered her gently upon the bed, himself with her.

'How much...' he said huskily, this man she loved. 'How much I love you...'

She lifted her mouth to his and slowly, sweetly, passionately and possessively, they started together on their journey to the future.

* * * * *

THE BOSS'S BABY
ARRANGEMENT

CATHERINE MANN

To Jeanette Vigliotti,
a brilliant professor and a dear friend.
So happy you are an unofficial
part of our family!

One

Xander Lourdes had loved and lost his soul mate.

Parked in an Adirondack chair by the Gulf waters, he knew deep in his gut he wouldn't find that again. Even after a year, his wife's death from an aneurysm cut Xander to the core, but he'd been working like hell to find solace as best he could in honoring her memory every way possible.

By parenting their baby girl.

And by revitalizing a wildlife refuge in his dead wife's beloved Florida Keys. He'd invested half of his personal fortune to revitalize this place. No great hardship as far as the executive angle went. He thrived on that part.

Although the fundraising parties? Like tonight? The endless schmoozing? A real stick in the eye. His preferred way to spend an evening was with his daughter, Rose, or in the office. These social gatherings tried his patience. For a moment his mind wandered back to how his wife had always stabilized and smoothed functions like this for him. She'd been a natural complement for him.

For his wife's memory, he endured the beachside gala.

Xander drank tonic water, half listening to the state politician rambling beside him about a childhood pet parakeet. Small talk had never been Xander's thing.

Waves crashed on the shore and a bonfire crackled at the high-end outdoor fundraiser. Tiki torch flames flickered, reaching toward the starlit sky as a steel-drum band played. Marshes *swooshed* with softer sounds in the distance, grasses and nocturnal creatures creating a night ensemble all their own.

A lengthy buffet table and bar kept the partygoers well stocked by the waitstaff currently weaving through the crowd of partiers talking or dancing barefoot on the sand, silk and diamonds glinting in the moonlight, tuxedo ties loosened. His brother—the head veterinarian— and his sexy-as-hell lady assistant led the dancing. The redheaded zoologist was just the sort to keep the party going.

Xander's wife, Terri, hadn't been much for dancing, but she'd loved music. When they'd found out she was pregnant, her first reaction was to track down a special device to play classical music for their baby in the womb. Music, she believed, could change a person's life—convey emotions stronger than any other type of language. This belief had also prompted her to find compilations for the animals at the refuge to soothe them. Terri had been his calm and support since they were in first grade, when Xander had been labeled an outcast for already performing three grade levels above the others.

They'd been inseparable since she approached him on

the playground that first day and he'd missed her every minute since she'd died.

His daughter—Terri's legacy—meant everything to him.

Washing down the lump in his throat with another swallow of tonic water, he nodded at something or other the politician said about expanding the bird care portion of the refuge's clinic. Xander tucked the info away for later. At least he had the executive power and the portfolio to make that happen, to control something in a world that had denied him control over so damn much.

There was no space tonight for thinking about that now. It wouldn't help the cause his wife had devoted so much time and energy to.

Her volunteer work here had been important to her. When Xander's brother had started at the refuge, Terri's interest ignited. And then she'd discovered her passion, starting foundations to try to channel more funds into reviving the place.

His brother, Easton, oversaw the medical aspect of the refuge as an exotic animal veterinarian with a staff of techs and zoologists. Easton had worked here back in the early days, more concerned with animals than with the money he could make at a bigger, tourist-trap outfit. Xander had supported the refuge's efforts with donations, but now his interest was more personal and yet also more professional. He'd been elected chairman of the board of directors. Terri had wanted him to take that role for years and now she would never know he'd fulfilled her hope that he could grow the refuge.

Damn.

He'd had enough of small talk.

Xander shoved out of his chair. "I appreciate your taking the time to chat and attend. If you'll excuse me,

I need to attend to some business, but my brother would thoroughly enjoy talking to you about those clinic additions. I'll get Easton off the dance floor for you."

Making a beeline for his brother who was still dancing with the fire-headed zoologist, Xander shouldered through the partiers, nodding and waving without stopping until he reached the throng of dancers. He tapped Easton on the shoulder.

"Mind if I cut in, brother?"

His eccentric younger brother turned on his heel, his forehead creased, a trickle of sweat beading on his brow. "What's up?"

Easton wore the Prada suit Xander had made sure was delivered for the occasion, but his brother hadn't bothered with a tie. No surprise. Dr. Easton Lourdes had always been more comfortable in khakis and T-shirts.

Xander tipped his head toward the politician still knocking back mixed drinks. "Donor at your nine o'clock. Needs your expertise on possible additions to the aviary in the clinic."

His brother's forehead smoothed and his face folded in a smile, all charm. "Can do." He clapped Xander on the shoulder. "Thanks again for this shindig. It's going to pay off big for the place."

Easton charged past like a man on a mission, leaving his dance partner on the floor alone.

Maureen Burke.

An auburn-haired bombshell, full of brains and energy. She was an Irish native who'd spent much of her life in the States, so her brogue was light. Her degree in zoology along with her rescue experience made her the perfect second-in-command for his brother. Lucky for them she'd received her work visa at exactly the right time. She was extroverted, but also all business. And a woman Xander didn't have to worry was out to take advantage of the Lourdes family fortune passed down for generations. A portfolio Xander had doubled and that women were attracted to when it came to dating Easton.

Maureen was an individual guaranteed not to mistake Easton's attention as interest and an invitation to leave ten voice mails. Maureen was much like Xander when it came to romance.

Not interested.

He'd learned she was divorced and, from her standoffish demeanor just beneath that plush-lipped smile, he got the impression it hadn't been a pleasant split. No doubt the man had been an idiot to let such a gorgeous, intelligent woman walk out of his life.

Xander extended his hand. "Sorry to have stolen your dance partner. I had to send my brother off. Dance with me."

"Dance? With you?" She swept her long red curls back over her shoulder, her face flushed from heat and exertion.

"Is that such a strange request?"

"I didn't expect you to know how to dance, much less to know an Irish jig."

He winced. "An Irish jig?"

She grinned impishly, gesturing to the stage with elegant hands, nails short but painted a glittering gold for the party. "Next up on the band's request list. Your brother double-dog dared me."

Double-dog dare? No wonder Easton had left the dance floor so easily and with a grin on his face. He'd set Xander up.

And Xander wasn't one to back down from a challenge. "I'm a man of many talents. Our mother insisted we boys attend dance classes as teens." He braced his shoulders. "Whatever I don't know, you can teach me."

"Good for your mama."

"And that dance?"

She propped a hand on her hip, her whispery yellow gown hitching along curves as she eyed him with emerald-green eyes. Finally she shrugged. "Sure. Why not? I would like to see the big boss give it a try."

"Remember, you'll have to help me brush up on the steps."

"We'll keep the moves simple." She extended an elbow. "Steel drums playing Irish tunes is a first, not too intricate but still fun."

He bowed before hooking elbows with her. Damn. He'd forgotten how soft a woman's skin felt. Clearing his throat, he mimicked her steps, mixed with a periodic spin. Her hair fanned across his chest as she whipped around.

His body reacted to the simple contact.

Had to be lack of sex messing with his brain.

But holy hell, the dance seemed to go on forever with his blood pressure ramping by the second until, thank God, the band segued to a slower tune. And still he didn't step away. In spite of the twinge of guilt he felt over the surprise attraction, he extended his hands and took her into his arms for a more traditional dance. The scent of citrus—lemons and grapefruit—teased his nose like an aphrodisiac.

Maybe the Irish dance hadn't been such a good idea after all.

He searched for something to say to distract himself from the gentle give of her under his touch, the occasional skim of her body against his. "I'm glad you're enjoying yourself."

"I enjoy anything that makes money for the refuge." Her eyes glimmered in the starlight, loose curls feathering over the top of his hand along her waist. "I love my work here."

"Your devotion is admirable."

"Thank you." Her face flashed with indecision.

"You don't believe me?"

"It's not that. But let's not talk shop right now and spoil the moment. We can talk tomorrow." She chewed her bottom lip. "I have an appointment to see you."

"You do? I don't recall seeing your name on my calendar."

"Not all of us have a personal assistant to keep track of our schedules."

"Am I being insulted?" He had a secretary, but not a personal assistant who followed him around all day like his brother did. Although his brother was known to be an absentminded-professor type.

"No insult meant at all. You've made a great future for yourself and for Rose. It's clear you didn't ride off your family fortune, but increased it. That's commendable." She shook her head, sending her curls prancing along his hand again. "I'm just frustrated. Ignore me. Dance."

Her order came just as the band picked up with a sultry Latin beat.

Maureen Burke danced with abandon.

Throwing herself into this pocket of time, matching the steps of this leanly athletic man with charismatic blue eyes and a sexual intensity as potent as his handsome face.

Brains. Brilliance. A body to die for and a loyal love of family.

Xander Lourdes was a good man.

But not her man.

So Maureen allowed herself to dance with the abandon she never would have dared otherwise. Not now. Not after all she'd been through.

She breathed in the salty air mixed with the scent of fresh burning wood from the bonfire. What a multifaceted word. *Abandon.* She danced with freedom. But she'd also been abandoned and that hadn't felt like freedom at all. The pain. The grief. Being given up on for no good reason other than the fact she wasn't a good fit for her ex-husband's life after all she had put up with. After she'd ignored the urgings of so many friends to leave him and his emotional abuse.

Rejection.

She'd known they had problems. Maureen was always willing to work at broken things. Hell, her never-say-die nature made her compatible and adept in a wildlife refuge. Vows meant something to her. She'd always expected if she ever got divorced it would be because of a major event—physical abuse or drugs. But for nothing more than "I love you but I can't live with you"? Like she'd filled their home with some toxic substance.

More of that negative thinking born of years of his tearing her down until finally—thank God, finally—she'd wised up and realized he was, in fact, the toxin.

So she'd let him go and left their home full of insults and negativity. Hell, she'd left County Cork to get as far away from him and the ache as possible. It wasn't like she had family or anything else holding her back. Her parents were dead and her marriage was a disaster. There'd been nowhere else for her to go except to the US and accept the job in a field of work she loved so much.

She allowed herself to be swept away by the dance,

the music and the pulse of the drums pushing through her veins with every heartbeat, faster and faster. Arching timbres of the steel drums urged her to absorb every fiber of this moment.

Too soon, her work visa was due to expire, and officials had thus far denied her requests to extend it. She would have to go home. To face all she'd run from, to leave this amazing place where *abandon* meant beauty and exuberance. Freedom.

The freedom to dance with a handsome man and not to worry that her husband would accuse her of flirting. As if she would run off with any man who looked her way. How long had it taken her to realize his remarks were born of his own insecurities, not her behavior?

She was free to look now, though, at this man with coal-black hair that spiked with the sea breeze and a hint of sweat. His square jaw was peppered with a five-o'clock shadow, his shoulders broad in his tuxedo, broad enough to carry the weight of the world.

Shivering with warm tingles that had nothing to do with any bonfire or humid night, she could feel the attraction radiating off him the same way it heated in her. She'd sensed the draw before but his grief was so well known she hadn't wanted to wade into those complicated waters. But with her return to home looming…

Maureen wasn't interested in a relationship, but maybe if she was leaving she could indulge in—

Suddenly his attention was yanked from her. He reached into his tuxedo pocket and pulled out his cell phone and read the text.

Tension pulsed through his jaw, the once-relaxed, half-cocked smile replaced instantly with a serious expression. "It's the nanny. My daughter's running a fever. I have to go."

And without another word, he was gone and she knew she was gone from his thoughts. That little girl was the world to him. Everyone knew that, as well as how deeply he grieved for his dead wife.

All of which merely made him more attractive.

More dangerous to her peace of mind.

As the morning sun started to spray rays through the night, Xander rubbed the grit from the corners of his eyes, stifling a yawn from the lack of sleep after staying up all night to keep watch over Rose. He'd taken her straight to the emergency room and learned she had an ear infection. Even with the doctor's reassurance, antibiotics and fever-reducing meds, he couldn't take his eyes off her. Still wearing his tuxedo, he sat in a rocker by her bed. Light brown curls that were slightly sticky with sweat framed her face, her cherubic mouth in a little cupid's bow as she puffed baby breaths. Each rise and fall of her chest reassured him she was okay, a fundamentally healthy sixteen-month-old child who had a basic, treatable ear infection.

A vaporizer pumped moisture into the nursery, which was decorated in white, green and pink, with flowers Terri had called cabbage roses, in honor of their daughter's name. A matching daybed had been included in the room for those nights they just enjoyed watching her breathe. Or for the nanny—Elenora—to rest when needed. A glider was set up in the corner and his mind flooded with memories of Terri nursing their baby in the chair, her face so full of maternal love and hope, all of which had been poured into putting this room together. A week before Rose was born, he and Terri had sat on the daybed, his arms wrapped around her swollen belly, as they'd dreamed of what their child would look like. What she would grow up to accomplish. So many dreams.

Now his brother catnapped in that same space, as he so often did these days, quirky as hell and a never-ending source of support. An image of his brother dancing with Maureen Burke flash through Xander's mind. His brother hadn't had much of a social life lately, either, and even knowing Xander would help Easton if the roles were reversed didn't make it fair to steal so much of his brother's time.

Xander pushed up from the rocker and shook his brother lightly by the shoulder. "Hey, Easton," he said softly. "Wake up, dude. You should head on back to your room."

His brother's eyes blinked open slowly. "Rose?"

"Much better. Her fever's down. I'll still take her to her regular pediatrician for a follow-up, but I think she's going to be fine. She's past needing both of us to keep watch."

"I was sleeping fine, ya know." His lanky brother swung his legs off the bed.

"Folded up like pretzel. Your neck would have been in knots. But thank you. Really. You don't have to stick around. I know you have to work."

"So do you," Easton said pointedly, raking his fingers through his hair.

"She's my kid."

"And you're my brother." His eyes fixed on Xander's. Steady and loyal. They'd always been different but close since their parents traveled the world with little thought of any permanent home or the consistency their kids needed to build friendships. They relied on each other. Even more so after their father died and their mother continued her world traveling ways, always looking for the next adventure in the next country rather than connecting with her children.

And, thank God, Xander's brother could work at any wildlife refuge around the world and he'd chosen to stay on here and help him. That meant the world to him. Easton had done special projects here for Terri, but this place wasn't on the scale of the other places where he could work.

Hell, it wasn't on Xander's scale. But for Terri, for Rose, too, he would put this place on the map. Whatever it took. This was his wife's legacy to their child.

"Thank you."

"No thanks needed other than getting this little one better." Easton smoothed an affectionate hand over his niece's head. "Well…and a bottle of top-shelf tequila to drink at sunset."

"Put it on the list." A long list, all he owed his brother. But he would find a way to pay him back someday. A kick of guilt pushed him to say, "If you need to move on to a larger job—"

"I wouldn't be needed. Being needed, making a difference—" he shrugged, eyes flicking to Rose "—that's what life's all about."

Xander swallowed hard. Terri had said that to him more than once. God, he missed her. "Fair enough." And before he even realized the thought had crossed his mind, he stopped his brother at the door. "Might you really be sticking around because of a certain red-haired zoologist?"

"Maureen?" Easton said with such incredulity there was no doubting the truthfulness of his statement. "No. Absolutely not. There's nothing going on between the two of us. We're too much alike."

Laughing lightly, he shook his head, scratched the

back of his neck and chuckled again on his way out the door, leaving Xander more confused than ever. Not because of his brother's denial.

But because of his own relief.

Two

Maureen listened for the familiar *click-click* of her key in her beach cabana door. The double click meant that the teal-colored cabana was, indeed, actually locked. One click meant a well-targeted gust of wind would knock the door in. She would miss these sorts of quirks when she moved out of the brightly painted cabana and tropical Key Largo.

But that wasn't happening yet. Shoving the thought aside, Maureen adjusted her satchel filled with notebooks and began her commute to work. A leisurely five-minute walk.

And today, with the sunshine warming her fair skin, she was content to take in her surroundings as she made her way to the Lourdeses' home residence, built on property they'd bought at the edge of the refuge. Sauntering to the main house—a white beach mansion that always reminded her of the crest of a wave in a storm—she let her mind wander.

Absently, she watched volunteers from town and from farther away gather and disperse on the dock on-site. Even from here, she could hear the bustle of their excitement as the crowd moved toward the fenced and screened areas beneath the white beach mansion on signature Florida Keys stilts.

Eyeing more volunteers who were gathering by the screened areas where recovering animals were kept, she scanned the zone for Easton. Not a trace of him.

Or Xander. After last night, her thoughts tilted back to the dance. To his warm touch, the way he looked after his daughter. The kind of person he was. And those damn blue eyes that cut her to the quick, pierced right through her.

She'd spent most of the night attempting to navigate her sudden attraction to Xander. Not that it really mattered. Instead of admitting that the dance echoed in her dreams last night, she attempted to turn her attention to more practical matters like the school group that was due at the refuge shortly.

Though located on Key Largo, the refuge's secluded location meant tourists didn't wander in haphazardly. The public could access the refuge only through a prearranged guided tour. This policy was one Maureen loved. It made the wildlife refuge into her own kind of sanctuary, one that often felt independent of the tourist traps and straw-hat community of the main part of town. The limited public interaction allowed her to enjoy the mingled scent of salt and animals. There was truly a wildness here that called to some latent part of Maureen's soul.

Surveying her watch, she noted the time. The school children would be here soon. That meant she had to find Easton quickly.

And if she happened to see Xander…well, that'd be just fine by her.

Though, if she were being honest, the thought of accidently on purpose running into him made her giddy. Flashes of last night's dance pulsed in her mind's eye again.

What would she do if she actually ran into him anyway? Running a hand through her ringlet hair, Maureen stifled a sigh as Xander came into view.

Well, she certainly was committed now. At least, committed to some harmless small talk with a man who had pushed her sense of wild abandon into the realm worthy of Irish bards.

Biting the inside of her lip, she dropped her hands to her sides. Xander's smooth walk was uninterrupted as he pulled on his suit coat.

He'd built an office extension onto the refuge when Terri, his wife, had started to volunteer. Terri had fallen in love with Key Largo and her volunteer work. Three years ago, when Maureen had just started with the refuge, Xander had commuted back and forth to Miami for work, using the office at the refuge as a satellite. After Terri passed away, he'd moved here full-time.

Maureen's thoughts lingered for a moment on her memories of Terri. She had been a quiet, gentle woman. It hadn't taken Maureen very long to figure out Terri's heart was bigger than most, and that her kindness and empathy were genuine. Wounded creatures were comforted by Terri's presence. When Terri had become pregnant, she'd begrudgingly performed office work, though Maureen could tell she'd rather have been among the animals.

After she'd passed away, Xander had poured himself into the refuge. In the beginning, Maureen felt like Xander was trying to find some other piece of Terri here.

Now she felt like the refuge had woven its charm for him, too.

Shrugging his suit coat into place, Xander jogged down the long wooden stairway leading from the home on stilts. "Maureen?"

He said it as if he didn't recognize her. But, um, well, maybe she had taken more time with her appearance today. Jeans with a loose-fitting T-shirt was her go-to outfit. Minimal makeup—maybe a wave of a mascara wand over her lashes, a pale lip gloss, her wavy hair confined in a high ponytail. But today she looked considerably…nicer. Her fitted shirt revealed curves, and she'd deepened her lip color, daring a deeper nude that made her seem a bit more put-together, a bit more…well, sultry.

"Of course. Do I look that different?" Maureen's tongue skimmed the back of her teeth, causing her to smile awkwardly, hands flying to a stray strand of her hair that fell in a gentle wave against her chest. So much for nonchalance.

His eyes flicked over her. Slowly—as if he was trying to work something out.

"From last night at the party? Yes."

"We have a group of schoolchildren coming in for a tour this morning," she explained quickly. "They're due any minute and we're shorthanded. Shouldn't you be at work?"

Tilting her head to the side, she squinted at him. His top lip curled up, a smile playing at the corner of his mouth. Raising his eyebrows, he took a step closer, winking at her, more lighthearted than she could remember him being in the past. "Shouldn't you, Maureen?"

The smell of pine drifted into the space between them. Xander's lip was still playfully curled up and she felt a thrill run down her spine as she stared back at him, noticing the way his hair was still damp from a recent shower. Her thoughts stopped there. It felt like ages before she responded.

"I'm looking for your brother." How did Xander manage to keep from perspiring out here in a suit when she already felt like she was melting in a sauna?

Or melting from a different kind of heat.

"Easton's running late. We were both up late last night with Rose."

"You two took care of her?"

"Why is that a surprise?"

"I just assumed someone of your means would lean more on the nanny or call her grandparents."

"My father has passed away and my mother, uh, travels a lot. As for my former in-laws, they can be rather… overpowering. And Elenora needs her rest to be on the top of her game watching Rose while I'm at work. I'm her father. And my brother worried, as well. He also pitched in early this morning when I needed to snag a shower for work. He should be down soon." Xander gestured toward the pathway leading to the offices. "Shall we go?"

She stepped forward, aware of him in step beside her, his shoulder almost brushing hers on the narrow, sandy path. "That's admirable of both of you to take care of Rose. How is she doing?"

"Ear infection, according to the emergency room doctor. I'll be taking her to her pediatrician to follow up today."

"Is there anything I can do to help?" Maureen's thoughts drifted to Rose—the kind of child that adults fawned over. She was sweet, affectionate and filled with life. Maureen had seen testament to that sprinkled all over his office in the form of finger paintings and photographs. A shrine to childhood and a dedicated father.

Maureen's own interaction with Rose always left a smile on her face. With tiny fingers, Rose would reach up to play with Maureen's leather bracelet, touching it carefully as if it was a magical totem. Out of habit, Maureen's own hand flew to her leather bracelet. Feeling the worn leather, she felt assured. This bracelet had been everywhere with her. A certifying stamp of endurance. "Thanks. But I think we've got it covered. Although I have to admit, it's ironic that it took me and my brother to do one woman's job."

"And somewhere women are sighing."

He laughed.

In the pit of her stomach her nerves became bramble-twisted, much like the palm fronds blowing and tangled by the wind. Those damn blue eyes—they disarmed her senses, unsettling her more than any sounds from wild creatures chattering. Especially today as his gaze darted from her eyes to her lips.

A faint tautness pulled at his cheeks.

Warmth crept up her neck, threatening to flood her cheeks with a schoolgirl blush. *Get it together*, her inner voice scolded. Taking the cue from her sensibility, she drew in a deep breath and straightened her blouse.

"You're needed here to take care of animals." Dropping his gaze, he nodded his head. The momentary flicker of attraction melted off his expression. Xander's tone and eyes returned to their normal bulldog, business-man-slate stare.

"Of course. She's your child and doesn't really know me well." She held up her hands. "I've overstepped and I apologize."

He sighed. "I apologize. You're being helpful and I'm being an ass. I have a reputation for that."

She stayed silent.

"Not going to deny it?" His lip twitched upward.

"I wouldn't dare call the big boss anything so insulting."

He laughed. Hard. "You are surprising me left and right. Not at all how I've perceived you in the past."

"You thought about me?" Words tumbled out of her mouth before she thought better of them.

"As your employer."

"That makes things tricky. And you've had…a difficult year."

"Fourteen months. It's been fourteen months and three days." His voice lost an octave, felt like a whisper on a breeze.

"I'm so very sorry for your loss." An ache of deep empathy pushed hard against her chest. She'd seen the love Xander and Terri had for each other, a love she'd hoped to have in her own marriage.

"Me, too." His eyes met hers as a gust of island breeze carried the scent of flowers and the sound of distant motors. "Rose means everything to me. She's all I have left of Terri. I would do anything for my daughter but sometimes—" he thrust a hand through his tousled hair, his head tipping back as he looked up toward the sky "—I just feel like I'm short-changing her."

She touched his arm lightly. "You're tired, like any parent. And you're an amazing father, here for her, along with your brother. And Rose truly has a wonderful nanny. Elenora genuinely cares about her."

"Of course she does. I can see the affection they share." Was this the kind of thing she was supposed to say to a man baring his heart and acknowledging his pain? Maureen found the familiar spot in her bottom lip and chewed, wishing she could say something—anything—to take the hurt out of his voice.

"I spend time with her every day."

"I know that, too." She hadn't realized how much she'd noticed about his routine before. "You don't have to explain yourself to me. It's clear you love her."

"I do. She's everything to me."

"She's a lucky little girl."

The space between them thinned and now, shoulder to shoulder, she noticed how the pine soap pushed against a symphony of coffee beans and mint.

Turning to face her, his blue eyes sparked. He took half a step toward her, his own lips parted slightly as he searched her expression.

She stopped chewing her lip and tilted her head to the side to stare back at him, stomach fluttering the longer his gaze held hers.

"Thank you for your help last night organizing the gala."

"Thank you for the dance last night."

They stayed like that for a few moments until the buses were pulling up and pulling them back into reality. Away from whatever had electrified the air between them.

A full day in the office left Xander desperate for some salt air and sunshine. He'd worked, taken Rose to the pediatrician and had just settled her down for a nap. He'd read her a story before she drifted off to sleep. With the nanny on-call, he'd decided to take his brother up on his invitation to check the water samples from the nearby swamp.

He tried to convince himself he was only going out on the boat to become better acquainted with the procedures so he'd be of more use at the next fund-raiser. The fact that Maureen also was on the boat was pure coincidence. Xander tried to tell himself that was an accurate representation of reality.

His attempt to delude himself, however, was a hard sell, it turned out. He couldn't deny he wanted to be there. He'd looked forward to seeing Maureen and finding out if this attraction to her was just an anomaly.

Easton, his assistant, Portia, Maureen and Xander were all in swimsuits as the low-slung boat putted its way through the water. He tried not to notice Maureen's toned legs and the way her lavender one-piece swimsuit hugged her curves. Even her messy wind-whipped ponytail was sexy as hell.

Maureen was also a stark contrast to Portia Soto, his brother's assistant. Portia was also in a one-piece bathing suit, but a long patterned sarong swaddled her body. Portia embodied prim and proper. No detail was too minute to escape her notice. Portia adjusted her oversize hat and sunglasses, though she looked anxious.

So far, Xander couldn't understand why Portia had taken the job as his brother's assistant. She was efficient and talented. Of that, there was no doubt. But she seemed to be timid the majority of the time, not necessarily the sort that came immediately to mind when thinking of staff for a wild animal refuge.

Easton sat beside his assistant, who'd plastered herself in the seat with her back pressed against it, her fingers gripping the edge. Poor thing. She looked absolutely miserable and terrified. And while Xander's first instinct was to talk to the trembling woman, he couldn't help how his eyes seemed to always find their way back to Maureen.

"Would you like to return to the shore? You don't have to come with us every time," Maureen said gently, touching Portia's arm.

"The doctor relies on my notes." She nodded to the

bag in her hand, though Portia's eyes darted nervously to the brackish water and swamp animals outside. Clearly this job pushed her limits and yet here she was, anyway.

"They are helpful," he said absently while leaning over the edge. Wind tore through the boat, pressing Easton's blue swim trunks and white T-shirt hard against his body.

Maureen clucked her tongue. "A gator's going to bite your arm off one day."

Portia turned green.

Maureen's brogue lilted like the waves. "I'm only teasing."

Portia looked down and eased one hand free to pull her recorder from her waterproof bag. She began mumbling notes into the mike.

Maureen angled down to Easton. "I think she's plotting your demise."

"Possibly. But we have an understanding. We both need each other."

"It just seems strange she would take a job that scares her silly."

"I pay well. Not many enjoy this. I trust her and that counts for a helluva lot. Besides, I'm convinced she has an adventurous spirit buried underneath all that starch." His grin was wicked as he turned to face Maureen. That was his brother all right—always pushing people's comfort levels and making them laugh.

"If she doesn't have a heart attack first."

Portia chimed in, hands once again finding the edge of the seat cushions for stability. "Or die from some flesh-eating bacteria."

Easton laughed, his chuckles echoing over the water before he returned to his work again.

Xander caught his brother's eye before Easton turned to face Maureen. Something sly passed over Easton's expression and he quickly raised his brow to Xander before fully focusing on Maureen. "I'm damn sorry you're going to be leaving us."

"Me, too. This is a dream job." Her lithe arm extended out to the impossible shade of green water that surrounded them. Her attention seemed fixed on an imaginary spot on the horizon and Xander followed her gaze, trying to imagine what she was thinking about. Did she want to go home? It certainly didn't seem so from her crestfallen face, and she had asked him to look into extending the visa to complete her work here. He hadn't heard back, but then, that news would have gone to her and apparently the answer hadn't been positive.

Still, her face showed such distress, Xander couldn't help but wonder if it was about more than work.

Easton let out a low whistle. "And you're sure there's no way to extend the work visa?"

"It's been denied. Your brother even had the company lawyers review my paperwork to help, but with things tightening down regarding immigration, my request has been denied..." Maureen glanced back at Xander, her eyes as green as the crystal waters.

Did she know he could hear them?

He did his best to seem disinterested and aloof, channeling years of cutthroat business meetings to school his features into a mask of neutrality.

Easton's eyes momentarily flicked back to Xander. For a brief moment he swore Easton's head nodded slightly. Was that a sign to pay attention? What did his brother have planned?

"Xander has a lot of his time and energy—and heart—invested in this place."

"That, he does. I was surprised to see him dance last night."

"Who would have thought he could dance a jig?" Easton winked over his shoulder at his brother, making it clear he knew full well his brother could hear every word. "Who would have thought he would dance at all? That has certainly been in question since Terri died."

"She was a lovely lady." Maureen's voice meshed into the sounds of the nearby birds.

Xander tried not to look desperate as he strained to hear the rest of the conversation.

"She was. We all miss her. Her parents do, too, obviously. We always will. But I can't help hoping my brother will find a way to move on." Easton's lips had thinned into a smile and he stuck her with a knowing glance.

Maureen shook her head and tendrils of red hair fell out of her loose ponytail. "You're reading too much into a dance."

"I didn't say a thing. You did." A taunting, brotherly tone entered Easton's voice. He lifted up his hands to her, palms out in an exaggeration of placation.

"I'm definitely not making a move on your brother." The words were jagged on her tongue. Even from his seat, Xander could see pain jutting into Maureen's normally fair, bubbly features.

"Again, I didn't say that. You did."

"I'm divorced."

"I know."

Shrugging her shoulder, she leaned against the rail of the boat. "It was ugly."

"So very sorry to hear that."

"The past is past. I'm focused on my present and my job."

"Is that the reason you're so determined to stay here? Because your ex is back home?" Easton's eyes flicked back to Xander who pretended not to notice. But the truth was that his heart pulsated in his chest as he continued to listen to their conversation. A bad divorce? He couldn't help but wonder what had happened.

"Staying here is certainly easier. Fresh starts often are."

"It's not over yet."

"I appreciate your optimism."

"Um, hello?" Portia's voice rang out, urgency coloring every syllable. "Um, Doctor?"

"Yes, Ms. Soto?" Easton turned to face her.

"I'm getting seasick." And with that, Portia pulled herself up to the railing, turned a particularly sunset shade of scarlet and hurled the contents of her stomach overboard.

Xander reacted, setting their course back to the dock. Portia needed land, and fast.

They weren't too far away. Within minutes the dock was in sight.

And so were Xander's in-laws. It was never a good sign when they showed up from Miami unannounced. A pit knotted in his stomach and he felt his jaw tighten and clench.

Xander leaped off the boat as soon as it stabilized and helped Portia out. She'd gone ghost-pale and her hands were clammy—clearly she was much more seasick than she'd let on. Once Portia's feet were on solid ground, she covered her mouth, nodded politely at Xander's in-laws and dashed up to the house, probably stifling the urge to hurl the whole way.

His in-laws surveyed the landscape with eyes that revealed complete disgust. His mother-in-law's gaze followed Portia up the slope to the house. Delilah's brow arched, a silent conversation seemed to unfold between her and Jake, Xander's father-in-law.

So the verdict was out on this place. They'd hated it and did little to try to disguise that.

Jake looked at Portia's disappearing form and then back at Xander. Disapproval danced in his gaze.

Xander stifled the urge to grind his teeth. Did they actually think he was interested in Portia? And was that really any of their business to pass judgment on his dating life? Of course they all missed Terri, but she was gone, for over a year, and that was the tragic reality.

Besides, he wanted to tell them they had it all wrong, anyway. Portia wasn't his type. Xander didn't know why they'd assumed she'd be the kind of woman he was interested in, and he didn't want them to believe he hadn't loved their daughter with his whole soul. Xander certainly didn't want them to think she'd been so easily replaced.

The protest nearly formed against his tongue when reality jabbed him. Portia was polished, quiet, reserved... As far as types went, she shared a lot of Terri's qualities.

But Portia had never crossed his mind. Not once. Not in passing. There was no draw to her. Not like there was to the fiery Maureen. Xander's eyes flicked quickly to Maureen. She was helping Easton dock the boat.

Turning his attention back to his in-laws, he surveyed them, trying to anticipate the reason for this unannounced visit.

Jake and Delilah Goodwin were good people, if intrusive. They were what the news media deemed helicopter parents.

Xander had always imagined their hovering had everything to do with the circumstances of Terri's birth. For years Delilah and Jake had tried to conceive but never could. The doctors had told them it was practically impossible for them to become pregnant. But somehow

Delilah had been able to conceive and carry Terri to full term. The miracle child. Their only child.

Terri had been pampered and sheltered her whole life. They'd treated Terri like spun glass, like a fragile thing that needed protection from everything and everyone. Now having a daughter of his own, he understood the motivation and desire, but Jake and Delilah had taken hovering to its extreme.

Xander watched as Jake gave Delilah's hand a quick squeeze. His business instincts told him the gesture was one of support. He understood that. Terri's death had changed everything.

Delilah straightened her heirloom pearls on her neck, the only piece of jewelry that spoke to their enormous wealth. They were kind people, but they were used to dictating orders. They weren't the compromising type.

"We heard our grandchild is ill and you're out here. Who's watching her?" Jack said, his voice even but stern.

"She's napping while Elenora watches over her. Rose has an ear infection. We went to the emergency room last night and the pediatrician today."

Laying a manicured hand to her chest, Delilah stiffened. "She could have a relative watching her."

"She does. Her father and her uncle." Xander kept his tone neutral, doing his best to remember that they didn't mean to be insulting or accusatory.

"Both of whom are out partying on a boat," Delilah continued, her voice shrill and unforgiving.

The correction was gentle but necessary. He wished Terri was here to help him navigate this. "Working."

"Okay, then. Working. She could have her grandmother all day."

"I'm appreciative of your offer to help. Who told you about the ear infection?"

Delilah waved her hand dismissively. "Someone on the staff when I phoned to say hello."

To check up, more likely. His in-laws made no secret of the fact that they wanted custody of Rose. He would feel a lot more comfortable welcoming them for visits if they weren't taking notes and plotting the whole damn time.

He ground his teeth and tried to be as reasonable as possible. He didn't want to upset his daughter's world by having her taken from her own father. "Rose will be awake in about an hour. If you would like to stay for lunch, you can play with her when she wakes."

He glanced over his shoulder, checking on his brother and Maureen. Easton was tying the boat off along the dock while Maureen gathered up the samples. But that wasn't what caught Xander's eye. A massive gator swam in the dock area and bumped into the boat. The low-slung boat was tipped off balance and his eyes darted to Maureen, who was leaning over the railing.

Three

Water swirled around Maureen as she plummeted into the murky bay off the side of the boat.

Swimming had never been an issue for her. In Ireland, her childhood adventures had often unfolded in rivers and lakes. The water called to her. When she was young, she'd hold her breath and dive in undaunted. She'd even told her parents she was searching for kelpie—mythical Irish water horses. They were dangerous creatures of legend—sometimes drowning mortals for sport. At eight, Maureen was convinced that she could find kelpie and clear up the misconception. Her inclination to help and heal ran deep, to her core.

But here, in the swampy waters of Key Largo, there was no mythical creature that might whisk her to the bottom and drown her. No, in this water, an alligator slinked by. An animal that actually had the capacity to knock life from her lungs.

She tread water, schooling her breathing into calm

inhales and exhales. Or at least, this was the attempt she was making. Boggy, slimy weeds locked around her ankle, twisting her into underwater shackles.

Adrenaline pushed into her veins, her heart palpitating as she tried to force a degree of rigidity into her so-far-erratic movements.

From her memory depths, she recalled a time not unlike this one. She'd been swimming in Lake Michigan after her parents had relocated to Michigan. She'd been caught in weeds then, too, but her father had been there to untangle her. And that lake had lacked primitive dinosaur-like predators, which had made the Lake Michigan moment decidedly less dramatic.

Eyes flashing upward, she caught the panic flooding Xander's face.

Ready to help her.

The weeds encircling her ankle pulled against her. *Damn.* How'd she managed to become so ensnared so quickly? The pulse of the tide slashed into her ears, pushing her against the boat.

A loss of control kicked into her stomach. She heard vague shouting. Easton? Maybe. His voice seemed far away.

The grip on her ankle pulled taut, forcing her below the surface. The more she tried to tread water, to grab hold of the boat, the more she was pulled down. A new sort of tightness tap-danced on her chest. A mouthful of salt water belabored her breathing.

A vague sense of sound broke through her disorientation. Xander's voice. That steadying baritone. "Maureen, I'm coming!"

Words drifted to her like stray pieces of wood. Her salt-stung vision revealed Xander's muscled form coming toward her. She made out the people behind him—

his in-laws. Even from here, blurry vision and all, she read the concern in their clasped forms.

In an instant Xander was there, face contorted in worry. With an arm, he stabilized her against the boat. Air flooded her lungs again.

"I'm okay. I can swim. I just need to get my foot untangled from the undergrowth."

"Roger." He started to dive.

She grasped his arm. "Be careful of the—"

His gaze moved off to the side where the gator lingered with scaly skin and beady eyes. "I see. And the sooner we get out of here the better."

He disappeared underwater, a trail of small bubbles the only trace of him. Sinking fear rendered a palatable thrum in her chest—a war drum of anxiety. The gator disappeared under water.

Time stood on a knife-edge.

Suddenly she felt a palm wrap around her ankle and release her from the weeds. On instinct, she drew her knee to chest.

Xander followed. The edge of worry ebbed but refused to fade.

"I'm sure you can swim. But humor me. You may not know you're injured."

"I don't want to slow you—"

"And I don't want to hang out here in the swamp with gators and God only knows what else in addition to the leaking gas. Quit arguing." No room for negotiation in that tone. It must be the same voice Xander used in boardroom meetings.

"Okay, then. Swim."

His arms around her, she felt warmth leap from his body to hers. Feeling small and protected for the first time in ages. The muscles in his arm grew taught and retracted as he moved them through the water. Steadying her breathing, pushing her fear far away.

The water gave way to mucky sand and he helped her wade through that all the way to the shoreline.

Her body shook of its own accord. As if by reflex, he wrapped her into a tight hug and her head fit snugly beneath his chin.

The world, which a moment ago was filled with panic and fear, stilled. His breath on her cheek warmed her bones with more intensity than the tropical sun.

In that space, adrenaline fell back into her bloodstream. But fear didn't motivate that move this time. Awareness did as he held her close, breathing faster, somehow keeping time with her ragged heart. His body felt like steel against hers as she pulled away from him, her eyes catching his, watching as they fell away to her lips.

She hadn't imagined it, then, noting his desire.

"Maureen?" Her name sent the world crashing back into place. Willing her eyes away from his, she looked over her shoulder to see his in-laws and Easton standing a short distance away.

Knowing he needed coverage, even if just for a moment, she turned to face them, careful to stay angled in front of Xander. As if he'd done it a thousand times before, his hands fell to her shoulders. A mild but welcome distraction.

Xander's in-laws were visibly distraught.

"Are you okay?" Xander's father-in-law asked, face crumpled like he smelled something rotting. Maureen nodded dully, afraid her words might betray something private and real about this moment.

The man shifted focus from Maureen to Xander. "And you?"

"Yes. Thankfully. More of a scare than any real harm."
His hands squeezed Maureen's shoulder blades before
dropping. Immediately she felt the echo of his absence
from her skin.

His mother-in-law sniffed in response. "Honestly.
What if that had been Rose? I'm just glad she wasn't out
here. A nature refuge is lovely, of course—" ice entered
her words "—but such a dangerous, unpredictable place
isn't so well suited for *our* grandchild."

Maureen squinted at the woman's response, which felt
more like a warning than anything else.

Hours separated him from the gator run-in and he still
couldn't think straight.

He'd always been a pro at compartmentalizing events,
locking his personal life away so he could focus on whatever task at hand. That proved infinitely difficult with
this afternoon's events.

As if his mind was a film loop, he kept revisiting Maureen falling in the water, a gator just a few feet away.
The moment she looked like she was struggling sent him
tumbling into action—a reflex and urge so primal, he
couldn't ignore it.

Nor could he ignore the way she'd looked, soaked to
the bone in her swimsuit. The feel of her shuddering with
relief when they were on solid ground. How that relief reverberated in his own gut as he'd looked at her full lips.

There was no denying how turned on he was. The
connection he'd felt to her in that beachside embrace
had made him so damn aware of her. Sure, she'd always
been attractive. He knew that, but there was something
so sexy about the way she'd endured the gator run-in.

He wanted her, down to his core. All day, his thoughts
drifted to her.

Did life ever get easy?

Watching his in-laws with his daughter provided a quick answer to that question. Delilah and Jake weren't mean—they were matter-of-fact. Particular. Things had to be just so.

Reflecting back on Terri's perfect makeup and clothes, he saw what a lifetime of being scrutinized could do. How that constant second-guessing had sometimes wrought Terri up with anxiety. Especially when her parents came for a visit. She'd agonize on the arrangement of pillows and the tenderness of the pasta. Her mother and father always had a critique, a method of alleged perfection. Deep down, he knew they meant well.

Seeing Delilah straighten Rose's bow and quietly comment on staying proper rubbed him the wrong way. He wanted his daughter to grow up confident in her own worth.

He wanted to bring up his child.

"You know, Xander, we could help you with Rose. Keep her until school starts. We're retired now and we can devote all of our attention to her." Delilah's polished voice trilled. She had been hunched over Rose, examining the little girl's drawing.

"Ah, well, I know she looks forward to seeing you both. I think that helps enough," he said sympathetically. The pain of loss seemed to form a permanent line on her brow.

"Barry, our family friend and lawyer, you remember him? He mentioned that the court might see an arrangement with us to suit Rose better. We know how hard you work. We have the time to devote to her that you may not right now." Jake stood behind Xander, resting a hand on his shoulder.

The blood beneath his skin fumed, turned molten. He

had to keep his cool. "Well, I know how much you love Rose. But it's time for her to nap. She's still not feeling well."

Smoothing her dress, Delilah nodded. "Yes, she does need rest."

"I'm sure you feel similarly. You both should probably get settled in your hotel." His even tone held a challenge in it. He needed separation from them. Boundaries.

Especially now, because their intent had come into full view. They were here to spy on his proficiency as a father.

A more sinister thought entered his mind. What if they just snatched her away? It echoed in his mind as he saw them off the property and as he walked back into the room where his daughter slept. He looked at Elenora, a woman in her fifties with kind brown eyes, and left instructions with a caution about the issue with his in-laws. Elenora had to stay with Rose, and if anyone tried to come on the property, he was to be alerted at once.

The woman nodded her understanding. Feeling satisfied, he walked to his other unofficial charge. He went to find Maureen. Needed to make sure she was okay after her accident. There had been no time to actually check on her—not with his in-laws so close by.

Striding over to the clinic—another retrofitted and well-windowed building—his pace quickened. An urgency to move filled him. The stress of his in-laws, their constant reminders of the danger of the refuge and the way he was raising Rose. It all slammed into him.

Opening the door to the clinic, the sour smell of oil assaulted him. He turned the first corner in the building to see Maureen and a gaggle of oil-soaked seabirds. When the boat tipped, oil had seeped into the water and drenched the feathers of about five birds. The refuge had rounded them up for cleaning.

Maureen worked quickly, using the Dawn dish soap generously to lift the layers of oil from delicate feathers. He studied her, once again reminded of the intense gut-kick he'd felt earlier when she'd fallen into the water. The fear of loss knotted. He hated that fear.

Maureen cooed at the birds, mimicking their squawks with absolute precision. From a distance, and if he didn't know any better, he'd felt like she was actually talking to them. A real conversation. Her heart seemed to soar with delight as every inky layer of oil was lifted from the feathers of the bird.

Easton, a few feet away in the exam room, diligently looked over every bird Maureen had expertly cleaned.

Her hair was wet and piled on top of her head in a loose topknot with a few spiral curls escaping. She wore surgical scrubs. Apparently she'd only taken a quick shower to remove the muck from herself before going to work again.

She probably hadn't even thought about getting her own ankle examined. So like Maureen. So tender.

As she stood rinsing a bird, a smile on her lips, he felt the world slip away again. Mesmerized by her grace and movements.

And so kind. That fact, her empathy and patience, it was the remedy he needed. One that might even strike favor with his hard-to-please in-laws.

Gently, Maureen worked the oil out of the bird's left wing feathers, careful not to squeeze too tightly and damage the delicate bones. Moments had fallen away before she registered someone lingering by the door frame.

Not just someone. Xander.

Heat flooded into her cheeks as she remembered the way their bodies had pressed up against each other after the gator run-in.

"Are you okay? That was quite a spill you took."

She shrugged her shoulders, tongue unable to articulate any of her whirring thoughts.

"What makes a girl—hell, anyone—want to wrestle with alligators?" He inched closer.

"They don't bite nearly as hard as the ones in the boardroom," she volleyed back, thankful to find her voice again. He unnerved her fully.

"Funny." A puff of a laugh teased against his teeth, leaving behind a serpentine hiss.

"And I can outrun them."

"Also funny. But seriously, why this career?"

A loaded question. Freedom. This career awarded her a sense of sky and life the way nothing else could. "Why any career? Why would you want to stay inside all the time?"

"I enjoy the corporate challenge and I have a head for business. Without that, places like this would close down. It almost did." A defensive edge filled his tone.

She flashed a toothy smile, raising an eyebrow as a soap bubble floated in the space between them. "True enough. And without me, places like this wouldn't exist. I wanted to be a veterinarian. I just had to find my niche."

"So someone threw an alligator in your pool and you knew?" His lips parted into an incredulous smile and she found it hard to concentrate. Averting her gaze, she turned back to the double-crested cormorant, the bird made its traditional guttural noise that sounded much like a grunting pig. Funny. Endearing. It helped her re-center, refocus on her work with the greenish-black bird that sported an adorable orange neck.

"I was actually out on a field trip for school. My work group got separated from the rest and we were lost, wandering around deeper into the moors. The fog rolled in and we couldn't see what was around our feet. It freaked out the others in the group, but I found that soup of nature…fascinating. I just wanted to reach down in there and run my fingers through the mist. I felt…connected. I knew." She gestured to the world around her. "This is what I'm supposed to do with my life."

"You are…an incredible woman."

She felt the blush heat her cheeks. His compliment shouldn't matter but it did. Her self-esteem had taken some serious dings during her marriage. "Thank you. I'm just a lucky one."

"Hard work certainly increases the odds of good luck."

"Still, life isn't always evenhanded." In fact, she felt like it was often like an out-of-balance scale. All the counterweights were askew. Looking at him now, leaning casually against the workstation, definitely riled her sense of evenhandedness. Being attracted to him was not without complications. Serious work-altering complications. And then, there was the problem of her work visa expiring.

His face went somber. "True enough."

"Oh, God." She touched his arm. "I'm sorry. I didn't mean to be insensitive."

"It's okay. Really. I can't spend the rest of my life having people measure their every word around me. I wouldn't want that for Rose, either. I want her to grow up in a world of happiness."

Searching for some level ground, she offered, "I'm sure she's being pampered to pieces by her grandparents."

His face went even darker.

"What did I say wrong?" Her stomach knotted.

"It's not you. It's just that my relationship with them has become strained since Terri died. They miss her, I understand that. We're all hurt."

"Everyone could tell how much you loved each other."

"We'd known each other all our lives." His voice was filled with a hollow kind of sadness.

"So you've known her parents as long, too. They should be like parents to you, as well."

He barked out a laugh. "If only it was that simple."

"I don't want to pry."

He shook his head. "You're not. They blame me for not taking care of her. I was working late when she died. If I'd been home on time, maybe I would have seen the symptoms, gotten her to the hospital in time..."

In his tone, she could hear how many times he'd re-played that night in his head. Played the what-if game. She knew how painful the potential of what-if could be.

"You can't blame yourself." Her voice was gentle but firm.

"I do. They do." Quieter still, he took a step forward, buried his face in his hands as if to shut out any chance of redemption. But Maureen knew a thing or two about "phoenixing"—the importance of being birthed by fire and ash.

"Easton told me the doctors said there was nothing that could have been done."

She reached a soapy hand for his, certain Xander needed a small show of comfort. Her heart demanded that of her.

"I wish I could believe that. I wish we all could."

"That has to have left a big hole in your life."

"It has."

"I'm so sorry." And she was. So damn sorry for how things had played out for him. For the burden of a future he'd glimpsed but could never have. She understood that sort of pain.

"I have our child. And I can't change things."

"Stoic."

He leveled a sardonic look her way. "The problem with that?"

"Nothing."

"Even I know that when a woman says nothing, she means something." He half grinned, an attempt at light in a shadowed spot. A good sign. A necessary one. And Maureen used that light to ask the question that had burned a hole in her mind all day.

"I just wonder who…"

"Who what?"

"Who helped you through that time?" Immediately she regretted the push for information. Stammering, she continued. "Th-that's too personal. Forget I said anything."

He waved his hand, dismissing her retraction. "Holding my daughter comforted me. There's no way to make the pain go away. Enough talk about me. What about you? Tell me your life history if you expect mine."

"I'm from Ireland." An evident truth and perhaps a cop-out answer meant to delay going deeper.

"Great mystery there, lass." He re-created a thick brogue, sounding like an Irishman in a BBC production. The gesture tugged a smile at the corners of her mouth.

"My accent's not that thick."

"True. And why is that?"

She looked up at him through her lashes as she finished the last bird's wing. "My father worked for an American-based company in Michigan for ten years."

"Is that what drew you back here?"

"Maybe. I needed a change after my divorce and this opening came up. I got the work visa. Here I am." That was the heart of the story. No lies, but nothing to sink his teeth into. Maureen was always much more comfortable asking people how they felt and what they needed than sharing her own details, especially after her divorce.

"And now it's time to go home." He tipped his head to the side. "You don't seem pleased about that. I imagine your family has missed you."

"They weren't pleased with me for splitting with my ex. They accused me of choosing my job over my marriage."

"Your husband wasn't interested in coming with you?"

"No, he wasn't. I didn't ask, actually. We'd already split by then, but my parents didn't know." She shook her head. "But I don't want to talk about that. Nothing more boring than raking over the coals of a very cold divorce." The need to change the subject ached in her very bones.

"Whatever you wish."

Time to shift back to Xander. To something of the present. "What brought you out here?"

"I need your help."

"Is there an animal loose?"

He held a hand to his chest, acting as if he'd been wounded by her insinuation. "I think you just insulted my manhood. I may not be my brother, but I can handle a stray critter."

Damn, he was too handsome and charming for his own good—or her sanity.

She considered his words for a moment before pressing further. "Snakes?"

"Sure." He nodded.

"Birds?"

"A net and gentle finesse?"

"A key deer?"

"I could chase it with the four-wheeler."

The image of Xander loaded up in a four-wheeler corralling key deer sent her giggling. She'd never seen this fun side of him before and she couldn't help but be enchanted by the flirtatious game. After all, it was safe, not likely to lead anywhere. "Gators?"

"Stay away from the gators."

She rolled her eyes. "Whatever. Quite frankly, I would rather handle the gator than wrestle the numbers and executives you deal with." She shuddered. "And living in an office? No, thank you."

"But you'll stay in the boat when it comes to the alligators from now on."

"Of course." She winked playfully at him, enjoying the lighthearted, no-pressure moment. "What did you want to ask me?"

"How's your work visa extension progressing?"

Ugh. Now that was a sobering turn to the conversation. This wasn't new information. The question confused her. "Not well."

"I can help you."

"You'll put in a good word for me?"

"I already did that and clearly that's not enough."

"Then what are you proposing?"

"That's just it. I'm proposing."

His words thundered in her brain, a reality she couldn't quite locate yet.

Proposing?

Four

The words hung heavy in the air between them. She blinked at him. Not a good sign.

Her head bobbed side to side, as if she was replaying his words. He watched as her practiced hands put the now-clean bird in a cage, the greenish hues of the feathers more vibrant, the orange neck glowing again. Astonishment pulled at her lips while the bird perched and gave its little grunting honk of joy. Maureen, however, stayed silent.

There was no enthusiastic agreement coming. He could see that now.

But that only made him all the more determined that this was the right path for both of them.

Maureen frantically scanned the room. Looking for Easton and the other technicians, no doubt, her eyes wide as she turned back to him. "Proposing what, exactly? A proposition?"

"Not propositioning you. Proposing *to* you."

"Pro...posing?" she stuttered in a shrill whisper. "To me? As in 'get married' proposing? You and I?"

"Pro-pose! Pro-pose!" screeched a three-foot-high parrot named Randy who kept watch over this workstation when he wasn't in the aviary. The parrot marched around a perch near the window, his presence somehow calming the traumatized new birds.

"A marriage of convenience. So yes, proposing we get married." This was a practical arrangement. A business deal that would suit them both. And damn lucky for them, they had the spark and heat that could make a marriage more than just a contract arrangement.

"So the work visa is no longer an issue and I could stay in the States?" Her teeth skimmed her bottom lip. He could see the reality of his offer taking root in her.

"And my in-laws won't stand a chance at taking my daughter."

Her brow furrowed. "You want a mother for your daughter? Is that fair to her to have her think of me that way and then I leave?"

"She has a mother and her mother is dead. I'm not asking you to replace her, not by a long shot. My daughter has a father who loves her more than anything on this earth and she has the best nanny money can hire in Elenora."

Maureen's shoulders relaxed down at least a little. "What exactly are you asking of me then?"

"I need my in-laws to quit threatening me. And I do know you will be a positive influence in Rose's life while you're here. I'm damn good at interviewing. I don't expect you to spend time with her if that's not what you want." He just needed a convincing façade to show the world. The appearance of cohesion. Unity. The sort of thing that would even appease Delilah. She could take this information back to their family lawyer. It'd be a helluva lot tougher for his in-laws to gain custody of Rose if a nuclear family manifested.

"Of course I would—"

Shaking his head, he leaned forward on the sink's countertop. "My mother-in-law—hell, everyone—will sense it if you're faking the emotion. It should be genuine."

"Won't she wonder why we married so quickly?"

"Let her wonder. This is a temporary arrangement. By the time your work situation is settled and my court battle is solid, then we can split. Rose'll be too young to understand. And I trust you to be kind."

She touched her forehead. "I need time to think about this. It's just so…calculated."

Xander made his fortune through careful calculations. He knew how to weigh options, to choose the most sensible path for the biggest gains. He had a knack for this sort of interaction. He couldn't help it if it appeared calculated. It was his skill set.

"You don't have the luxury of time and neither do I, so think fast. Our futures—Rose's future—depend on your decision."

All of his years in boardroom coups and takeovers had taught him two things: when someone would cave and when someone wouldn't. Examining her lip-chewing and her continuously wringing hands, he could see Maureen's resolve crumbling. Not only for her future—he knew how much she wanted to stay in the States—but also for Rose. For the child who needed to be protected. Xander knew Maureen couldn't turn her back on any living being in need. Especially not a vulnerable little girl.

Damned if that didn't make Maureen all the more appealing to him—and perhaps a bit riskier than he'd anticipated.

* * *

Xander took his seat at the head of the dining room table. Dinner with his in-laws. An informal affair, as always, since he opened up his dining room to anyone still on the grounds volunteering. It wasn't unusual for people to come and go, filling a plate of food and joining the family or making their own little groupings out on the patio area. The cost of the food was nothing to him compared to the compassionate volunteer help of the people who helped fulfill Terri's mission here.

And he appreciated the love and attention they showered on Rose. She had quite an extended family, not blood-related but connected by affection.

He was doing his best to build a life for her here and he hoped like hell his former in-laws could recognize the depth and thought he put into parenting. He did not take this responsibility lightly. Neither did his brother.

And now that Maureen had agreed—albeit reluctantly—to his proposal, all would see he had a stable environment in place here for Rose. In fact, he'd asked Maureen to bring Rose in after the little one woke from her nap to help set the stage of their connection.

The three of them.

Xander had to keep his cool and not let the threat of a custody battle cloud their visit. Even Easton was keeping his normally outrageous personality in check, seated at the other end of the table.

Xander lifted the wine carafe. "I trust your hotel suite is comfortable?"

He poured Delilah a glass of wine. Her manicured fingers touched the base of the wine stem, gray eyes steadily focused on the merlot cascading from bottle to glass.

Jake answered, "Of course. It's a beautiful hotel. Big bay windows. Polite bellman."

He cast a look at his wife. The nod she gave back was practically imperceptible, but the subtle gesture didn't escape Xander's notice.

"You know, Xander, we love Rose. We see so much of Terri in her."

Xander stopped pouring the wine. "I know. I see that, too."

"Where is she, Xander? Our visit was too short today," Delilah pressed.

"She's sleep—" His voice trailed off as Maureen entered the dining room. With Rose. "—ing."

His in-laws followed his gaze, resting on Maureen and the child. *His* child, who looked so damn comfortable in her arms. Rose's face had regained color and her eyes, finally cleared of their earlier drowsiness, sparkled with interest. Rose giggled and blew baby kisses at her uncle Easton, who winked back.

After examining the sweet expression of ease on his daughter's face, Xander's gaze drank in the curves exposed by Maureen's lilac-colored sundress. Heart hammering, he swallowed. Hard.

Delilah practically leaped out of her chair, pushing to see her grandchild.

"I'll take her off your hands. It's late and Xander shouldn't keep you here after hours."

"Actually, I'm here for dinner." If she noticed Delilah's disappointment as the woman slid back into her chair, Maureen didn't let on.

Brow furrowing, he tried to read Maureen's expression for a hint of what she was thinking. And quickly, before his in-laws read the silent exchange between them. But he wasn't going to argue. In fact, he had to admit to being charged by the way she kept him on his toes. "Yes, I'll take Rose while you help yourself to dinner." He gestured to the sideboard with the plates and supper buffet, china serving platters laden with crab-covered snapper, coconut shrimp, asparagus and diced red potatoes. Small baskets of fluffy biscuits and hushpuppies rested at the end of the line of steaming offerings.

Maureen shook her head. "It's okay. I'll hold her until one of you finishes your food. I've missed her today." With admirable dexterity, she held Rose on one hip while putting together a dessert-size plate of finger foods for the toddler—fries, a roll, fruit and cheese. Rose carried a sippy cup of milk in her chubby fist.

"Go on, eat. I really don't mind." She kissed Rose's forehead, brushed back her baby curls with her hand, and sat in the chair next to Easton. Bouncing her knee up and down, she began to sing softly to Rose. Melting his heart with every movement. And Rose... She looked so happy in Maureen's lap. So natural—as if they'd spent a lifetime together and this was routine.

His in-laws said nothing, looking at each other side-long before heading to the buffet across the massive dining area, two more volunteers gathering up plates to head out the French doors to the lanai—Don and his wife always stayed late, such loyal helpers using their retirement to give back to the community. Lips tight, Delilah shoved up from the table to refill her plate, her husband following her. To keep the peace?

Draining his glass of wine, Xander let out a long sigh, eyes still fixated on Maureen, completely preoccupied as she adorably moved her mouth to create an exotic bird noise. Easton fished a toy bird out of his pocket.

Portia leaned toward Xander, following his gaze. "They're not like us."

"Are you saying Maureen belongs with him and not with me?" he asked softly.

His brother's assistant sipped her glass of wine, her voice low, as well. "No, just that they're alike in spirit."

"In spirit? I'm a man. Speak in less woo-hoo kind of terms." The idea that Maureen would be better suited for Easton set Xander's skin on fire. The suggestion bothered him more than it should have.

"I mean we're the organized, feet-on-the-ground sorts. They're the dreamers." She gestured with her wineglass, as if pointing to the vastness of space.

"They're scientists." He raised a brow at her. Scientists and dreamers didn't seem to go hand in hand. Too poetic.

"They're Dr. Doolittles. They talk to the animals and live on different plains than you and I. They don't care about convention or practicality. Their hearts are huge and defy practicality or reason. They're different."

And it was that difference that set him ablaze. But he saw his opening—the way to announce the arrangement. With his father-in-law in earshot, Xander said, "If you're congratulating me on the engagement, this is a strange way to go about it."

"Engagement?" Portia squeaked.

He cocked an eyebrow, glancing around the room quickly to see if anyone else had overheard.

Portia held up a hand and quieted her voice again. "Who am I to say anything about secret relationships? We all have our private lives."

Secret relationships? What could she possibly mean by that? Had people speculated that Maureen and he were… together before this? How would his in-laws feel if they caught wind of that? The last thing he needed was more tension or trouble from them.

Before giving any more thought to Portia's comment, his eyes fell back to Maureen a few chairs down at the lengthy table.

Out of her chair now, she raised Rose to the ceiling, simulating a plane sound. His baby girl's peal of laughter warmed the room.

Tipping her head to the side, Portia added, "Maureen's quite lovely."

"Yes, she is." Lovely. Unpredictable. Sexy. And the perfect business partner for this arrangement.

"Treat her well when you take her shopping for the ring."

"Why are you telling me this?"

"You'll have to sort that out for yourself. Besides, you're the boss. I wouldn't presume to give you advice." She smiled.

"Even if I asked for it?"

"No need to ask." She tapped his phone. "Add more features to your data planner and you can just look up the answers."

Maureen cut into the snapper with practiced ease, balancing Rose on her lap. Shoveling the fish into her mouth, she enjoyed the savory fusion of lemon, garlic and pepper.

A few bites later she felt satiated and cut up the biscuit on Rose's plate, feeding her small pieces. Rose devoured the food. *Sweet girl.* The return of her appetite said good things about her recovery.

Though she'd played it smoothly, entering with Rose on her hip, Maureen's nerves pulsated in her chest. All throughout dinner she'd felt the gaze of Xander's in-laws. As she cut up Rose's food, she could practically hear their running commentary assessing how well she was doing.

Rose lifted her small, chubby fingers, stretching and grasping toward her uncle. She squirmed in Maureen's lap, eyes fixated on Easton.

"Mmmmmmmmmmm," Rose blurted, bouncing more emphatically.

"Easton, I think you are being summoned," Maureen said, planting a kiss on the toddler's blond hair.

Easton turned, setting his plate down at the table. A little giggle emanated from Rose as Easton stuck out his tongue at her, his voice descending into a wild birdcall.

"I'll take her from you." Easton scooped Rose up off of Maureen's lap, zooming her like a rocket ship. Hardly the normal dinner-side antics, but Easton's free spirit was what made him a brilliant boss.

"Go on, Maureen, get seconds. Thirds. Tenths. Enjoy yourself, will ya?" Easton sat in the chair next to her. "You barely put anything on your plate."

She shrugged. The few bites she'd eaten had been enough. Her nerves were starting to get the better of her. "I'm fine, Easton. But thank you. I'm going to put my plate away."

"Suit yourself."

Maureen pushed out from her chair, eyes locking with Xander's. His blue gaze sent electricity into the core of her being. Grabbing her plate from the table, she arched her eyebrow at him, hoping he would understand.

They needed to talk. So much felt up in the air. Not that Maureen wasn't up for adventure, but she could use some bearings at this point.

She maneuvered past the conversations taking place in the dining room, entering the kitchen. Scraping the food bits off her plate into the kitchen sink, she took a steadying breath. Running the water from the faucet, she flipped on the garbage disposal.

The grinding noise stifled Xander's footfalls, but Maureen saw him in the reflection of the big window. Even in a shadowed, distorted form, he sent butterflies leaping down her spine.

"So…" His voice was a sexy growl. "You're fully on board with my proposal, then?"

Turning off the water, she grabbed an orange-colored plush towel, leaning against the counter. "Tentatively."

"Tentatively? What can I do to persuade you more fully?" He took a step toward her with a smoldering smile.

She bit her lip. "More defined terms would be a decent start." Maureen couldn't let this devilishly handsome, tall, dark and sexy thing derail her from getting to the truth.

"Hmm. Well. As my wife, you'd get to stay in the States. Continue working for my brother and doing your job here, at the refuge."

"Right. That's my benefit. What do you get? Exactly?" She pinned him with a stare.

"You'd have to help me at the fundraisers, mix and mingle at work events. A stable parental figure for Rose—" he stepped closer, lowering his voice "—and a way to keep my in-laws from taking my daughter. It's not forever. Just for a bit. Until everything settles down on both our ends."

Maureen pressed her palms into the cool granite countertop, leaning back. Considering.

"I know how it sounds. But we don't have the luxury of time." Another step toward her.

Cocking her head to the side, she crossed her arms. "We don't?"

"Your work visa is going to expire. My in-laws want Rose. If it's going to happen, we can't afford to delay. We have to close the deal. Now."

Pursing her lips, she took a step toward him. "Is this how you close all your boardroom meetings?"

The heat between them was nearly tangible. Her face was inches from his.

A haughty laugh crinkled his expression. "Things don't have to stay so…businesslike. Not if you don't want them to."

She swallowed, eyes lingering on his lips. Damn. She wanted to grab him, pull him close. Feel him against her. "So you're saying, we can get engaged, married, and… explore?"

"Explore the heat between us…see where it takes us." He drew closer, lips barely brushing hers as he spoke. The smell of sandalwood anchored her. Maureen's heart thudded. She wanted him. Bad.

"I can see where this takes us."

He touched the side of her face, running a finger down her neck. "So is that your final answer?"

Her mind wandered away from the kitchen. What would it be like to be with—even if only fake married— a man that made her so reckless with her heart? The heat between them made her want to damn caution and practicality.

"My final answer? I'll do it."

As the lightning feathered across the sky, Maureen realized there was nothing typical about a date with Xander. The first indication of his adventurous nature evidenced by an impromptu date night to Miami. Via private jet. Just the two of them.

That level of grandeur had been offset by the burgeoning storm. Even that had a certain charm to it. He seemed willing to risk, to push. So different from the life she'd had when she'd been married. Everything had been dictated for her, controlled and regimented.

No, Xander reminded her of the storm outside. Full of life and flash. A force to be reckoned with. She liked this aspect of his personality.

The dark sky didn't bother her one bit. Tropical rains were standard South Florida fare. So much for the sunshine state. And this tropical depression didn't warrant any kind of alarm. She'd quickly adopted the South Florida vibe that if you buckled down for every tropical depression, you'd never get a damn thing done. The only time to become concerned was when the bad weather turned into a tropical storm or hurricane. Not that she'd experienced either, but tropical depressions had seemed relatively minor in damages and stress.

Peeling her eyes away from outside the limo's tempered glass, her thoughts drifted back to Rose and Xander.

Rose's need for stability had lit a maternal instinct in Maureen. Sure, she'd always had a penchant for lost souls, the ones that wandered. But this was different. She'd seen Xander with his daughter, knew that the best place for Rose was with him.

So when Xander had asked her to go with him to Miami on his business jet to further stage the ruse of their engagement, she'd accepted.

Of course, that didn't mean the idea of deceiving his in-laws and the government sat well with her, but she also couldn't imagine Rose being taken from her father, from her home.

Maybe it was more Maureen's own history unsettling her. A false engagement and marriage gave her the same sort of feeling she'd gotten when she'd been talked into skydiving. The rush of adrenaline and exhilaration coalescing with fear.

He'd insisted on dinner in Miami at an upscale restaurant, Bella Terre.

He'd left his in-laws to watch Rose. And, he had admitted on the flight over, he'd left Easton and Portia to watch Delilah and Jake. An insurance that nothing would go wrong—at least nothing that his in-laws could use in a custody dispute. After spending dinner with them last night, Maureen understood and shared his concerns. They clearly loved Rose, but they wanted to manage her.

The limo stopped in front of Belle Terre, rain streaming and pooling against the window. The chauffeur popped open the door, extending a sturdy hand. He helped her out of the car, giant umbrella already extended overhead. In an instant Xander's body pressed against hers, the warmth of him teasing her senses to life as he took the umbrella from the driver and offered her his arm. She couldn't deny how damn sexy he looked, all dark-haired and charming.

As they stepped into Belle Terre, the sound of a Spanish guitar flooded her ears. Not a murmur, not a whisper or a trill of laughter pushed against the sound waves. What? That didn't make sense. Scanning the floor of the restaurant, she realized they were the only ones there. Aside from the waitstaff, of course.

Xander's breath whispered against her ear. "I rented this place. Just for us."

Her breath caught, drinking in the crystal chandelier, the rich, gold chairs.

The whole place looked like a fairy tale. Lace lingered against the white tablecloths, and as they made their way to the center of the room, she noticed the guitarist off in the corner.

He'd pulled out all the stops. So much effort, but she felt out of place in this extravagance. As he pulled her chair out for her, the scent of his woodsy cologne danced in the space between them. His fingers brushed against her bare shoulder and she stole an appreciative glance at the way his tailored suit hinted at his broad, muscular chest. Touching a hand to her neck, she fumbled with the small, teardrop-diamond necklace that rested at the center of her collarbone. The necklace, her mother's, was the finest thing she owned, and added glamour to her simple floor-length black-chiffon dress.

"You didn't have to go to all of this trouble. I already agreed to your plan."

"This engagement is going to come out of the blue. If we want people to believe we're in love, if we want to convince them all, then we need, well—" he spread his arms wide "—moments like this."

"Why not just make them up? We could get our stories together."

A true fiction uncomplicated their arrangement. But being here with him pushed up her attraction to him, made her remember the press of his body at the dance, on the beach.

Those were the kinds of feelings that needed to stay leashed to ensure the success of their deal.

As if in answer, ripples of thunder filled the room, reminding her to stay focused. A tropical depression didn't cause the damage of a hurricane. And those memories of how he felt against her? Potentially devastating.

His eyes glinted like sexy shards of lightning snapping across the table. "You must confess, this is easier and a helluva lot more fun."

She averted her gaze, tearing away from the heat of his eyes. *Focus elsewhere. Fast.* Staring at the plate of lavish food the waiter set in front of her, Maureen's stomach leaped in anticipation. Lobster. Escargot. Shrimp. "It is lovely."

"You're lovely."

"I don't smell of fish and I'm not wearing scrubs. It's likely the contrast." Her mouth dry, and needing to divert his attention, she speared a shrimp with her fork.

"What about the night you danced by the fire? I've seen you dressed up before." Flashes of the dance materialized before her eyes. Maureen wanted to press into the simplicity of that moment.

"True." She reached for her chardonnay. A sip—then two—later, she turned to stare out the window, watching the rain bubble on the thick cut of glass.

"And I noticed then. I also noticed when you were waterlogged in the swamp covered in seaweed." He refilled his wineglass.

She smiled for an instant before her mood darkened. "And your in-laws arrived. It must be difficult for them seeing you engaged again."

"They'll have to get used to it since we will be married soon. Very soon. The custody battle outweighs their personal reactions." He broke the shell of his lobster easily. "And we'll have much to look forward to with the refuge expanding."

As Xander continued to talk about plans for the coming year, her stomach knotted until she barely noticed what she ate. What type of wedding was he going to want? Her mind skated back to her own first marriage, that day in a massive church when she'd expected her vows to last forever.

Xander stroked a finger across her forehead. "Smooth that frown away. Only happy thoughts tonight. This is a new start for both of us," he said in a way that was completely truthful regardless of who listened in.

The waiter, a short man with a mustache like the Monopoly game banker, removed their dinner plates with a great flourish. In exchange, he brought molten chocolate cake to the table, served along with two gleaming silver forks.

"Happy thoughts. Of course." She forced a smile. "You're right, and you've gone to so much trouble, I must seem a horrible ingrate."

His fork edged into the chocolate cake, the melted fudge trickling out onto the plate.

Though she felt full, a small indulgence of chocolate seemed like the right call. A spoonful of sugar to help the deception go down. Or something like that.

"Maureen, stop worrying about what I think. Let's focus on you. And more thoughts about how beautiful you are now, and with that seaweed, and when you wear surgical scrubs."

Her shoulders rolled with her laughter. "You're quite a charmer."

"Not really. Not usually." He reached across the table to twine one of her curls around his finger. "You make it easy."

He tugged her toward him ever so gently. More thunder rolled.

"I'm not exactly a girly girl."

"You are entirely feminine. Alluring. Sexy."

Confused and more than a little rattled, she sagged back in her seat. He tugged her lock of hair ever so slightly before he let go. Were the compliments just for show? She was attracted to him and he knew it. Would he take advantage of that to enhance their ruse? She hated to think of all this male seductiveness serving as gossip for the waitstaff.

The cake lay in ruins on the plate. A bite left. Maybe two. He scooped up the last bit onto his fork. Lifted it to her lips. She took the cake off the fork, her eyes trained on his.

A small smile played on his lips and he snapped his fingers.

On cue, men in tuxedos and women in plain black dresses wheeled out carts that glittered like water in subdued light. Rows of velvet-lined cases glittered with wedding rings. Scores of them, each prettier than the last. Pressing a napkin to her mouth, she dabbed at any chocolate residue.

Was this actually happening?

Xander pushed back his chair and held out a hand for her to stand. "Choose whatever ring you want."

She pressed her fingers to her racing heart. "I couldn't do that."

"Of course you can." He took her hand and squeezed gently, tugging her upward.

"There's no need for you to go to such expense—" In fact, the amount of carats that surrounded her caused her anxiety. Too much. It was all too much.

"Expense is not an issue." He waved his hand.

"Or you could choose. Then I won't feel guilty." Heat torched her cheeks and she could almost feel her freckles popping all the more hotly to the surface.

He slid his arm around her bared shoulders until his mouth brushed her ear. "The waiters and jewelry staff have ears. Learn to be a better actress, my love."

He nipped her earlobe and she battled a wave of heat that was only partly from all that raw masculine appeal. Be a better actress? Oh, the man was getting away with too much. She simmered silently even as her body hummed from his touch. "Now, what engagement ring would you like?" he pressed, his voice sending pleasant shivers down her spine. "With a wedding band, too, of course. Let's make this a night to remember."

Two could play at this game, damn him. He wanted an act? She turned her face and nibbled his bottom lip, releasing slowly. "If you insist, *my love*."

His gaze tracked the movement of her mouth in a telltale sign that shot a thrill through her.

For a moment they stayed there, breathing one another's air. Locked in the drumroll moment, heat and fire building, the Spanish guitar swelling to an aching crescendo. His hand went to her jaw, his touch setting her ablaze, that familiar pull between them descending over her.

She knew then that she was no match for him in this seductive game. Her heart beat so fast she swore he must've heard it.

Her lips touched his in a perfect meet, in a kiss igniting all the sparks she had been trying to ignore for weeks. Longer even? Now those feelings flamed to life, fast and hot, coaxing a delicious warmth at just a stroke of his hand up her spine.

The glide of his mouth over hers, the parting his lips. An invitation she couldn't resist.

Five

This kiss fired his blood.

Her lips pressed into his, tongue searching and meeting until he already throbbed in response. He'd known she would be hot, that there was a connection, but this was so much more than he'd been prepared for. On instinct, his hands leaped to the back of her head, cradling and holding the kiss that seemed to kick up a notch with every passing moment.

Xander tasted her greedily, as if she might fall away off the earth if he slowed. And he had no intention of slowing. Not anytime soon.

But then a clap of thunder, one that sounded overhead, grounded him. Reminded him that they were in a restaurant. That there were boundaries in place.

He could—and would—have more of her later.

Another crack of thunder, more intense than the last. It reverberated through him, blending with his pulse. Pushing him. He felt a storm rage in his chest, building with intensity, building to get his hands on Maureen.

Xander cradled her face in his hands, passion still pumping through his veins. "How did any man ever let you go?"

A slight retreat shone in her eyes. So quick, he'd almost missed it as she spoke. "Why does anyone get divorced?"

"You don't need to brush off the statement. I'm serious. You're an incredibly smart, fascinating, sexy woman."

"I appreciate you saying that. And I could feel that attraction a few seconds ago." Her voice turned husky and low, eyebrows arching.

He liked her this way—fiery and challenging. She'd been so quiet at the beginning of dinner he'd wondered where this strong, determined woman had gone. She seemed overwhelmed by the more traditional, lavish gestures, and he'd made note. Next time, he would try to find a way to romance her that was more in keeping with her hands-on, passionate personality.

"That's more than attraction. It's damn near twenty-four-seven fascination." And even that description felt like an understatement. He drew his chair closer to hers.

"The feeling is mutual." With preternatural grace, she grazed her fingertips along the top of his thigh. Tempting. He eased back into his chair. "I'm seriously trying to talk here."

"And I'm trying to distract you from discussion." She scrunched her nose.

"Why?"

"I don't want this to get complicated," she said tightly, easing back. "We've made it clear this is a deal."

He angled his head to the side, his eyes narrowing.

"What happened to make you so closed off, so defensive?"

"Are you calling me insecure?" A hint of her Irish brogue slipped out. Exotic and powerful.

"If I wanted to use the word 'insecure,' I would have."

A moment passed. The world so still as she considered him, and in the spaces between breath, he could hear the steady drumbeat of the rain.

She bit her lip, looked him up and down, then eased back, relenting. "I shouldn't have snapped." She gestured around the dining room. "You've made everything so lovely tonight."

The hint of insecurity in her tone felt foreign to him. Maureen always had an air of confidence to her actions, even her subtle movements. Had this layer of vulnerability always been there, somehow latent and overlooked?

"Maureen, snap all you want. If I say something that upsets you, let me know. Fire up that Irish temper."

"That's a stereotype."

"Not with you."

Her lips pursed tight.

"What did I say wrong?" The evening was devolving before his eyes. He needed to figure out how to diffuse this. "Maureen? Tell me."

Leaning back in her chair, she loosened a chest-heaving breath. "I don't want to be the bitter woman who talks crap about her ex until other people yawn or run for the hills."

"You aren't. For that matter, I can't recall hearing you say anything more than irreconcilable differences."

"It was. Totally irreconcilable. I thought when we said 'till death do us part, in sickness and in health,' that's what it meant. He apparently thought it just meant until you get on my nerves and I'm just not 'happy.'" She glanced up. "I told you I can sound bitter."

"That had to be hard, having someone you love walk away for no tangible reason. He sounds like an ass."

He wanted her to know that he would never judge her for any degree of bitterness about someone so willing to walk away. That wasn't his style.

"He was an ass. Which makes me feel worse for putting up with a man who belittled me that way. The more he criticized me about getting on his nerves, the harder I worked to make him happy and the more he complained." She drew circles on Xander's shoulder absently. "I guess neither of us was very happy."

"I refer back to my original statement about him being an ass."

"There are two sides to every breakup and I'm sure he has his." Her gaze went past him, far past him. As if she was imagining how that breakup might be partly her fault. Taking the blame and somehow internalizing it.

"I've watched you this past year with the animals, with my daughter—hell, even with the way you put up with my brother. You're a good person."

"Thank you." She swallowed hard. "That means a lot to me."

"You deserve to hear it often."

"I definitely don't want to sound pathetic." Her hands flew to the sides of her temples, red curls twining around her fingers.

"You don't. You sound caring. You are kind." He cupped the back of her neck, his thumb caressing her cheek. "And you are very sexy."

"As are you." The more familiar smile and lightness edged back into her voice.

"Even if I'm all buttoned up and not the type to wade around with alligators?"

"I've seen you work with a diaper. That's far more impressive—and fearsome." Her freckled nose crinkled.

"I would have to agree. Scary stuff."

Her shoulders braced as if she'd been waiting for the right moment to broach a difficult topic. "I do want to be clear, just because we're engaged and that kiss was…undeniably full of toe-curling chemistry, that doesn't mean we'll automatically be sleeping together."

"I can't say I'm not disappointed. But then, I did state this is a marriage of convenience. When we have sex is your call." This whole marriage proposal was surreal enough for him when he'd expected to stay single for life. But he couldn't deny the lust he felt for Maureen, and the timing was right for them to help each other.

"If," she said. "If we have sex." The defiance and correction felt loaded with electricity.

A practical challenge he wanted to meet. "When."

His hand wandered back over her cheek. She leaned into his touch, eyes fluttering shut.

He brought his lips just out of reach of hers and he felt the sigh ripple from her body to his. "Time to choose your ring."

Helping her up from the table, they walked past the rows of diamonds. He watched her expression as she studied the options. Her eyes seemed to linger on a pear-shaped diamond. A pause he caught. She pushed past that ring and pointed to a small, round diamond. Traditional. Plain. The smallest one of all the ring cases.

"This one is beautiful," she said, smiling. She sent a small eye flick back to the case where the pear-diamond ring sparkled.

"Anything for you, my love." He gestured to the attendant. "We'll take the pear ring from case number three. The one in the middle."

Maureen's face flushed as the man handed Xander the ring she'd been eyeing.

He knelt down, sliding the ring on her thin finger. Eagerly, he put his lips to her finger, kissed the placement, then her wrist. When he stood, he kissed her gently on the cheek, wanting the moment to be special for her. And also knowing that if he went further, he might lose control altogether.

He pushed aside memories of Terri and what they'd shared. He had to. This was too important for his daughter.

Maureen's eyes were soft. Words seemed to press at her mouth, but found no audible track.

A familiar sound pushed against his pocket. His brother's ringtone. Immediately, Xander reached for his phone, hoping Rose was okay.

"Easton? Is Rose all right?"

Maureen's face grew pale so Xander put the phone on speaker.

Easton continued, "She's fine. But the weather's been upgraded to a tropical storm and it's predicted to be a bad one. You need to get the plane off the ground right away while it's still safe, if you plan to come home, which I assume you do. We really need your and Maureen's help to lock down the clinic and deal with any aftermath at the refuge."

Damn it. These kinds of storms could wreak havoc on wildlife, something Maureen understood, as well, as she was already reaching for her purse.

Xander extended a hand to her as he finished with his brother. "Say no more. We're leaving now."

* * *

The return flight left Maureen wrestling with a tangle of ragged nerves and stress. Was it crazy of her to be just a little bit grateful for the storm because it had distracted them from the attraction raging as fiercely as the winds outside the jet? Of course. And yet she couldn't deny as much anxiety about her feelings for Xander as she experienced about the worsening weather. The turbulence and reality of a storm coming for their refuge left her queasy and uneven.

When they'd made it back to the house, Xander's in-laws were gone. Easton said they'd blamed their departure on the weather, but they'd been upset over Xander and Maureen's engagement. Not that she could blame them.

She didn't have long to consider their reaction, though. They didn't have long to secure all the animals. Hurrying into her office, Maureen changed quickly out of her evening gown into pants and a shirt she kept stashed in a locker, piling her flowing hair into a tight ponytail.

Randy cawed from his perch, his feathers ruffling when the thunder boomed loudest. She spoke softly to him as she grabbed a rain poncho on the way out the door.

Xander and Easton were already pulling tarps over a few cages that could remain outside under the deep eaves of one of the buildings, leaving enough of a gap at the bottom to ensure fresh air even as the tarps kept out the more severe weather.

The three of them moved silently through the yard, reaching the main animal shelter.

Wind whipped at her, stinging her cheeks. So there was a huge difference in pure fury between a tropical depression and a tropical storm.

On rote memorization, she secured the animals. Talked to them in soothing tones.

Putting the storm shutters down in the avian center, the feel of the cool metal of her engagement ring pressed on her finger.

An odd feeling, really. After her divorce, her finger had ached in her wedding band's absence. So much had been promised with that little piece of metal. When she'd taken it off after her divorce, the ring's absence had left her with a lot of questions.

The clang of her ring sparked something in her. It felt strange to have another promise around her finger. At least she knew the bounds of this one.

While wings flapped nervously and the new arrivals squawked unhappily, Maureen checked all the birds, making sure they had food and water to tough out the hours of a tempest's barrage.

Through the sheeting rain, she could hear Easton trying to coax one of the big cats into the sheltered portion of their habitat, but Sheekra wasn't having it. Most cats hated the rain, but the cougar liked to sit in a tree during a storm. Xander was latching the door to the coyote shelter while Maureen dragged some of the goat feed under cover so it wouldn't spoil. Once the animals in the clinic and outdoor sanctuaries were secured, the trio raced back to the house to the storm shelter, rain pelting furiously on their backs, urging them inside.

Dripping wet, they made their way to the shelter at the center of the main house on stilts, which was protected from rising tides and secured from glass breaking through. As they ran, water puddled behind them.

Easton tossed towels at Maureen and Xander. She pressed the fabric to her face, mopping water beads that clung to her skin.

She glanced around the storm shelter. Rose sprawled on Elenora's lap, fast asleep as her sitter dozed lightly in a fat rocking chair. Looking at the child, Maureen could have almost forgotten the storm outside. The little girl epitomized peace.

The well-equipped room featured a few sofas, a generator and a fridge filled with drinks. A shelving unit pressed against the back wall was stocked with a variety of food. A reminder that these were the other kinds of dangers of living in Florida. Natural predators aside, the weather could turn life-threatening.

Easton weaved past Maureen to Portia. She sat at a table, pencil pushed into her hair, papers scattered in front of her. They began talking quietly, inventorying the status of the refuge.

Xander motioned for Maureen to join him on the blue-and-white-striped overstuffed sofa.

A crash that cut to Maureen's core pulsated above them. A low whistling sound seemed to respond. Destruction. This was the sound of destruction.

Her body shook of its own accord.

Xander pointed to the well-secured windows and the supplies. "You're okay here in the storm shelter. This place is solid. We have a top-notch generator."

Did she really look as shaken as she felt? "I understand in theory. And I researched all about hurricanes and tropical storms before I moved here, even after, because of the care needed for the animals. I just didn't expect it to be so…much."

So much? Ha. That was an understatement. From beyond the walls of the storm shelter, she heard the sounds of branches scraping against the house. The burnt smell of up-close lightning wafted into the room.

"You don't need me to tell you this isn't even the

worst." That casual feeling about storms in South Florida left her. Pressing herself into him, she let his presence steady her.

The warmth of his strong arms slowed her racing pulse and helped her to take a deep breath. "Thanks."

"No problem." He tucked her closer, his soft cotton work shirt carrying a hint of his scent—a blend of something smoky and sandalwood.

"I can't believe Rose is sleeping right through this." Safer to think about his daughter than the way he smelled, even if it made Maureen want to bury her nose in his shirt.

"Storms are soothing for some. Lucky for us, she's one of those people." He rubbed Maureen's arm, his touch steady and sure. "You should try to rest, too. There will be a lot of work to do afterward, cleaning up and taking care of trapped and displaced animals."

A reminder that straightened her spine.

"And that's the reason I didn't let the storms scare me away. There's a challenge and a need here. A lot to be learned and good work to be done." How were the animals doing? Concern for them ripped through her soul. She might not like the storm, but she could rationalize it. But the animals? They didn't have that benefit.

"True enough." His voice seemed distant, and his attention drew away from her. She could feel it in the way he shifted on the sofa.

"Is there a problem?"

"I'm just thinking, remembering."

"About when your wife volunteered here."

He nodded. The pain of her absence visibly hit him as his eyes lingered on Rose.

"She wasn't scared at all, was she? Her daughter's just like her." A palpable thunder rattled through Maureen.

"Terri grew up in Florida. We all did. So while we have a healthy respect for the fickle weather, we understand it."

The internalized environment. It made sense to her. The cold of Ireland, the natural state of overcast skies and misting rain. It was a part of her. So she understood how his environment molded him. How could it not?

A crash seemed to shake the shelter. Perhaps a tree falling? It sent her closer to him, to the muscled planes of his chest. His arms pulled her close.

They were a hairbreadth apart. Lips so close. Just like they'd been in the restaurant. All she wanted to do was to lose herself in him, indulge in more kisses and enjoy the bliss of that courtship of the mouths, something she'd lost over the span of a controlling and ultimately loveless marriage. She wanted to have the storm fade as she found courage to trust in his embrace.

But with so many people here with them, she held herself at bay.

Rose awoke to what Xander had identified as a falling tree. She was bleary-eyed, calm, but definitely awake.

Maureen had taken some animal figurines off the shelves and brought them to the floor. Rose climbed into her lap, clearly interested in the menagerie.

His daughter. Maureen. What a sight. Long red curls curtained the little girl's face as she played. Maureen's knees bracketed her and Rose used a chubby hand to steady herself on one of Maureen's legs.

He couldn't keep himself from thinking about Terri, though. His thoughts fell back to his life with the wife he'd lost. On the future he'd imagined for them since they were kids. She'd left him. Not by choice, of course, but her absence created a space in his life that, even fourteen months later, he felt. Phantom pain encircled him the way an amputee still felt a missing limb.

More than that, though, he'd lost his mother shortly after. Not in a permanent, delineated way like with Terri. Growing up, Xander and Easton had been well-traveled, following his parents on adrenaline-fused adventures. Adventures that made him feel like the world had magic in it. When Xander's father died in a mountain climbing accident, his mother had been like a ball that suddenly lost its tether. She'd skidded and skirted out of his life. Hadn't even checked on him when Terri died. Wasn't there for him. Or Rose. She'd simply checked out, a bohemian spirit that refused to settle. Another fracture, another point of departure that ripped into his soul.

He didn't want anyone else leaving his life.

Under no circumstances could that happen with Maureen.

Rose's infectious laughter colored the room. Easton and Portia and some of the other staff stirred from sleep.

"Shh-hh. Shh-hh. We have to make quiet noises. What sound does this snake make?" Maureen asked, lifting a rubber snake in front of Rose.

"Hisssssss," Rose said proudly, taking the fake snake in her hand. She wriggled it in the air.

Xander moved from his chair to sit on the ground in front of her. "You're good with her."

Maureen flashed a smile his way. "Thank you."

"I know I've indulged her."

She stayed quiet.

"Okay, I've spoiled her."

Maureen shook her head, giving Rose a quick hug. A grin bloomed across the toddler's mouth. "You've loved her. She lost her mother. She needed to feel secure and she's attached to you."

"And she's spoiled."

"And you'll do something about that at the right time." She handed Rose a rubber tiger. The baby made a growling noise.

"You handle her tantrums well."

"I'm not her parent."

"Her boo-boo lip protruding doesn't move you the way it tears me apart." And it did. All that talk about being able to resist his little girl's charm had cracked.

"It moves me. I just—" she shrugged "—think it's easier for me to be the bad guy."

"That's a nice way to put it. I'm working on it, though. I have to. I'm just still finding my footing on parenting. It's tougher than I could have known. I don't want to spoil her, but I want her to feel loved and confident."

"For what my opinion is worth, I think you're doing a great job. Every child deserves as good." A heavy sigh passed through her and her gaze fell away from his with hesitancy and resignation. He recognized that look. Had seen Terri exhibit a similar reaction.

"Your parents were critical?"

"Strict. The divorce was difficult for them to accept." Maureen's normally full lips thinned.

"I'm sorry. You deserved support."

"Thank you for the sympathy but, honestly, it made me stronger in the end. I'm here, forging a new path."

This woman embodied resilience. He admired her for that. Wanted to drink that into his essence. Starting a new path wasn't easy. Especially when he'd thought his life had been planned out.

"I'm sorry the stress of getting engaged to me brought back bad memories." He hadn't anticipated what it might be like for her, his plans taking shape around his own needs and a desire to keep her working at the refuge.

"Nothing to apologize for. You're saving me from having to give up the work I love. Thank you for filing the paperwork so quickly." She heaved a sigh of relief. "You kept me from having to go back to all the reasons I left in the first place."

"Are you hiding here until you're ready to return?" Maybe the question wasn't fair. But he needed to understand her motivations. Maureen's veiled past made it difficult to understand her full perspective.

"Hiding? That's a harsh word. I'm not sure if I plan to go back. I just know my destiny is here for now."

Stroking Rose's feathery hair, she added, "One day at a time."

Perhaps that sentiment was her marching orders. Kept her from feeling the weight of forever.

"Fair enough." His hand found hers and he stroked her palm, his thumb moving along the band of the ring he'd placed there what felt like another world ago. He could sense her tiredness, her fraying. "Do you mind if I ask you one last question?"

She eyed him warily. "Okay, shoot."

"Can you help teach me that trick for getting my daughter to stop pitching a temper tantrum?" He tried for levity, adding in a grin for good measure.

Her shoulders lifted with her laugh. A good sound. A needed one. He had this well in hand, damn it. Friendship and attraction. Just that. Good. Satisfying. Not dangerous, not something that would shatter his world again.

"I'll try my best." She took Rose's hand in hers and played with her pinky finger. "But I suspect we may have to work on how tightly she has you wrapped around that tiny finger of hers."

"You may have a point."

The still room seemed to inhale and hold its breath.

Everyone slept. His eyes met hers and her lips parted slightly. His desire and longing for her returned.

They were engaged now and kissing her would sell the cover story even more. But beyond cementing their story, he wanted to feel her against him. Craved it. Ached to have her in bed, to be inside her, to wake up with her next to him and see all that magnificent red hair splayed across the pillow.

He nearly took his chance on his wife-to-be but then the radio blurted emergency signals.

The room burst into life as the radio host gave an update on the tropical storm. The worst had passed them by, moving on toward Miami. They could re-enter the main part of the house now.

And maybe even find some privacy.

Six

The tropical storm had ruffled the landscape of the refuge. Xander surveyed the grounds, noting the damage. An uprooted tree from the east of the property found a new home just outside the bird sanctuary. Speaking of which, glass speckled the ground outside the aviary. That'd been the first place Maureen dashed to. She'd wanted to make sure those birds that couldn't survive on their own in the wild were safe.

The busted glass was thankfully the most substantial damage any of the buildings sustained. Xander made a mental note to put the hurricane shutters for the newly constructed part of the refuge on rush. The tropical storm's damage reminded him a hurricane would be devastating by comparison. They needed to make sure all of the windows were secured.

Of course, other miscellaneous pieces of shrubbery decorated the lawn. Palm fronds, bushes, branches and garbage scattered the area, looking like discarded wrapping paper after an eager child's Christmas morning.

Alongside Easton and Xander, volunteers began reclaiming the space. A crew had arrived on-site early, setting up a tent with bottled water and boxed lunches for the group, acting as command central for the cleanup efforts. By now, most of the new arrivals were either piling up debris or acting as company for some of the more unsettled animals. While cleaning up after the tropical storm frustrated him—he hated lugging and stacking branches—he'd been glad for the minimal damage. Tree branches were annoying, sure. But if they'd lost a building and the animals inside? That would be much harder to come back from.

Xander worked in silence, stacking palm fronds one on top of the other in what looked like a woodsy edition of Jenga. Easton added to the pile, too. The other volunteers spread out around the yard, giving Easton and Xander a small degree of privacy.

He'd always been close to his brother. That's how he knew Easton was weighing his approach to something he wanted to discuss. His indecision rendered itself visible in the way he carelessly tossed the branches and licked his lips.

Easton cast a sidelong glance at Xander, jaw set and voice quiet. "Are you sure you know what you're doing?"

"I can lift a branch and work a saw. It's not like I never leave the office." He could still steer this conversation.

"That's not what I'm talking about and you know it."

Xander kept working silently. He wasn't interested in advice right now and if his brother wanted to confront him, he would have to work for it.

Easton tugged off his heavy-duty work gloves. "Come

on, brother. You're not really going to pull that old silence act, are you? You pretend like I don't know you."

"Say what you want."

"You got engaged to Maureen to ensure your custody of Rose is secure."

"I'm marrying her." No discussion. Just the matter-of-fact delivery that had made him such a success in the business world. Xander chucked another piece of a palm tree onto the wobbling stack.

"For real? And what does she think about this—" He sighed. "She gets to stay in the States. Aren't you worried about the legal implications of a fake marriage?"

"It will be a real marriage." The words pressed out of his clenched teeth. This was *his* life, not his brother's. He didn't have any right to comment.

"What does Maureen think? How honest have you been with her? Because I'm not buying for a second that you're in love with her." Easton held up his hand once he saw a protest form. "Oh, I get that you're in lust with her. But love? Nope. I've seen you in love before."

Pain lanced Xander at the reminder of all he'd lost. Damn it.

"What makes you think anything Maureen and I discuss is any of your business?"

"I'm family." He folded his arms across his chest, staring.

Xander inhaled deeply, drawing closer to his brother. Undaunted. "Then be supportive, damn you."

A command and a warning all at once.

Easton nodded, but his body tightened into hard lines. "I'm your brother, so I'm the one person not afraid to stand up to you."

"Maureen and I understand each other." The arrangement benefited them both. She'd chosen to accept his offer.

"Do you realize how vulnerable she is?" Easton's octave dropped, eyes scanning Xander's.

"I know her past with her ex-husband."

"Then tread warily. Because you may be my brother but she's my friend, and if you break her heart, I will kick your ass."

"I'm not going to hurt her and you're not going to kick my ass."

"If worse comes to worst, I have the gators on my side."

He playfully slugged Xander on the shoulder before stepping away toward a group of volunteers.

Xander watched his brother walk away, but his eyes settled on Maureen. She emerged from the bird sanctuary. Hair piled high into a ponytail, gloves and trash bag in hand. Ready to work. Even now, she looked stunning. This storm-torn element reflected a truth about Maureen, he noted. That her heart sung for these moments of reconstruction, that her earthy vibe and huge heart rendered her beautiful.

His mind wandered back—had it really only been a few hours ago when she'd spoken of her ex-husband?—to the pain and calluses he'd uncovered.

He warily regarded his brother's warning about hurting her. He didn't want to be so significant to her that he could cause her emotional pain.

And yet, their engagement, his proposal…it had to be right. He needed to keep custody of Rose and Maureen needed to stay in the States. He'd put them on this course and had to see it through. They were too far in to go back now.

And besides, he wanted to take that kiss to its very satisfying conclusion in bed.

* * *

Cleaning up after the storm had left everyone sticky with sweat and dirt. In her short time in the Keys, she'd learned a shower wasn't the first way to clean up after muck and grime attached to skin. The ocean, now settled and calm, claimed the first rite of cleansing.

This system of ocean cleansing before an outright shower jibed with Maureen's sensibilities. If nothing else, it'd proved an excuse to literally immerse herself in this landscape. Two years later and Maureen still found the water enchanting. She loved how there were multiple incarnations of water on this small island. The boggy area she'd fallen into represented only part of what Key Largo offered. That swampy ecosystem supported specific types of creatures, had its own scent and flavor. And then there was the ocean access—unreal colors of turquoise sparkling in the sun. For such a small island, Key Largo's nuances fascinated her.

As she looked around, she felt suddenly aware of how the wildlife refuge had become its own ecosystem, one she felt part of. The group of dedicated volunteers who had showed up today astounded and humbled her.

They'd waded into the water, too, ready for a little bit of fun after a morning that had everyone's muscles aching. The whole area seemed alive with chatter and laughter. No one had bothered changing, charging headlong into the water, clothes and all. A minor form of recklessness she enjoyed.

Even Portia had joined in the impromptu beach excursion. Maureen watched as a wave fell against Portia's back, soaking her clothes. Easton's whooping laugh filtered on the breeze.

Maureen's breath hitched a bit as Xander approached. Self-consciously, she adjusted the strap of her green tank top. When she'd started the cleanup this morning, she'd been in a T-shirt and shorts. The Florida sun had warmed her, prompting her to discard the black shirt in favor of the tank top. Layering clothes was a leftover habit from Ireland she'd yet to break.

As he approached he discarded his shirt, tucking it into the pockets of his shorts. Heart quickening, her eyes fell on his muscled chest. Why did he have to be so damn sexy?

His smile caught her off guard, pairing nicely with his dark hair. He had that old-school-movie-star glamour, effortless charm.

Just like that, he made his way to her. Their bodies so close. And she became aware of just how thin their physical barriers were.

She flashed him a grin as he took her hands, leading them deeper into the ocean. The small waves caused them to brush more and more against each other. And move farther away from Easton, Portia and the volunteers. A semblance of privacy.

Maureen splashed water at Xander, trying to maintain a lightness in their communication that ran counter to the unease mounting in her gut. "What a relief that we're all okay and the refuge only suffered minor damage."

"We've been lucky this hurricane season."

"I read up on the storms before moving here, preparing myself, and so far I feel over prepared."

"The time will come you'll use that knowledge, now that you're staying." His hand brushed her cheek, sending shivers down her spine. The warmth of his fingertips almost made her forget what had plagued her mind all morning during the cleanup.

She raised her eyebrows. "Maybe there won't be one during my time here, since I'm not staying permanently."

Her forehead creased. "We never did talk about how long this marriage is supposed to last."

She stared down at the ring on her finger where her hand rested on his forearm, her skin so pale next to his while the diamond sparkled in the sunlight.

"We can figure that out later. This isn't the time or the place to discuss it, anyway, when someone could walk up and overhear."

"Of course, you're right." She curled her toes in the soft white sand.

He wrapped his arms around her waist. "We should be persuading people we're a couple, an engaged couple, a totally enamored couple." His hands skimmed up and down her back, inciting pleasurable shivers. "It's not that difficult to be convincing. You are a gorgeous woman, Maureen, and that smart mind of yours is every bit as sexy."

His words held her spellbound. He stared a moment at her and she felt the press of the waves knock them even closer. As if by instinct, his grip on her waist tightened. The squeeze encouraged contact, underscoring her desire to get closer. His wet thigh brushed hers, igniting a rush of longing so strong it threatened to pull her under faster than any wave.

And so she kissed him, tasting the salt on his lower lip. Warming up to this moment she'd been thinking about—no, *hoping* for—all morning. His right hand cupped her head, keeping her with him. As if she had any thought of backing away. Anticipation fired hot inside her, deep in her belly, radiating out to tremble through her limbs. Making her weak with desire.

He drank her in, pushing farther with his tongue until the space between his body and hers melted away. So much so that they were unaware of the approaching wave.

It rocked them, pulling them gently underneath the water, but their bodies remained entwined. Eyes closed, lips still pressed together. Even with the water closing over her, the only tangible relationship was the feel of his body and hers. How she wanted to luxuriate here, in this feeling of weightlessness. To surrender full control to the moment as his body pressed more firmly to hers. Her breasts ached for his caress and she could feel him against her, broadcasting how much he wanted her, as well.

An urgency for air disrupted that need, however. They pushed their way to the surface with quick inhales.

And then he pulled her back, folding her into him. Kissing her deeply. Hungrily. The sounds of the seagulls and volunteers returning her to the moment in a way she didn't want. For a secluded refuge, there sure were a lot of people around all the time.

Don, a volunteer with spiked hair, shouted in their direction, "Get a room, you two."

She thought that sounded like a brilliant idea. And, oh, God, what was she thinking to let herself get so aroused in a public place? She could barely catch her breath.

Xander lifted an eyebrow at her. "Interested in a room?"

She splayed her hands along his chest, trying to slow her racing heart rate. "I thought you said I would call the shots on the issue of when—or if—we sleep together."

"I did ask."

"True." She looked down at her hands, her engagement ring sparkling in the bright Florida sun, a reminder that she needed to think carefully about her decisions when it came to him. "But this is all so new to me. Let's take our time."

"Ah, the lady would like to be romanced."

She laughed lightly. "Perhaps the man should be romanced, too."

"We chase each other?"

"We do have a wedding to plan." This romance would leave her with whiplash if she wasn't careful. She needed to remain in control of the situation.

"Are you suggesting we wait until the wedding night?"

"Is that such an outrageous idea? Especially considering how quickly this all came about?"

Cupping her face, he let out a groan. "Sounds like an incredible invitation to foreplay. But keep in mind, we get married in a week."

"Not much time to plan a wedding."

He rubbed a thumb along her bottom lip. "And an eternity to get you into my bed."

Sleep held Xander in the hazy world of the past. In that most vulnerable time, when there were no safeguards in place to stop the memories that could slay a man, he was tormented by memories he'd been fighting hard since the word *marriage* became a part of his life again.

He stood at the altar of the church, eyes trained on the big oak door. Waiting for her. Anticipation of the future coloring his stance, making his heart palpitate. The moment stretched before him like an eternity. Easton leaned in next to him. "Delilah's straightening out the flowers on the pew. For the third time."

Was she? Xander hadn't even noticed. His sole focus had been on waiting for Terri to come through those doors. So they could start their lives together.

"Today I don't even care." He meant it, though he did avert his gaze to see Delilah fuss over the lilies by their parents. Xander's mother looked at him, joy painting her

face in a serene, eye-shining smile. She squeezed his father's hand. Xander nodded at them, his father winking in response. Perfection. This was what it looked like.

"I know. I just thought it'd help distract you. Dude, you look intense right now." A small, nearly inaudible laugh.

"Ah. Always looking out for me, aren't—"

The doors opened. This was the moment. The organist began playing "Here Comes the Bride."

All of the air was knocked from his lungs. Terri radiated as she approached, her slender frame accented by the A-line skirt. Her blond hair styled in perfect ringlet curls.

Jake walked next to her, looking at Xander with a fierceness.

"Take care of my baby girl," he mouthed to Xander.

In response, Xander nodded. Of course he would. He'd shield her from anything.

Grasping Terri's hand, Xander had never felt more certain about anything in his life. That they'd live happily ever after. Have kids. The works.

But then she started seizing. Shaking. On the ground. Voices pushed against him.

Paramedics appeared. An aneurism. That's what they were saying.

This was all wrong. Not like this.

And it wasn't like this. Where was Rose?

He looked at Terri, her body stilling after the seizure. Life flooding out of her eyes. Pain flooding his. The pink rose she'd been holding lay limp in her hands.

He went to pick up the rose, but it fell away from his grip, becoming—

Sheets?

Blinking, Xander kicked aside the blankets in his California King bed and took in his surroundings. He heard the steady beat of waves against sand, the feel of his Egyptian cotton sheets and his tossed pillows.

A damn nightmare.

A helluva way to cap off an exhausting twenty-four-hour period. Sweat soaked his sheets and even trickled down his chest.

No way he could stay in bed after that piece of the past shredded him. Space and air. That's what he needed. Anything to get those images out of his mind.

He'd never been much of a runner. Instead he'd found swimming to be what set his mind right. In times of stress, personal or business, he'd found a few laps brought him solace.

And he needed that now.

Quietly he slipped out of his room to the grand pool. He'd brought in a special designer, wanting this to be a kind of sanctuary for Rose, too. So he'd pulled out all the stops. Salt water and Olympic length, he'd also had a faux water cliff constructed on the back wall. Water-falls had been added, giving off a very distinct lagoon feeling. Even the hot tub had been incorporated into the tropical feeling. Live palms were interspersed in the de-sign, shading the hot tub and adding texture to the cliff.

As he closed the sliding-glass door behind him, he no-ticed he hadn't been the only one with this idea.

Water rippled behind a redheaded mermaid. The hair webbing behind her, parting to reveal a topless Maureen.

While swimming topless was a European custom he appreciated, his desire ramped up. Without a second thought, he shucked his blue shorts and dove in after her.

Seven

Water flowed over Maureen's body, washing away the tension of the day, the storm. Her desire for a man still in love with his dead wife.

A man Maureen had agreed to marry.

What had she been thinking?

Why couldn't he have been a troll?

She swam harder, faster, desperate to wear herself out to the very last atom of energy so she could fall into a dreamless slumber. She was a strong swimmer, a part of not only her job but also from having grown up on the craggy shores of a waves-tossed Irish village. She wanted to swim in the ocean tonight but fear of sharks and riptides had kept her in check at the last minute, opting for the pool instead. No one stirred this late at night, anyway. She could be alone with her thoughts.

A whoosh of water rippled over her. From the fountain or water features? She opened her eyes and realized…

Xander swam in front of her, side-stroking, studying her through the crystal waters. God, he was so muscular and broad-chested.

He matched her pace, stroke for stroke. Tendons in his arms rippled with each strong sweep through the crystal water. Definitely nothing troll-like about this man. Instead he exuded power and seduction with every ripple that broke against his tanned skin.

Not ready to come to full reality, to words, Maureen pushed on. Since their impromptu dinner at Belle Terre, they'd yet to be alone together. Even at the restaurant, waitstaff and musicians had stood at an attentive, audible distance. Now this midnight swim felt different from that night.

Cresting the water for a moment, she stole a glance at him and the lanai beyond. Alone. They were actually alone. No Easton or Portia or volunteers.

The thought simultaneously thrilled and terrified her. Never before had two equal but opposite forces begged her muscles for movement. So she kept swimming, kept doing her laps, all too aware of the throaty sound of his breathing, of his lips searching for air.

A phantom trace of the kiss from the ocean lingered in her thoughts when she pushed off the side of the pool, more determined than ever to keep swimming. As if swimming in this pool with him and not throwing herself at her very sexy, fake fiancé would prove to Maureen once and for all that she was in control.

He kept time with her. To an outsider, they must have looked like synchronized swimmers. Every so often, on the lap exchange, she'd catch his eye. A watery grin and challenge arched in his eye. They went on lapping until Maureen lost count, until her lungs and limbs burned with exhaustion. Finally, they both stopped at the side by the water feature.

Gasping, she asked, "What brought you out here tonight?"

"What brought you?" he asked back, not in the least winded, which almost made her roll her eyes but also gave her a moment of pleasure to appreciate his strength.

Treading water, she shrugged, keeping energy in her limbs. "Trouble sleeping. I guess I'm too ramped up from all the stress of the storm and cleanup. Relieved, too, but over-revved. And you?"

"The same. Adrenaline."

Xander pulled himself out over the pool's lip and into the hot tub, settling on the far wall. She followed, aware of him and appreciating the way his gaze lingered on her exposed breasts.

But the appreciation also made her aware that she needed to be more careful. Put boundaries up. Though the water teased and wrapped just above her breasts, she scanned for her bikini top. Too exposed, too quickly.

She nibbled her lip and reached for her stretchy Lycra top on the concrete. And wrapped the front tie bandeau around her again.

Xander smiled, his eyes heavy-lidded and sexy. "Damn shame to cover up such beauty."

"Someone else could be awake. I shouldn't have been so reckless. I forget I'm not in Europe sometimes."

"Well, I won't so easily be forgetting the loveliness I saw, regardless of what you're wearing." His lips tipped in a crooked grin, eyes lingering from mouth to bikini top and finally flicking back to her eyes. Rattling her to the core.

"I'll simply take that as a compliment, you wicked

man." She flipped her red hair that already had begun to form little ringlets.

"I'm your wicked fiancé." He floated toward her, the movement of the water sending anticipatory chills down her spine.

"Yes, you are, and we agreed this is in name only."

She was telling it to him as much as she was telling it to herself.

"How long do you think we'll be able to hold on to that sterile farce with all this attraction and chemistry damn near electrocuting us as we sit here in the water?" He motioned lightly with his fingers in the space between them, the light tremors pressing into her chest. How she wanted him to actually touch her. But she needed to keep her head. For both their sakes.

"I believe sex would complicate things tremendously when we have to say goodbye."

"It doesn't have to, not as long as we agree to get on as amiably as this, friends. It could be fun, exciting... Think of the adventures we could have in this exotic locale."

Oh. Was she just a way to live out what never was with Terri? The thought gutted her like a fish at market. That would never work, not for either of them. It wouldn't be fair to Terri's memory or to Maureen's world. "I won't be a part of you replaying your past."

His face went somber. "I wouldn't dishonor either of you that way. Anything between you and me is just that, about the two of us. New experiences. New adventures."

"I want to trust that." And she did want to trust that. But, damn, their scenario exploded with complications and unhealed wounds. A dangerous combination.

"You want to trust me. You want *me*. Because I sure as hell want you."

She glanced down, his thick erection visible enough through the material of his shorts and the hot tub swirls. "I can tell."

He grinned. Definitely wicked.

She splashed him. "Wipe that look off your face."

He tossed back his head and laughed and Lord, that was every bit as enticing as his smile, his face.

His body.

"Maureen, I truly meant what I said. We'll take our time. Wanting and acting on those desires are two different things. When you're ready, clearly—" he glanced down with a wry smile "—I'll be ready, as well."

"And meanwhile?"

His thigh grazed hers. "I'll be doing my best to romance you and entice you to make that night one to remember."

The dwindling golden rays of late afternoon glinted off the deck of the glass-bottomed section of the yacht. But nothing looked more radiant than Maureen.

She stood a few feet away from him, her wild hair ablaze in the light, loose curls against ivory skin and a green shift dress. Slow, smooth jazz stirred on the breeze, coming from the small band stationed at the end of the yacht in front of the makeshift dance floor where high-powered couples pressed cheeks.

Xander watched her eyes take in the fish darting in and out of the coral. A bemused smile on her lips.

For him, this sort of gathering felt stale and stifling. At least it had for the last fourteen months. He'd always found excuses for attending the minimum amount of social gatherings since Terri's death. Too many questions. Everyone gave him a sympathetic headshake.

With Maureen by his side? Everything changed. He

wanted to show her a fine evening, to romance her. She deserved that. So he'd confirmed his RSVP for the company's glass-bottomed boat charity event.

He scanned the crowd, noting the sheer variety of movers and shakers. A lot of these guys were politicians whose plastically constructed trophy wives made the Stepford wives look like a leper colony. Local celebrities from the Miami sports teams sipped champagne, huddled among the wealthiest people Miami-Dade County had to offer.

A glittering world. Xander could almost forget there'd been a tropical storm as he looked toward the shore. A few knocked and battered trees, but most of the lush greenery remained intact. A tropical oasis beckoning.

A part of him worried he was letting go of Terri's memory, yet he also couldn't help but indulge in Maureen's company that reminded him he was still alive, something he'd avoided thinking about or feeling since Terri's death.

And the people on the glass-bottomed section of the yacht were all potential partners, investors and promoters. He turned to the bartender, handing over his downed bourbon-on-the rocks glass. An older man and his wife sidled past Xander, bumping in to him.

"Oh, so sorry, love," the older lady with gray-blue hair crooned. Her voice sounded real and genuine, something often lacking at gatherings of the elite and wealthy. She and her husband looked like the kind of people he liked to chat with at events like these.

"Not a problem at all," Xander murmured, waving his hand.

Her husband, an older gentlemen dressed in a fairly modest black suit, cleared his throat. "You and your girl remind us of, well…us when we were younger. Hold on to her," he added, winking before walking away with his wife.

"Thank you, sir." Xander knew he and Maureen were selling the engaged couple act well. Truth be told, she made it damn easy. Maureen's natural beauty, her kind heart. Their intense chemistry. The role seemed like a perfect cast.

Looking back toward Maureen, he realized he wasn't the only one appreciating the way her body curved. A tall blond man approached her, eyes hungry.

A wave of jealousy coursed in Xander's blood, bubbling in his stomach. He cut the blond man off at the pass, planting a kiss on her forehead, placing his palm possessively on her spine.

"Dance with me, my love," he breathed into her ear.

She nodded, her slender hand folding in his. He pulled her to the dance floor, his hand finding purchase again along the small of her back. She was his. He didn't want to question why he felt that way, not now. He just wanted to hold on to this moment, this attraction. He just had to pick the right moment to make his move to win her over into his bed.

"You reminded me of the Little Mermaid a few moments ago."

"For real? So you've had a Little Mermaid crush since you were, like, ten years old?"

He choked on a laugh then shook his head. "Maybe. But make no mistake, my feelings now are one hundred percent adult, feeling drawn to the siren song of a luscious adult mermaid."

"For real? That's…intriguing." Her voice was a sigh on pink lips.

"Yeah. When you were standing there, looking at the

fish with the coral backdrop. You looked like part of that landscape. Like I said, a siren."

"Mmm."

Her subdued response tipped him off that her mind trailed elsewhere.

"What's wrong?"

Pulling back slightly from the intimate slow dance, she squared to look at him. "This is your life? Full of parties and gatherings with the wealthiest people in the country?"

He mentally regrouped, trying to gauge where this was coming from, where it might be leading. And what that meant regarding turning the page on his past with Terri.

"I'm a person with a chance to make a difference. I do that my way. You do the same in your way."

"What about all the waste here?" Heat entered her syllables, infusing them with accusations and distaste.

"Be more specific." He couldn't address her concerns until he understood them better, but he recalled her discomfort at Belle Terre, almost as if she didn't dare enjoy the opulent dinner.

"The decadence? You know, like endless escargot and party bags with gold and sapphire jewelry."

"They chose how to spend their money and that money went into a business's pocket, feeding back into the economy. And the majority of the people on the yacht donated heavily to charity, as well." He couldn't help his defensiveness. He knew the people here could solve a lot of the world's problems with the kinds of checks they wrote. And they frequently did just that. "So your problem is?"

He glanced around the deck, taking note of Jerry Ghera, the world-famous surgeon who'd given up his private practice to be part of Doctors Without Borders.

Sure, the lights, the band, the food was lavish…but a lot of these people were kind and generous.

Pausing, she nibbled her bottom lip. "I sounded judgmental, didn't I?"

"Were you being judgmental?" Every time Xander thought he'd pegged Maureen, figured her out, a surprise leaped out at him.

"What did Terri think of this lifestyle?"

The tempo quickened so he increased their pace, spinning her around and then back to him. "She wasn't comfortable in large groups."

"So it wasn't the money for her, just so many people?"

"Basically, yes. Her parents are quite well-off." A problem only because of the power that came with their wealth and what it might mean for his daughter. He'd never given their wealth—any of the wealth—much thought before.

"I didn't realize that."

"Terri's money is all in a trust for Rose."

"And Rose's maternal grandparents?" She pressed into him, leaning in as he led her toward the center of the dance floor.

"They could pitch one helluva battle for custody of Rose if they decided to dig in deep."

The Irish anger leeched from her face. Concern touched her brow, causing it to furrow and her eyes to widen. In a lower voice, she asked, "Have they been in touch or made threats?"

"No. Nothing since our engagement announcement." He thrust his hand through his hair. "I want to find a way to trust them so they can spend more time with her. But I'm terrified they'll leave the country with her."

"Do you seriously think they would go to illegal lengths?"

"They loved their daughter and I understand that. God, I understand a parent's love for their kid. But Rose is my daughter. My child." He closed his eyes for a moment. There'd be time to deal with all of that later. He sighed hard before continuing. "Enough of that kind of discussion. You're supposed to be having decadent fun."

"It is a lovely party," she admitted finally, although it was obviously not the kind she'd ever throw.

He winked. "I enjoy the way you dance."

"Are you teasing me?" Her head titled to the side, a strand of hair falling into her face.

Lifting his hand from her side, he tucked the curl behind her ear.

"Your moves are sexy as hell, lass. I would never tease you about that. In fact, now that I'm thinking about it, maybe I don't want them seeing you dance."

An overpowering stillness rippled through Maureen's body, like someone had fastened her with a pin like a Victorian moth. Her normal grace and fluidity vacated her features, a retreating shift he felt as tension rippled through her.

"Maureen? What's wrong?" Trying like hell to read her face, to understand what had happened.

"It's nothing." Her lip jutted, brow furrowed, and her voice sounded distant and cold. Not a terribly convincing liar.

"Clearly, it's something."

Her eyes, filled with rage and resignation, met his. "My ex had a jealousy issue. A bad one."

Damn. His brother's veiled warning about how bad her ex was entered his mind again. "Did he hurt you?"

"Physically? God, no." She held up her hands. "Forget I said anything. Really. I don't want to talk about this."

Maureen pulled back, shifting her weight onto her slender heels. Leaving the dance floor and him.

He needed her to understand that he shared little in common with her ex. He'd never been the kind of man to emotionally or physically hurt a woman. Didn't have it in him for that level of manipulation.

Determined to make his point, he searched the crowd for her until he found her chatting with a group of women around a champagne fountain. Her glorious red hair drew him like a beacon. Lightly, he touched her arm, fixing her with a stare.

A shudder unfolded beneath his fingertips, but she stayed. In the truest way he knew how to convey his understanding, he kissed her. Lightly, on the forehead. Then softer still on her mouth. The tension in her stance eased.

Xander held out his hand. "Keep dancing with me. We won't talk. Just…dance."

In response she drew closer in his arms, practically melting into his body. The light scent of her jasmine perfume enveloping him as a sigh ricocheted through her body.

Damn. This woman… She could become a living flame, and when she burned, it was bright and fearsome. He admired the hell out of her spirit. And her willingness to stay here, pressed up against him, meant he might be getting through to her. Winning her over, after all.

With a week left until the wedding, he hoped Maureen would begin to trust him. To separate him from that scumbag ex of hers. If he played all his cards right, kept that boardroom bravado, she would be his.

And he would have to learn to overcome the twinge in his gut—in his heart—that suggested he was somehow betraying Terri. Because no matter how many times he told himself he and Maureen were just helping each other out, he knew damn well he wanted her.

Wedding planning.

Words that normally involved a small group of girl-friends pouring over websites and bridal magazines, mimosas in hand. Picking out decorations that reflected the couple's collective personalities.

This meeting with Portia? Opposite of that.

Not that Maureen minded. She'd done the months-of-planning wedding before. And her real wedding had ended with real pain, despite the hours of primping and making her wedding day look like a spread in one of those magazines.

Even with Portia's assistance, and the knowledge that somehow this wedding wasn't real, she still felt nervous. For a variety of reasons.

The biggest of which? Her conflicted but ever-present attraction to her fiancé. Her *fake* fiancé. A reality that continued to crash into her soul.

"So talk to me about what you'd like your wedding to be like. The vibe you are going for. I'm great at organizing and getting things done quickly," Portia said, taking a seat next to Maureen. Portia clicked her retractable pen and wrote the wedding date at the top of her legal pad.

A week to go until the wedding. A week and nothing planned yet. *Not a big deal. Not a big deal.* If she told herself that enough times, would it become true?

"The exact opposite of my first one," Maureen quipped, folding her legs into lotus position. She ran her fingers on the light fabric of her capris, thinking back to her wedding.

"What was your first one like?" Portia asked.

A loaded question. "In a nutshell? Too big."

And not by Maureen's choice. Her parents, her now ex-husband—they'd all wanted the big white wedding. A huge bridal party, a guest list of over 200 people. A wedding dress that had practically swallowed her whole in yards of fabric. A cathedral-length train. She wanted this wedding—real or not—to feel nothing like that.

"You don't strike me as the big wedding type, anyway."

"I'm not interested in replaying the past in any capacity. Which reminds me—" a blush burned on Maureen's cheeks "—I should extend the same courtesy to Xander. Any chance you know what his wedding was like?"

Portia chewed at her lip, shaking her head. "No. Do you want to call and ask him?"

Oh, heavens no. Maureen had to think quickly on her feet. "I don't want to bother him at the office."

Portia laid the pen to the center of her chin. "We could always look at his wedding album. It's in the family room."

"Great. That'd be perfect." Maureen exhaled a little too quickly. Portia's eyebrows inclined slightly, but she didn't press.

"I'll be right back." Portia set her pad and pen on the driftwood coffee table, flitting out of the room. Moments later she returned, album in hand.

Moving the chairs together, Portia and Maureen sifted through the album. For a moment Maureen felt intrusive, looking at these photos.

Her heart burst as she took them in. His smile, bright, unfettered by heartbreak. She wished he could still look like that, feel like that. Terri and Xander had been a beautiful couple. Their wedding, also very traditional, had been set in a large church.

"Oh, look at Easton," Portia said, laughing at the picture of Easton dancing next to Xander's in-laws. Always a ham.

Maureen's emerald eyes slid to the next picture, the one that showed the huge dance floor filled with couples.

"I think it's safe to say, you and Xander both did that big white wedding before. So, what's the opposite?" Portia said, closing the album.

"When I was a little girl in County Cork, I always wanted to get married at one of the old, mossy country chapels. Something situated in nature. And something that only has room for the few people that actually matter," Maureen said wistfully, recalling the green and mist.

Portia snapped her fingers. "There's a small, old, Spanish-style chapel on one of the nearby barrier islands."

Nodding, Maureen said, "That could work. Can we check it out?"

Portia shrugged. "As long as we don't take a dip with any alligators, I don't see why not."

Within about fifteen minutes Portia and Maureen had made their way to one of the smaller boats. Portia took up her familiar boat position—clinging to the railing and concentrating on filling her lungs with air. Maureen laughed, admiring her friend's willingness to constantly fling herself into the jaws of anxiety.

The Sunday-afternoon sun stretched long rays in front of them, singeing warmth into Maureen's skin. She drove the boat with a steady hand, anticipation rising as the shoreline of the small barrier island drew closer.

Visible from the shore was a small Spanish chapel. Climbing ivy shrouded the curved façade of the building, with the exception of the wood door. An elaborate bronze cross jutted from the curved roofline. Exotic tropical plants surrounded the chapel, flanking it in natural beauty.

As Maureen anchored the boat, Portia stood on wobbling legs. "What do you think?"

"It's perfect. This is definitely the place." A true smile pushed loose.

"So now that we are here, tell me your vision. I'll help make it tangible."

Maureen blinked, letting her Irish imagination have full rein and dance before her.

"Small. The family and some of the full-time staff for the guest list. Will you be my bridesmaid?" Maureen asked.

"Of course, I will. That's an easy enough request. What else? Colors you have in mind?" Portia pressed, pen to paper.

"Light and natural colors. Orange flowers. They feel like they could have come from this landscape, don't they?"

Portia nodded, scribbling on her legal pad. "Dress?"

Maureen took a moment, letting the image wash over her. "I want Rose to be in a flowing white dress, one with peonies that ripple out of the fabric by her precious feet."

"Gorgeous. What about flowers for her? Perhaps a flower wreath headband?" Portia offered, trying to ride in the direction of Maureen's vision.

Maureen nodded in agreement. "Yes. A beautiful flower crown of orange and white flowers with nice green leaves twined together."

"And how do you envision your dress?"

A pause. Her first wedding dress had been stifling and rigid. The landscape here beckoned for something more natural. "Something strapless. And with ruffles from the waistline down. The kinds of ruffles that look like cascading waves."

"Now *that* I know we can find. And you will look like a fairy-bride in a dress like that. I'll make a few calls to bridal shops as soon as we get back. This is going to be a beautiful ceremony."

Maureen's eyes lingered on the chapel. The echo of a childhood plan rendered real. Or real enough. She could practically picture Rose as the flower girl and Xander, all tall, tan and handsome, standing with her in that chapel.

Tears threatened to blur her vision, a lump pushing in her throat. She knew the wedding would be stunning, and go off without a hitch.

But the wedding night… That was another story. What would it be like after a day of fairy-tale romance? Could she resist Xander when it was just the two of them?

Or, better yet, did she want to?

Eight

Xander slipped on his aviator sunglasses as he stepped outside. Looking for Maureen.

Less than a week until their wedding. Until he could have her. But for now, he'd settle just to see her. Maureen's presence had a steadying effect on him, like a constant drumbeat in a song.

He had a sneaking suspicion of where he'd find her today. His paces eating up the ground fast, he made his way to the wild bird sanctuary and rehab facility. The covered screen area rose high as a palm tree, maybe about twenty feet tall. Maureen worked in the screened area, every bit the sexy wood nymph.

Her hair twisted on her head in a messy ballerina bun, she wiped beads of sweat from her brow. The Florida sun worked overtime, heating the air, turning the midday afternoon sticky with unbridled humidity.

And she still looked damn good.

Xander stood back a moment, drinking her in. She hadn't noticed him yet. He recognized one of the birds from the boat oil spill. The bird seemed to test its wings, stretching them as it perched on her arm.

She cooed at it. Patient. Encouraging. The bird cocked its head at her, as if trying to understand.

"There we go. You've got it." As if in response, the bird bristled its chest, white feathers puffing. But it made no attempt to leave her arm.

"Maybe later, love." She sat the small bird down on a nearby branch. It chirped at her as she turned her attention to an African gray parrot. One with a splinted broken wing. She scrutinized the wing, nose crinkling as she inspected it.

As he approached, Xander noted the way the days out in the sun had left her skin slightly pink. A sunburn, but it colored her fair skin in the appearance of a fixed blush.

Stepping up behind her, he cleared his throat. "Shouldn't you be planning the wedding?"

"We could just go to a justice of the peace."

"We could, but we're looking to make this appear as legit as possible for both our sakes. Need I remind you how high the stakes are for you and for Rose?" The words came out sharply, but damn it, she needed to take this seriously.

Stroking the African gray's feathers, she returned the bird to the low branch.

Casting him a glance over her shoulder, she replied, even-keeled as ever. "You can calm down. Portia and I have everything mapped out. Portia and I already called the caterer and florist this morning. All will be taken care of."

"And your dress?" The dress he wanted to see and then promptly relieve her of.

She chewed her full bottom lip. "I, uh, I'll have one."

"I certainly hope so."

"I have evenings to shop." Her voice wavered and her hands went to her hair, a sign of fraying nerves.

"There are parties planned, you know. As my wife, there will be more functions to attend. It will be good for the refuge, too."

"I understand and I can handle it."

He hooked his arms around her. "Part of this whole deal is appearing like a couple. Starting now."

The heat of her sunburn radiated warmth between them, adding to the electric nature of their embrace. He pulled her closer, bodies practically one. His hand traced up the small of her back, gently outlining her spine, hinting at her generous curves. He wanted her. Not a week from now. But now.

Ever since that night in the hot tub with her, the level of his craving had ratcheted up too high to ignore.

She blinked up at him flirtatiously. "Are you asking to kiss me?"

"Do you want me to?"

Her eyes went sultry. "Well, in the interest of being a good, engaged couple."

He laughed softly. Angling his head to hers, he kissed her. Slowly and thoroughly, long enough to feel her body go limp in his arms. A victory that only made him ache.

Before he lost his senses, he pulled back, away from the fierce temptation her mouth presented. "I have a wedding gift for you."

Her eyes went wide. "You do?"

"Easton and I hired extra help for today so you can have the afternoon and evening off with Portia and your friends here."

"Doing what?" She nibbled her enticing bottom lip, trying to ferret out the information.

He grinned, wishing he could work on that lower lip of hers himself, but he knew that kissing her again would be his undoing. "It's not a gift if it isn't a surprise."

The owner of Je T'aime, Darling passed out five flutes of champagne. Maureen nodded her thanks to the shop owner, wishing it was socially acceptable to down the whole glass before the toast.

Nerves jumbling in her stomach, she surveyed the women that accompanied her as she searched for a picture-perfect dress. Portia sat next to a thin, athletic, brunette woman in a yellow sundress—Allie, one of Maureen's good friends and one of the hardest-working volunteers at the refuge. Jessie, the wife of Don the security guard, reapplied bright pink lipstick before taking the champagne off the tray. Two other volunteers sat on the couch. Maureen's impromptu wedding-dress-shopping gang assembled.

"Now, Portia called ahead and let me know the styles you were interested in. And your size. I've pulled a collection of about five dresses for you to try on. We can add from there." The shopkeeper smiled warmly, pointing to a dressing room. "I'll be standing right in the main area if you need me."

With that the woman turned on her heels, disappearing in a rustle of chiffon behind pale pink curtains.

Maureen smiled at her collection of friends, still apprehensive about picking out a dress.

"To Maureen, the beautiful bride," Allie said, raising her glass.

"To Maureen!" the ladies echoed, full smiles as they raised and clinked their glasses together.

With a practiced, steadied hand, Maureen raised and clinked her glass, slamming the champagne back.

"Well, go on. We want to see you in those gorgeous gowns!" Portia grabbed the empty flute from Maureen, ushering her to the dressing room. "Just remember, we can have anything rush-altered. I've got seamstresses on speed dial."

"Is there anything you don't have covered?" Maureen laughed, slipping into the oversize dressing room. Eyes catching immediately on the floor-length mirror, she noticed how the five gowns were each carefully laid on their own hooks. All waiting for her to try.

"No, not if I can help it." Portia squeezed her hand before returning to the couch with the other ladies.

Maureen gravitated toward the gown in the right corner—a strapless, mermaid-cut ivory dress that had ruching all the way from waist to the floor. She slid out of her blue sundress and into the mermaid gown. Taking a glance in the mirror, she twisted her face in displeasure.

Because this dress pressed the unreal reality of her impending wedding on her? She couldn't tell.

Still, she gathered the dress in her hand, walked out to stand in front of her friends.

"It's a beautiful gown," offered Allie, eyebrows rising as she sipped her champagne.

"But?" Maureen pressed, needing further clarification.

"It hides your pretty curves. So restricting, too. You're like the ocean, love. Movement and passion. You need a dress that shows that exuberance, reflects you," Jessie said, fluffing her blond bob.

Maureen nodded, chewing her lip. She did want a gown that spoke to the vibe of this place she loved so much. The untamed, unstructured grace. "I'll try another."

Back into the dressing room. This time she selected an A-line cut. It, too, was strapless, but a true white. An attendant came out with a series of belts to add to cinch in the waist, starting with a simple braided ribbon. Not right. Then more of a low-lying chain, which wasn't quite right, either.

Then…yes, the attendant placed a wide belt of intricate beads along Maureen's waist, cinching it with ribbons in the back to give the right effect until the band could be fitted and sewed on. From beneath the belt, waves of fabric coalesced, folding in and out like sea water.

She didn't even bother to look at herself in the mirror before striding out to her group. "Well?"

Maureen glanced at her friends on the couch, and then past them, to her reflection in the mirror.

The dress was…

"It's you. Someone stole your spirit and made a dress out of you," Portia breathed, smile widening. All the ladies nodded.

Admiring herself in the mirror, Maureen spun, luxuriating in the swish of fabric, the freedom it promised.

"Can you go tell the shop owner I've made my selection? I don't need to try any more."

"You've got it." Portia stood up from the couch. "And Xander has booked the spa for us. That's up next."

After Maureen changed into her clothes and paid for her dress, the group of ladies found their way back to the limo. The chauffeur set a course for the Oasis Spa, an exclusive resort known for their Swedish massages, kelp-based facials and gel mani-pedi combos. An afternoon of pampering for her and her friends, courtesy of Xander Lourdes.

The limo ride went quickly. Maureen did her best to concentrate, to stay present and calm. But guilt crept into her thoughts. All the levels of deceit gnawed at her ability to enjoy such a kind gesture.

As they entered the marbled room, Maureen's jaw dropped. A water feature trickled down a rock wall, the soft babble of water soothing her along with the scents of lavender and eucalyptus in the air. Calm guitar music melted into the background, layering luxury into the very air. A spread of chocolates, grapes, chocolate-dipped fruits, pastries and cheeses covered a long table. Five plush chairs were arranged in a circle, primed for conversation.

First up, pedicures for the ladies.

"You know, Jessie, I always knew Xander and Maureen would hit it off," Allie said, a sly smile playing on her face.

"Did you, now?" Maureen asked, popping a grape in her mouth.

"Oh, yes. You balance each other. The timing just had to be right. But I saw the spark months ago."

Months ago? He hadn't even been on her radar then. Not in a real way.

"Oh, yes, I can see that, too. He's always had that intense gaze for her, hasn't he?" Jessie agreed, clearly enjoying the pedicure. Her normally tensely furrowed brow seemed to release all tension.

"Ah, yes. And here they are today. Inseparable. In love," Portia added.

A bit *too* quickly, Maureen noted. Wondering, briefly, if she knew the nature of the ruse.

Best not to dwell on that. Instead, Maureen focused on relaxing. Living in the moment, drinking in the layered scents of incense and nail polish. Letting the conversation fall away as her personal attendant shaped her nails.

While their face masks were still setting, her friends told her to close her eyes. More surprises?

"Okay. Open them." Portia urged, placing a shirt in her hand.

Eyes blinking to readjust to the light in the room, she read the shirt. *Bride.* She willed her mouth to smile. "Thank you. It's so kind."

And a lie. But for a minute she wanted it to be true.

"That's not all. We've gotten you something to make your big night and your life together just a little sweeter," Allie said, pulling a perfectly wrapped box out from under her chair.

"Or saucier." A wicked grin escaped Jessie's lips.

Oh, Lord. She was worse than a liar. She was a downright fraud. All of the effort these women had put in on such short notice…

"You all…you all didn't have to do this." Maureen's voice cracked, a hint of shimmering tears beginning to line her eyes.

"Of course, we did. It's not every day you get married. And it's certainly not every day you get married to such a handsome, generous man," Allie chided, unaware that this, in fact, was not Maureen's first jaunt down the aisle. The first wedding had been in earnest and ended in flames. Could a wedding constructed in falsehood somehow fare better? She shoved that thought away.

"Anyway, I want you to open mine first," Jessie said, pushing her silver-wrapped box in front of Maureen. Jessie took a bite of chocolate fudge, motioning Maureen to hurry up.

With shaking fingers, touched and humbled by the attention of these kind woman, she tore through the wrapping paper, lifted the cardboard lid to reveal five smaller boxes, all with little cards affixed to the lids. Each card had a jingle about panties—when to wear each pair. One for the honeymoon. One for their first fight. One for Valentine's Day.

Maureen's face turned upward, light dancing in her eyes. "This is hysterical."

"I thought you'd appreciate them." She winked, biting into a chocolate-covered strawberry.

Maureen unwrapped the rest of the gifts—a few pieces of delicate, lacy lingerie, an embroidered pillow with their names and wedding date, and a tiny, glittering frame.

"Thank you so much. I really appreciate all of this."

"Of course, Maureen. We wanted you to have a special, albeit hastened, bridal shower. Which reminds me. I wrote down all of your reactions to your presents. It's a list I like to call 'Things I Will Say to Xander on Our Wedding Night.'" Portia's smile reached her eyes.

"What?"

"Oh, just listen. 'Things Maureen Will Say to Xander in Bed.' Ahem. 'This is hysterical. This is so precious! Lord, this is so tiny! Beautiful and delicate. What a pretty shade of pink!'"

Peals of laughter erupted from around the spa room. Her fake bridal shower had been so much more spontaneous and comfortable than her real one. After another two hours of massages, the limo arrived to take them all back to the refuge. Back to Xander. She wanted to thank him for his kindness, to show how much she appreciated him.

She rushed back to her room, slipped into a backless black dress. The front was a deep cowl neck that tastefully nodded to the nature of her curves. Ready to see him. Ready to unwind from the day together.

So eager to see him it almost scared her.

* * *

Two hours later, and dinner on the water still made her heart sing. Xander had made reservations at a small, local restaurant. They'd eaten the catch of the day on the deck, watched the sun sink heavy on the horizon and exchanged stories about their childhoods. Gotten to know each other.

The night offered them a degree of comfort—stars dipping in the sky. The lack of true light pollution meant the stars were out in full force, crowning the end of a pretty amazing day. Maureen felt like she lingered on in a fairy world. A slumber that she didn't want to wake from. The whole day had been wonderful. Brilliant.

He helped her into the Mercedes. The touch of his fingertips leaving her wanting. He closed her door, loosened his tie on the way around and climbed into the driver's side. The ride back to the refuge was about five minutes. Too short before they'd part.

Xander parked the Mercedes in the driveway and turned to face her. An eternity passed between them and she stared at his lips, his eyes. He looped his tie around her neck and tugged her toward him. Melting into the feel of him, Maureen inhaled his spicy aftershave, rich with sandalwood and spices and *man*. Greedy with need, their mouths met, parting instantly as they tasted each other for the first time after denying the attraction for so long.

As Xander tunneled his fingers through her hair, it slipped loose, tumbling around them both in a sensuous cloud. Strands spiraling midway along her back tickled down her spine, tingling along her already sensitive skin.

Maureen gripped the lapels of his jacket. Her fingers clenched tight as she strained to get nearer, desperate to deepen the closeness she felt with him, blocking out the rest of the world. Twining her fingers in his hair, she held his face to hers, devouring him, ravenous after what felt like an eternity of waiting. Had this attraction been lurking even longer than she'd allowed herself to acknowledge?

A low groan rumbling in his throat, Xander's leg pressed against hers, the muscles firm, exciting. He covered her body with his, muscled arms lowering her into the corner of the seat. His hand trailed up her leg, stopping to grasp her hip and pull her against him, hard with need.

Maureen arched her back as something uncomfortable prodded her spine. When her body bowed upward, Xander groaned in response and pressed her deeper into the cushioned seat.

"Ouch!" Maureen reached behind her back and tossed a pen case aside.

"Sorry," Xander mumbled against her lips, groping to locate any other possible sharp objects that might distract her. He tossed the pen box over the seat to land in a thudding heap on the floor on top of his briefcase.

"It's okay." Maureen pulled his face back for another mind-drugging kiss.

Xander slipped her dress down one shoulder and cupped her breast, brushing a thumb across the tightened crest, sending sparks of desire through her. When he lowered his mouth to replace his hand, Maureen couldn't control the desire to roll her hips against his. A new music coursed through her as they resumed their dance.

She pushed away any concerns, wanting to revel in him. She'd spent enough time pretending. She wanted something real.

She wanted him.

"Birth control," Xander moaned.

His chest heaving, he rested his head against her

breast. Puffy gasps of air dried the damp peak, the painful chill almost as stimulating as his warm, moist kisses.

"You have my mind so muddled I can't think straight half the time." He raked his fingers through his mussed hair. "I can't believe I let things go this far in the driveway, where anyone could walk up on us. Give me a minute to clear my head and figure out where we should go."

Maureen struggled to control the passion singing through her body as she watched Xander, his eyes closed, his breathing ragged. She'd been so determined to wait, but something, maybe the edginess of the storm or the visions of him with his family or just his magnetism altogether, created a different storm inside her and she knew.

She didn't want to wait any longer.

"My place."

"What?"

"Go to my place." Maureen cupped his face in her hands and explained with urgency, "It's private and I have condoms."

His eyes opened wide as realization dawned. "Yes, ma'am."

Rolling off her, Xander turned on the Mercedes and slammed it into gear just as she snapped her seat belt into place. Their labored breathing filled the luxurious car as they made record time through the dirt roads to her cabin. Every stop sign became a sweet temptation as they stole hot, passionate kisses, becoming more familiar with the flavor of each other at every intersection.

After four years of abstinence, she owed it to herself not to wait one minute longer. She stroked up his arm. "Drive faster."

"And you have condoms?"

"An unopened box of a dozen."

"Twelve!" Xander's brow creased into deep furrows

while he stared at the road as if pondering a quadratic equation. "Well, at least that's in the ballpark if you give me a couple of days. It is a weekend, after all."

"If only you had one in your wallet."

With a low growl of sexual arousal, he put the car in Park and reached for her again. "You're driving me crazy."

The second Xander slid to the middle of the front seat, Maureen straddled his lap. She couldn't remember when sex had been fun. And this was so wonderfully abandoned and impulsive, and a huge turn-on.

The skirt of her dress hitched up as she knelt, her feet dangling off the edge of the seat. She fumbled with his belt, having difficulty managing even in the luxury sedan, leather creaking as she moved.

Xander's jaw slid open.

Even though it couldn't go further until they reached her place, the thick press of his arousal through his pants pressed against the core of her, sending sweet sparks of pleasure through her.

Not one to lag behind, he slid his hand under her dress and skimmed his fingers along the edge of her panties.

When he gripped her hips, his fingers grazed across her stomach. She grabbed his wrists and moved his other hand to cup her breast under the silky fabric flowing around them both in a fiery cloud.

Tap-tap-tap.

Maureen flinched.

Xander's head pivoted toward the sound.

Someone with a flashlight strobed the beam in their direction, illuminating Xander's eyes, full of heat and desire. Xander's hands snaked from under her dress with lightning speed.

"Good evening. Is everything okay?" Don, a volunteer, shouted through the window. The older man had worked security detail for a major corporation before retiring, and now volunteered those skills to patrol the refuge at night.

Maureen pressed the electric button, thankful the Mercedes was still running. Easing off Xander's lap, she almost toppled over when he clamped his hands on either side of her dress to hide the considerable evidence of his arousal. The exotic scent of tropical flowers in the night air drifted through the open window as the security guard shuffled his feet.

"Hi, Don. Uh, nice weather." She shifted, sitting on Xander's knees and praying very hard that this nightmare would end—soon.

"Yes, ma'am, mighty nice." Grin spreading across his craggy face, Don thumped his flashlight against his palm, the beam flickering through the dark like a laser show out of control.

"Uh-huh." Maureen unclenched her hands, tight with building desire.

Xander injected into the awkward silence, "How's little Donny Junior?"

"Just fine. He and his wife have a baby on the way."

Maureen felt Xander's glance her way as she focused with undue concentration on the files littering the floor of the car.

Xander cleared his throat. "Tell them I said congratulations."

"Sure will." Don tapped a foot against a tire. "Night, Mr. Lourdes. Good evening, Miz Burke."

She nodded and smiled awkwardly.

Xander waved. "Good night, Don."

With a low chortle, the volunteer security guard turned and strode off into the darkened parking lot.

Maureen raised the window and turned back to Xander just as he adjusted his pants. She clenched the armrest, unsettled by the interruption and by how quickly she'd been swept away by desire for this man.

"Maureen, don't you think you could have helped me out with Don?"

"Nope. I can still barely put two thoughts together." Maureen pressed a hand to her mouth, a hysterical giggle bursting free.

"What?" An indignant expression stained Xander's face as he flopped back against the seat.

"Think about it, Xander."

His shoulders lifted and fell, chuckles rumbling low in his chest. "You make me act like a sixteen-year-old again, making out in a car."

"You must have had a very different life at sixteen than I did. Sorry I didn't consider Don when I, uh, jumped you."

"Don't worry about it. We have a dozen condoms waiting for us at your place."

Nine

From the Mercedes to the cabin door seemed to take an eternity. She stepped in front of him, her slender calves visible in the subdued moonlight, teasing him even more. The promise of her skin against his drove him to madness as she fumbled to slip her keys in the door.

And each step gave him too much damn time to think about the step he was taking—sleeping with a woman for the first time since he'd lost Terri. But she was gone, and he had to move forward with his life. He shut down thoughts of the past that threatened the present.

He wanted this, and Maureen deserved his full attention.

The lock clicked open like a gunshot starting a marathon race, spurring him to action. They stepped through the frame and he kicked the door closed behind him, kissing her deeply. The soft press of her body against his sent his passion into overdrive.

Her hands wandered over his shirt, undoing each button. Shrugging off the fabric, he broke their embrace. To look at her. To *see* her.

Maureen's wild red hair framed her face, falling just above her breasts. A hunger danced in her green eyes as she stood, pressed against the white wicker sofa in the center of her small living room. The modest cabin was filled with photographs of exotic locales and remnants of her Irish roots in the form of a Celtic Cross centered on the wall behind her. A woman who knew no real borders.

He approached her again, kissing her exposed shoulder, running his hand to the zipper on the back of her satiny dress edged with the gentle rasp of lace. He wanted nothing between them. He couldn't remember when he'd felt so out of control as he'd been in the car. That wasn't his style. He ran the show, called the pace, took things slow and careful. Yet they'd almost forgotten birth control.

Above all, he had to remember to be careful with her, to think of her needs. He didn't want to think about Terri now, but she'd been so delicate. Hell. He shoved thoughts of her aside and focused on this moment and what Maureen wanted. What Maureen needed from him. What he needed from her.

Not that reasonable thought was any easier to find now than in the Mercedes.

She felt exquisitely smooth and soft to his touch. Memories of her bare breasts the day in the hot tub grotto blared into his brain, a vision seared on the backs of his eyelids that he couldn't wait to re-create. Tugging her dress down, down, he unveiled her delicate yellow bra, an expanse of sheer lace with strategic roses stitched to cover the rosy tips.

With a groan, he stripped off the yellow ribbons that

served as straps, letting the lace peel down and away. Her back arched, tilting those beautiful breasts toward his mouth. Inviting his kiss. He palmed one creamy weight in his hand, lifting her for a taste.

She hissed a sigh between her teeth, her knees giving way as she fell deeper into him. He anchored her waist with one arm as he rolled one taut nipple between his teeth—gently plucking and licking. Her hair spilled over his arms as she strained to get closer. He molded her waist and hips with his hands, dragging the dress fabric down and off.

Their clothes fell away in a trail on the way to her bedroom, pooling haphazardly on the wood cabin floor.

Entering her bedroom, she pulled out a box of condoms from her driftwood nightstand. They were still sealed. She made no further moves as he joined her near the bed.

He looked at her, questioning. Hoping she still wanted him.

A mischievous look entered her eye. "You can ask."

"Ask what?"

"When I bought them. Why I have them. I bought them after your proposal."

"For this?" He lifted his hand to her face, touching the softness of her wild curls.

She leaned in, kissing the outline of his top lip. "It's been inevitable."

A roar of victory filled his brain as finally, finally, she understood what he'd known in his gut since that impulsive proposal burst from his mouth.

"Nice to hear you acknowledge what I've felt since our first dance together," he said, skimming his lips over hers.

She teased her fingers along his bristly jaw, then back

around to the back of his neck, stroking up into his hair. "Because I want you as much as I believe you want me."

Pulling her closer, their bodies pressed together, he reveled in the brush of their bare flesh against flesh, their legs tangling. One hand between her shoulder blades, his other against her spine, he lowered her onto the thick duvet and covered her body with his. The mattress gave beneath them, her curves molding to his, sending his need into intense overdrive.

The ceiling fan stirred gusts of air over their rapidly heating flesh as his hands learned the terrain of her every curve. As she reciprocated. It was so natural. So right.

And so well lit, thanks to the bedside lamp.

He couldn't have dreamed anything more perfect. And he wasn't sure how much longer he could wait.

Just when he thought he'd reached the breaking point, he saw her pat the bed for the box of condoms and, yes, he was more than happy to assist. Quickly.

At the last instant she snatched a packet from his hands and tore it open. Maureen sheathed the throbbing length of him with deliberate—oh, so deliberate—control. Slowly. Almost torturously slowly, and her smile said she understood well how close she danced to the very hot flame of desire.

His hands tangled in her hair, he kissed her, thoroughly, sealing their lips, their tongues mating as he pushed inside her body for the first time. Felt the hot clamp of her around him, drawing him in, welcoming him.

Bringing him such intense pleasure he almost flew over the edge right then and there.

But he held on, holding still until he had enough self-control to move again, with her, in and out, thrusting and guiding her hips with the rock of his against hers.

He took each kittenish gasp of pleasure into his mouth, grazing kisses along her jaw, then her neck as her head flung back, exposing the graceful arch. Her riotous red hair splayed over the pillow like a fire he would never forget. Ever.

She pushed against his shoulders, rolling him to his back, her magnificent hair draping forward in long, tangled curls over her shoulders, skimming the tops of her breasts. His hands slid from her hips up to cup the weight of her, his thumbs grazing her until her nipples tightened into peaks of pleasure.

The *hmm* of bliss rolling up her throat and between her lips encouraged him as much as the roll of her hips as she rode him, drawing out the pleasure between them.

He pulled her closer to him, needing to feel the curve of soft breasts in his palms. Leaning forward, she kissed his neck, breath heavy and urgent. Hand slipping on her back, pushing her farther. Needing more of her.

He gritted his teeth to hold back the urge to come. Now. Hard and fast. But he wasn't finishing without her. He was determined to see the ecstasy of release stamped on her face, flushing her bare flesh.

Audible moans rose from her, encouraging him to hold on longer. The long red curls that shadowed her face a moment ago flipped back. She arched in pleasure as her body throbbed around him with ripples of her orgasm, massaging him into a release that sent his head pressing back into the pillow.

Then in a flash, he rolled her to her back again and thrust once, twice more, drawing an additional moan of pleasure from her.

He sighed deeply, pulling her to his chest. No words, just the sound of labored breathing growing calm. Her leg snaked around his, breasts and thighs against his side.

She mumbled against him, kissing his shoulder. "That was…perfect."

He skimmed his mouth along the top of her head. "Damn straight it was and the next time will be even better if possible. I have plans for you, lady."

"Hmm—" she hummed against him "—I like the sound of that…" Her voice trailed off.

"Maureen?"

"Yes," she said in a whisper.

"Are you with me?"

"Uh-huh," she murmured. "Just deliciously mellow and recharging for the next…round…"

Maureen's breath slowed more, sleep finding her.

Sweat trickled on his brow, cooling him physically.

Emotionally? He revved up thinking of the next time he'd have her once she woke. For now, though, he couldn't help but be glad for the chance to get his thoughts together. Because his world had just been rocked. He hadn't felt this way in a damn long time.

Not since Terri. He hadn't had sex since his wife had passed away. Fourteen months and it all had come down to this moment. A moment he had angled for. Wanted. And, more importantly, *enjoyed.*

But that didn't change the fact that conflict swirled like a burgeoning hurricane in his heart. Maureen rolled slightly away from him, the sudden space between their bodies sending a brief chill through him. Already aching over that absence, he knew his feelings for Maureen had transitioned. Not tonight, exactly. He couldn't tell when it had happened.

Xander was starting to experience more than just lust for her. Something so much more. Something that scared the hell out of him. He felt disloyal to the memory of Terri as he lay in bed, tangled with Maureen.

And for Maureen. Would this complicate how she approached their marriage of convenience?

His thoughts picked up force, that familiar tightness in his gut howling.

Distance and space. He needed that now. Needed to sort all of this out. Carefully, Xander pulled his arm out from beneath Maureen. She stirred but didn't wake. Even sleeping, her expression seemed kind.

The last thing he wanted to do was hurt her. Gathering up his clothes, he dressed. Taking one last look at her, he noted the way the covers dipped with her hourglass figure. His eyes slid to the box of condoms. Eleven left. Part of him wished he could have used more tonight. He wished a lot of things and had damn few answers to his questions.

Dressing the next morning, Maureen told herself she wasn't upset Xander hadn't been in bed when she'd woken. That was fine. Really.

She'd curled up beside him again and drifted often, expecting a morning of leisurely wake-up sex. And instead found a cold pillow that still carried a hint of dampness from his showered hair.

Maureen went through a rational list of reasons why he'd left before she woke up. He did have a child. And with his in-laws breathing down his neck, he probably needed to make sure he didn't appear negligent or selfish. That explanation seemed satisfactory.

Besides, even though she and Xander were technically engaged, his early morning departure effectively eradicated the possibility of too much gossip around the refuge. Another aspect she greatly appreciated. Appearing engaged and in love was one thing. Having people watching him slip out of her cabin and fill in lurid details was another altogether. This was all still so new to her.

She refused to let her mind wander to more sinister reasons. There'd be no good in that.

Over the past few days he'd been so kind to her. Filled her hours with surprises—the spa day with her friends, dinner. Maureen desperately wanted to do something for him. So he'd know how much she appreciated his gestures and actions. Before this all fizzled away and she was forced back to reality with only a couple of days left until the wedding.

Her wedding, the reality that she would really be staying in the States, reminded her of her home in Ireland and all of the things she'd left behind. She was committed to staying here, wanted to stay in the States, but daily she'd had to remind herself that might not be possible. It still might not be possible for any number of reasons if—when—she and Xander split. If she were to survive that transition, she wanted to make sure she and Xander parted as good friends. Maureen needed to build her fake marriage on something real.

She and her ex were like an arsonist and a lit match. While the flaming love sounded poetic, its reality manifested in destruction. Damaging. The ashes of that life still swirled around her.

After her fake marriage ended, she didn't want to find herself again in a burn pit of ruins. *After*. The reality of *after* bit at her, nipped at her mind.

What did she want after? To really return to Ireland? To leave Xander and Rose? The refuge?

So many pounding questions she couldn't deal with. Instead, she dressed in coral-colored shorts and a flowing white top, and went to pick up pastries for Xander. A small surprise, but food always had a way of easing tension between people.

Knocking on the door to the main house, pastries in

hand, Maureen's thoughts entered the now-familiar circle in her mind. Xander. What did he do for fun? He didn't appear to have any hobbies. His interests seemed to be work and caring for Rose.

Part of her wondered if he didn't allow himself any quiet time. Time when he'd have to face realities he seemed desperate to escape. Or maybe that was just her. She'd always pushed into work in moments of stress and uncertainty. Maybe he did the same.

The door swung open, interrupting her thoughts. The afternoon sun soaked into Xander's cool blue eyes and tanned skin. Sexy still. Her belly did a little backflip, nerves prickling her face into a smile.

"I brought pastries." She extended the box to him.

"You'll be bringing those to go. I was actually headed to come surprise you. I've got a whole afternoon and evening planned for us. And Rose." There was a lightness in his voice that didn't fully reach his eyes.

Maureen blamed it on the strength of the sun, taking the gesture of an impromptu date more seriously than the lack of sparkle in those eyes. She tried to guess the nature of the date from his clothes: khaki shorts, a polo shirt that matched his eyes and leather boat shoes that finished off his casual look so different from his office suits and formal tuxedos.

He'd been prepared for her. Within five minutes, the little trio packed into the limo. The nanny had already left ahead of them to set things up in the hotel. Rose chattered in her car seat, grabbing for Maureen's hair. They set out for a tiny neighboring island where a street market filled with entertainment and life flourished like a school of vibrant fish.

Maureen carried Rose on her hip, relishing the smile on the baby's face. She liked the way Rose drank in the scenery, cooed at the street musicians. So aware for one so young. A natural-born observer, perhaps a future scientist in the making.

"Xander, last night was…beautiful," Maureen said softly, her gaze focused away from him, "but I can't help wondering why you didn't say goodbye."

He paused for an instant before answering. "I didn't want to wake you."

"Hmm," she said softly. "That sounds a bit like a cop-out to me."

His shoes thudded along the boardwalk. "You're a smart woman. So, okay, I'll be honest. It was the first time I've been with anyone since Terri died and I needed to gather my thoughts."

She glanced up at him. "It was a first for me, too, since my divorce. That takes a lot of trust on both of our parts, I'm thinking."

He nodded. "I believe you're right."

Silence fell between them again, more comfortable in some ways but also more intense as they both openly acknowledged the shift in their relationship. This wasn't just about Rose or paperwork or interfering in-laws anymore.

Xander stroked Maureen's back as they walked. For a few brief, shining hours she felt a sense of togetherness. Like they were a real couple, a real family. Like she'd actually gained entrance into this world. That there wasn't a fake marriage tied to her pear-shaped ring that glittered in the fading light.

They paused on the brick-paved street. Maureen leaned into Xander. Wrapping his arm around her shoulder, they watched a street performer juggle a pineapple and a sword. The action made Maureen a little queasy, but the juggler moved with a dancer's grace. A small, collapsible black table stood in front of him. With break-neck speed, the juggler tossed the pineapple to the table, grabbed the sword by the hilt and sliced open the fruit.

"Impressive," Xander murmured right as Rose began to cry hysterically. Maureen's maternal instincts stimulated, she began to rock Rose, speaking in a soothing voice.

To no avail.

Glancing at his bronze-faced watch, Xander cleared his throat. "I think she's exhausted. It's a little past her bedtime. Come on, let's go to the Dolphin's Tale and meet the nanny. She'll put her down and we'll have time alone. Just you and me. No more talk or interference of the past."

The promise of his words struck a chord in her, reassuring her.

They walked down the street, to the quaint but well-appointed bed-and-breakfast. The dying light sinking into the ocean seemed to absorb the fair pink color of the building, making it part of the sunset. Elenora was waiting in the lobby for them.

"Shall we?" Xander extended his arm to Maureen. She grabbed it, nodding. "I hope you don't scare easy." A laugh rolled off his tongue like a stray wave on a calm day.

"Why?" She squeezed his arm, having enjoyed the day more than she possibly could have imagined a couple of weeks ago.

Not that she would have imagined any of this two weeks ago. Could it be real so fast? Or was it as simple as the plan he'd stated at the outset?

Old insecurities were difficult to shake.

"You'll see." He maneuvered them toward a party boat

designed to hold a couple dozen tourists, the craft moored at a nearby dock.

They boarded the boat and the guide began telling legends of ghosts and vampires. Tracking over to a smaller island's shore, the tour group followed the guide on the sand, huddled close to hear about gruesome deaths and hauntings that chilled Maureen, making her hold tighter to Xander.

"What made you think of this?" Maureen asked on the way back to the main island, wind causing her hair to have a life of its own.

He shrugged, looking at the water below the railing. "I tried to imagine the date a scientist would have never considered."

"Vampires. Good guess."

"So you've never been to Transylvania." He laughed but his gaze seemed to travel past her.

What was he thinking? Were his thoughts drifting back to his dead wife in spite of what he'd said earlier?

"Can't say that I have. I still remember coming to the States as a child and realizing how the size of everything is…overwhelming. But in an amazing way. I love my home country and I miss so much about it, but the space here, the expanses and vast differences in terrain that offer so much for my mind to ponder…I feel at home here, as well. It wasn't hard to run here when I needed to leave."

"God, Maureen…" Night wind tore at his jet-black hair. "I'm sorry taking the job on Key Largo happened under duress." His answer seemed more rote than governed by feeling. This couldn't all be in her head. Something was definitely off.

"I don't want to talk about that. I love my job. I love being here. And we had an amazing night out." She tried to shift the focus back to the positive. Putting them back into the moment of this lovely night. They both seemed to need that.

"Okay," he said, turning to her, the light entering his eyes again as he rejoined the lighter mood she'd sought, "so no Transylvania trip as a kid. What about vampire crushes as a teenager?"

She smiled, toying with the button on his polo shirt. "What teenage girl hasn't read some kind of vampire hot-hero story and imagined being in love forever?"

"That's the appeal? The forever part?" He guided her onto an empty bench seat, shrouded in a bit of darkness and privacy from the other passengers.

"And the sexy charisma. The machismo. You have that—without the fangs."

"I can still bite. Lightly, of course, and in just the right places." He kissed her neck, playfully nipping it.

She shivered. "You're bad."

"I thought I was a starched-shirt businessman."

"You're a…surprise."

"That's good. I used to wonder why you and my brother didn't end up together." Was this why he was distant? Fear of a crush on his free-spirited younger brother? That kind of fear she could squash.

"Three reasons."

"Care to share?"

She sipped the bottle of water the guide had distributed earlier in the evening. "We're too much alike. There's no chemistry. And I think he has a thing for Portia."

"Portia? For real? They can barely stand working together. I've never even been sure why he keeps her on the payroll other than the fact most people wouldn't put up with him. I'm even more bemused as to why she stays."

She cast him a sidelong glance as the boat drew closer to the dock. Could he really be that oblivious? "And that should tell you something."

"Good point."

Leaning against the rail, she inspected her leather bracelet as the boat pulled up to the dock. The boat came to an abrupt stop, causing Xander to press against her slightly.

"I'm not sure and, certainly, I've never seen anything concrete. It's just an impression I get sometimes," she said as the crew finished tying off the boat and placing the debarking plank so the passengers could leave.

They made their way to the exit, falling into line with the others in the group.

"You have good instincts. That's clear." He helped her down off the boat ramp, his grip light and loose.

"Thank you. That's a lovely thing to say." While he hadn't stopped touching her all night, she could hear the distance in his voice.

"It's just the truth." Grasping her hand, they meandered on the sidewalk. Bars filled with loud, live music jumbled together. Their discordant mingling reminding Maureen of the play she'd studied while at university—*The Rites of Spring*. The disorientation extended beyond the framing of the various bands' sounds. She didn't know how to ease whatever troubled Xander.

"Still, thank you for the compliment."

"You deserve it and so many more. You're an incredibly resilient, compassionate and accomplished woman—which all makes you even hotter than you already are, which is mighty damn hot."

Playfully shoving him away, she stopped on the corner before the Dolphin's Tale, eyebrows raised incredulously, more than a little concerned. A horribly failed marriage could do that to a person. "Are you for real or playing me?"

"I hope you know me well enough to realize I shoot straight from the hip. I always have. Dishonesty in business and life gets you nowhere fast." He closed the distance, grabbing her hand. His intense eyes fixed on her, undoing her doubts slightly. This was the most honest he'd been all day. She could tell he meant it.

"I have to agree. Honesty is crucial. Dishonesty always comes back around. Karma's a bitch."

"A bitch with vampire fangs." He gave her a long, sensual look of promise.

This evening's date had clearly brought up more questions than answers, leaving her more confused and unsure than ever. She should be content. All would be well when it came to enjoying their short-term marriage of convenience.

She twisted the ring on her finger and wondered at the odd squeeze of her heart that warned her she could be getting in over her head.

Leading her up the wooden stairs of the Dolphin's Tale, he noticed a shift in Maureen's demeanor. She seemed subdued. A far cry from the siren in the pool the other night. Or from the woman he'd taken to bed last night and, damn it, that was his fault—for bailing on her after their night of sex. He'd let his own mixed emotions about making love for the first time after Terri's death lead him to disregard Maureen's feelings.

Unforgivable.

Thoughtfully, he opened the pale yellow door, stepping into the main lobby of the bed-and-breakfast. Tasteful experimental coastal art framed the room; it had a lot in common with an art gallery showroom. The harp-

ist played in the back corner, her fingers nimbly plucking an old crooner's song about paper moons and love.

Placing his hand on the small of her back, he led her
to their room, sending her inside. Stepping up to the
bamboo drink cart, he opened the bottle of chardonnay,
pouring Maureen a glass. She lingered a few feet away,
absently placing her soft brown purse on the glass living room table. Leaning against the overstuffed couch,
she stared into the bedroom off to the left. The plush ma-
hogany four-poster was framed in billowing white tufts
of sheer fabric. An inviting space.

He laughed softly. "I brought my own this time."

She turned on her heel and looked at him through her
eyelashes. "I like a man who thinks ahead. Impulsive is
nice, too."

"I can do that. Think fast on my feet. But keep in
mind I'm the analytical type, the kind who has a very
distinct plan to bring you complete and utter bliss. Soon.
Very soon."

Her lips parted, driving him wild. "I'll be right back.
Don't go anywhere," he replied huskily.

Slipping from the room, he checked on Rose and
the nanny before rejoining her. Elenora reported Rose
had fussed, but slept soundly now. On her way out of
the room, the nanny handed over the baby monitor. He
smiled, ready to return to Maureen.

Pausing outside the door, he thought about where
this—all of this—was heading. He could sense that Maureen felt how he'd coiled like a pygmy rattler today. Xander's retreat had had little to do with her, though. Mostly,
his distance had been from a lifetime of too many endings and partings.

Hand on the decadent crystal doorknob, he focused
fully on this moment. This woman.

He needed more than just sex from her and a business deal. He needed the oblivion being with her could bring. A tangible, incredible connection between them. Something to stand on. Her caring heart, her banter. Maureen's empathy made him want to be better. Opening the door, he smiled at her. Ready to try harder than before. Feeling as light as the breeze that drifted in from the window overlooking a blackened sea and dew-dripped stars.

When he returned, she stood, sipping the glass of wine he'd poured for her, lingering at the threshold of the bedroom. He approached her, eager as ever. He took the wineglass, set it aside and eased her back on the bed, her legs draped off as he skimmed her dress up.

She laughed softly. "The wicked man is back."

"Do you want to talk?" He nuzzled the inside of her thigh. "Or do you want to see just how bad I can be?"

He snapped the edge of her panties.

"Talking finished," she said succinctly just as he nuzzled between her legs.

He swept off her satin underwear and found the core of her, inhaling her feminine scent of jasmine and desire. With a flick of his tongue, he heard her moan, caught a glimpse of her twisting her hands in the covers. He continued to push her, feeling her hips pulse up to him beneath his tongue. Her breath growing more clipped, more hitched. His own desire ramping up—

Only to be interrupted by the nursery monitor shrieking to life. A deep wail blared through, followed by another. And another, each more urgent than before.

Ten

Rose's wails tore at Maureen's ears, spurring her limbs to move. Xander snapped back, gaze flying to the baby monitor and then to Maureen. He pulled on sweats and a T-shirt as she yanked her panties on, trailing after Xander out of the bedroom, heading for the door. As she passed the couch, she grabbed a robe, feeling the need for more coverage, but she didn't break stride.

The urge to make sure Rose was okay flooded Maureen's awareness. Popping open the door to the baby's room, Maureen tightened the robe's tie. From the corner of her eye, Maureen noticed Elenora's sleep-bleary face emerge from the bedroom as the woman headed for the crib.

Maureen's gait broke into a near-run, needing to check on Rose herself. Lifting Rose out of the crib, a relief washed through her.

Elenora extended her arms. "I'm sorry she disturbed you both. I can take her."

Maureen shook her head. "I've got her. Truly, no worries. It's okay, Rose, sweetie." Lifting the toddler to her shoulder, she patted her back. Maureen had never spent much time around babies, but there seemed to be a natural maternal instinct she must have tapped into.

Elenora stepped away, waiting in the shadows.

From a distance, Maureen had watched Rose grow up. She'd known Rose for the baby's entire life. But over the last few days, and especially tonight, a chord had been struck. A shift, perhaps, as she realized the larger role she would be playing in this little girl's life. One that represented every complicated aspect of her relationship to Xander.

Maureen would be moving into the house, living with Rose, would become her stepmother. And inhaling the baby shampoo scent, feeling that soft little cheek against hers, Maureen realized that stepping back when the marriage ended was going to be far more complicated than she'd considered in the mad rush to the altar as a way to solve their immediate problems.

Nevertheless, a new feeling of closeness, affection, love for this little life twisted in her heart. She made *shush-shush-shushing* noises as she rubbed soothing circles on Rose's back, the cotton footie pajamas soft against her palm.

Xander walked up behind Maureen. She could feel the heat of him before she heard him, felt his hand on her shoulder.

"Is Rose okay?"

Maureen felt the baby's soft, plump cheek. Turning to face him. "She doesn't feel feverish. Maybe just a baby dream or gas pain?"

Elenora, reaching for Rose, added gently, "I can take her now."

Maureen glanced at Xander and saw the answer in his eyes, an answer that mirrored her own instinct. "We're going to stay with her until she falls back asleep, and then we'll keep the monitor with us. Please, you go ahead and rest."

Xander slid his arm along Maureen's waist. "Yes, please, rest. We'll need your help with Rose tomorrow since we'll be busy with company and finalizing wedding plans."

Maureen's stomach fluttered. Wedding finalization? Only two days left until they exchanged vows. Until their lives were tied. Until this little girl would be her stepdaughter.

And Xander would be her husband. At least temporarily.

Back home again the next day, Xander sat on a beached piece of palm that had probably floated in with the storm. Elbows on his knees, his blue eyes scanned the lapping turf in front of him. A few gulls added their sounds to the rhythm of waves and the soft laughter of Rose.

The objective of the early afternoon? Wear Rose out so she napped soundly since she'd snagged a catnap on the trip home this morning. That would free up some time to finalize wedding details with Maureen.

Wedding details.

As he thought about the ceremony only two days away, his heart tightened. He hoped Maureen felt welcomed and like a part of his small, fractured family. He wasn't sure why it was so important, but he needed her to. Even as he still grieved over the loss of Terri—he would always love her—he knew he had to do this. Hell, he wanted to. Maureen was a good fit in his life. She'd helped him wake up again. This was good for him and for Rose.

So far, his in-laws had made it clear they wanted no part of seeing their son-in-law get remarried. And while he was sad they felt that way, at least the decision was made. He hoped over time they could have a more amicable relationship and accept Maureen.

A vision filled his head of how at ease she was with his child. When they'd spent the night at the bed-and-breakfast, Maureen had sprung for Rose with feline grace and a mother's power. A natural-born nurturer.

A fact Xander had always understood about her, but in that moment he'd seen how deep that inner chord vibrated.

Even now, on the beach, he watched Rose's easy smile. A trusting one. Her shining eyes on Maureen's delicate face. No doubt about it. A bond had been forged between the two of them.

Maureen sat crouched in the shallow crystalline water of a recently developed tide pool. She splashed the cool water on Rose's legs as unadulterated laughter erupted from his daughter's lips.

The scene seemed perfect. Downright natural. He scraped sand between his toes, understanding gathering in his mind as a gust of wind knocked into his chest, the salt heavy on the air and the faint spray of water finding his cheek.

When Maureen left…

Lord. The thought scared the hell out of him. No, she wasn't Terri. He knew that. But Maureen was a woman who deeply cared for Rose. Showed her love and support. Bonded with Rose.

And when she left after the end of this fake marriage? What would happen to Rose?

Devastation.

He knew the feeling. Even though his own mother had

left him in his later years, he understood what kind of vacuum that created. A damn hole that billowed open, the result of trusting in a vanishing act.

Maureen caught his gaze, a smile gracing her fair skin, tugging all the way up to her eyes. She began to sing an old Irish song to Rose. In her pink-and-white swimsuit, Rose clapped her hands together, enjoying the sound of Maureen's soft voice.

Damn. That gaze. That heart. He didn't want to lose that. They'd begun to forge a real friendship and their banter made him feel alive. He didn't want to lose that, either.

No, he had to find a way to convince her to stay. And not just for a year. Or even five.

Maybe forever? Something he damn well should start thinking about. The thought gave him qualms, no question, because the thought of having her around permanently sounded good. Too good. It was getting harder and harder to convince himself he was just doing this for Rose.

Xander leaped from log to shore, going to join the ladies who held his heart captive.

Checking her watch, Maureen looked at him. "Time for Rose to nap already?" Her eyes scrunched, squinting in the sunlight.

"It appears that way. I'll carry her." Xander hoisted Rose into his arms. But she grabbed for Maureen.

"I've got her," she said, glowing slightly. "I'll put her down, and I'll be back soon." Taking Rose on her hip, she squeezed his hand, that familiar electricity pulsing in her gaze. Dropping both his hand and gaze, she made her way back to the main house.

Xander put a palm to the back of his neck, massaging it gently as he watched her walk away.

A low whistle sounded behind him. Easton. He'd forgotten his brother was coming to meet him to go over his best-man duties.

"Dive, shall we?" Easton said with a theatrical wave of his hand, alluding to the water in front of him. He had two sets of gear slung over his back.

A dive would probably clear his head. "Done."

They suited up, pushing into the crystal water, heading to the reef.

Once submerged, Xander did his best to feel present, notice the parrot fish, the flow of the anemones and smaller tropical sea creatures. The reef looked like the home of a mermaid queen—and that brought his mind straight back to Maureen.

He motioned to Easton to go back up to the surface. Xander loved the way the sun looked like stained glass from beneath the water and how, since he was a kid, breaking the surface always made him feel like he busted through glass.

Once they both reached the surface, they began treading water, removing the gear so they could talk.

"Know what I love?" Easton said, voice cutting into the air.

"A good, adrenaline-filled vacation?"

Easton's lips curled into a smile. "Well that, obviously, but that I'm a best man twice to my big brother. Seriously. How are you doing and what do you need from me?"

How was he doing? What a loaded question. Xander stayed quiet for a moment, considering how to answer.

In the pause, Easton continued. "The flavor of the speech would be a good place to start."

"Oh, well, nothing that will turn my bride scarlet. Or me, for that matter."

"So I shouldn't mention the run-in with Don the security guy?" Easton winked, devilish mischief in his eyes. Xander stared at him, laughing slightly. "I'm kidding and you know it. My toast will be funny but tasteful. Just like last time."

"But this isn't like last time." Xander breathed, arms moving through the water with more determination than before.

"I know it's not. Mom's not going to be there this time."

Xander had known this, but the reaffirmation of her absence cut still. "Do you think she'll ever stay in one place?"

"Mom is the actual embodiment of wanderlust. I know we all traveled a lot, but I get the feeling Dad had reined in Mom's tendency for that vagabond life." Easton tilted his head, started heading for the shore.

"Yeah. I think you are right. He balanced her out. Grounded her." Xander kicked his feet beneath the water, gaining forward motion, slinging seaweed.

"Listen, I know I accused you of just being in lust the other week…but something seems to have shifted with you two."

"Something has. I think." But was it enough? The women in his life wandered in and out of his story so easily. Too easily. Terri. His mother.

He wouldn't add Maureen's name to that list.

The ground buzzed with movement. Volunteers with flowers, tables and chairs flooded the grounds, transforming the great yard of the refuge into a beautiful rehearsal dinner area.

Maureen sat perched on the edge of an oversize wood chair on the main house's balcony. Watching her fairy-tale wedding come together. And it was a fairy-tale wedding, wasn't it?

She had to keep reminding herself this was scripted, fictional, fabricated. Her heart could not take any more abuse or ache. Still, she couldn't stop the rush of attraction—and more—that caught her unaware every time he walked in the room.

Even when his name was mentioned. She was completely and totally infatuated with this man. She liked him, respected him. Found her daydreams drifting to thoughts of him and plans for ways they could spend time together, ways to help him find more fun in life so she could see that smile spread across his handsome face.

She caught sight of Portia and Easton directing the catering company around. They'd be up here soon, to finalize details. To make sure the whole event went off without a hitch.

Xander set down his tall glass of lemonade on the table, calling her back to their plans.

The honeymoon.

"So, we've narrowed it between Greece and Sicily. But, my Irish lass, I want you to have the final say." He grabbed her hand, stroking his thumb over hers.

The warmth of his gentle touch made her belly flip. She kept thinking she would get used to this—the incredible way he made her feel every time he put his hands on her. But, if anything, each time they were together amped up her attraction. Tilted her whole world on its axis until she seemed to always lean toward him.

"So much pressure, sir."

He looked at her sidelong. "You can handle it."

She chewed her lip, looking at the two vacation itineraries before her, both of which would start with a night in a local cabana before a flight somewhere romantic the day after the wedding. "Sicily."

"That's what I was going to pick, too." He raised her hand to his lips, kissed it gently, sending sparks through her.

Still holding on to her, he looked at her, blue eyes as soft and clear as summer. "Have you ever thought about having children of your own?"

The question became a harpoon lodging in her chest, and she let herself collect her breath by glancing at the wedding preparations: a floral arch being delivered, exotic blooms unloaded in sprays from a truck, and the food van—so much food.

Finally, she turned back to Xander to answer his question, which had caught her so unaware. "Of course I've thought about it. But after my divorce I realized my work is my family. The animals I save and work with are, in effect, my children."

"But you could still have a baby, too."

She shook her head. "I'm not marrying again." Her heart couldn't allow it.

"You already have." Xander gestured to the bustle below.

"I meant after we finish our arrangement."

His dark eyebrows knotted, a storm descending on his face. Shifting to a serious tone, he leaned forward. "But this—as you call it—*arrangement* is going well. We get along. We're compatible in bed and out. You're fantastic with Rose. We could build a family."

Build a family? A fake family?

She wanted him. Cared for him and Rose. But to be with a man who didn't love her. And to be with a man who wouldn't ever love her? She couldn't do that. Couldn't break again like that.

"You're backing out of our agreement."

He blinked at her. "What?"

"You're scared of losing Rose so you're trying to bribe me into staying longer." That had to be what this was about. No other explanation seemed logical.

"Damn it, no. You've misunderstood my meaning altogether. I was being honest. I think we could build a great life together."

Her Irish temper surged, a storm of her own infusing her voice with anger. And pain. "And so you're offering me a baby if I stay?"

"You're twisting everything I'm saying. We're going to be married. Why not stay that way? You said you're not waiting for another man. So let's share our lives. Be friends."

"Friends?" The last time she checked, marriage was about more than friendship. *Love.* There had to be love, too.

"With benefits and a ring, and a family and common interests. It's actually a stronger foundation than most marriages out there. Think about it tonight."

So, the stiff-shirt businessman returned. The engagement and marriage had been calculated. Sure. But this? A whole new level.

He leaned in to kiss her. But feeling deceived, she angled away under the excuse of conferring with the florist, wondering if she could really go through with this, after all.

The next morning Xander stood outside Maureen's cabin, rolling the simple gold band between his fingers. Maybe it was bad luck to see the bride before the wedding, but he needed to look into her eyes before they said their vows. While he didn't expect the unrestrained joy of his first wedding, things still felt too unsettled.

He'd been trying to reconcile his feelings for Terri,

a love he feared he might never know again. But then, too, he was afraid to let what he felt for Maureen really flourish since it seemed like he would be robbing his first marriage of the bond he'd always felt for Terri and he didn't want to let go of that for Rose's sake.

After their seaside argument, Xander had wanted to run for the hills and stay a single man forever, parent his child and hire the best damn lawyers possible to reach an amenable arrangement for his in-laws to safely visit their granddaughter. He would live a satisfying life watching his daughter grow up, work the hours he wanted and watch football games on a wide screen TV with his brother.

Later that night, Xander had thought through his options as he lay in bed staring at the ceiling, missing Maureen. Though a calculating businessman, his rationale for wanting Maureen to stay had little to do with logic. But to persuade her, he needed to present it in a way that made practical sense. Rose grew more and more attached to Maureen by the day. To rip her away from Maureen would completely fracture Rose's young life.

And, damn it, he wanted Maureen in his life, too. He couldn't deny that. They had a solid friendship. Chemistry. A mutual desire to stay here. Tons of things in common. She was the one he wanted to vent to and laugh with. He'd become quite fond of the way her nose crinkled, and her fiery spirit. That didn't diminish his love for Terri. The women were different. Comparing would be unfair to both of them.

Standing outside Maureen's cabin on their wedding day, with the sun beaming in a cloudless sky, he still couldn't decide what it was about her that entranced him beyond the normal realm of sexual attraction. She wasn't at all his type. Yet when they were together, he felt alive, happy…in a way he hadn't in a long time.

In the midst of all the confusion, one thought remained clear to Xander. He wanted Maureen. He wouldn't let it take anything from his marriage with Terri, but he would enjoy being with Maureen.

Xander tucked the ring into the inside pocket of his charcoal-gray suit coat. He rang the bell and stepped back, leaning against a porch post.

Maureen answered, half dressed. She wore a pale blue satin gown, her makeup soft and natural, accenting her Irish eyes. Everything about her glowed, Xander thought, as his gaze swept down.

Even her nail polish shimmered.

Looking more than a little nervous, Maureen wiggled her toes, emphasizing that sparkly pedicure. "You caught me before I had a chance to finish dressing. Portia and Jessie are inside. Don't let them catch you."

Relaxing into the safety shield of banter, Xander resumed his lazy position against the post and gestured with a small nod of his head. "Come here and they won't, lady."

Maureen smiled stiffly, unsettled by his words. "Who me?"

"Yeah, you."

She padded across the porch, stopping just in front of him. A breeze blew the skirt of her dress across his legs. The scent of her shampoo and her jasmine perfume teased his senses.

He skimmed his knuckles across her velvety cheek. "Do you mind if I muss you up a bit?"

"Please." Her arms rested by her sides as she pressed her full length to his.

Xander slipped one hand behind her head and cupped her neck. With the other, he palmed her waist, his hand tightening instinctively as the feel of her tingled up his arm. Maureen slid her hand inside his jacket, her fingers spreading wide against his chest, digging past his shirt, imprinting his skin.

He guided her face to his, pressing his lips to hers, flicking his tongue along the seam of her full mouth. She opened, begging for more, needing the reassurance of connecting on any level they could find after their tense, uncertain time apart. With a gentle moan, Maureen slid her arms around Xander's neck, deepening their kiss. Their mouths mated with the familiar yet unexplainable frenzy both had come to accept as inevitable.

And in less than two hours they would be married. For better.

Or worse?

Eleven

In the end, Maureen ditched her shoes just before entering the chapel, wanting instead to make her vows in the ruins of the old church with the soles of her feet pressing into the cool stone slab of the floor. She needed to ground herself in reality, even if only through the sense of the ground beneath her feet.

This wasn't a real wedding.

They were entering this union for practical reasons only.

She couldn't afford to forget that. Her heart couldn't take another round of marital rejection.

Nerves dancing in her stomach, she held her small bouquet of white peonies as a trio of guitarists began playing, their stringed music filling the space with a harp-like quality that carried a hint of local flair. Perfect.

Except, was it really?

Her mind floated back to a letter she'd been terrified to read but had read anyway. Moments before the ceremony—a choice she regretted now. A wildlife refuge in Killarney had offered her a job.

A job in her home country. She'd applied when she'd thought the expiration of her work visa was inevitable.

She didn't even want the job. Not really. But knowing she had this option—a plan of her own that could have been in play—knotted her gut with tension and fear and the realization of how high today's stakes were. How important it was to make the right choice.

Her growing feelings for Xander made her feel out of control. Filled with an urgency to flee.

But she knew better. She had to go through with this for so many reasons, not the least of which being that she couldn't let Xander and Rose down.

Portia stood just ahead of her, ready to do her maid of honor walk down the aisle with baby Rose on her hip. Before they began the trek to the altar, Maureen leaned down to kiss Rose's cheek and handed her a mini bouquet of peonies. The flowers complemented the floral orange-and-white crown in the girl's golden curls. As the two walked between the benches of volunteers, friends and family, Rose giggled, her bouquet bouncing like an erratic orchestra conductor's baton. Those baby giggles elicited a lot of clucks and laughs from the guests in the pews.

The butterfly nerves picked up speed in Maureen's tummy as she stood alone, just out of sight of the church's occupants. This was different from her first wedding in so many ways. Unlike her last wedding, her father wasn't here to escort her down the aisle. She tried to bury the thought, will it back to the dark recesses of her mind and think of the reasons this marriage was right. Good. Safe?

Her hand wandered up to her own flowers. The stylist

had woven them seamlessly into her hair. To her relief, it seemed like they weren't going anywhere.

The setting, the music, those ancient stones, made her feel like a fairy princess from all the Celtic stories she'd read as a child. If this was to be her fabricated narrative, she wanted the story to have some degree of authenticity, to represent her wildness. Would Xander find that part of her too impractical over time? Would the friendship and passion withstand day-to-day living?

As she made her way to Xander, her bare feet taking in the cool stones along the aisle, her heartbeat roared in her ears. He stood at the altar, a genuine smile radiating from his lips to his eyes. Damn, he was sexy in his suit, with his blue eyes and dark hair. This tall, looming alpha male who'd somehow become such a huge part of her life.

A light breeze carrying the scent of salt and blooming flowers seemed to urge her toward him, tousling her hair slightly, making her feel truly like a water nymph in her dress that mirrored the waves of the ocean, and for a moment, her nerves stilled.

A moment only. Was his smile real? Or was he hiding thoughts of his first wedding? An ache over the loss of his wife? Maureen swallowed hard and pressed forward.

Easton stood next to Xander and shot a quick wink her way. He shifted on his feet, shoulder brushing against a lush green leaf that poked out from the side of the old Spanish-style ruins.

Hibiscus plants and vibrant flowers in sunset hues lined the aisle in homage to their tropical location. Out of the corner of her vision, she saw the smiling faces of the volunteers. They pressed up against each other, hands held to mouths and ears, bowing and flowing like marsh grass. Wisps of words like "She's stunning!" and

"Look at the love in his eyes!" caressed her ears. A fairy tale indeed.

Portia smiled at her, holding Rose still on her hip. Her one-shoulder coral gown complementing her fair complexion, the light breeze pushing loose strands of her hair.

Maureen reached the altar, gave herself away, and took her position next to Xander as they both turned to face each other. His hands were warm as they clasped her chilly shaking ones.

Out of the corner of her eyes, her gaze flitted once more to the crowd of people, and she counted those who weren't actually there. Xander's mother had sent an email from Tibet, confirming her inability to attend. She wondered, as the last few notes of the music reverberated, if Xander felt sad about that. Or if, since this was an arrangement, after all, he felt indifferent.

Also missing were his in-laws. Or, his former in-laws. Once Maureen said "I do," their definition would shift. Another way for him to lose more of Terri.

Shoving that thought aside, too, Maureen looked at Xander. He reached for her hand, his touch reassuring and stabilizing. Anchoring. The leap of her pulse only scared her more with fears that she'd let him mean too much to her, too fast.

Rose fussed in Portia's arms, pointing toward Maureen. She lifted Rose from Portia, smiling as the little girl's face lit up, glowing as bright as the sun. Xander touched Maureen's cheek with a gentle stroke of fingertips and emotion in his eyes, a gratitude that she'd allowed his daughter to share in the spotlight of this big moment.

They'd opted to write their own vows rather than go the traditional route and repeat pledges of forever love that would have resembled their first weddings—and also wasn't truthful to their reasoning for this marriage. They'd opted for promises to keep. Honesty.

Maureen had labored over what to say and was relieved that Xander went first. "Maureen, I promise to be here for you. To pledge my every effort to take care of you, to keep you safe, to remind you daily what an incredibly fascinating and alluring and giving woman you are."

"I promise to make you laugh and remember to enjoy life outside the office, to live life to the fullest." She smiled, planting a kiss on Rose's forehead.

The remainder of the ceremony reminded Maureen of a dream. Before she knew it, she locked her lips on his, the strength of his embrace pressing into her. The sparks were there, no question.

Would it be enough?

Flower petals were tossed over them as they left the church to go to the outdoor reception set up just off to the side near the shore. Her toes skimmed over the bright white rocks. Seagulls danced above their heads, circling.

As they moved toward the reception area outdoors, by the ocean, her place of peace, Maureen took in the sounds of the waves crashing, the contained chaos of an unfolding reception. Portia calmly directed people to their tables, smiling, handling the crowds with grace. Maureen appreciated Portia's presence.

Maureen felt like one of the dolls in "It's A Small World"—a smile painfully painted on her face. Volunteers and guests lined up to see her and Xander, offering their congratulations.

All of the smiling and handshaking had her feeling a bit like an animatronic version of herself. The gestures occurring by rote.

Xander and Maureen had split up at the reception to cover more ground to say thank you to their guests. Her hands slid to grasp and hug guest after guest, but her mind focused on that letter she'd gotten in the mail last night.

The lilt of a brogue snapped her attention into focus, her eyes searching for the owner of the voice. Andrea Yeats, the only one of her friends who had been able to fly out for the wedding on such short notice. They'd grown up together, filtering in and out of church together—a dynamic duo.

Andrea raised the glass of merlot to her plump lips, sipping as she nodded at Xander. Shaking her chestnut, curly hair, Andrea lowered her voice, stepping closer to Xander. "I'm so happy for the two of you. You know the old saying there's fault on both sides of a divorce? Well, in their case…she did everything she could to hold that marriage together."

A knot lodged in Maureen's throat. She didn't want to talk about Danny, not this way, and especially not in front of others.

"Andrea—"

But her friend pressed on. "Maureen, you can play nice and be the bigger person, but I don't have to. He was a narcissistic ass. There's no other way around it. He was mentally abusive. He belittled her to death with a thousand paper cuts. It took a lot of courage for her to break away and come here."

"What precipitated the move?" Xander's interest manifested itself in his body language. In the way he leaned on the table.

Maureen had heard enough. Time to take control. "My parents passed away in a ferry accident. Something seemed to click inside me and I moved on. Now, let's move on from this conversation and enjoy the day."

Andrea turned scarlet. Not even her thick, constellation-like freckles could mask the embarrassment gracing Andrea's cheeks. Sheepishly, she wrapped Maureen in a quick hug. "I'm sorry. My mouth ran away with me, love. I just adore you and want to make sure this fella knows how lucky he is to have you." She smiled at them both. "Congratulations. Truly."

With a nervous nod, Andrea excused herself, a predatory swagger in her step as she approached Easton.

With the ocean echoing in the distance at their outdoor reception, Xander slid his arm around her waist and stayed silent, sensing that Maureen didn't want to talk about what had just happened. She was right. This day should be about happiness.

He'd finally claimed her as his own.

Yes, he'd had thoughts of his first wedding today and he would always miss Terri, but Maureen had helped him move forward with his life. Her beautiful, bold personality had shaken him from his fog and brought him back to life again.

He just hated that Andrea had made Maureen so uncomfortable, hurting her with reminders of the past. And, yes, he felt vaguely guilty for prying into her history, but she'd said so little and he wanted to know.

Maureen played with the tips of her curls, fidgeting as her brow furrowed. "Andrea didn't care for my ex-husband." Cool indifference laced her words. She grabbed his hand, pulling him aside, toward the edge of the crowd at the bar.

"Everyone should have a loyal friend." He pulled Maureen close, his hands trailing along the soft exposed skin on her back.

She nodded, chewing on the edge of her bottom lip. "I'm glad she came to visit."

"Are you homesick?" He searched her eyes. Tried to figure out what had her so distant. Learning about the death of her parents... It had changed the way he regarded her. How traumatic that must have been to lose her parents and realize her marriage was a shambles all at once. She'd been truly alone in the world. No wonder she'd made such a large move to start over somewhere fresh without reminders of all she'd lost.

Perhaps she felt their absence acutely today. He felt the absence of his mother like a deep twist of a knife in his gut. And at least she was alive, just not in the picture. He'd missed his dad today, though. The finality of him not being here hurt Xander deeply. He imagined that feeling would intensify if both of his parents were deceased. Guilt stabbed at him now that he'd never thought to ask details about her family, her past. She'd listened to so much he'd shared, drawn him out more than anyone else had been able to.

"Are you homesick?" he repeated since she'd ignored his question the first time. He would be better about listening to her from now on.

"Obviously, I'm trying to stay away from there. I went so far as to marry you, didn't I?" She turned away from him, pulling out of his grasp.

"And a horrible fate that is, right?" He skimmed his knuckles gently across her cheek.

She looked around at the crowd with nervous eyes and linked fingers to draw him behind a palm tree a bit farther from the guests so they wouldn't be interrupted. "Xander, I'm sorry for what I said. That didn't come out right."

He wrapped his arms around her, his back blocking them even further from others in hopes of making it clear they wanted this time alone, if anyone did stumble on them. "You don't need to apologize. I was only teasing." His voice faded to a lull as he realized he really needed to start things off with her by being honest. "What she said about your ex—"

"I told you he walked out on me."

"You didn't tell me he was abusive."

"He never laid a hand on me."

His hand swept over her cheek again, keeping his touch gentle even as anger pulsed through him at the man who'd treated her so poorly. "That's not the only way to abuse someone."

"Andrea talked too much. I'm fine now, happy here, feeling confident and like myself again." A dismal tone edged her voice. She crossed her arms over her chest, shutting down on him.

"You're safe here." He glided his hands down her arms until she relaxed, then pulled her close. "I want you to know that."

"I do." She swallowed hard. "What made you such an expert on emotional abuse?"

"I'm not an expert, but I'm human. And I've dealt with some employee situations..." Her head pushed off his chest to stare at him, eyebrow raised, a bemused smile on her face. He continued, a laugh on his lips. "That sounds lame and impersonal even as I say it. Why don't you tell me about your situation?"

She buried her face back against his chest, shaking her head, a sigh shuddering through her bones. "Andrea said enough. It's in the past. I'm working to restore my life and rebuild my career. Now, can we really stop talking about this? Haven't I said before that I don't want to be one of those individuals who vents nonstop about the ex," she muttered against his shoulder.

"We're married now. This is about making our history." Xander wanted her to feel comfortable talking to him about anything. Everything. The small stuff. The details and stories that shaped her. He wanted her to trust him deeply.

She pulled away from him, her eyes lined with phantom pain. "He was…charming in the beginning. And I fell fast. Looking back, I can see signs I should have paid more attention to."

"Such as?"

"We really should have talked about this before, and maybe this isn't the right time."

He held up a hand, walked over to the waiter and took two champagne flutes, hoping to ease her nerves. His own anger was boiling just below the surface at the man who'd hurt her, but he would keep that under control. For Maureen. He would listen and learn and make sure she had a better marriage this time.

Xander brought the drinks back and guided her farther away from the crowd for even more privacy, finding a bench under a swaying palm in a dim corner.

He passed a drink to Maureen and said, "Maybe we should have talked more, but I would argue we've covered a lot of ground in a week. Now we have plenty of time."

He clinked his glass with hers, and encouraged her to continue.

"My family was so volatile with what you would call a stereotypical Irish temper." She traced along the crystal base, circling with one finger. "Danny kept things light, funny. He was witty. Sarcastic sometimes, but so very witty. I was charmed. We fell fast. Married just as fast. Before long I realized 'light' meant he didn't appreciate deep discussions, especially if that meant addressing a problem. Sarcastic wit turned biting. Hurtful.

Anything to shut down a conversation that challenged his perceptions."

Xander could see how much the memories pained her. He'd give anything to make her feel better. "And if avenues for discussion were shut down, I imagine that made it tough to express your frustration or hurt."

She shrugged lightly. "I used to think it was my fault for being unable to take criticism." She looked at him. "I thought I loved him, or that at least we could find that love again. And then, out of the blue, he told me he wasn't happy, and left. It hurt, but I'm a stronger person now. Much stronger."

"That strength shows. You're strong and compassionate." He met her honesty with his own. He had seen firsthand how deeply Maureen cared for those around her... how much more so she must have felt for a man she'd been in love with. Those feelings didn't just erode overnight. The death of a marriage—for good reasons and bad ones—still had consequences in the heart.

"Thank you." Tears pushed at her eyes.

He pulled her closer, needing to show he cared.

"The breakdown of a marriage is tragic." The end of love hurt. By death or divorce. He knew that too damn well.

"But I truly am better off."

"I believe you are." He kissed her cheek. Her nose. Her lips. She sighed, falling into him more before continuing to speak.

"It just galls me that I didn't see the truth sooner. That made me doubt myself for a very long time."

"And now?"

"I'm doing better."

"Getting married again must have been difficult for you," he said, his hands roving over her arms.

"But this isn't about love. That gives me a level of emotional protection."

Her words felt like a wall coming between them.

He didn't have time to process that. Not now. Easton and Portia approached them.

"It's showtime." Easton's words slurred slightly.

Portia laughed, adjusting her one shoulder strap. "What he is trying to say is that it's time for us to send you lovebirds off."

She gestured to the crowd, which parted like the Red Sea, leading to a stretch beach buggy with a chauffeur waiting to take them to a cabana on Key Largo for their first night as man and wife before departing to Sicily for a proper honeymoon. All the trappings of romance intact.

After watching the chauffeur disappear down the thin, sandy lane, Maureen turned to face Xander. Her husband.

God, how strange that word felt. This day had been surreal enough without Andrea showing up and eliciting that whole conversation about Danny that Maureen just wasn't ready to have yet.

And then there was the job offer still looming over her that she hadn't told Xander about. Not that it mattered now. She wasn't going to take it. But she should tell him.

Before she had time to process all the tumult of the day, much less their new roles, Xander swept her off her feet. Literally.

Six hours as man and wife. She knew him as a boss. A friend. A lover. But this? This was…beyond anything she would have considered happening.

Moonlight bathed them in silver as he carried her toward the door of the cabana. The ocean provided the soundtrack—a mounting sound of waves and night birds. Each step up to the cabana caused him to draw her closer, the scent of sandalwood intoxicating her. Over the threshold and into the cabana, he took her.

Xander let her slide out of his arms, her bare feet touching the grain of the wood. He pushed her gently against the wall, kissing her deeply.

She wanted more of him. Angling into his kiss, she pushed farther. He pressed his hand on her hip, sending an electric pulse through her limbs.

She raised a hand to his jawline. He leaned into it for a moment, her fingers taking in the way his chin curved. His head tilted to the table at the center of the living room.

She followed his gaze, settling on the baskets filled with gifts—a collection of jasmine and vanilla massage oils, lotions and rainbow-colored condoms. A gift from Easton, according to the tag.

A bucket filled with ice and champagne took position to the left. Another basket brimmed with chocolates and dried fruits.

Platters of exotic cheeses, grapes, chocolate-dipped strawberries and crackers covered the remainder of the table. True decadent indulgence.

Xander picked up a chocolate-covered strawberry and fed it to her. Eyes on him still, she bit down into the fruit, enjoying the contrast of bitter dark chocolate and sweet strawberry. He discarded the top of the strawberry, brushing her top lip with his thumb before grabbing one of the oils and a condom from the basket.

"Coming?" His question came out breathy. She nodded, following him to the bedroom.

Rose petals speckled the ground and the bed. He kissed her hand, traced the edge of her collarbone, sending shivers down her spine. Helped her out of the gown.

"Let me spoil you. Pamper you." He gestured to the bed.

"You're too kind," she mumbled, climbing onto the silken sheets. He rubbed the oil between his hands and then pressed into her shoulders.

"Relax, Maureen. There's no reason to be so tense." He worked on her shoulders, releasing the tension with every stroke. "Everything's going to be okay. More than okay."

He began kissing her neck, back, hip. She turned over to face him, propping herself up on her forearms to kiss him.

Xander pushed her back down, hand grazing her thigh. His mouth sought hers, body pressed against hers. Urgency entered with his tongue. Roving hands teased her nipples.

Her hand wrapped around the length of him, stroking, caressing, her thumb rubbing along the tip of him until he growled with the intense pleasure of just how perfectly she seemed to know how to move him.

His desire for her grew with each movement. She became slick with feminine want. Their normal fire and frenzy changed tonight, replaced with a calm burn. A steady burn.

He kept kissing her. Her hands pulled him closer, raking lightly down his back. Her nails scored his skin ever so lightly, just enough to relay her desire.

Xander eased inside her, each thrust slow and deep as his eyes held hers. Her hips rocked against his, every move of their bodies releasing the sweet scent of the shared fruit mixed with a growing perspiration of need. Building desire. She slid her heels up the backs of his calves, higher still until her legs locked around his waist.

The urgent need to find completion built inside him, along with the realization that once—hell, twelve times or more—wouldn't be enough.

The need was becoming greater with each passing

day. The sweet clasp of her body around his sent his pulse pounding in his ears, his heart pounding against his chest. His whole body throbbed from want of her. Maureen. Her name echoed in his mind again and again.

Even while he burned to reach completion, still he took them to the edge—holding back then pushing her closer until she was wild with need. He reveled in the flush of desire spreading over her flesh, attesting to her pleasure. Her hands twisting in the sheets and rose petals alike until he brought her to a crashing release. His final deep thrust and hoarse shout made it clear he'd followed her over that edge with every bit as much bliss, their bodies connected as they rolled to their sides, panting.

As their breathing slowed to a more even pace, chests rising and falling in time together, her heart grew heavy. All of the complications of this arrangement came crashing down on her. With a weighty realization. She loved him.

She loved Xander.

And what scared her in the pit of her stomach was that even though he cared for her, even though she suspected he might one day come to love her, he would never care for her as much as he'd loved Terri. The thought rocked her.

"When was the last time you went stargazing?" he asked, kissing her.

Hesitancy flooded her. "Um. Ages ago."

"Let's change that." He handed her a silk robe out of the closet and put his clothes back on. Xander disappeared for a moment, returning with the basket full of chocolates and dried fruit in hand.

"Come with me." He opened the balcony door of the cabana. She followed, wrapping the silk against her bare skin, taking in the mesh of starred horizon and cool ocean, her revelation knotting in her stomach.

On the porch there were two oversize chairs. Maureen sank into one and Xander reached for her hand, staring at her with dreamy eyes. Melting her heart a little bit more. The world unbalancing.

Until a masculine brogue cut through the air.

"I've come for my wife."

Ice chilled her blood. She didn't even have to look over her shoulder to know.

Andrea wasn't the only person from her past to have come to the States today.

Danny had arrived.

Twelve

Maureen went rigid next to Xander. She'd inhaled sharply, eyes falling in the direction of the voice.

In the muted light of moon and stars, the form of a somewhat muscular man manifested. He approached them, features coming into focus with every step.

Danny.

Maureen's ex. Fists tightened, more than ready to slam the guy's teeth through his face if it became necessary. The urge to send Maureen inside wailed in Xander's head. Standing up from the chair, he looked down at the man, unwilling to resort to violence unless absolutely necessary.

Damn, but he hoped it would be necessary.

Danny's bronzed, buzzed hair practically glowed in the moonlight. Xander noticed how his handsome face seemed to be chiseled by bitterness.

How in the world had he found them? For the last two years Maureen had flown under the radar. He racked his brain. No matter what, he'd make sure she was safe. That thought coursed through his mind on full-blast.

"What are you doing here? And, more important, who the hell do you think you are to call yourself my husband?" Maureen lobbed pure fire at him, blazing and glorious.

"Fine, ex-husband. But I've come here to win you back, love. I miss you." His brogue was thick and deep. But Xander thought the man's swagger was a bit cartoonish, as if he was trying to put on some kind of machismo show.

Through clenched teeth, Xander said tightly, leaving no room for doubt, "She's not just engaged. We got married today."

"I'm too late?" Shock pushed his mouth into a faux grin dripping with malice. He took a few steps closer. "I heard she was engaged and the wedding was soon, so I came running. But married? Already? I screwed up the time change or something, I had plans for—"

The jackass had actually planned to burst into their wedding? Xander's eyes narrowed. "How did you even know about the engagement?"

Maureen sighed. "Andrea. Tossing it in your face that I've rebuilt my life."

Danny sneered. "She enjoyed every minute of crowing over that."

Xander put a protective arm around Maureen, damned determined she wouldn't be facing this demeaning jerk alone. "I'm her husband. She and I got married." He held up her hand to show off her ring. "It's official. Ring, certificate and all."

Danny whistled lowly, his attention narrowed on Maureen. "That is quite a rock. You landed a big fish. No wonder you don't want me."

Maureen stepped forward, her chin tipped high and proud. Strong. "Danny, I didn't want you before. I don't want you now. And the feeling was mutual, so I have no idea what you're doing here. I believe it's best you state your business and go off somewhere to sightsee or something."

Xander tucked her back at his side. Even knowing she could handle herself, he didn't want her to think she had to do this alone. He wanted to support her, to protect her. To let her know how amazing she was and how undeserving of this kind of jerk show. "Clearly this is a surprise to you, but this is how things are. Now, if you'll kindly leave—"

Danny shook his head, tapping his chin. "Something's fishy and I'm not going anywhere until I get some answers to—"

Glancing at Maureen, Xander noted the way her body had begun to shake with anger. Distress marred her face, but she wasn't backing down. Damn it, she didn't have to face this alone. No one, especially not Danny, would ever harass Maureen. Not while he was around. "You're on private property. You will only be allowed to stay if my *wife* wants you to be here." He turned to her and cocked an eyebrow. "Maureen?"

She shook her head.

Xander shrugged. "It's final, then. Your visit is done. If you wish to speak with my wife, you may, of course, call, or better yet, send a certified letter."

Danny's voice became more agitated, louder. "But I'm the one that left—"

Standing her ground, Maureen stared him down with strength and fire in her eyes. "And you'll be leaving now. Having you out of my life is a blessing. I moved forward. I have an amazing job." She leaned closer to Xander.

"And a wonderful husband. You and I no longer have any connection. So please, don't contact me again."

A calculating look entered Danny's steely eyes as his gaze moved from Maureen to Xander and back again, a laugh lodged in his throat. "Your job… And this is your boss." A slow, smarmy smile ticked at the corners of his mouth. "Convenient you got married right before you had to come home. Wasn't that job offer you got from the university big enough for you?"

Xander took him by the arm. "This discussion is over. I'm calling security."

With admirable speed, Don, still wearing his suit from attending the wedding, came to pick Danny up. Xander helped Don secure the man in the car, closed the door and watched him drive away. Satisfied to see him gone. And return to Maureen.

He wanted to make sure Maureen was safe. And not just tonight. But forever. He wanted to shield her as best he could. Because he…because he loved her. Truly and deeply loved her. It took nothing away from what he'd felt for Terri. In fact, Terri had taught him to love and he knew now that the greatest gift he could give her was to let love into his heart again.

And without question, he loved Maureen every bit as deeply as any love he'd ever felt before.

Tears cascaded down Maureen's fair cheeks. She shook uncontrollably, hands wrapping around herself. "I feel awful. He all but said we married for my green card and he's right."

Xander touched her lips then thumbed away her tears. "I needed a mother for my child to ensure she stays with me."

"Great. We pulled a fast one on the courts twice."

"Do you believe Rose is where she belongs?"

"Absolutely."

"Are you happier married to me than you were to him?"

"That's not even a fair question. I could be happier married to just about anyone."

"Then are you happy here, in the house…" He leaned closer. "In my bed." He touched her mouth again. "You don't even need to answer that. I heard your joy loud and clear that night before we stepped out on the porch."

Her cheeks flushed. "Loudly?"

"Delightfully so. And I look forward to making that happen again and again."

A part of the conversation with Danny gnawed at him. She seemed calm now, but he had to ask, had to know if she was making arrangements to leave him. "So tell me what he meant about that big job offer at the university."

She shook her head. "There's nothing to discuss."

"But it's a big deal," he pressed, hoping to get something out of her.

She shrugged.

His body chilled all the way to his soul. "Are you taking it?"

"No," she insisted quickly. "Of course not."

Then he asked the question he had to know. "If the job had been offered earlier this week, would you have accepted it?"

She looked away quickly. Too quickly for his liking. "Uh, Xander, I should double-check my suitcase for our trip."

He clasped her elbow gently. "Are you sure you still want to travel after the upset you've just had?"

She finally met his eyes. "The fact that you're asking offers the answer already. Maybe it's best that we delay any honeymoon plans."

"Is that what you really want? No honeymoon? Not even an attempt at starting this marriage off on a positive note?"

Her eyebrows shot up. "This is already nowhere close to a positive note. I think we both need to stop this discussion before we say something that can't be taken back. This is a marriage of convenience. Let's not lose sight of that."

She tugged her arm free and walked away, closing the door with a finality that echoed to his toes. He was losing her before he'd even fully had her.

Not her, too. He couldn't lose another wife. He couldn't go through that again in any way.

He couldn't lose Maureen.

A familiar sound buzzed in his pocket. Easton's ringtone. Of course.

He fished the phone out of his pocket, sliding to accept the call.

"This is your best-man courtesy call. Your jet is fueled and ready for the Lourdes party of two first thing in the morning."

"Forget it. Cancel the flight. Maureen and I had a disagreement." He sank onto a chair, running his free hand through his thick hair. Wondering how he'd gotten to this place so quickly. He didn't want to lose her.

"A fight over what, if you don't mind my asking?" Easton sighed. "You didn't do something dumbass like murmur your first wife's name during sex…"

"God, no. Thanks for the vote of confidence," he quipped back with a levity he was far from feeling.

"But you still love Terri." His brother's question was more of a statement.

"I will always love her." There would never be a moment where he'd be able to stop those feelings. But he now knew that he had a bigger capacity for love than he'd imagined.

"Of course you will."

"I'm not sure how another woman would feel about that," Xander admitted.

"If she were alive today you would still be married."

"We would." Xander snagged a grape from the fruit basket and rolled it between his fingers.

"Of course you would. But you also need to ask yourself honestly…will you be able to love another woman as much as you loved her? Because no woman wants to be second best."

Easton's tone was level but firm. Perhaps this was what Easton had been hinting at when he'd promised to beat Xander's ass if he hurt her. Because Maureen, a woman whose past marriage had been filled with emotional games, had developed a callus around her heart. She'd become accustomed to not being enough.

And just making that connection—realizing that he had, however unwittingly, treated her the same way as that ass of an ex-husband he'd met tonight—made Xander furious with himself.

Having heard every damn thing he needed to, Xander ended the call, understood with crystal clarity that he needed to follow after her. Now.

Tossing the grape into the waste can, he charged through the cabana to find her sitting on the overstuffed pale peach chair, her delicate legs tucked beneath her. Palm to chin, she gazed absently into space. Years of pain were written in her posture. The letter from the university hung limply in her hands.

"I don't know how much I have inside left to give. But I'm trying, Maureen. I want this to work between us. I want to give it a real try. The question is—" he tapped the letter "—do you?"

Her hesitation, her lack of an answer, was all he needed. Whatever she felt for him, for his daughter, for this island, didn't come close to what he felt for her. But then, when had she been shown how deeply a man could love a woman? Certainly not by that jackass she'd been married to the first time.

She wrapped her arms tightly around herself. "I think it's best we cancel the honeymoon and go back to the house."

Watching her close him out, Xander realized that he could lose her, really lose her. Forever, in fact, if he didn't put his heart on the line and let her know how much she meant to him.

Rattled.

Unsettled.

The feelings coalesced inside her, becoming a pressure system of anxiety. She'd known this wasn't at all the right time to travel and maybe some of that had to do with the shock of seeing Danny again. She knew Xander was a far better man. But that didn't mean he loved her and it didn't change the fact that they'd entered this marriage for convenience's sake only.

So Sicily? Now? No. She wouldn't have been able to enjoy herself or their time together.

She'd told Xander they should go back to the house and rethink their plans.

They'd told the volunteers and family she had a sinus infection and couldn't fly. Not a tough sell since her sinuses were stuffed after she'd cried her eyes out in the shower.

But with work covered, she had nothing to do, so she'd

sought comfort in playing with Rose at the beach. They sat together on a blanket with a pile of blocks.

Rose sat in her lap, humming a made-up tune that seemed to mimic the sounds of the nearby parrots. A call-and-response of innocence and wonder.

This little girl had quickly taken up residence in her heart. Made her want to stay.

Scooting out of her lap, Rose picked up the building blocks and began stacking them together. Smiling back at Maureen, still singing her little ditty.

Handing over a block, Rose giggled. "Yooouuu." Her bell-like voice was small and sweet.

Maureen stacked her yellow block on Rose's green one. The little girl clapped, bobbing her head from side to side. Clearly amused and satisfied by the progress they'd made.

But Maureen didn't share in the toddler's delight. The fight with Xander had left her shaken and heartsick. When she'd seen Danny, standing there in the moonlight, the life she'd fled crashed back around her.

All the strength and healing fell away in that moment. She knew Danny didn't care about her one damn bit. He'd showed up only to unsettle her. To beat her back down. Just another move in his emotionally abusive chess game.

He'd been forcibly removed from the property and given a restraining order.

But the damage to Maureen had already been done. Before he'd left her, she'd become unsure of her place and worth. Those feelings returned, fully visible, in the heated exchange with Xander.

Xander. Whom she loved.

That thought scared her, rendering her completely vulnerable. The jumble of insecurities stilled her tongue when she should have spoken up.

Of course she wanted to stay. Wanted to be in Rose's life. And Xander's.

The block tower had grown quite high and, with a devilish look in her eye, Rose pushed on the middle pieces. The whole thing tumbled, eliciting peals of laughter from Rose.

How appropriate.

But then Rose began to build the tower again. Maureen admired her tenacity. Her willingness to simply start again.

Handing over a green block, Maureen said, "Parrot."

Rose took the block, nodding. She picked up a yellow one, handing it to Maureen. "Puppy."

"That's right, love," Maureen said softly.

A rustle of sand caused Maureen to turn around. Xander approached, plopping down on the beach blanket next to them. He was dressed in khaki shorts and an old white T-shirt, and there was something decidedly off about him. His face was tense, his eyes sad. "We need to talk."

Her stomach flip-flopped with a sense of dread. "Should I take Rose back to the house?"

He shook his head. "If you don't mind, she's happy. Let's let her keep playing."

"Okay, then. What did you want to say?"

He tossed a block from hand to hand. "I had a talk with my brother. He has a brilliant mind and some damn good insights, ones I always listen to when I remind myself that I should do more listening."

"Were you always close?" Maureen asked, watching the movements in his eyes. "You don't talk much now, so it's tough to tell."

"We're both so wrapped up in our work there isn't as much time. We work all hours. We've talked more in my time here than… God, in I don't know how long." His hand went to his hair, a shrug in his shoulders.

"And when you were children?"

"Our parents were very into letting us learn through experience."

The statement gave her pause. "What do you mean?"

"They weren't helicopter parents, other than the fact they strapped us into helicopters at a young age to tour the Andes. We were homeschooled for real, except home was around the world."

A bohemian lifestyle. It explained so much about Easton's approach. Even the way he talked to people. "That sounds like your brother's style, but not so much yours."

"Are you insinuating I'm uptight?" Arms immediately crossed over his chest.

Rose hummed louder, chanting random words into her melody. Maureen handed the baby another block, which she took as fast as a snapping turtle.

"Not by a long shot. You're sexy and exciting. But you're a businessman and a family man. Not a hippie veterinarian." And, honestly, she enjoyed that about him. He was her naturally occurring counterweight in so many ways.

"I realized that fast and made my own plans accordingly."

"What kind of plans?" Maureen added a block to Rose's tower. Rose high-fived her, then toppled the tower.

"Lots of plans, some better than others. I planned to go to college and get my business degree to start my own company. My brother was clear he wanted to be an exotic animal veterinarian."

"Which you both did. What were some of your other boyhood plans?" In the span of five minutes, some of the harshness of the morning ebbed away. She felt as though, for the first time, he trusted her with the vulnerable bits of his life. Maureen wanted him to keep sharing.

"We decided to catch the biggest fish for a local contest. The grand prize was five thousand dollars."

"Wow, that's a lot of money for a fish." She knew fishing contests drew a lot of attention, but hadn't really understood the appeal.

"It was for the serious fishermen, but we had big dreams and bigger egos. We were certain we could make it happen."

"And did you?" Resting her face on her palm, she leaned forward.

He waved, a smile tugging at his lips. A bit of the Xander she knew and loved peeking through. "Wait for the story. Give it time to breathe."

"You're seriously telling me to slow down and relax? Mr. Fast-Paced Executive?"

"I'm learning. Anyhow, I built the boat. My brother researched the fishing channels. I adapted the dynamics of the craft to his calculations." He picked up a block, handing it to Rose.

"How did the competition turn out?"

"We caught the most fish, but not the biggest. We lost by two ounces."

"Seriously? Only two ounces? That must have been a huge fish." The tropical fish of Florida astounded her. So different from the fish in the streams and lakes of Ireland, so vibrant and mammoth.

"We ate well. We filled the freezer with the extra, then started a campfire to grill the rest for Mom and Dad by suppertime." He gestured with his hands, as if drawing that freezer back to the present.

She tried to picture a younger Easton and Xander hauling in the fish. The image made her laugh.

"That's really thoughtful."

"Um, Mom turned white and passed out and Dad gave
us one helluva lecture about going out on the water without an adult."

"How old were you?"

"Ten and eleven." That sly smile returned. He looked
at her sidelong, his blue eyes complementing the state of
the sky. Piercing and intoxicating.

"What did they think the boat you'd been building
was for?"

"They assumed it would be for local villagers on our
latest family expedition. And it was. Once we finished
with it."

She nodded, thinking she understood. But she wanted
clarity. Time to be brave. "Where were you going with
that story just now?"

"I was making a couple of points, really. The first
point, the less pertinent one, is that for a long time I
thought you and my brother might be an item because
you have so much in common."

Shock rippled through her, then amusement. A laugh
of disbelief snorted free. "Me? And Easton? Seriously?"

He nodded.

"Clearly you realized that's not the case at all. No
disrespect to your brother. He's a brilliant veterinarian,
but he's a friend and a work companion. Nothing more."

"Okay, I believe you."

She took the block from his hand, reading hesitancy
in his eyes. "But what?"

"He's the sort of person you would be with at that
university job, the world you're from." He paused, inhaling deeply before continuing. "Are you taking the job?"

"No," she said without hesitation. "Of course not. We made promises to each other."

His hand fell to rest on his daughter's head, his eyes still searching Maureen's. "So you're staying because of Rose? So she doesn't risk a custody battle?"

And in a flash she realized, holy hell, he was every bit as insecure as she was when it came to giving his heart again. She lifted his hand from Rose's head, linked fingers with his and went out on the biggest limb of her life. "I'm staying because of you and what's happening between us. I hope you believe me."

His throat moved in a long swallow and he squeezed her hand. "Obviously I haven't been thinking with the clearest of minds for a while, not since Terri's death. I will always love her, but I hope you understand that doesn't mean I can't fall in love with another woman just as deeply."

Her heart leaped at his words, at his implication. Could it be? Her hearing intensified, causing her to lean closer, hand touching his thigh.

"Once I realized how close I was to losing you, to your work visa expiring and your leaving for Ireland, I acted fast. Just like with the boat, I knew on some level what had to be done."

"But your in-laws? They were a threat—"

He waved a hand dismissively. "They're coming around, I believe. They love Rose, but they don't want to be parents again. They already sent flowers this morning with a congratulations and a request to come for a lunch visit to discuss how to be helpful, involved grandparents." He tapped his temple. "On some level, I knew they would see reason."

"But I didn't." She eyed him. "You manipulated me?"

"I did what I needed to in order to make you stay. To

give us this chance at a life together, because, Maureen, I love you. If we waited here while someone counted every grain of sand on the beach, there wouldn't be enough time to explain how much you mean to me. And if you'll give me a chance, I'll prove it to you and, hopefully, with time, you'll come to love me in return."

Relief coursed through her as she saw the truth in his eyes. She'd spent so long telling herself not to believe in the fairy tale, but maybe it wasn't a fairy tale. The truth had been building all along and she'd been so worried about being hurt again, she hadn't allowed herself to see it.

She caressed his face. "How beautifully lucky for us that I already am in love with you."

Urgency filled her. She'd found courage again. Leaning in to kiss him, she angled her head below his. A tender kiss transferring from her lips to his. Electricity melded with comfort, the kiss feeling like a long-overdue homecoming.

His hand braced her chin, fingers soft.

Maureen felt a smaller hand touch her cheek three times. They broke the kiss to see Rose beaming at them. She kissed Maureen's cheek, then Xander's. A ripple of laughter passed between them all. Everything settling into place. Together.

Xander scooped up his daughter and wrapped an arm around his wife's waist. "What do you say we put Rose down for a nap and we make new honeymoon plans? Together."

She leaned against his shoulder, her arm sliding around his waist, as well. "I like the sound of that, husband. Very much."

* * * * *

LET'S TALK
Romance

For exclusive extracts, competitions
and special offers, find us online:

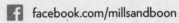 facebook.com/millsandboon

 @MillsandBoon

@MillsandBoonUK

Get in touch on 01413 063232